sepharad

ANTONIO MUÑOZ MOLINA

sepharad

Translated from the Spanish by
Margaret Sayers Peden

HARCOURT, INC.
Orlando Austin New York San Diego Toronto London

Requests for permission to make copies of any part of the work should
be mailed to the following address: Permissions Department, Harcourt, Inc.,
6277 Sea Harbor Drive, Orlando, Florida 32887-6777.

www.HarcourtBooks.com

This is a translation of *Sefarad*

Library of Congress Cataloging-in-Publication Data
Muñoz Molina, Antonio.
[Sefarad. English]
Sepharad/Antonio Muñoz Molina;
translated from the Spanish by Margaret Sayers Peden.—1st U.S. ed.
p.   cm.
I. Peden, Margaret Sayers.   II. Title.
PQ6663.U4795S4413   2003
863'.64—dc21   2003005538
ISBN 0-15-100901-5

Text set in Adobe Garamond
Designed by Linda Lockowitz

Printed in the United States of America

First U.S. edition
A C E G I K J H F D B

For Antonio and Miguel,
for Arturo and Elena,
with the wish that they live fully
the future novels of their lives

CONTENTS

"Yes," said the usher, "they are accused,
everyone you see here is accused."
"Really?" asked K. "Then they are my comrades."

—FRANZ KAFKA, *The Trial*

sepharad

sacristan

WE HAVE MADE OUR LIVES far away from our small city, but we just can't get used to being away from it, and we like to nurture our nostalgia when it has been a while since we've been back, so sometimes we exaggerate our accent when talking among ourselves, and use the common words and expressions that we've been storing up over the years and that our children can vaguely understand from having heard them so often. Godino, the secretary of our regional association—which has been rescued from its dismal lethargy thanks to his enthusiasm and dynamism—regularly organizes meals where we enjoy the food and recipes of our homeland, and if we are disgruntled that our gastronomy is as little known by foreigners as our monumental architecture or our Holy Week, we *like* having dishes that no one knows about, and giving them names that have meaning only to us. Oh, there's nothing like our *gordal* and *cornezuelo* olives! Godino exclaims, the plump ones and the long, pointed ones! Our rolls, our *borrachuelos*—we dream of those sugar-sprinkled pastries with a light touch of brandy—our layered pasta, our Easter cakes, our *morcilla*—our sausage has rice, not onion—our typical gazpacho, which is nothing at all like Andalusian gazpacho, and our wild-artichoke salad . . . In the private room of the Museo del Jamón, where those of us on the directors' council often meet, Godino gluttonously hacks off a piece of bread and before dipping it into the bowl of steaming *morcilla* makes a gesture like a benediction and recites these lines:

> Morcilla, *blessed lady,*
> *worthy of our veneration.*

The owner of the Museo is a countryman of ours who, as Godino says, often personally oversees the catering of our feasts, in which there isn't a single ingredient that hasn't come from our city, not even the bread, which is baked in La Trini's oven, the very oven that to this day produces the mouthwatering madeleines and the Holy Week cakes with a hard-boiled egg in the center that we loved so much when we were kids. Now, to tell the truth, we realize that the oily dough sits a little heavy on our stomachs, and though in our conversations we keep praising the savor of those *hornazos,* which are absolutely unique in the world and no one but us knows the name of, if we start eating one, we quit before we're through, even though it's painful to waste food—something our mothers always taught us. We remember the early days in Madrid, when we used to go to the bus station to pick up a food package sent from home: cardboard boxes carefully sealed with tape and tightly tied with cord, bringing from across all that distance the undiluted aroma of the family kitchen, the delicious abundance of all the things we have missed and yearned for in Madrid: *butifarros* and *chorizos,* sausages from the recent butchering, *borrachuelos* sparkling with sugar, even a glass jar filled with boiled red pepper salad seasoned with olive oil, the greatest delicacy you can ask for in a lifetime. For a while the dim interior of the armoire in our boardinghouse room would take on the succulent and mysterious penumbra of those cupboards where we kept food in the days before the advent of refrigerators. (Now when I tell my children that back when I was their age there was no refrigerator or television in my house, they don't believe it, or worse yet, they look at me as if I were a caveman.)

We had been away from our homes and our city for long, long months, but the smell and taste of them offered the same consolation as a letter, the same profound happiness and melancholy we felt after talking on the phone with our mothers or sweethearts. Our children, who spend the whole day glued to the telephone, talking for hours with someone they've seen only a short while before, can't believe that for us, not only in our childhood but our early teens as well, the telephone was still a novelty, at least in ordinary families, and because the system wasn't as yet automated, calling from one city to another—ringing someone up, as we said then—was a rather difficult undertaking that often meant standing in line for hours, waiting your turn in a public telephone office crammed with people. I'm not exactly an old man (although at times my wife says I seem ancient enough), but I remember when I had to call my mother at a neighbor's house and wait until they went to get her, all the while hearing footsteps in the wooden booth at the telephone company on the Gran Vía. Finally I would hear her voice and be overcome by an anguish I have felt only rarely since, a sensation of being far away and of having left my mother to grow old alone. We both would be nearly tongue-tied, because we used that exotic instrument so seldom that it made us very nervous, and we were consumed by the thought of how much we were paying for a conversation in which we barely managed to exchange a few formalities as trite as those in our letters: Are you well? Have you been behaving? Don't forget to wear your overcoat when you go out in the morning, it's getting cold. You had to swallow hard to work up the nerve to ask the person you were talking with to send a food package, or a money order. You hung up the telephone and suddenly all that distance was real again, and with that, besides the desolation of going outside on a Sunday evening, there was the contemptible relief of having put behind you an uncomfortable conversation in which you had nothing to say.

Now that distances have become much shorter, we feel farther and farther apart. Who doesn't remember those endless hours on the midnight express, in the second-class coaches that brought us to Madrid for the first time and deposited us, done in from fatigue and lack of sleep, in the unwelcoming dawn of Atocha Station, the old one, which our children never knew, although some of them, just kids, or still in their mama's womb, spent arduous nights on those trains that carried us south during the Christmas vacations we looked forward to so much, or during the short but cherished days of Holy Week, or of our strange late fair that falls at the end of September, when the men of our parents' generation picked the most delicious grapes and pomegranates and figs and allowed themselves the luxury of attending the two bullfights of the fair: the one on Saint Michael's day, which opened the fair, and the one on the day of Saint Francis, which was the most splendid, the "big day," our parents called it, but also the saddest because it was the last, and because the autumn rain often spoiled the corrida and forced the mournful closing of the few carousels we had in those days, completely covered over with wet canvas.

TIME LASTED LONGER THEN, and the kilometers were longer. Not many people had a car, and if you didn't want to spend the whole night on the train, you got on the bus we called the Pava, which took seven hours, first, because of all the twists and turns on the highway toward the north of our province, and also because of the cliffs and tunnels of Depeñaperros, which were like the entrance into another world, the frontier, where our part of the world was left behind on the last undulating hillsides of olive trees, and then the endless plains of La Mancha, so monotonous that sleep seemed to bleed into exhaustion and prevail over discomfort and you fell fast asleep and with a little luck didn't open your eyes again until the bus was approaching the lights of Madrid. What a thrill it was to see the capital from afar, the red tile roofs and, high above them, the tall buildings that impressed us so strongly: the Telephone Building, the Edificio España, the Torre de Madrid!

But it was another emotion that moved us most, especially when our illusions about the new life awaiting us in the capital began to wane, or when we simply began to get used to that life, the way you get used to everything and, as you do, lose your taste for it, the way liking turns into boredom, tedium, hidden irritation. We preferred the emotion of that other arrival, the slow approach to our home country, the signs that announced it to us, not kilometer markers on the highway but certain familiar indications seen from the small window of the train or bus: a roadside inn, the red color of the soil along the banks of the Guadalimar River, and then the first houses, the isolated street lamps on the corners, if we arrived at night, the sensation of already being there and the impatience of not quite having arrived, the sweet feeling of all the days that lay ahead, of vacations begun and yet still intact.

There was in those days one last house, I remember now, where the city ended on the north, the last one you left behind as you traveled toward Madrid and the first you saw on the return, an ancient little hotel with a garden, called La Casa Cristina, which was often the meeting place for the crews of olive pickers and also the place where we bade the Virgin farewell when at the beginning of September her image was returned to the sanctuary of the village from which she would be brought the following year, at the time of the busy pilgrimage in May, the Virgin to whom, as children, we came to pray on late-summer afternoons.

Maybe the limits of things were drawn more clearly then, like the lines and colors and names of countries on the maps that hung on the schoolhouse walls: that small hotel with its tiny garden and its yellow street lamp on the corner was precisely where our city ended. One step farther and the country began, especially at night when the lamp glowed at the edge of the darkness, not lighting it but revealing it in all its depth. A few years ago, when I was on a trip with my children, who were still small—I remember that the second one was holding my hand—I tried to take them to see La Casa Cristina, and along the way I was telling them that it was near that hotel that the owner of the olive groves would hire my mother and me to work as pickers. I told them how icy cold it was as we walked through the dark city in heavy wraps: I wearing my father's corduroy cap and wool gloves, my mother in a shawl that completely enveloped her and covered her head. It was so cold that my ears and hands were frozen, and my mother had to rub my hands with hers, which were warmer and rougher, and blow her warm breath on my fingertips. I would get choked up when I told them about those times, and about my mother, whom they had scarcely known. I made them see how much life had changed in such a short time, because it was nearly unimaginable for them to think that children their age had to spend the Christmas vacations earning a daily wage in the olive groves. Then I realized that I had been talking for a long time and wandering around without finding La Casa Cristina, and I thought I'd lost my way because of all the talking I was doing, but no, I was right at the place I'd been looking for: what wasn't there was the house. A man I asked told me it had been torn down several years before, when they widened the old Madrid highway. Whatever the case, even if La Casa Cristina had still been on that corner, the city wouldn't have ended there: new neighborhoods had grown up, monotonous block after brick block, and there was a multisports complex and a new commercial center the man showed me with pride, as if pointing out impressive monuments to a foreigner. Only those of us who have left know what the city used to be like and are aware of how much it has changed; it's the people who stayed who can't remember, who seeing it day after day have been losing that memory, allowing it to be distorted, although they think they're the ones who remained faithful and that we, in a sense, are deserters.

My wife says that I live in the past, that I feed on dreams like the idle old men who hang around playing dominoes at our social center and attend the lectures and poetry readings that Godino organizes. I tell her that I am like them, more or less, as good as unemployed, almost permanently "between jobs," as they say now, no matter how hard I try to start business deals that don't come to anything, or accept nearly always short-lived, often fraudulent jobs. What I don't tell her is that at this point I would really like to live in the past, to sink into it with the same conviction, the same voluptuousness, that others do, like Godino, who when he eats *morcilla* stew, or remembers some joke or the nickname of one of our paisanos, or recites a few lines from our most famous poet, Jacob Bustamante, flushes with enthusiasm and happiness, and is always planning what he's going to do when Holy Week comes, and counting the days till Palm Sunday, and especially till the night of Ash Wednesday, when it's time for the procession he participates in as a member of the brotherhood and also as director. "Just like our renowned Mateo Zapatón, who's retired now in La Villa y Corte," says Godino, who knows an unbelievable number of our paisanos by their proper names and nicknames although he has lived his whole life in Madrid, and calls everyone "illustrious," "esteemed," "distinguished," hitting that *uished* so hard, the way they do in our town, that more than once he's sprayed saliva as he says it.

It's true, many of us would like to live in the immutable past of our memories, a past that seems to live on in the taste of some foods and those dates marked in red on the calendars, but without realizing it we've been letting a remoteness grow inside us that no quick trip can remedy or increasingly infrequent telephone calls ease—forget the letters we stopped writing years ago. Now that we can make the three-hour trip swiftly and comfortably on the expressway, we go back less and less. Everything is much closer, but we're the ones drifting farther away, even though we repeat the old familiar words and stress our accent and though we still get emotional when we hear the marches of our religious association or recite poems by the "distinguished bard who gives meaning to the word," as he is introduced by Godino—who is flattering and admiring him but at the same time pulling his leg—the poet Jacob Bustamante, who apparently paid no attention to the siren song of literary celebrity and chose not to come to Madrid. He's still there, in our city, collecting prizes and accumulating benefits because he's a civil servant, as is another of our local glories, maestro Gregorio E. Puga, a composer of note who also ignored the siren song scorned by Godino in his day. They say (actually, Godino says) that maestro Puga concluded his musical studies in Vienna brilliantly, and that he could have found a position in one of the best orchestras of Europe had the pull of his hometown not been so strong, but he returned instead with all his diplomas for excellence in German, in Gothic lettering, and very quickly and very easily, in a competitive examination, earned the position of band director.

WE LIKED TO COME BACK with our children when they were small, and we were proud to find that they were fond of the same things that had enchanted us in our childhoods. They looked forward to Holy Week, when they could wear their costumes as little penitents, the child's cape that left the face uncovered. Almost as soon as they were born, we enrolled them as members in the same associations our fathers had enrolled us in. When they were a little older, they would get antsy in the car, asking, from the moment we left, how many hours till we got there. Born in Madrid, they spoke with an accent different from ours, but it made us proud to think, and to tell one another, that they belonged to our land as much as we did, and when we took them by the hand on a Sunday morning and led them down Calle Nueva, just as our parents had led us, and lifted them up as a float passed so they could get a better look at the donkey Jesus rode as he entered Jerusalem, or the green, sinister face of Judas on the Last Supper float, we were consoled by the sense that life was repeating itself, that time didn't pass in our city, or that it was less cruel than the nerve-racking and jumbled pace of life in Madrid.

But the children have been growing up without our realizing it, turning into strangers, unsociable guests in our own homes, locked in rooms that have become dark dens from which sounds of insufferable music issue, and smells and noises we prefer not to identify. Now they don't want to go back, and if one of us tells them something, they look at him the way they would at a pitiful old man, at some worthless bum, as if it were a snap for a person to find a secure and decent job after the age of forty-five. And they've forgotten all the things they liked so much, the thrill of the tunics and hoods (Godino insists that our word is *cowls*) that covered their faces like storybook masks, the noise of the trumpets and drums, the taste of the candy cigarettes that were sold only in Holy Week and the red caramel *pirulís* on a stick, spiraled with sugar, that we bought at the street stall of a small man appropriately nicknamed Pirulí; he died a few years ago, even though to those of us who'd been seeing him since we were children, he seemed as frozen in time as Holy Week itself. Our children are no longer drawn to the attractions of the fair, and it's as if only we, their parents, have retained some trace of nostalgia and gratitude for the modest carousels of all those years ago, the merry-go-rounds, as we called them as children and as we taught our children to say. Nothing we like has meaning for them now, and when from time to time they stand and stare at us with pity, or indifference, making us feel ridiculous, we see ourselves through their eyes: worn-out old-timers whom they don't feel the need to thank for anything, who irritate and bore them more than anything, nobodies they walk away from as if wanting to rid themselves of the dirty, dusty cobwebs of the time to which we belong: the past.

TO LIVE BACK THEN, in the past, what more could I want? But a person no longer knows where he lives, not in what city, not in what time, he's not even sure that his is the house he returns to in the late afternoon with the sensation that he's a nuisance, even though he may have set out very early, not knowing precisely where he was going or for what reason, looking for God knows what job that would allow him to feel he was once again doing something useful, something necessary. At one of the last meals held by the association, the one we had for the purpose of awarding Jacob Bustamante our Silver Medal, Godino scolded me affectionately because it had been two years since I came home for Holy Week. I explained to him that I was going through a difficult phase, hoping that he, a man of so many resources and acquaintances, might offer a helping hand, but of course I didn't ask for his help straight out, because of my pride and the fear of losing face in his eyes. My dejection and wounded honor kept me more removed than usual from the activities of our regional association, though I tried never to miss the meetings of the board and was scrupulous in paying my monthly dues. I wandered from morning to night, not myself, from one place to another in Madrid, from one job to another, following promises that never came to anything, opportunities where for some reason or other

I always failed, meaningless jobs that lasted a few weeks, a few days. I spent hours waiting, doing nothing, or had to rush to get to something that eluded me by a few minutes.

One morning, while I was crossing Chueca Plaza with my heart in my fist and my eyes straight ahead in order not to see what was around me—the drug dealers, the people with terrible diseases, the spectacle of sleepwalking men and women with faces of the dead and the shamble of zombies—I ran into my paisano Mateo Chirino, the man who was called Mateo Zapatón when I was young, not only because of his trade as a cobbler but also because of his size; he was much larger than most men in those days and, as I remember, wore huge black heavy-soled shoes, legendary shoes he must have spent a lifetime repairing. I noticed that he seemed to be wearing the same enormous shoes, although now they'd been stretched out of shape by his bunions. I was wearing the dark suit I wore for job interviews and carrying my black briefcase and files. I had been accepted, on trial, as a commissioned salesman of supplies for driving schools. Planted in the middle of Chueca Plaza, in an oversized overcoat and a dark green Tyrolean hat outfitted with the obligatory feather, Mateo Zapatón stood staring benevolently at something, the very picture of a robust, lazy fellow with time on his hands, and he rose from those black shoes as from the pedestal of a statue or the stump of an olive tree, so deeply rooted he seemed in the neighborhood of Madrid where he was living and where he gave the impression of being as comfortable as he had been in our distant, shared hometown.

His face, too, was just as I remembered it, as if impervious to the wear of time. To a child, all adults are more or less old, so when you grow older and see those persons again after years have gone by, it seems as if they haven't changed at all. It was a cold winter morning, one of those disagreeable workday mornings in Madrid when the facades of buildings are the same dirty gray as the cloudy but rainless sky. I was rushing as always, harried from running late to meet a client, the owner of a driving school on Calle Pelayo. I'd made the mistake of coming in my car, and the little bit of time I'd left for having a cup of coffee was lost looking for a parking place in impossible streets filled with traffic, pedestrians, unshaven transvestites, thugs, drug addicts, distributors, and trucks loading and unloading, blocking the sidewalk and provoking a blare of horns that were the last straw for my already shattered nerves.

It was late, I hadn't eaten, I'd left my car so badly parked that it would probably be towed, but seeing Mateo Zapatón, and the pleasure of the recollections that seeing him awoke in me, was stronger than my haste. As tall as ever, erect, with the same placid expression, big nose, and slightly bulging eyes, cheeks ruddy with cold and good health, though sagging with age, his step as firm as when he used to march in his penitent's robe ahead of the Last Supper float, guiding the huge cart sponsored by the association's board of directors.

That float was one of the most spectacular of all Holy Week, and it had the most figures: the twelve apostles seated around a linen-covered table, with Christ standing at one end, one hand on his heart and the other raised in a gesture of benediction. The gold fringe encircling his head vibrated with every majestic turn of the wheels over the cobbled or paved streets of that time, with the same slight shiver that flickered the flames in tulip-shaped globes and rippled the white tablecloth on which the bread and the wine were arranged for the liturgical sacrifice. All the apostles were looking toward Jesus, and each had a small white light focused on him that dramatically illuminated his face. Everyone except Judas, whose head was turned away in a gesture of remorse and greed, focused on the pouch that held the coins of his betrayal, half-hidden behind his chair. The light that struck Judas in the face was green, the bilious green of liver dysfunction, and everyone in town knew that those features, which we children despised as much as those of the villains in the moving pictures, were those of a tailor who had his workshop on the corner of Calle Real, very near the cubby of Mateo Zapatón.

Godino told me the story, not without promising that he would tell me others even juicier. The figures on the float, like almost all the figures displayed during Holy Week, had been carved by the celebrated maestro Utrera, who according to Godino was one of the most important artists of the century but hadn't received the recognition he deserved because he had chosen to stay in our hospitable though isolated city. Because he was such a genius, Utrera was naturally a dedicated bohemian, and he was always consumed by debts and pursued by creditors, one of whom, the most persistent and also the one man to whom Utrera owed the most, was that same tailor on Calle Real who made Utrera's monogrammed shirts, his closely fitted waistcoats, the suits as snug as Fred Astaire's, even the floating robes Utrera wore in his studio. Whenever the debt reached an unacceptable level, the tailor would present himself at the Royal Café, where the authors and artists' club headed by Utrera met every afternoon, and would publicly call the sculptor a reprobate and a thief, shaking a sheaf of unpaid bills in his face. Very dignified, small, ramrod-straight, packaged, as it were, in the elegant Fred Astaire–model suit he had not paid for and had no intention of ever paying for, the sculptor would gaze at a different part of the room while waiters and friends subdued the tailor, whose eyes were bulging and face was dripping sweat from anger, and who ended up leaving as empty-handed as he had come, though not without having ignominiously recovered from the floor of the café the bills that had fallen from his hands in the heat of his tirade, as valuable proof of an insult he threatened to rectify in court. Imagine everyone's shock, Godino told me, anticipating the punch line with a broad smile that lighted his clever and jovial face, when a few weeks later, the first Wednesday of Holy Week, at the first appearance of the newly carved Last Supper (the old one, like almost everything else, had been burned by the Reds during the war), the tailor saw with his own eyes what malevolent gossips had already told him, the news that was flashing around the city, in Godino's words, "like a trail of gunpowder." The contorted face of Judas, the green face that turned away from the kind but accusing face of the Redeemer to examine, in his greed, the badly hidden pouch of coins, was the tailor's living likeness, exact and faithful despite the cruel exaggeration of the caricature: the same bulging eyes that had looked at the sculptor in the café as if wanting to bore holes in him. "Or petrify him, like the eyes of the Medusa," said Godino, who as he warmed up to his tale would utter his favorite words . . . "And the Semitic nose!" With that adjective Godino would make a face and thrust his head forward, looking as the tailor must have looked when he discovered his likeness on the figure of Judas, and would twist or wrinkle his nose, which was small and turned up, as if merely pronouncing the word "Semitic"—which gave him so much pleasure that he repeated it two or three times—had the virtue of making his nose as prominent as that of the tailor and of Judas, as the nose of all the cruel soldiers and Pharisees of the Holy Week floats: the Jews spit on the Lord, as we children used to say when we played our games of floats and parades. In the paved and dirt streets of our day, we held our juvenile versions of Holy Week and paraded playing small plastic trumpets and drums made from large empty tins; we even pulled floats fashioned from wood or cardboard boxes and wore capes made of old newspapers.

BOTH MEN HAVE BEEN DEAD a long time now, the irascible tailor and the morose, bohemian sculptor, but the vengeful joke one played on the other survives in the grim, still green-lit features of the Judas of the Last Supper, even though with every

Holy Week there are fewer people who can identify them as the tailor's or who remember the stories of the past that Godino spins, whether inventing them out of whole cloth or just embroidering them, I don't know. Nor would there be many who recognize the other real model for the apostles, the Saint Matthew who is turned toward Christ, half devout, half frightened, his raised eyebrows underscoring the amazement in his eyes, because this is the moment when the Master has just said that one of the twelve will betray him that night and everyone is alarmed and scandalized, gesturing wildly, asking, "Master, is it I?" In the midst of that uproar no one pays attention to the green, rancorous face of Judas or notices the swollen pouch of coins that our mothers pointed out to us when we were children and they held us up in their arms as the float passed by in the procession.

I didn't need Godino to explain to me that the noble Saint Matthew, straight of back and red of cheek, was the living image of Mateo Zapatón, who thus had his instant of public glory on the same night of Holy Week that the bill-collecting tailor was covered with ridicule. After the sculptor Utrera, when he had money or the prospect of collecting some, had the measurements for a new suit taken in the tailor shop, he would cross Calle Real and order hand-cobbled shoes from Mateo, or during hard times he would bring old pairs to be repaired. But unlike the tailor, Mateo Zapatón never reminded Utrera of past-due bills, partly because of the man's somewhat cowardly nature, which made him inclined to accept half measures, but partly too because he had a fervent admiration for the sculptor, which swelled to the point of abject gratitude every time the maestro came by his shop and stayed several hours to chat with him, offering him his blond-tobacco cigarettes and telling him stories of his travels through Italy and of his life in the artistic circles of Madrid before the war.

"Friend Mateo," the sculptor would say, "you have a classic head that deserves to be immortalized by art." Said and done.

Mateo never charged Utrera a cent, but he considered the debt canceled when, with a surge of vanity and modesty, he saw his unmistakable face among those of the apostles, as well as his husky shoulders in a very typical posture: looking sideways and upward from the low cobbler's bench where he spent his life. Being a penitent and a board member of the brotherhood of the Last Supper, could he imagine a greater honor than inclusion among those who supped with the Savior? Every characteristic, the entire persona of the evangelist saint, was of a prodigal fidelity, except for the beard, which the flesh-and-blood Mateo did not have, although at times he seemed to be on the verge of letting it grow, an inconceivable daring in those years of carefully tended mustaches and shaved faces. The tailor shop sat almost directly across from the cobbler's shop, but whenever the aggrieved tailor met Mateo on the opposite sidewalk, he would lower his head or look away, his face greener and his nose more Semitic than ever, and Mateo, like so many others, would have to clamp his hand over his mouth to keep from exploding with laughter, his cheeks flaming a bright red more appropriate for a giant figure in Valencia's festivals than for the image of a pious evangelist.

IT GAVE ME A LITTLE START of pleasure to see that face in the middle of a hostile city, a face tied to the sweetest memories of my hometown and childhood. When I was a boy, my mother often sent me to the door of Mateo Zapatón, who without knowing anything at all about me used to pat my cheek and call me Sacristan. "Mercy, Sacristan, this pair of half soles didn't last very long this time!" "Tell your mother I don't have change, Sacristan. She can pay me when she comes by." The shop was very narrow and high-ceilinged, almost like a closet, and it opened directly onto the street by way of a glass door, which Mateo closed only on the most severe winter days. All the available space, including the sides of the chest he used as a worktable and counter, was covered with posters of bullfights and of Holy Week, the two passions of this master cobbler, glued-on posters, yellowed by the years, some pasted over others, announcements of corridas celebrated at the beginning of the century or at last year's fair, all in a confusion of names, places, and dates that fed Mateo's chatty erudition. He was almost always surrounded by his troop of friends, with a cigarette or tack between his lips, or both at once, a tireless narrator of historic anecdotes from the world of bulls and famous taurine maneuvers, which he knew at first hand because the presidents of the corridas often asked him to act as an official adviser. His voice would break and his eyes fill with tears when he was recalling the doleful afternoon when he watched from a row of seats on the sunny side of the bullring in Linares as the bull Islero charged Manolete. "He's going to hook you, don't get so close," he had shouted from his seat, and he bent forward as if he were in the plaza and cupped his hands to make a megaphone, his face tragic with anticipation, living once again the instant when Manolete could still have saved himself from the fatal goring, "the fateful goring," as Godino always said when he imitated the madly waving arms of the impassioned cobbler as he told that tale. Godino always promised some great and mysterious story about Mateo, a secret about which only he knew the most delicious details.

I WENT UP TO MATEO there in Chueca Plaza, and he looked at me with the same broad, benevolent smile he had worn when he welcomed the shoppers and the circle of friends who gathered at his cobbler's shop. I was moved to think that he recognized me despite how much I'd changed since the last time we saw each other. Just then another coincidence came to mind that linked him to my oldest memories and, without his knowing, made him a part of my childhood. In the space next to Mateo Zapatón's was the barbershop my father used to take me to, the one where my grandfather always got his haircut and shave, Pepe Morillo's shop, which was doing less and less business as his oldest customers died off and young people were letting their hair grow. Now his door was closed as tightly as Mateo Zapatón's and the Judas-face tailor's, like so many of the shops on Calle Real that once had been busy, before people gradually forgot to go by there, turning it, especially at night and on rainy days, into a ghostly, abandoned street. But in those days Pepe Morillo's barbershop was as animated as Mateo Zapatón's shoe repair, and often, on mild April and May afternoons, the clients of both shops would take chairs out on the sidewalk and smoke and talk in one single gathering, which was observed from the other side of the street, from the darkness of his empty shop, by the brooding tailor, who would wring his hands behind the counter and sink his head deeper between his shoulders, ever more closely resembling the Judas of the Last Supper, the misanthrope with the green face and hooked nose slowly pushed toward bankruptcy by the unremitting advance of mass-produced clothing.

My father, holding my hand, used to take me to Pepe Morillo's barbershop (back then "hair salon" was a woman's word), and I was so small that the barber had to put a little stool on the seat in order for me to see myself in the mirror and for him to be comfortable as he cut my hair. His face smelled of cologne and his breath of tobacco when he bent close with the comb and scissors, and he shaved my neck with a little electrical machine. I could hear his strong, fast breathing and feel the touch of capable adult fingers on the nape of my neck and on my cheeks, the rare pressure of hands that weren't those of my mother or father, familiar yet strange hands, suddenly brusque when he doubled my ears forward or made me bend way over by pushing the back of my head. Every time he trimmed my hair, almost at the end, Pepe Morillo would say, "Close your eyes tight," and I knew he was going to trim the bangs to just above my eyebrows, cutting toward the middle of my forehead. Damp hair would fall on my eyelids, tickle my plump cheeks and tip of my nose, and the cold blades of the scissors would brush my eyebrows. When Pepe Morillo told me I could open my eyes now, I would be surprised by the round, unfamiliar face in the mirror, with protruding ears and straight bangs above the eyes, and also by my father's smile as he looked approvingly at my reflection.

I remembered all this as if I were reliving it when I unexpectedly ran into Mateo Zapatón in Chueca Plaza . . . and something else that until that moment I hadn't known was in my memory. Once, as I was waiting my turn and reading a comic book my father had just bought for me, I felt thirsty and asked Pepe Morillo's permission to get a drink. He pointed to a small, dark interior patio at the rear of the barbershop, through a glass door and down a dark corridor. When you're a boy, the farthest places can be reached in only a few steps. As I pushed open the door, I think I was a little dizzy; maybe I was getting a fever and that was why I was so thirsty. The paving tiles were white and gray, with reddish flowers in the center, and they echoed as I walked across them. In a corner of the tiny patio, where a number of plants with large leaves added to the humidity, there was a pitcher on a shelf covered with a crocheted cloth, one of those clay water pitchers they had back then, a brightly colored, glazed jug in the shape of a rooster, made, I remember precisely, by potters on Calle Valencia. I took a drink, and the water had the consistency of broth and the taste of fever. I went back down the hallway, and suddenly I was lost. I wasn't at the barbershop but in a place it took some time to identify as the cobbler's shop, and the person I saw was the flesh-and-blood apostle Saint Matthew, although he was wearing a leather apron and not the tunic of a saint or a member of the brotherhood, and he was beardless, with the stub of an unlit cigarette in one corner of his mouth and a tack in the other. "Mercy, Sacristan, what in the world are you doing here? You gave me quite a turn."

JUST AS I HAD THEN, I looked at Mateo and didn't know what to say. Up close he seemed much older, he no longer resembled the eternal Saint Matthew of the Last Supper. Neither his gaze nor his smile was directed at me: they stayed absolutely the same when I spoke his name and held out my hand to greet him, and when I clumsily and hastily told him who I was and tried to remind him of my parents' names and the nickname my family had back then. Limply holding my hand, he nodded and looked at me, although he didn't give the impression that he was focusing his eyes, which until a moment before had seemed observant and lively. His hat, more than tilted to one side, was skewed on his head, as if he had jammed it on at the last moment as he left the house or put it on with the carelessness of someone who can't see himself well in the mirror. I reminded him that my mother had always been a customer in his shop—then shops had patrons, not customers—and that my father, who like him was also a great fan of the bulls, had often been present at his gatherings, and at those in Pepe Morillo's barbershop next door, which communicated with his via an interior patio. Mateo listened to those names of persons and places with the look of one who doesn't completely connect with things so far in the past. He bowed his head and smiled, although I also thought I noticed an expression of suspicion or alarm or disbelief in his face. Maybe he was afraid that I was going to cheat him, or assault him, like many of the thugs who hung around that area—you saw them all the time, kneeling in clusters beside the entrance to the metro and dealing in God knows what. I had to go, I was very late for an appointment that was probably futile in the first place, I hadn't had breakfast, my car was double-parked, and Mateo Zapatón was still holding my hand with distracted cordiality and smiling, his mouth half-open, his lower jaw dropped a little, with the gleam of saliva at the corners of his lips.

"You don't remember, maestro?" I asked him. "You always called me Sacristan."

"Of course I do, man, yes," he winked and stepped a little closer, and it was then I realized that now I was the taller. He put his other hand on my shoulder, as if in a benevolent attempt not to disappoint me. "Sacristan."

But the word didn't seem to mean anything to him, though he kept repeating it, still holding the hand that now I wanted to get free, feeling trapped and nervous about continuing on my way. I pulled back but he didn't move, the hand with the soft, moist palm that had clutched mine still slightly raised, the hat with the tiny green feather twisted around on his forehead, standing there alone like a blind man, in the middle of the plaza, supported on the great pedestal of his large black shoes.

copenhagen

SOMETIMES IN THE COURSE of a journey you hear and tell stories of other journeys. It seems that with the act of departing the memory of previous travels becomes more vivid, and also that you listen more closely and better appreciate the stories you're told: a parenthesis of meaningful words within the other, temporal, parenthesis of the journey. Anyone who travels can surround himself with a silence that will be mysterious to strangers observing him, or he can yield, with no fear of the consequences, to the temptation of shading the truth, of gilding an episode of his life as he tells it to someone he will never see again. I don't believe it's true what they say, that as you travel you become a different person. What happens is that you grow lighter, you shed your obligations and your past, just as you reduce everything you possess to the few items you need for your luggage. The most burdensome aspect of our identity is based on what others know or think about us. They look at us and we know that they know, and in silence they force us to be what they expect us to be, to act according to certain habits our previous behavior has established, or according to suspicions that we aren't aware we have awakened. To the person you meet on a train in a foreign country, you are a stranger who exists only in the present. A woman and a man look at each other with a tingle of intrigue and desire as they take seats facing each other: at that moment they are as detached from yesterday and tomorrow and from names as Adam and Eve were when they first looked upon each other in Eden. A thin and serious man with short and very black hair and large dark eyes gets onto the train at the station in Prague and perhaps is trying not to meet the eyes of other passengers coming into the same car, some of whom look him over with suspicion and decide that he must be a Jew. He has long, pale hands and is reading a book or absently staring out the window. From time to time he is shaken by a dry cough and covers his mouth with a white handkerchief he then slips into a pocket, almost furtively. As the train nears the recently invented border between Czechoslovakia and Austria, the man puts away the book and looks for his documents with a certain nervousness. When the train reaches the station of Gmünd, he immediately peers out at the platform, as if expecting to see someone in the solitary darkness of that deep hour of the night.

No one knows who he is. If you travel alone on a train or walk along the street of a city in which no one knows you, you are no one; no one can be sure of your anguish or of the source of your nervousness as you wait in the station café, although they might guess the name of your illness when they observe your pallor and hear the rasping of your bronchial tubes, or when they notice the way you hide the handkerchief you used to cover your mouth. But when I travel I feel as if I were weightless, as if I had become invisible, that I am no one and can be anyone, and this lightness of spirit is evident in the movements of my body; I walk more quickly, with more assurance, free of the burden of my being, my eyes open to the incitement of a city or a landscape, of a language I enjoy understanding and speaking, now more beautiful because it isn't mine. Montaigne writes of a presumptuous man who returned from a journey without learning anything: How was he going to learn, he asks, if he carried himself with him?

BUT I DON'T HAVE TO GO far in order to undergo this transformation. Sometimes, as soon as I leave the house and turn the first corner or walk down the steps of the metro, I leave my persona behind, and I am dazed and excited by the great blank page my life has become, the space where the sensations, places, people's faces, the tales I may hear, will be printed with more brilliance and clarity. In literature there are many narratives that pretend to be stories told during a journey, at a chance encounter along the road, around the fireplace of an inn, in the coach of a train. It's on a train that one man tells another the story Tolstoy recounts in "The Kreutzer Sonata." In *Heart of Darkness,* Marlow tells of a journey toward the unexplored territory along the Congo as he is traveling up the Thames on a barge, and when he sees the still-distant glow of the lights of London through the night fog, he recalls the bonfires he saw on the banks of the African river, and he imagines much older bonfires, fires the first Roman sailors would have seen when they sailed into the Thames for the first time more than two thousand years ago. On the train on which he was being deported to Auschwitz, Primo Levi met a woman he had known years before, and he says that during the journey they told each other things that living people do not tell, that only those who are on the other side of death dare say aloud.

In a dining car, traveling from Granada to Madrid, a friend told me of another trip on the same train when he met a woman he was kissing within the hour. It was summertime, in broad daylight, on the Talgo, which leaves every day at three in the afternoon. My friend's fiancée came to see him off, but shortly thereafter he and the stranger had locked themselves in a rest-room, with a terrifying urgency and joy and desire that neither cramped quarters nor problems keeping balance nor the pound-ing on the door by impatient travelers could disrupt. They had thought they would say good-bye forever when they reached Madrid. My friend, who was fulfilling his military service, had no profession or income, and she was a married woman with a small child, a little unstable, given to both fits of reckless excitement and black spells of depression. My friend told me that he liked her very much although she frightened him, but also that he had never had such pleasure with any woman. He remembered her with the greatest clarity and gratitude because with the exception of his wife, whom he married soon after returning from the army, she was the only woman he had ever slept with.

They continued seeing each other in secret for several months, repeating the sexual intoxication of their first meeting in board-inghouse rooms, the darkness of movie theaters, several times in her home in the bed she slept in with her husband, watched from the crib by the large, tranquil eyes of the child clinging to the bars to hold himself up. When my friend was discharged they agreed that she would not come to see him off on the midnight express that was to carry him back to Granada. At the last moment the woman appeared. My friend jumped from the train and as he put his arms around her felt such a surge of desire that he didn't care if he missed the train. But he took it the next day, and they never saw each other again. "It frightens me to think what must have become of her, unstable as she was," my friend said, his elbows propped on the bar of the Talgo diner, sitting before the coffee he still hadn't touched and staring through the window at the desert landscape of the northern Granada province, or turning toward the slamming door that led to the other cars, as if with the im-possible hope that the woman would appear all these years later.

Listening to him, I was envious, and sad too that nothing like that had ever happened to me, that I had no memories of such a woman. She smoked joints, took pills, sniffed coke, he told me, and he was afraid of all those things, but he followed her through all her strange behavior, and the more frightened he was the more he desired her. "I wouldn't be a bit surprised to learn that she ended up on heroin," he told me. "Some mornings I wake up remembering that I've dreamed of her. I dream that I meet her in Madrid, or that I'm sitting on this same train and see her coming down the corridor. She was very tall, like a model, and she had curly chestnut hair and green eyes."

TODAY'S TRAINS, whose seats aren't arranged so we're forced to sit face to face with strangers, are not conducive to travel stories. Instead, there are silent ghosts with headphones covering their ears, their eyes fixed on a video of an American film. You heard more stories in those old second-class coaches, which had the flavor of a waiting room or a room where poor families eat. During my first trip to Madrid, as I dozed on the hard, blue plastic seat, I listened in the dark to my grandfather Manuel and another passenger tell each other tales of train trips during the winters of the war. "In the battalion of assault troops I served in they marched us all up to a train in this same station and made us get on, and although they didn't tell us where they were taking us, the rumor spread that our destination was the front along the Ebro River. My legs trembled at the thought all night, there in the dark of the closed coach. In the morning they made us get off and with no word of explanation sent us back to our usual posts. A different battalion had been dispatched in our stead, and of the eight hundred men who went no more than thirty returned. Had that train taken us to the front," my grandfather said, "I wouldn't be telling you this story," and suddenly I thought, half asleep, if that journey along the Ebro hadn't been canceled, my grandfather probably would have died and I wouldn't have been born.

Everything was strange that night, that rare and magical night of my first trip; it was as if when I got on the train—or earlier, when I arrived at the station—I had abandoned the everyday and entered a kingdom very much like the world of films or books: the insomniac world of travelers. Almost without leaving my home I had been nourished by stories of travels to far-off places, including the moon, the center of the earth, the bottom of the sea, the islands of the Caribbean and the Pacific, the North Pole, and that enormous Russia that Jules Verne's reporter named Claudius Bombarnac traveled through.

As I recall, it was a June night. I was sitting on a bench on the train platform between my grandmother and grandfather, and a train, not yet ours, arrived at the station and stopped with a slow screech. In the darkness it had the shape of some great mythological beast, and as it approached, the round headlight on the engine reminded me of Captain Nemo's submarine. A woman was leaning against the railing of the observation platform; I was instantaneously overwhelmed with desire, the innocent, frightened, and fervent desire of a fourteen-year-old boy. I wanted her so badly my legs trembled, and the pressure in my chest made it difficult to breathe. I can still see her, although I don't know now whether what I remember is in fact a memory: a tall blond foreigner wearing a black skirt and a black blouse unbuttoned low. I looked at her windswept hair and the brightly painted toenails of her bare feet. A deep tan brought out the gleam of her blond hair and light eyes. She moved a knee forward, and thigh showed through the slit in her skirt. The train started off, and as I watched she moved away, still leaning on the rail and watching the disappearing faces observe her from the platform of that remote station. Midnight in a foreign country.

In shifting tatters of dreams, the woman appeared again as I dozed and my grandfather and the other man kept talking in the darkened coach. Through half-opened eyes I could see the tips of their cigarettes, and when my grandfather or his companion took a drag, their country faces were visible in the reddish glow. Oh, the acrid black tobacco that men smoked then. As I watched those faces and listened, their words dissolved into sleep, and I felt myself on one of the trains they were telling about, past trains of defeated soldiers or deportees who traveled without ever reaching their destination, stopped for whole nights beside darkened platforms. Shortly before he died, Primo Levi said that he was still frightened by the sealed freight cars he occasionally saw on sidetracks. "I served in Russia," the man said, "in the Blue Division. We got on a train at the North Station, and it took ten days to reach a place called Riga." And I thought, or half said in my sleep, Riga is the capital of Latvia, because I'd studied it in the atlases I liked so much and because one of Jules Verne's novels is set in Riga and his books filled my imagination and my life.

Now I understand that in our dry inland country night trains are the great river that carries us to the world outside and then brings us back, the great waterway slipping through shadows toward the sea or the beautiful cities where a new life awaits us, luminous and true to what we were promised in books. As clearly as I remember that first train trip, I remember the first time I stopped at a border station; in both memories are the brilliant night, anticipation, and fear of the unknown that made my pulse race and my knees buckle. Scowling, rough-mannered policemen examined our passports on the platform at Cerbère Station. Cerbère. Cerberus. Sometimes stations at night do resemble the entrance to Hades, and their names contain curses: Cerbère, where in the winter of 1939 French gendarmes humiliated the soldiers of the Spanish Republic, insulted them, pushed and kicked them; Port Bou, where Walter Benjamin took his life in

1940; Gmünd, the station on the border between Czechoslovakia and Austria where Franz Kafka and Milena Jesenska sometimes met secretly, within the parentheses of train schedules, within the exasperating brevity of time running out the minute they saw each other, the minute they climbed the stairs toward the inhospitable room in the station hotel where the rumble of passing trains rattled the windowpanes.

What would it be like to arrive at a German or Polish station in a cattle car, to hear orders shouted in German over the loudspeakers and not understand a word, to see the distant lights, wire fences, and tall, tall chimneys expelling black smoke? For five days, in February 1944, Primo Levi traveled in a cattle car toward Auschwitz. Through cracks in the wood planks where he pressed his lips to breathe he glimpsed the names of the last stations in Italy, and each name was a farewell, a step in the voyage north toward winter cold, toward names of stations in German and then Polish, isolated towns no one had yet heard of: Mauthausen, Bergen-Belsen, Auschwitz. It took Margarete Buber-Neumann three weeks to travel from Moscow to the Siberian camp where she had been sentenced to serve ten years. When only three had passed, they ordered her onto a train back to Moscow, and she thought she would be set free; the train, however, did not stop in Moscow, it continued west. When finally it stopped at the border station of Brest-Litovsk, the Russian guards told Buber-Neumann to hurry and get her belongings together, because they were in German territory. Between the boards nailed over the window, she saw the black-uniformed SS on the platform and understood with horror and infinite fatigue that because she was German, Stalin's guard were handing her over to Hitler's guard, fulfilling an infamous clause in the German-Soviet pact.

The great night of Europe is shot through with long, sinister trains, with convoys of cattle and freight cars with boarded-up windows moving very slowly toward barren, wintry, snow- or mud-covered expanses encircled by barbed wire and guard towers. Arrested in 1937, tortured, subjected to interrogations that lasted four or five days without interruption, days and nights during which she had to remain standing, then locked for two years in solitary confinement, Eugenia Ginzburg, a militant Communist, was sentenced to twenty years of forced labor in camps near the Arctic Circle, and the train that carried her to her imprisonment took an entire month to cover the distance between Moscow and Vladivostok. During the journey, the women prisoners told one another their life stories, and sometimes when the train was stopped at a station, they put their heads out a window or to a breathing place between two boards and shouted their names to anyone passing by, or tossed out a letter or a piece of paper on which they'd scrawled their names, with the hope that the news that they were still alive would eventually reach their families. If one of two survives, if she gets back, before doing anything else she will look for the other's parents or husband or children and tell them how her friend lived and died, give evidence that through hell and in the farthest reaches her friend never stopped thinking of them. In the Ravensbrück camp, Margarete Buber-Neumann and her soul mate Milena Jesenska made that vow. Milena told Margarete about her love affair with a man dead for twenty years, Franz Kafka, and she also told her the stories he had written, stories Margarete hadn't read or heard till then and for that reason enjoyed even more, like the age-old stories no one has written down and yet are revived whole and powerful as soon as someone tells them aloud: the story, say, of the surveyor who comes to a village where there's a castle he is never able to enter, or the one about the man who wakes one morning turned into an insect, or the one where police come to the director of a bank one day and tell him that he is going to be tried, although he never learns what accusation was brought against him.

The love affair between Milena Jesenka and Franz Kafka is crisscrossed with letters and trains, and in it distance and written words count more than real meetings and caresses. In the spring of 1939, a few days before the German army entered Prague, Milena sent to Willy Haas the letters from Kafka that she had kept, the last of them coming to her sixteen years before, in 1923. On the journey toward the death camp, in the dark stations where the train would stop all night, she must have remembered the emotion and the anguish of those secret journeys of other days, when she was married and lived in Vienna and her lover lived in Prague, and they would meet halfway in the border town of Gmünd, or the first time they met, after several months of exchanging letters, at the station in Vienna. Before they started writing, they saw each other only once, in a café, scarcely noticing each other, and now suddenly he wanted to reclaim from the fuzzy fringes of memory the face of this woman. *I warn you that I cannot remember your face in detail. I remember only your moving away between the small tables in the café: your figure, your dress… I still see them.* He has taken the train in Prague, knowing that at the same time she has taken another in Vienna, and his impatience and desire are no stronger than his fear, because he knows that within a few hours he will hold in his arms a physical woman who is scarcely more than a ghost of his imagination and their letters. *Fear is unhappiness,* he wrote to her. He fears that the train will arrive and he will find Milena standing there, her light-colored eyes searching for him, and also fears that she had second thoughts at the last moment and stayed in Vienna with her husband, who does not make her happy, who deceives her with other women, but whom she doesn't want or is unable to leave. He consults his watch, looks at the names of the stations at which the train is stopping, and is tormented by an urgent wish for the hours to race by, to already be there, but also by the fear of arriving and finding himself alone on the platform of the station in Gmünd. And he fears the impetuous physical presence of Milena, who is much younger and healthier than he, more skillful and more daring in sex.

Unconscious memory is the yeast of imagination. I did not know until this very moment, while I was trying to imagine Franz Kafka's journey on a night express, that I was in fact remembering a journey I myself made when I was twenty-two, one sleepless night on a train to Madrid, on my way to a rendezvous with a woman with light eyes and chestnut hair. I had sent her a telegram minutes before buying my second-class ticket with borrowed money and foolishly leaving everything behind. When I reached the station at dawn, there was no one there to meet me.

What would it be like to approach a border checkpoint and not know if you would be turned back, if the uniformed guards who examined your papers with cruel deliberation, looking up arrogantly to compare the face in the passport photograph with the fear-filled face struggling to seem normal and innocent, would prevent you from crossing to the other side, to the salvation only a few feet away? After meeting Milena for the first time and spending four days with her, Kafka took the express from Vienna to Prague, nervous about getting to his job the next morning, feeling a mixture of happiness and guilt, of sweet intoxication and intolerable amputation, for now he couldn't bear to be alone and who knows how long it would be before he could meet his lover again? When the train stopped at the station in Gmünd, the border police told him that he could not continue on to Prague; one paper was lacking among his numerous documents, an exit visa that could be issued only in Vienna. On the night of March 15, 1938, when Kafka had been dead for almost fourteen years, safe from all worry and guilt, that same express, which left Vienna for Prague at 11:15, was filled with refugees— Jews and leftists, especially—because Hitler had just entered the city, welcomed by crowds howling like packs of wild beasts, their arms uplifted, shouting his name with the hoarse, collective roar of a raging ocean, yelling *Heil* to the Führer and to the Reich, clamoring for the annihilation of the Jews. Uniformed Austrian Nazis boarded the Prague express at intermediate stations and looted the baggage of the refugees, whom they beat and subjected to insults and curses. Many passengers had no papers, and at the border station the Czech guards prevented them from continuing. Some leaped from the train and fled across the fields, hoping to cross the border in the shelter of night.

What would it be like to arrive by night at the coast of an unfamiliar country, to jump into the water from a boat in which you have crossed the ocean in darkness, hoping to leave the coast far behind even as your feet are sinking into the sand? A man alone, with no documents, no money, who has come from the horror of illness and slaughter in Africa, from the heart of darkness, who knows no word of the language of the country to which he's come, who throws himself to the ground and crouches in a ditch when he sees the headlights of a car, maybe the police, coming toward him.

IT SEEMS WE ENJOY reading travel books more when we are traveling. At the beginning of the summer of 1976, after wrapping up my courses, I took a train from Granada and during the trip read Proust's account of a journey to Vienna in *Remembrance of Things Past*. Two years later, on a September evening, I went to Venice for the first time, and remembered Proust and his painful propensity for disillusionment as I visited places I had wanted so long to see. Talking with Francisco Ayala about the pleasure of reading Proust, I discovered that he, too, connected it with the simultaneous pleasure of a journey. In nineteen forty-something, when my friend was living in exile in Buenos Aires, he taught at the provincial University of Rosario. He traveled once a week, first by train to Santa Fe, then in a bus that ran along the banks of the Paraná. He always carried a volume of Proust, and it seemed to him that reading Proust now was even more delicious than the first time, because when he looked up, he saw vistas from the other side of the world, was instantly whisked from the streets of Paris in 1900 and from the cloudy beaches of Normandy to the immense uninhabited spaces of South America he was passing through by train and bus. Suddenly the book was his only tie with his previous life, with a Spain lost to him, a Spain he might never return to, and a Europe that still had not emerged from the cataclysm of war. He was reading Proust on a bus traveling along the sealike vastness of the Paraná, and the volume he held in his hands was the same he'd read so often on streetcars in Madrid.

Once, at one of the stops, he looked up and saw a white-haired old man who had just got on, wearing a worn overcoat and carrying an equally worn briefcase. He was struck by his air of melancholy and poverty; the face reflected illness and exhaustion, the face of an old man whom the years had not spared life's bitterest dregs. In an instant of shock, disbelief, and embarrassed compassion, he recognized in this old man riding a bus in a remote town in Argentina a man who had once been president of the Spanish Republic: Don Niceto Alcalá Zamora. Afraid that Alcalá might recognize him as well, he turned his face toward the window and buried himself in the book. When he looked up again, after the next stop, the man was no longer on the bus.

ON A JOURNEY YOU HEAR a story or by chance find a book that sends out ripples of concentric rings that affect succeeding discoveries. Once on a train to Seville, at a time when I was very much in love with a woman who fled from me when I most desired her and who pursued me when I tried to break away, I was reading *The Garden of the Finzi-Continis* and bestowed on Giorgio Bassani's beautiful and ungovernable Jewish heroine, Micol, the features of the woman I loved. The final failure of the novel's protagonist sadly anticipated mine, which I saw with a clear-sightedness I wouldn't have been capable of on my own.

I remember a cheap, dog-eared copy of Herodotus's *Histories* that I found in a street stall in New York, and also Captain John Franklin's journal of his trek to the North Pole that I had leafed through by chance in a secondhand bookshop and then read ravenously in a London hotel, a narrow, high-ceilinged bedroom of perverse geometry and a dressing room scarcely larger than an armoire but writhing with angles of expressionist decor. In 1989, having arrived in Buenos Aires during the southern hemisphere's autumn, I spent hours lying on the bed in my room listening to the rain drumming against the windows, the same rain that prevented me from going outside to walk the streets I wanted so badly to explore. For hours, to offset the claustrophobia of my confinement, I read the first book I had discovered by Bruce Chatwin, *In Patagonia.* Now I know that precisely during the time I was reading Chatwin's book, the author was dying of an illness whose name he did not want to divulge to anyone. A rare infection contracted in Central Asia through food or an insect bite, his friends said, to conceal his disgrace and avoid speaking the word that was already akin to the sore that centuries ago announced the horror of the plague.

So I read Chatwin in Buenos Aires as he was dying in London. My journey through Argentina was thus part truth and part literature, because as I read I was traveling to the great desolate spaces of the south, though my itinerary had ended in the nation's capital, in the room of a hotel I seldom left because of the rain. What a rest for the soul, to be far from everything, completely isolated, like a monk in his cell, a cell with every comfort: a firm bed, a telephone within reach, a remote control for the television. The rain absolved me from the exhausting obligation of touring and provided the perfect excuse for spending hours doing nothing, lying or half sitting propped up on two pillows, with a book in my hands that told of a journey to the ends of the earth and in which other, much older journeys were recalled: that of Charles Darwin in the large sailing ship *Beagle,* that of the Patagonian Indian who traveled with Darwin to England, learned English and English ways, visited Queen Victoria, and after a few years returned to his southern clime and to the primitive life he had left, now forever an alien wherever he lived.

IN COPENHAGEN, a Danish woman of French and Sephardic heritage told me of a journey she had taken as a child with her mother through recently liberated France, toward the end of autumn 1944. I met her at a luncheon in the Writer's Club, which was a palace with double doors, marble columns, and ceilings with gilded garlands and allegorical paintings. At a window I watched as one of the tall ships passed, looking as if it were gliding down a street: it sailed along one of the canals that lead deep into the city and suddenly give a street corner the surprise perspective of a port.

That was early in September, about eight years ago. I had spent a couple of days wandering the city, and on the third an editor friend invited me to lunch. My memory is filled with cities that have greatly pleased me but that I visited only once. Of Copenhagen I remember especially images from my first walk. I left the hotel and started walking at random, and soon I came upon an oval plaza circled with palaces and columns; in the center was the bronze statue of a horse, the color bronze acquires because of humidity and lichen, a grayish green like the sky or like the marble of the palace I was told was once the Royal Palace.

In all the cold and baroque space of that plaza cut through from time to time by a solitary car (as I heard the sound of the motor, I heard also the whisper of tires on the cobblestones) there was no human presence other than mine and that of a soldier in the red coat and high furry shako of a hussar who was unenthusiastically standing guard with a gun over his shoulder, a gun with a bayonet as anachronistic as his uniform.

Not knowing which way to go, I let the streets lead me, as I let myself be led by a trail in the country. Across from the bronze horseman began a long, straight street that dead-ended at a dome, also verdigris bronze, of a church adorned with golden letters in Latin and a variety of statues of saints, warriors, and individuals dressed in frock coats along the cornices. The church resembled those baroque churches of Rome, one just like another, that give the unpleasant effect of being branch offices of something, maybe the Vatican or the financial offices of God's grace.

A statue ensconced on that facade undoubtedly represented Søren Kierkegaard. Stooped over, as if watching something below, hands behind his back, he did not have that attitude of elevation or of definitive immobility typical of statues. After death, after a century and a half of official immortality, of rubbing elbows with all those solemn heroes, saints, generals, and tribunes of the historic pantheon of Denmark, Kierkegaard—that is, his statue— still had a transient, temporary, restless demeanor, a look of uneasiness about walking alone through a closed and hostile city, casting sidelong glances at people he scorned and who scorned him still more, not only for his hump and large head but for the incomprehensible extravagance of his writings, his fervent biblical faith. He was as exiled and stateless in his native city as if he had been forced to live on the other side of the world.

I looked for the way back to the hotel. In less than an hour my editor—whom in truth I scarcely knew—would be coming to pick me up. On one long, bourgeois street of clothing and antique shops I saw a tiled roof projecting rather absurdly from a whitewashed or painted wall in which there was a wooden door with metal hinges and doorknocker and a window grill filled with geraniums. I, who on that Saturday afternoon had felt so far from everything on my walk through the empty streets of Copenhagen, had found a Spanish oasis called Pepe's Bar.

A WOMAN WAS SEATED beside me at a large oval table in the Writer's Club. As has happened other times, the luncheon was in my honor, but no one was paying much attention to me. Before each of us was a card with a name. The woman's name was an enigma and a promise: Camille Pedersen-Safra. I can't resist the attraction of names. She told me she'd been born in France, into a Jewish family of Spanish descent. Pedersen was her married name. While the other guests were laughing and heatedly talking, relieved at not having to make conversation with a stranger they knew nothing about, she told me that she and her mother escaped from France on the eve of the fall of Paris, in the great exodus of June 1940. They had returned to that country only once, in the autumn of 1944, and both realized that after only those few years they no longer belonged to the country of their birth, from which they would have been deported to the death camps had they not escaped in time, and to show their gratitude they had become Danish citizens. Denmark, too, was occupied by the Germans and subjected to the same anti-Jewish laws as those of France, but unlike the French Vichy government the Danish authorities did not collaborate in isolating and deporting Jews, did not even apply the law making them wear a yellow star.

Camille Safra had been six at the time of their flight from France. She remembered her displeasure when her mother shook her awake in the middle of the night, and the strange, warm, and vaguely pleasant sensation of traveling wrapped in blankets in a trailer behind a truck, beneath a canvas being beaten by the rain. She also remembered sleeping in kitchens or entryways of houses that weren't hers, places where there was a strong odor of apples and hay, and she sometimes had flashes of mysterious routes along moonlit country roads, held in her mother's arms beneath the shelter of a wet woolen shawl, listening to the creaking of a cart and the slow hoofbeats of a horse. She remembered, or dreamed of, lonely lights on street corners and in barn windows, the red lights of locomotives, and series of lights in the windows of trains she and her mother did not succeed in boarding.

In her memory, the journey into exile had all the sweetness of childhood well-being, the way children settle comfortably into the exceptional and give dimensions to things that adults cannot know and that have nothing to do with what is being experienced. When she left France, Camille was still submerged in that mythology; but by ten or eleven, when she and her mother returned, her adult sense of the real was nearly established. She had precise images now, colored with a sadness that was the reverse of the mysterious dream of the first journey.

She was a redheaded woman, stocky, energetic, careless in her dress, with features more central European than Latin and pronounced by age. I've seen Jewish women very much like her in the United States and in Buenos Aires: women of a certain age, fleshy, negligently dressed, lips brightly painted. She smoked a lot, unfiltered cigarettes, and conversed brilliantly, leaping between English and French according to her needs or limitations in expression, and she drank beer with a superb Scandinavian panache. She wrote book reviews for a newspaper and a radio program. The editor who had brought me to the luncheon, and who in the heat of conversation and the beer seemed not to remember I was there, had mentioned her influence when he introduced me, indicating that a favorable review from her was important to a book, especially one written by an unknown foreign author. I had the firm and melancholy conviction that the book, my reason for being in Copenhagen, would not attract Danish readers, so I was feeling remorse in advance for the bad deal the editor was getting from me, and I forgave him and was even grateful that at this luncheon at the Writer's Club he had abandoned me to my fate. In any case, the event was not that successful; there were unoccupied tables in the large dining room with its mythological paintings. Before serving, the waiters had removed those settings.

I also noted with annoyance as Camille Safra was talking that she hadn't said a word about the Danish edition of my book. She told me that her mother had died several months ago, in Copenhagen, and that in the last conversation she'd had with her the two of them agreed about details of that journey to France, especially something that had happened one night at a hotel in a small town near Lyon.

They were looking for relatives. Few had survived. Old neighbors and acquaintances looked on them with suspicion, perhaps fearing that they'd come back to make some claim, to accuse them or ask for an accounting. Camille's mother had taken her to that small town—she didn't give me the name—because someone had told her mother that one of her sisters took refuge there in early 1943. They found no record of the sister's having been arrested, though neither was there any information about where she might be—and they never found out. People disappeared in those days, said Camille Safra, trails were lost; her aunt's name was not on any list of deportees, repatriated, or dead. They came by train very early in the morning and ate a breakfast of cold coffee, black bread, and rancid butter in the station canteen. They asked questions of several unsociable early risers, who looked at them sullenly and refused to give the simplest information for fear of compromising themselves, since at that time collaborators were being flushed out.

Hungry, disoriented, strangers in the country that four years before had been theirs, their feet aching after walking all day, they found themselves, when night overtook them, in an open area near the shelter of a streetcar stop. They couldn't return to Paris until the following morning. The streetcar had left them at a plaza with closed-up shops and with a monument to the fallen of the First World War; nearby was a street lamp lighting the sign of a hotel that called itself the Commerce.

They rented a room. They went upstairs to go straight to bed because the electricity would be turned off at nine. Sitting on the bed beneath a bulb that faded to pale red then revived to shed an oily yellow light, they shared a package of food they'd been given by the Red Cross. Then, dressed, and with their arms around each other, they lay down, icy feet touching beneath the thin blanket and threadbare bedspread. Her mother, Camille Safra told me, never locked doors; she was terrified of being trapped, of losing the key and not being able to get out. In the shelters, when the air-raid sirens sounded, she had attacks of sweating and panic. If they went to the movies, as soon as the film was over she rushed to the exit, for fear that everyone would leave before her and they would lock the doors, thinking the theater was empty.

Mother and daughter woke at dawn. Through the window, beneath the beating rain, they could see a rustic patio with chicken coops and an area of garden. They took turns washing with the icy cold water in the pitcher beneath the washstand and dressed in the drab, dignified, and inexpensive clothing they always wore, clothes that never kept them warm, just as there was never enough food to satisfy their hunger. When her mother tried to leave the room, the knob wouldn't turn, the door wouldn't open.

"I told you last night not to turn the key."

"But I didn't, I'm sure."

The key lay on the dressing table opposite the bed. They inserted it in the lock, turned it this way and that, but nothing happened. The key didn't click, it seemed not to meet any resistance, merely turned ineffectually in the lock. It wasn't that it didn't fit because it was the key to a different room. The mechanism appeared to function, but the door simply didn't open.

The mother grew nervous. She rattled the doorknob and the key, beat on the lock, bit her lips. She said in a low voice that if they didn't get out, they would miss the train to Paris and couldn't go back to Denmark, would have to stay forever in France, where they had no one, where no one had given them so much as a smile of welcome, not even recognition. She took the key from the lock but then couldn't get it back in, and when she finally did, refusing to let her daughter help her, she turned it so hard that the key broke in half.

"Why don't we ask for help?" said Camille.

"They'd laugh at us, two ridiculous Jews. Who ever would expect to be locked in like this?"

They tried the window: it, too, was impossible to open, although they didn't see any latch, and of course there was no lock. They had to ask for help. A few minutes later, her mother, now out of control, her jaw hanging loose and her eyes glassy with fear—the fear she'd suffered during the flight that had saved her daughter four years before—beat on the door with desperation, yelling for help.

It was with relief that they heard footsteps on the stairs and along the hallway. The owner of the hotel, with the help of a wire, managed to extract from the lock the half of the key that had broken off, but when he introduced the master key, the door still wouldn't open. From both sides, the door was pushed, shaken, and pounded, but it remained firmly locked, and the wood was too thick and the hinges too solid for them to batter it down.

Her mother was choking. She had sat down on the bed, in her black traveling clothes—ancient overcoat, small hat, and wide, misshapen shoes—and was breathing open-mouthed, nostrils flaring, wringing her hands or burying her face in them, the way she had when mother and daughter went down into the shelters during the raids at the beginning of the war. We'll never get out of here, she kept saying, we shouldn't have come back, this time they won't let us leave. Camille then made a decision she was still proud of forty years later. She threw the washstand pitcher at the window, and as the glass broke, the cool, damp morning air flowed in. But it was too high for them to jump down to the patio, and the ladder someone went to look for never appeared.

They never did get the door open. An hour later the manager opened a second, sealed door hidden behind an armoire that the two of them struggled to pull away.

Despite all this, they caught a train to Paris that same morning. Her mother led her by the hand, squeezing hard, and told her that they were going back to Denmark and that she would never again set foot in France. In the train compartment, she was as pale, and looked as worn, as if she'd been traveling a long, long time, like many of the refugees and exiles in those times who were seen wandering around stations, waiting days, entire weeks, for trains to arrive that had no schedule or precise destinations, because in many places tracks had been twisted and bridges destroyed by bombings or sabotage. One gentleman with an air of genteel penury very like theirs offered the girl half of the orange he unrolled from a very clean handkerchief and peeled with extreme tidiness while they had tried not to look or notice the tart, tempting aroma that filled the air, erasing the usual odors of sweaty clothes and tobacco smoke. He was the first person to smile at them since they arrived in France. They struck up a conversation, and the mother told him the name of the town and the hotel where they'd spent the night. When he heard it, the man stopped smiling. He was also the only one they'd met who spoke without caution or fear.

"That was a good hotel before the war," he told them. "But I'll never go in it again. During the occupation the Germans converted it into a barracks for the Gestapo. Terrible things happened in those rooms. People passing through the town plaza heard screams, though they acted as if nothing were wrong."

When she stopped talking, Camille Safra shook her head slowly and smiled with her eyes closed. When she opened them, they were moist and shining. Those eyes had been beautiful in her youth, when she traveled with her mother through France on that train and had shyly and enviously looked at the orange the man in her car so carefully peeled on his white handkerchief. She told me that toward the end of her mother's life, in the hospital room where Camille spent nights beside her bed, her mother waked at times from a nightmare and asked her not to lock the door, breathing through her open mouth, staring at her with eyes wide with fear, fear not only for her approaching death but also, and perhaps worse, for the death she and her daughter had escaped forty-five years before.

At the end of the luncheon at the Writer's Club, several toasts were made with excessive fervor. I don't remember whether any was in my honor, but perhaps they were in Danish and I didn't understand them. The clearest memory I have of that trip to Copenhagen, aside from the misanthropic statue of Kierkegaard and the Andalusian red tiles of Pepe's Bar, is of the journey the woman named Camille Safra made during the rainy, lugubrious autumn of the war's end in Europe. While traveling, you hear and tell tales of journeys. "Wherever a man goes, he takes his novel with him," Galdós writes in *Fortunata y Jacinata*. But sometimes, looking at travelers who never say a word to anyone but sit silent and impenetrable beside me in their plane seat or who drink their drink in the dining car or stare at the monitor showing a movie, I wonder about the stories they know and aren't telling, about the novels each carries inside, the journeys lived or heard or imagined that they must be remembering as they travel in silence at my side, shortly before disappearing forever from my sight, their faces forgotten, as mine is to them, like those of Franz Kafka on the Vienna express or Niceto Alcalá Zamora on a bus traveling through the desolate landscape of northern Argentina.

those who wait

AND YOU, WHAT WOULD you do if you knew that at any moment they could come for you, that your name may already be on a typed list of prisoners or future dead, or suspects, or traitors? Maybe right now someone has penciled in a mark beside your name, taking the first step in a proceeding that will lead to your arrest and possibly your death, or to the immediate necessity of leaving the country, or temporarily, merely, to the loss of your job or of certain minor perks you wouldn't find too hard to give up. They notified Josef K. of his trial, but no one arrested him; it didn't even seem that they were watching him. You know how it goes, or at least you should be able to imagine it, you've seen what happens to others close to you, neighbors who disappear, or had to flee, or stayed as if there were no danger, no threat to them. At night you've heard footsteps on the stairs and in the hall that lead to the door of your apartment, and you feared that this time it was for you, but the footsteps stopped before they reached your door, or went by, and you heard the pounding on another door, and the car you heard drive away later took someone who could have been you, although you prefer not to believe it, telling yourself they have no reason to arrest you or any of yours, at least for now. You never did anything, never stood out in any way. You belonged to the Party since you were very young, and Comrade Stalin's picture hangs in the dining room of your home. You're a Jew, but only by blood, your parents brought you up in the Protestant religion, and to love Germany. In the summer of 1914, as soon as war was declared, you enlisted, you received an Iron Cross for bravery in combat, you don't belong to any Jewish organization, you don't feel the least sympathy for Zionism: you are, intimately, by education, by language, even physically, German through and through.

It is hard to get from one day to the next, to break with everything, with ties of the heart and habits of daily life, hard not to be crushed by the thought of losing your home, your books, your favorite easy chair, the normalcy you have always known; hard to endure despite the pounding on the neighbors' door or the shot that in an instant has cut short a life, or the rocks thrown through the windows of the tailor shop or the neighborhood grocery where one morning a coarsely painted Star of David appeared along with a single word that in its brevity contains the greatest insult: *Juden.* You plan to do your buying at the usual shop every day, but today in front of it a group of men wearing brown shirts and armbands with swastikas are holding a placard, *Anyone who buys from Jews is backing the foreign boycott and destroying the German economy,* so you lower your head and change course as unobtrusively as possible. You go into a nearby shop, hiding your shame; after all, the boycott of Jewish businesses is in effect only on Saturdays, at least it was in the beginning, the spring of 1933, and if the next day, or that same afternoon, you meet your usual shopkeeper, who knows you didn't come to do your shopping, you can look away or cross the street instead of going up to him and shaking his hand, or not even that, speaking a few normal words, showing a sign of fraternity that's not necessarily Jewish, simply human, like lifelong neighbors. Things happen little by little, very gradually, and if at first you prefer to imagine that things aren't that serious, that normalcy cannot be shattered so easily, the prophets of doom irritate you more than ever, those who point to the threat that grows nearer because they articulate it, that might go away if only they would pretend not to notice it. You wait, you do nothing. With patience and a low profile it will not be difficult to wait out these times. In 1932, traveling on a boat down the Rhine, Maria Teresa León saw thousands of small swastika-printed flags stuck into tiny buoys and bobbing along on the current. On Thursday, March 30, 1933, Professor Victor Klemperer, of Dresden, notes in his diary that in a toy-shop window he saw a child's balloon with a large swastika. *I can no longer rid myself of the disgust and shame. Yet no one makes a move; everyone trembles, hides.* But Professor Klemperer does not plan to leave Germany, at least not at this time, for where will he go at his age, almost sixty, and with a wife who is ill, and now that they've bought a small bit of land where they hope to build a house? *So many people beginning new lives other places, and here we are waiting, our hands tied.* But who in his right mind can believe that a situation like this will last long, that well into the twentieth century such barbarism and senselessness can prevail in a civilized country? Surely the Nazis, so brutal, so demented, will be rejected by the German people in the end, and the international community will refuse to acknowledge them. Except sometimes, when you think you're getting away from danger, you are hypnotically drawn to it, as if by a magnet, the powerful desire to be caught and thus end the anguish of the waiting once and for all. But neither is an expatriate safe. In remote Mexico, in a house turned into a fortress, protected by armed guards and barbed wire and concrete walls, Leon Trotsky waits for the arrival of Stalin's emissary, who will come slipping past barred doors and guards and stand alone before him and fire a bullet into his head, or lean over him with the solicitude of Judas and sink a climber's ice pick into the nape of his neck, as efficient as a bullet. It is summer, August 1940. Klemperer, no longer a professor, notes undramatically in his diary that after July 6 Jews are forbidden to enter public parks. In France, in the late, warm twilight of early June, three men fleeing together before the advance of the German army went deep into a forest. One of them, the oldest, most corpulent, and best dressed, turned up several months later, hanged, his decomposed cadaver fallen to the ground and half hidden beneath the autumn leaves. The branch on which he hanged himself, or was hanged, had broken beneath his weight. A German fleeing Germans, but also once a Communist, though the Communists had declared him a traitor and decreed his execution. The two fleeing with him were Soviet agents who had traveled to France with the one goal of finding and killing him. Not even hiding among the throngs of refugees from the war, or behind a cement wall topped with broken glass and a tangle of barbed wire, will you be safe. You escape your country and become stateless, and one morning when you wake in the room of a hotel for foreigners, where you are living in miserable conditions, you hear loudspeakers shouting orders in your own language, and out the window you see the same uniforms you thought you had saved yourself from by crossing borders and distance. In 1938 the Viennese Jew Hans Mayer escaped from Austria; with false documents he traveled across a Europe of black predictions and hostile borders, took refuge in Antwerp, Belgium, and only two years later the same boots and armored cars and martial music that invaded Vienna were echoing through the streets of this city in which he had never ceased to be a foreigner. In 1943 he was captured by the men in leather coats and snap-brim hats from whom he had been running since 1938, more precisely, since the night of March 15, just after Hitler entered Vienna, when he, Hans Mayer, took the 11:15 express to Prague. He had pictured the scene of his arrest for so many years that when it finally came, he felt he had already lived it. Only one thing he had not foreseen: those who arrested him, asked the first questions, and delivered the first blows did not have the faces of men of the Gestapo, or even of police. *If a member of the Gestapo can have a normal face, then any normal face can belong to the Gestapo.*

In Moscow, the night of April 27, 1937, Margarete Buber-Neumann noticed that one of the KGB agents who came to arrest her husband was wearing small, round rimless glasses, which gave his very young face an intellectual air. That impression is substantiated by Nadezhda Mandelstam, who suffered from the harassment of the secret police and says that the youngest of them were known for their sophisticated tastes and a weakness for literature. At one in the morning, there was pounding on the door of their room in the Hotel Lux, where employees and foreign activists of the Comintern were housed. In 1920, Professor Fernando de los Ríos had lodged there, sent by the Spanish Socialist Workers Party with the task of reporting on Soviet Russia. He had interviewed Lenin and was surprised by the man's resemblance to the Spanish writer Pío Baroja, and by his scorn for the liberties and the lives of common people.

With beating hearts we fixed our attention on the sound of boots coming closer and closer. As happened every night, Margarete—Greta—had lain awake in the dark, listening to footsteps in the corridors, jumping every time the lights in the stairway were turned on. If the lights on the stairs and in the corridors of the Hotel Lux were turned on after midnight, it was for the KGB men, who prowled the dark, empty streets of Moscow in black vans everyone called crows. They didn't use the elevators, maybe out of fear that some mechanical failure or interruption of electrical current would allow a victim to escape. But the victims never escaped, they didn't even try, lying motionless, paralyzed, in their rooms, in the bleakness of their lives, and when finally the KGB did come for them, they offered no resistance, didn't fight or scream with rage or panic, didn't have a weapon ready to shoot their way out or blow their head off at the last instant. For years Heinz Neumann, leader of the German Communist Party, knew that he was a marked man, that his name was on the list, and still he went with his wife to the Soviet Union after the triumph of Nazism in Germany. He did not try to take refuge in a different country but lived in Moscow, aware of how the circle of suspicion and hostility was tightening around him every day, how his old friends stopped talking to him, how one after another comrades disappeared, those he had trusted but who had turned out to be traitors, Trotskyite conspirators, enemies of the people. Now no one visited him and his wife in their room in the Hotel Lux, nor did they visit anyone for fear of compromising them, of contaminating others with their always imminent disgrace, postponed day after day and night after night. If the telephone rang, they sat looking at it without daring to answer, and when they picked up the receiver, they heard a click and knew that someone was listening. There was a time when they covered the telephones with blankets or heavy clothing because a rumor said that even when the receivers were down it was possible to hear conversation in a room.

In the summer of 1932, Heinz Neumann and his wife had been Stalin's personal guests at a resort on the Black Sea. The night of April 27, 1937, when the pounding comes at their door, Greta Neumann is lying wide awake in the darkness, but her husband doesn't wake up, not even when she turns on the light and the uniformed men enter. The three of them stand around the bed, and one of them, maybe the youngest, the one with the rimless glasses, yells his name, but Neumann turns beneath the blankets and faces the wall, as if refusing with all the strength of his soul to wake. When finally he opens his eyes, *an almost childish horror floods his features, and then his face turns slack and gray.* While the men search the room and examine each of his books, husband and wife sit facing each other, and both feel their knees trembling. A piece of paper falls to the floor from one of the books, and the guard who picks it up identifies it as a letter from Stalin sent to Neumann in 1926. "Worse and worse," murmurs the guard, folding it back again. The husband and wife's knees touch, each with the identical tremble, like an ague that can't be stopped. Outside the room, in the hotel corridors, as outside their windows, they begin to hear the faint sounds of people waking up, of the city coming to life before the first light of day. *The dawn came slowly behind the window curtains.*

In 1935, Professor Klemperer was let go from the university, but because of his status as a war veteran he continued to receive a small pension. It would be a few years before he would be forbidden to drive a car, own a radio or telephone, go to the movies, have a pet. Professor Klemperer and his wife, always in such delicate health, given to neuralgia and melancholy, liked cats and films, especially musicals, very much.

They have been threatened, they know that at any moment they can be put under arrest or killed, but in the street the sunlight is the same as it always has been, cars drive by, stores are open, neighbors greet one another, mothers hold their children's hands on the way to school and before they leave them at the fence in front of the entrance squat down to turn up the lapels of their overcoats or to wrap them more tightly in their mufflers and caps. One November day in 1936, Professor Klemperer, who was taking advantage of the forced leisure of his retirement to write a scholarly book on eighteenth-century French literature, arrived at the university library, but the librarian who had helped him every day for many years told him, with distress, that she was no longer authorized to lend the professor books, and that he shouldn't come back anymore. You have been marked, sentenced. In the reading room you cannot enter now, people are bent in thought over opened volumes, under the soft light of the low, green-shaded lamps. You go outside, knowing that your days are numbered, that you should seize what time you have left and flee, at least make the attempt, but the man at the kiosk sells you your newspaper just as on any other morning, the bus makes its usual punctual stops every few minutes, and then it seems to you that the curse is in you, something that makes you different from the others, more vulnerable, worse, unworthy of the normal life they're enjoying, though you stubbornly believe that maybe it's due to some error, some misunderstanding that will be cleared up in time. In May 1940, Professor Klemperer is denounced by a neighbor for not having properly closed his windows during a blackout; he is arrested and locked in a cell, but released after one week.

Waiting for an inevitable disaster is worse than the disaster itself. On September 1, 1936, Eugenia Ginzburg, a professor at the University of Kazan, a Communist leader, editor of a Party journal, and wife of a member of the Central Committee, receives the notice that she is forbidden to give classes. She is a young and enthusiastic mother of two small children, a fervent adherent of each and every one of the Party's directives, convinced that the country is swarming with saboteurs and spies in the service of imperialism, traitors whom it is right to unmask and punish with the greatest firmness. Every day in meetings of cells and committees, in the newspapers, on the radio, new arrests are announced, and Eugenia Ginzburg is surprised by some of them but remains convinced of their necessity and justice.

One day she learns that she herself is under suspicion: nothing very serious, it seems at first, but it is irritating, and even unpleasant, a mistake that must eventually be resolved since it is unthinkable that the Party would accuse an innocent, and she, Eugenia Ginzburg, does not find in herself the least shadow of guilt, not the slightest uncertainty or weakness in her blind revolutionary faith. You believe you know who you are, but suddenly you've become something others want to see in you, then you've become a stranger to yourself, and your own shadow is the spy following your footsteps, and in your eyes you see the look of your accusers, those who cross the street to avoid saying hello or lower their head when they pass. But life is slow to change, and at first a person refuses to notice the alarm signals, to question the order and solidity of the world that has begun to break apart, the everyday reality in which large holes, pits of darkness even at midday, begin to open, where at any moment you may hear loud pounding at the door of the dining room where your children have lunch or do their homework, and the ring of the telephone cuts the air like an icy steel blade, like a fatal shot.

Eugenia Ginzburg is summoned at odd hours to meetings that turn out to be interrogations; it is suggested to her that she will be punished, because at one time she was connected with the university, or worked in the Party with someone who was a traitor, or didn't denounce someone with the proper revolutionary zeal. But the meeting, the interrogation, ends, and she is allowed to go home, and if there are people who have begun to pretend they don't see her or change course if she is walking toward them, others tell her to be calm, give her advice, say that nothing will happen, she'll see, everything will work out in the end. Only one woman warns her of the danger: her husband's mother, who is an old and maybe illiterate woman from a small village, shakes her head with resignation and remembers that all this happened before, in the times of the czars. *Eugenia, they're setting a trap for you, and you must run away while you can, before they have your head.* But why would I, a Communist, hide from my Party? I must show the Party that I'm innocent. They speak in low voices, trying not to let the children hear, afraid that the telephone, even though the receiver's down, will allow someone to listen. On February 7, Eugenia Ginzburg is called to yet another meeting, which is less disagreeable, and at the end of it the comrade who has been interrogating her gets to his feet with a smile; she thinks he will shake her hand, maybe tell her that the misunderstandings and suspicions are clearing up, but the man asks her rather casually, as if remembering a minor bureaucratic detail he'd almost overlooked, to leave her Party card with him. At first she doesn't understand, or can't believe what she's heard: she looks at this comrade and the smile disappears from his serene face, then she opens her handbag and looks for the card she always carries with her, and when she hands it to him, he takes it without a glance toward her and puts it in one of his desk drawers.

For eight days she waits. She stays home, in her room, not answering the telephone, barely noticing what is going on around her, the presence of her children, who move quietly, as if in a house where someone is ill, the company of her husband, who comes and goes like a shadow and raps quietly at the door and says in a low voice, "Open up, it's me." Now they begin to doubt whether innocence is enough to save her, they burn papers and books, old letters, any manuscript or printed page that might draw attention during a search. At night they lie awake, silent and rigid in the darkness, and shiver every time they hear a car coming down the silent street or see headlights through the window, flashing diagonally across the walls of the room. Their fear lasts from the moment they hear the car in the distance until it fades and is lost at the end of the street. In Kazan, as in Moscow, the only cars moving about at such hours are the black vans of the KGB. *Russia is very large, Eugenia, take a train and go hide in our village. Our little summer house is empty and the windows are sealed, and it has a garden with apple trees.*

It happened during the day, on the morning of February 15, and they didn't knock at the door, they called by telephone. How can the everyday life you love and know, that's filled with routine and things taken for granted, end so suddenly, and forever? How can this cold morning with the bright light on the snow that seems like so many others be the last? Eugenia was ironing, and her son was having breakfast at the kitchen table, drinking from a large cup. Her daughter had gone out to skate. The telephone rang, and at first she and her husband stood looking at it, not moving, not looking at each other. But it could be a call from anyone, maybe from the school, maybe their little girl had fallen while she was skating and the teacher was calling to tell them to come get her, that it wasn't serious. After several rings, her husband went to the telephone, lifted the receiver, and nodded as he listened to what they were telling him.

"Eugenia," he said, wanting, in vain, to make his voice sound normal, "it's for you." Maybe the boy dipped a piece of bread in his cup of milk and didn't even look up. "Comrade," said a young, well-mannered voice on the telephone, "would you have a moment sometime today to come by our office?"

Eugenia Ginzburg buttoned up the boy's overcoat and sent him out to skate with his sister. She pulled his cap down tight, covered half his face with his muffler, went with him to the door, waved good-bye as he walked off down the snowy street, and never saw him again. No one had come looking for her, no one had pointed a gun at her, handcuffed her, or shoved her into a black van, she just went out as she did any morning and walked toward the station; she could blend in with the crowd converging on the platform as a train approached, and get on, and maybe no one would notice her face. "I'm not doing anything," she had told the well-mannered man on the phone. "I'll come right now." She'd wanted to go alone, but her husband insisted on going with her. Outside, when she heard the familiar sound of the door closing behind her, she thought calmly that she would never hear it again, that she would never step across that threshold again. They walked in silence across the unbroken snow radiating whiteness in the gray February morning. They didn't hug each other when they went their separate ways at the entrance to the building where the men were waiting for her: to say good-bye would have been to recognize the abyss opening between them. Her husband said, "You'll see, you'll be home by suppertime." She nodded and pushed open the door. As she went in, she turned back and saw him standing motionless in the snow in the middle of the street, his mouth open and eyes afraid. For years, in disciplinary cells, in the stinking cars of trains that never reached their destination, in icy barracks in deserts of snow, in the hallucination of fever and hunger, in the debilitation of forced labor, in the eternal dusk of the polar circle, Eugenia Ginzburg saw that face, the expression she wouldn't have caught if she hadn't turned that one time before pushing a door that opened to the busy sound of footsteps, voices, and typewriters.

Three weeks later, on March 8, 1937, Rafael Alberti and María Teresa León, who were on a trip to Moscow, were received by Stalin in a large office in the Kremlin. María Teresa León remembered him as bent over and smiling. *He had short little teeth, as if his pipe had worn them away.* They talked about the war in Spain and about Soviet aid to the Republic. On one wall was a large map of Spain, with pins and little flags indicating the positions of the armies. On another, a map of Madrid. Stalin asked María Teresa León if it would bother her if he lit his pipe. He talked with them for more than two hours, promising them weapons, planes, military instructors. *He smiled at us the way you smile at children you want to encourage.* Many years later, far from Spain, lost in the duration and distance of exile, María Teresa León remembered Stalin with a kind of distant tenderness. *To us he seemed slim and sad, burdened by something, maybe by his fate.*

WHEN THEY BEGAN the deportation of Jews from Dresden, Professor Klemperer felt temporarily safe because he was married to an Aryan woman. *For the moment, I'm safe. As safe as someone can be on the gallows with a rope around his neck. Any day now a new law can kick the platform from under my feet, and then I'm a hanged man.* Men came to get Greta Buber-Neumann on June 19, 1938, but when they showed her the arrest warrant, she pointed out that it bore a date that was nine months old, October 1937. It must have been mislaid in all the red tape of the interrogators and murderers, the intellectuals with round eyeglasses and exquisite ideas about literature and the need to purify the Revolution with blood. Or maybe someone had deliberately kept it in a desk drawer, examining it day after day at an office desk the way you study a valuable manuscript, in an office with the noise of typewriters and heavy doors and locks. Someone decided to prolong for a year the day-and-night torture of the German woman who went from jail to jail in Moscow, vainly seeking news of her husband, and who kept a suitcase in her small, icy room, packed with a few things she needed for the moment she was arrested and shipped to Siberia. She never learned how or when Heinz Neumann died. With a letter and a packet of food under her arm, she went to Moscow in the midst of the tumultuous preparations for May Day, keeping away from the crowd as if she had the plague or leprosy, a foreign woman who didn't speak Russian well and who couldn't trust anyone, because her former comrades were either arrested or dead or had turned their backs on her. A figure among the throngs, not wanting to see the red flags or the posters strung above the streets or hear the music thundering over the loudspeakers, the heroic march from *Aida,* she recalled years later, and Strauss waltzes. On April 30, 1937, Greta Buber-Neumann walks to Lubyanka Prison, hoping to find her husband, who was arrested three days before, and everywhere she sees portraits of Stalin, in the shopwindows, on the fronts of houses, on movie theater doors, portraits encircled with flower garlands or red flags bearing the hammer and sickle. When she passes a group of people who have stopped to watch as workmen with pulleys and ropes raise an enormous portrait of Stalin that covers the entire front of a building, Greta turns away and presses harder against her belly the package of food and clothing that she may never be able to deliver. *If only I could never see that face again.* In the Opera House square they have just raised a wooden statue of Stalin—more than ten meters tall and mounted on a pedestal encircled with red flags: Stalin, walking energetically in a soldier's greatcoat and cap. What would you do if you were that woman lost in a vast foreign and hostile city, if they had taken away your passport and the temporary ID that classified you as an official of the Comintern, if they had thrown you out of your job and were about to throw you out of the room you shared with your husband, a room you still hadn't straightened after the search, still hadn't made the bed where you spent your last night with him, not sleeping for a minute, still hadn't picked up the books they threw on the floor and then stomped on or the stuffing from the mattress they expertly gutted looking for hidden documents, weapons, proof? You wait in the room, sitting on the unmade bed, stupefied, hearing steps in the hotel corridor, watching as the gray light of the afternoon slips toward darkness. They will come for you too, and you even wish they would hurry, you have your suitcase packed, or the bundle you will take with you, but days go by, weeks, months, and nothing happens, except that you've become invisible, no one looks you in the eye, and when you stand in line in the police stations and prisons beside the relatives of other prisoners and your turn comes, they rudely close the little window in your face because it's late. They won't tell you whether or not your husband is locked up in there, or pretend they don't understand the words you speak in Russian, words you have prepared so carefully, repeating them as you walk down the street like a crazy woman talking to herself. Ever since the Germans entered Prague, Milena Jesenska knew that sooner or later they would come looking for her, but she didn't hide, didn't stop writing in newspapers, she only took a few precautions; she sent her ten-year-old daughter to spend a while with friends, and she asked someone in whom she had absolute faith, the writer Willy Haas, to keep for her the letters from Franz Kafka.

In a distant park, one you reach after a long ride in a streetcar, almost on the outskirts of Moscow, Greta Buber-Neumann makes a date to meet an old friend, someone as frightened as she, but nonetheless loyal. You are that woman who jumps from a moving streetcar and turns to see if anyone is following, then takes another streetcar, and when she gets off, following a circuitous route, arrives at a suburban park bathed in the afternoon light. There will be people around, old men with canes and overcoats and leather caps, mothers holding the hands of children swathed in mufflers and heavy coats. Greta and her friend see one another from a distance but do not approach one another until they are sure no one is following. "Can't we get away somehow?" he asks. "Do we have to have our throats cut like rabbits? How have we been able to accept all this for years without questioning it, without opening our eyes? Now we have to pay for our blind faith."

The next time, the man doesn't come. Greta waits until nightfall, then goes back to her room without bothering to check whether she's being followed. She imagines, with sadness, almost with sweetness, that her friend has managed to escape.

One night in January 1938, the knock at the door finally comes. They haven't come to take her away, however, only to confiscate the last belongings of the renegade Heinz Neumann. Uniformed police collect the few books Greta hasn't sold for a pittance in order to buy food, and some of her husband's old shoes, and as they leave they hand her a receipt. Someone tells her that the friend she used to meet in the park was arrested as he tried to board a train for the Crimea.

They came one morning very early, on July 19, and when she realized that they had finally come for her, she felt only a kind of relief. They drove her to Lubyanka Prison in the backseat of a small black van, sitting between two men in sky-blue uniforms who didn't look at her or speak a word. This time her knees didn't tremble, and at her feet was the suitcase she'd kept packed for so long. She remembered the last thing she saw in a Moscow street before the van drove through the prison gates: a luminous clock glowing red in the early dawn.

On July 12, Professor Klemperer refers in his diary to some friends who left Germany and found work in the United States or England. But how do you leave when you don't have anything? He, an old man with a sick wife, with no knowledge of any foreign language, with no practical skill, how do you leave the house you've finally managed to build, the land Eva has almost made into a garden? *We have stayed here, in shame and penury, as if buried alive, buried up to our necks, waiting day after day for the last spadefuls of dirt.*

silencing everything

STARTLED AWAKE, I am stiff with cold, and I don't know where
I am, even who I am. For a few seconds, I have been a blaze of pure
consciousness, without identity, without place, without time,
only the waking and the sensation of cold, the darkness in which
I'm lying curled up, wrapped in the sheltering warmth of my own
body, on my side, hands between my legs and knees up against
my chest, my feet icy despite the boots and wool socks, my fingertips numb, my joints so stiff that if I try to move, I may not
be able.

There's something more than the cold and the darkness like
the bottom of a well, like a breath of moist stone and frozen,
plowed earth. The smell of manure too, manure mixed with mud,
an ocean of mud and manure that swallows up military boots,
horses' hooves, the wheels and tracks of war machines. What has
woken me is a sense of danger, a reflection of alarm so powerful
that in one second it dissipated all the weight of sleep. Quicker
than my still groggy consciousness, my right hand feels beneath
the blankets in search of the gun. The Spanish wool gloves, the
harsh sleeve of the gray military tunic stained with dry mud, the
feel of the greatcoat I'm using as a pillow and of the mattress of

damp straw on which I was sleeping: each is a feature added to my identity, to this persona that nevertheless observes from without, someone groping among rough fabrics for the cold metal of a Luger. But my whole arm feels heavy as lead, still paralyzed by sleep and cold, and an automatic instinct of caution warns me that I mustn't make a sound. I hold my breath, hoping to hear something, a whisper that barely scratches the silence. I want to evaporate in the darkness, to lie as motionless as those insects whose defense mechanism is to be mistaken for a blade of grass or a dry leaf.

It's the danger that has reminded him of who and where he is. Danger, not fear. He never feels fear, just as he cannot remember ever having felt envy. He feels the cold, the hunger, the exhaustion of brutal marches, the desperation of always sinking in endless mud—from the beginning of autumn, when the rains came—in a sea of mire and manure that swamps everything: men, animals, machines, dead and living.

A second ago it was barely a spark of alarm in the void of darkness, as anonymous as the tip of a cigarette glowing for an instant beyond the mud and the no-man's-land—in the vast nothingness of the plain obliterated by mud, which in a few weeks will become a desert field of snow. Now he knows, remembers. In old Spanish to remember means to wake up. The professor of literature is lecturing, walking from one side to the other on a dais dusty with chalk and echoing hollowly beneath his feet. He wears round eyeglasses, a rumpled suit, and draws from a dangling cigarette as he speaks passionately of Jorge Manrique and recites long sections of his poetry. He doesn't know that within a few months he will be shot, his nearsighted eyes squinting in the headlights of a truck. He remembers "the sleeping soul" and thinks of his favorite student in the Instituto Cardenal Cisneros in Madrid. His mind brightens, and he wakes completely. Memory explodes in him as if he had walked into a dark room where objects begin to take shape, the outlines of furniture and windows. His animal instinct for danger makes him listen again for the sound that woke him. A staccato, metallic sound, insignificant to anyone who doesn't know it, but unmistakable: the whisper of a gun lightly brushing against something, a rifle against the clothing on a shoulder. He raises his head a little and sees a ray of light beneath the door, between the chinks of the badly joined boards that separate the lean-to where he's sleeping from the main room of the hut. He could have chosen to sleep there, the German officer in charge of billeting told him, he'd be near the fire and wouldn't have to endure the stench of the manure. When he arrived the first night, the Russian woman and her child had already retired to the lean-to, or, more accurately, had hidden in it, leaving the only bed for him. Arms about each other, mother and child become a single mound of rags, two pairs of eyes frightened and shining in the light of the flashlight. He told them in German to come out, that they didn't have anything to fear, he told them using signs that he didn't want the bed, that they should take it. The woman shook her head, murmured in Russian, cuddled her child, the two of them rocking back and forth. The child had thin blond hair and sunken cheeks, and large blue circles smudged the transparent skin beneath his eyes.

But the light filtering from beyond the door doesn't come from a fire or candle. It's a flashlight being turned on and off; he can hear the click of the switch, which someone is sliding very quietly: not the woman, because he is sure she doesn't have a flashlight, she didn't even have candles until he brought her a handful from the commissary, or matches to light the fire. There was nothing at all in the straw-thatched log hut stranded in the midst of the mud and the chaos of the roads to the front, untouched by the disaster, nothing but the large iron bed that ended up there through God only knows what whim of fate, the bed that he'd refused to sleep in, despite instructions from the officer in charge of billeting.

He hears voices in the hut, barely whispers, but men's voices, not the woman's or the child's. Footsteps too, boots, which he doesn't exactly hear but rather feels as vibration on the ground where he's lying. The flashlight is turned on again, and again he hears the sound of a rifle against cloth or a leather belt—specifically, the sound of the ring that fastens the sling to the rifle butt. Now the beam is turned in his direction, and the straw and the nest of blankets and greatcoat in which he's lying are striped by threads of light coming through the cracks. Something blocks the light, a body brushing against the planks of the door. It's the woman, he's sure; he recognizes her voice, even though she is speaking very quietly, repeating one of the few words of Russian he's learned. *Niet.*

Now he guesses, understands, but still isn't afraid. Russian guerrillas. They operate behind our lines, sabotage installations, execute and hang from telegraph poles known collaborators with the Germans. They make raids at night, and at dawn there is no trace of them except for the corpse of someone they've hanged or strangled in silence. They don't run, they vanish in the darkness, in the limitless expanse of plain and woods, a space that no army can encompass or conquer.

He thinks coolly, trying to make the numb fingers of his right hand respond and find the pistol; they're carrying rifles, but they're not going to shoot me, they won't want to waste a bullet or have shots heard so near our guard posts. How strange to remember Jorge Manrique at this moment: *How death comes, silencing everything.* They will push open the plank door, and one of them will shine the flashlight on me and point a pistol at me, and maybe before I can get up another will bend over me and slit my throat, expertly stepping to one side to avoid the spurt of blood. The blood will steam in this cold. Everything soaked, heavy with blood: blankets, greatcoat, rotted straw mattress, and me dead... no, not me, someone else, because the dead lose all trace of identity. I will be dead without having touched my pistol, paralyzed by the cold that stiffens my hands, my entire body, as if I were wrapped in a premature shroud that prevents me from moving, as when you are sleeping and your muscles don't respond to your will, and you wake up with one arm so numb that you have to move it with the other arm as if it were made of wood.

What terrifies me is not dying but being mutilated. At the moment I'm safe from that. I won't be blown up by a howitzer or have my legs ground into the mud under the tread of an armored car. Someone, at any moment now, will push open that old plank door and cut my neck with a Russian Army machete, or with a nicked kitchen knife, or a rusty old sickle, and I won't move or do anything to prevent it. I'm lying here in the dark, staring at the streaks of light still in my eyes even though the flashlight was turned off, and I'm waiting like a steer to be slaughtered by some Russian guerrilla who's never seen my face, who will forget it as soon as he's cut my throat, because no one can remember a dead man's face, it becomes anonymous as soon as the life has left it, and that's why we have so little sense of the death all around us, rotting in the barbed wire, bloating in the mud, the piles of dead that we sometimes sit on to rest as we eat our rations.

Now he understands why he can't find the pistol. The woman took it while he was asleep; she must have slipped her hand beneath the doubled-up greatcoat he uses as a pillow and then crept away on her large bare feet, broad like her face and hips, in which there is a kind of stubborn, mulish strength despite the hunger and misfortune of the war that has upended the only world she knew and taken her husband. Shot by the Germans, she explained sketchily with gestures and mimicked sounds, as the child clung to her like a limpet, clutching her skirt with tiny, filthy hands so thin they were delicate, his frightened eyes fixed on the uniformed stranger, eyes huge in the starved face, as was his broad forehead, his entire head, compared to the scrawny torso and the skinny legs and arms as fragile as the limbs of some amphibian creature.

I offered them food, both mother and child, one of my rations or a tin of conserves, and they looked at my extended hand as warily as beaten dogs. The woman pushed the little boy, said something in a low voice, but he didn't budge, didn't take what I was offering but merely clung more desperately to his mother's skirts, never taking his eyes from the slice of bread or packet of crackers I'd brought. I could see the thread of saliva running down his scrawny neck, which didn't seem capable of supporting the weight of that enormous head. I put my offering on the table and went into the lean-to to rest, or I walked away a bit from the hut—*izba* is the Russian word. When I returned, the food was no longer on the table, but neither the mother nor child was chewing, they'd eaten it all, gulping it down with the choking haste of hunger, or else they'd hidden some in their clothing or beneath the bed, and they looked at me as if they feared that I wanted something from them, that I would demand they give back what no longer existed: two pairs of blue eyes bored into mine, staring at me with the knowledge that I could kill them without thinking twice.

Until this evening, I'd never seen them eat. I'd been out several days with guards and patrols on the front line; there'd been rumors of a Russian attack, and I hadn't been able to go back to the *izba* to sleep. I'd barely slept at all in the last three or four nights. Worse than the hunger and cold in war is the lack of sleep. When I went past the battalion command post to start my watch, I was handed a package of food my family sent from Spain. I reached the *izba* dead with hunger and weariness and found with relief that neither woman nor child was there, though I couldn't imagine where they might have gone. They must have been scrabbling through the mud somewhere, looking for food like stray dogs around some of our camps. But the fire was going, so I opened my package, which was filled with delicious sausages—almost impossible to believe they'd traveled untouched across the whole of Europe and half of Russia to reach me—and began roasting a few. What incredible delight in the midst of such misery, the sputter of the red grease bursting the casing, the smell of the seasoned, roasting meat. Then I became aware that the woman and her child were standing in the doorway, looking at me, looking at the sausages I was roasting over the fire. Maybe all they'd had to eat on the days I didn't bring anything was potato peels. I set the package on the table and motioned for them to come in. This time when the woman pushed, the boy didn't resist. With both hands he picked up a sausage I'd put on a plate and gobbled it down without lifting his head, grunting like an animal.

The woman watched but didn't come closer. I let her see I was leaving. I came in here and closed the door, I wrapped myself up in my blankets and folded the greatcoat to use as a pillow. I'd barely closed my eyes when I was swept away by the sleep I'd missed for so many days. Then the woman knocked very softly at the door. I could see her large body through the openings in the planks. I told her to come in and got to my feet. She came in, words tumbling out in Russian and making strange gestures as if crossing herself. She had red grease all around her mouth. Before I could say anything, she was kneeling before me and covering my hands with kisses, with tears and saliva and sausage drippings.

Now I hear her voice again, and although she's speaking so low that the only thing I can distinguish is sound, her voice has the same monotonous tone of supplication I heard this afternoon. *Niet,* she's saying, *niet.* The flashlight flicks on, goes out, and it's the woman's large body that has blocked the light. If I can work the stiffness out of my fingers and pick up the pistol and cock it before the men come to kill me, I might get at least one or two of them. When they shine the light in my face, I'll raise my hand and shoot, and in the confusion maybe I can save myself. But that simple act is as impossible as if I were planning it in a dream. I do nothing, I lie rigid on the floor, half propped up against the wall, listening to those murmuring voices, counting the seconds I have left before I die in these desolate northern reaches of the world, less than one kilometer from Leningrad, the city we were always on the verge of conquering but never reached, the city I'll never reach now, even though on clear days we see its golden cupolas gleaming in the distance, on the edge of the plain.

But there is no fear in me, not even now. I hope they come soon and that the pain doesn't last too long. The flashlight goes out, is turned on again, and my heart lurches, thinking that *now* they will push open the door. *Niet,* the woman says, and after the muted sound of a male voice I hear a cry from the boy that sounds something like the mewing of a cat.

No more voices. They'll come in, and I can't move this hand to pick up my pistol. A door opens, but it isn't the door in front of me, it's the other one, of stouter wood, the door of the *izba,* and as it opens a blast of wind touches me. I feel the vibration of boots on the ground. I hear that slight noise of a rifle, the sling ring clicking against the butt. Now the door has closed, and everything is darkness and silence once more.

With faint gratitude, but also with the indifference that has been growing in him as the war proceeds, he understands that the woman has saved his life. She has convinced the guerrillas not to kill him, telling them that he isn't a German and doesn't act like them despite the uniform with the lieutenant's insignia. Maybe she showed them the package of food, or what was left of it, maybe she gave them something to ease their hunger.

A German lieutenant takes his place in the hut a few days later, when he goes to serve in the front line. The first night, the

German claims the iron bed, while the mother and child sleep on the floor of the lean-to, and the next morning he is found strangled with a wire and hanged from a telegraph post near the hut. The mother and child are barricaded in the hut and it's set afire, and when everything has burned to the ground they flatten the area with a tractor and stick a sign in German and Russian in the mud reiterating the punishment reserved for those who collaborate with guerrillas.

Wait a minute. He shudders as a chill runs down his spine; he is huddled in the darkness, feeling the sheets, a pillow he should find a pistol beneath. *These things haven't happened yet. I can't be remembering something that hasn't happened. In April or May of 1936, my literature professor couldn't know that at the end of that summer he would be shot and thrown into a ditch.*

Confused again, he is on the verge of waking and doesn't know where he is or who he is. Where am I if not in a Russian hut near the Leningrad front in the autumn of 1942? I'm wearing not a German winter uniform but lightweight pajamas, there is no rough cloth of a military blanket, no stink of manure or the rotted straw of the mattress I dropped onto a few hours ago, dead with fatigue, not roused from sleep by the stealthy sounds of guerrillas who came to kill me.

Now, yes now he feels panic, lost somewhere in the tangle of unreliable memories and the chaos of time, and vertigo, because in a single instant his mind has leaped more than half a century and an entire continent. He is tempted to reach over to the night table and turn on the lamp, but he chooses to lie quietly, curled up as he did that night fifty-seven years before, a whole lifetime in one lightning flash, in that instant when you're dozing but jerk awake as your head drops. He listens attentively to the quiet whir of the alarm clock, the distant hum of the refrigerator, the muted night traffic of Madrid. He looks at who he was as if watching a stranger, seeing himself from the outside, feeling curiosity and a certain tenderness, as well as the satisfaction of learning that he wasn't a coward, and the surprise of having survived where so many perished. He knows that his lack of fear, like his lack of envy, is not something to be proud of but simply a part of his character. He sees the youth who was so passionate about philosophy and literature and the German language in a public institute in Madrid, the young man who wasn't born in time to fight in the Spanish Civil War but enlisted in a fit of reckless, toxic romanticism to go to Russia. He sees himself leaping over a trench, at the head of a squad, shooting a pistol and shouting orders, all the while feeling invulnerable. He sees coming toward him, emerging from a mist, a platoon of Russians with upraised swords.

But of all his successive identities the strangest, the most unreal, is the one he has experienced now, tonight, just awakened from a memory as vivid as a dream. Who is this eighty-year-old man turning clumsily in the bed, who knows he will lie awake until dawn, seeing the faces of dead men and places that don't exist, the Russian woman and the benumbed child hiding in the folds of her ragged skirt, the flames of the fire glowing on the leveled plain of mud, the face of the executed professor without his eyeglasses? He wishes he could fall asleep and for a few minutes or seconds have *now* again become *then*.

valdemún

COMING OUT OF THE last curve of the highway, you will suddenly see all the things she never saw again, the last things, perhaps, she remembered and felt a surge of nostalgia for as she lay dying in her hospital bed, caged among machines and tubes in a room where the air was burning with July heat, the thin cloth of her sick-room gown clinging to her sweaty back. She was always thirsty, and she mumbled words, working parched lips that you moistened with a wet cloth, and she imagined or dreamed she was sitting on the bank of a river in the shade of large trees swaying in a breeze as cool as the current, the clean, swift water where she dabbled her bare feet one summer morning in her early youth. Irrigation ditches snaking through heavy shade, gurgling water hidden beneath thickets of blackberries and willows, scales of gold glittering in the sun, clean pebbles on the bottom shining like precious stones, and in the eddies, spongy masses of eggs brushed the feet with the same delicate feel as water or mud, and bubble-like protuberances, imperceptible to the untrained eye, betray the presence of half-submerged frogs. She swallowed saliva and her throat burned, and once again her mouth was dry, her rough tongue licking lips that you didn't moisten because you fell asleep, overcome by the exhaustion of so many sleepless nights, now in the hospital and earlier at home, when they released her after her first stay and it seemed she would recover, would regain her health even though she was fragile and frightened. But once she was back home, it was obvious that she belonged in the hospital, for in those few days she had become a stranger to the place and things that once had formed the framework of her life. She would walk with a strange air through the kitchen or the living room in her bathrobe, as if she couldn't find her way, get lost in a corridor or stand before an open closet, looking for something she didn't know how to find, trying unsuccessfully to resume the domestic patterns of the time when she was well, the simplest tasks: preparing a snack in midafternoon, changing sheets.

Then she was back in the hospital and growing worse, her heart weaker than ever, but her face, colorless against the sanitary white of the pillows, took on an expression of serenity and surrender, and she stopped asking when she could go home. At night she was delirious with thirst or fever, or from the tranquilizers and injections they gave her to calm her unruly heart, and she imagined or dreamed that she was looking down on the swift, transparent river, dipping her cupped hands into the water and lifting it streaming and sparkling in the rays that slipped through the trees. But just as her lips touched the water, it escaped through her fingers, and she was still dying of thirst, and some part of her that remained lucid accepted that she would never again see the stair-stepped houses on the hillside or the valley of orchards with the ever-present sound of water in the irrigation ditches and the breeze in the treetops and waving willows. She twisted and turned in the bed, in the tangle of tubes and straps, moaned, half sleeping, half awake, and then you sat up with a start in your synthetic-leather armchair, with a rush of anguish and remorse for having dozed off when she might need something, might ask and you wouldn't hear, might die there beside you, gone forever without your knowing.

YOU WILL SEE PERFECTLY, at a precise point in the distance, what you saw as a little girl when you arrived every year for your summer vacation, and what she saw before you were born, when her eyes began to look out on the world, eyes like yours, preserved in your face after her death, the way a part of her genetic code is preserved in every cell of your body. Dead twenty years, she still looks through your eyes at what you will discover with a thrill of happiness and sadness when the car takes the last turn and spread out before you is the landscape that was a paradise not only after it was lost to you but also in the time you enjoyed it with the rare clarity of a child, unaware how sensations from your mother's childhood were being repeated in you, just as the shape and color of her eyes are repeated in your face, the hint of sweetness and melancholy in her smile. The fertile river valley was covered with green orchards of pomegranates and figs and crisscrossed with paths of loamy soil beneath the concave shade of the trees—poplars, beeches, willows—a water-saturated vegetation nourished by land so gravid that it welcomed with unique delicacy the tread of human feet, yielding slightly to the weight of a body, absorbing it with a welcome as hospitable as that of a river breeze.

"I want to be buried here, I don't want to be alone when I'm dead, surrounded by strangers in a cemetery as big as a city," she used to tell you. I don't mind dying, but I don't want to be buried where no one knows me, among strange names, that would be like living again in one of those apartment buildings where I was an outsider, stuck in my house waiting all afternoon for my children to come home, and my husband after nightfall, reserved or talkative, bragging about his job or bad-mouthing the people in his office, superiors or subordinates, names I hear and get used to but then stop hearing and forget, just as I get used to the new cities where his work takes us and where I never have time to get completely settled, never have what I want most: my own things, furniture I've picked out, a routine, that's what I miss the most, being able to settle sweetly into the passing of time, to get established, to occupy a secure place in the world, as I did as a child living in my small town, and although I always had a head for fantasy and imagined journeys and adventures, I enjoyed the safety of my home, my brothers and sisters, the presence of my father, the joy of looking out the window of my room and seeing the valley with its flowering almond and apple trees and, high above them, the bare tops of the mountains, with that color earth that's the same as the houses on the road to the cemetery where I want to be buried.

It makes me sad to leave life so soon and not see my children grow up or sit again with my sister to count and make a list of supplies in the large kitchen that looks out on the garden and the valley. Really it's more sadness than fear I feel, but there's something more, something I didn't count on, a strong desire to be relieved of tormented nights, medicines, sudden crises, trips in the ambulance, hospital rooms, all the tubes and machines. I used to imagine that it all would end and I would get well, but now I know I won't; even though they tell me they've found a new medication, I know that the time I have left will be exactly like now, or worse, a lot worse, as my heart grows weaker. I long to rest as I did when I was young and behind in my sleep. I would jump into bed and pull the covers over my head and close my eyes tight to get to sleep as quickly as possible. I would cover my mouth to hold back the giggles that burst out like the water in the public fountain when you pressed the copper or bronze handle down too hard. The water roared into the jar, cool and deep as the mouth of a well, all those years ago, before there was indoor plumbing and we women went with our water jugs to the fountain high on the hill, where there were always swarms of wasps. My sister would complain that since she didn't have hips, the full jug always slid down her side. Oh, that summertime water, how I would love to wet my dry, cracked lips in it now, in the drops sweating through the cool belly of the jug, feel against my cheeks the cool beads of moisture, the pores breathing in the clay. That's what I want, the only thing I want now, to fall asleep, to sink as I do when they give me a pill, or, better, a shot I can feel spreading through my bloodstream, through my whole body. Things fade: faces bending over me, beloved voices growing fainter, distant, and each time it takes a stronger effort not to let myself go along, as gently as closing your eyelids when you fall asleep.

The voices of my two daughters, and their faces so alike and so different, blend into the same sensation of tenderness and farewell, their hands clasp mine, covertly looking for my pulse when I'm lying so still I seem to have died. I have an idea what my older daughter will think when she's lived as many years as I have, "How strange, I'm as old as my mother was when she died," and she will wonder what I would have been like had I gone on living. She will finish the courses she's wanted to take ever since she entered college: she will be a teacher, marry her boyfriend, follow the path that she picked out when she was little and that she's never veered from. But what's to become of the younger one? Only sixteen and still amazed by the world, dazzled by the wealth and confusion of her imaginings. One day she wants to be one thing, and the next the opposite, one minute she's taking in everything but then suddenly only one thing pleases her, and for her there's no hurry or urgency, not about growing up or what to study or finding a boyfriend or getting married. She still lives as if she were floating, so weightless that any idea can sweep her away, the way I was when I was her age, full of dreams inspired by the movies, the novels I read behind my father's back, every day painting a different future for myself, cities and countries I'd travel through, but I wasn't bitter about being stuck in the village, I loved the house so much, though now I'll never see it again, the paths in the country, the water in the ditches, the fun my girlfriends and I had on Sunday afternoons, the summer night dances, protected by my father's kindness and my sister's affection. At least she will live longer than I do, will look after my daughters, she who never had a husband or even a boyfriend, her hips so slight she couldn't rest the water jug on them on the way back from the fountain.

YOU WILL TRY IN VAIN to remember the sound of her voice, for she stopped visiting you in dreams years ago. Again you are only guessing what she would have thought, the words she wanted to say to you but didn't have time, the advice that would have served you well, that might have kept you from making so many mistakes. Or maybe she followed you, protected and guided you without your knowing, present and invisible in your life, like the spirits your aunt lighted candles to, flickering lights floating in basins of oil on dressers and night tables and trembling like ghosts in the shadows. Maybe she came to you in dreams you didn't remember when you woke, told you things that saved you from the greatest dangers in your life, the quagmires in which so many of your generation lost their way, neighbors, friends of your teenage years who ended up as living dead, numbed, with unseeing eyes and a needle in one arm, aged, wiped out in what should have been the best years of their youth. You could have suffered the fate of your cousin, who also visited you in dreams after her death, who shared childhood summers in your small town, the two of you almost like twins when your mother died, standing at her funeral with your arms around each other, but she was always wilder than you, more daring in everything: childhood games, then sexual explorations with the first boyfriends, the excitement of a speeding motorcycle, the vertigo of a joint, and later, daring in matters of greater danger, perils you easily could have fallen into yourself, even though you panicked when you saw the restlessness and trouble that never left her eyes.

You will see the plain, green as an oasis, and above it the hill-sides with houses clinging to steep streets, supported by vertical buttresses or rocks where ivy and brambles clamber and figs sprout. You used to climb there with your cousin, always behind her, frightened but spurred by her boldness, and both of you would end up sweaty and panting, your knees as raw as those of the boys. You will hear the gurgling of unseen water in the ditches, and your eyes will search out the cypresses that line the road toward the bare peak of the hill, ending at the walls of the cemetery, which are the same harsh brown as the naked earth that suddenly is like desert, though only a short distance from the water and the green of the valley: desert and oasis, the peaks scored by dry gullies, stained rust red, the highest house already eroded by the dryness, the other houses abandoned many years ago, their shutterless windows empty of glass, their roofs caved in, their walls the color of clay, like adobe ruins in a desert slowly returning to dirt and sand. And at the top, above the last almond trees and ruined houses, at the end of the winding cypress-lined road where an occasional light is visible at night, that is where I want you to bury me, with my family and lifelong neighbors, among names I've heard since I was a little girl, in a cemetery so small that we all know one another, with a sweeping view of the hillsides and the valley and the overhanging houses of the village that makes your head swim.

You are on your way, and long before the name you loved so much when you were a girl appears on a sign at the side of the road, you will be excited, hypnotized by the pull of return, by the strong current of time that carries you back at a speed greater even than that of the car on the flat, straight highway, still barely out of Madrid, still near your present life and several hours and hundreds of kilometers from your destination but rushing toward it. Your face changes without your noticing, making you look like the person you were at four or five—the age of your first memories of that trip—and also the person you were when you were sixteen and your mother died. She pressed your hand on the mussed sheet of the hospital bed and said something you couldn't understand, and with the words barely out of her mouth, her moist hand softly released yours, with a kind of delicacy, and then it wasn't at all your mother's hand, the one you'd known and stroked so many times, pressed during those nights of agony and sleeplessness, it was the hand of a dead woman, neutral and inert when you held it to your face. Exhausted and in tears, you called to her for the last time, refusing to accept that she had left with no warning, in a few seconds, like someone slipping away to avoid the pain of a long farewell.

I keep sneaking glances at you, observing you. Driving, I turn toward you and see a new expression in your face, a look developing as we drive, and from that I get some hint of what you were long before I met you, a secret archaeology of your face and soul. I had handed you the telephone, which rang at a strange hour, almost midnight, and as you nodded and listened, your face became different from any face I'd seen in the years I lived with you.

Your previous life is a country that you've told me many things about but that I will never be able to visit: your past, your previous lives, the places you left behind, never to return, summer-vacation photos. The ring of the telephone broke the silence, the calm of the house, and when you hung up, after listening and nodding and asking questions in a low voice, the long ago erupted into your present, into mine, and enveloped us both—though I didn't yet know it—in its mist of sweetness and distance, of loss and regret. "You remember my mother's sister, who took such good care of us after Mother died? Now she has cancer, less than a week to live, a few days, he said, my cousin who's the physician, the brother of that cousin of mine who died so young."

You are grateful for your sadness, because it atones a little for the remorse you feel over how long it's been since you went to see her . . . really, since you even thought of her. It was enough for you to know that you loved her, that she had been the one warm, strong presence in your life for many years, your slender mother, or shadow of your mother, whom she closely resembled although without half her charm, a less attractive version of her younger sister. You didn't have to go see her, even call her, because she was with you, planted almost as deeply as the memory of your mother, but it never occurred to you that she was receiving no sign of that love from you. You realized too late that you made no effort to be with her during the last bitter years of her lonely life, in the large house where no one came to spend the summer. In all the hustle and bustle of life there had always been other things to do, more demanding things, like creditors. As if she would always be there, in that house, which changed as little as she, always ready to welcome you no matter how much time had passed. She, the house, the town belonged to a realm unaffected by your forgetfulness and long absences. If you were careless about your job, some misfortune might overtake you; if you failed to see a friend, you might lose him; you left nothing to chance either in love or in looking after yourself, never let things become routine, in all your actions, feelings, desires there was an edge of anxiety. You had been stripped so bare when your mother died, and overnight the daily order of your house was broken, so you could no longer trust in the permanence of things. Even as you enjoyed what you had, you knew how temporary it was, how inevitable loss was; and when you succeeded at something—a job, a friendship, a house—you never believed it was truly yours or that you deserved to celebrate it calmly. Which was why you always did things with vehemence, as if it were the first and last time, why you liked to decorate the places where you lived with carefully chosen objects, so that wherever you were, it seemed you'd lived there forever, given their careful arrangement and intimate relationship to you, except you felt that you had just arrived and might leave at any moment. In you, and in everything that had anything to do with you, one saw the sure hand of carefulness as well as the fragility of all that could be shattered or lost, all that was subject to chance.

Only the distant past was stable, a foreign country that long predated my arrival on the scene, a place you told me many things about but could not be found on any map, but only in the forbidden land of time. The three Moorish syllables of its name did not describe a location, they were merely a sound, a call that was familiar to you but had no resonance in my memory. All it took was the telephone ringing at midnight, and now haste, death, and guilt have invaded our static kingdom, and you realize that every day, every hour, every minute holds a threat, and you glance at the speedometer out of the corner of your eye, at the clock on the dashboard, calculating the kilometers yet to go, the days or hours of life left to your aunt, whom you imagined as safe from old age as she was in that black-and-white photograph taken in her youth, where she wears a summer dress and stands arm in arm with your mother, the two of them so much alike, yet one is striking and attractive and the other isn't; both laugh, innocent, for in their future no illness or death exists, and you and I are not even possibilities.

The place-names along the highway invoke your childhood, space transmuting into time as the signs mark the kilometers. You gaze out the window, recognizing the landscapes you saw long ago, and your eyes take on a faraway look. It's the beginning of summer vacation, and your excitement and impatience to get there are much more powerful than the weariness of so many hours in the car. Each roadside name and each number are a promise repeated every year, and yet it never loses its glow of happiness. You can't remember the sequence of the summers, though you might organize them according to the episodes of your childhood, but the sequence has come to a sudden conclusion in a hospital room on a chokingly hot day in July, as you observe the waxen face of the woman who has just died and is already losing her resemblance to your mother. In your mind all those summers become one broad and serene river, and all the trips are variations on the theme of approaching paradise. Sitting in the front seat, in your mother's lap, looking at the highway and gradually falling asleep as you gaze at the profile of your father, who was driving and smoking, or back toward your brother and sister, who were fighting in the backseat and surely resentful of you because you were the smallest and in the arms of your mother, who was still young and in good health, or didn't yet know she wasn't, or at least didn't let your brother and sister and you find out. But maybe even then, as she held you in her arms and let her thoughts roam, she was feeling in her breast the labored thudding of her heart and thinking that she might die and never see you grow up, never know what would become of you, that this summer trip to the town where she was born just might be her last. When the car made the final turn, and as you beheld the paradise of the orchards on the plain and the stair-stepped houses on the hillside, maybe she was looking up toward the sere, reddish peak where the cemetery was and thinking, "That is where I want to be buried, with people I love and who know me, not in one of those cemeteries in Madrid filled with nameless dead."

FINALLY, DRIVING INTO TOWN, you will see the name in the headlights and only then realize that you're slightly carsick, and bored. The old joy of arriving is scarcely a flicker. It's winter now and totally dark, and although from a distance the lights have given you the sensation that everything might be the same, little by little you see that things are not as you remember: the road is paved where you remember cobbles with grass growing between the rounded stones, encroaching buildings transform the street corners and block the view, and the shop where your mother and your aunt sent you as a girl to do the shopping, where you bought rolls and treats and soft drinks and Popsicles in the summer, is closed and looking run down. My cousin was a lot more adventurous than I. Whenever she could get away with it, she would take some coins from her mother's apron and drag me with her to buy ice cream and chocolates. As for me, I take everything in, look at what you point out, and study your face as we drive up a steep, narrow street toward the house where your aunt lies dying. I know I'm not seeing what you're seeing, the ghosts that have welcomed you the moment you arrived and are escorting you or lying in wait as we go up a paved hill and along a dimly lit street on which many of the houses are boarded up.

We're almost there. The house is at the top of the hill, and you used to arrive panting with excitement, running up the street ahead of your brother and sister, and with your two childish hands you'd push open the large door that was closed only at night, at bedtime. Now, too, the door is half open, and there are lights in all the windows, lights that suggest wakefulness and alarm in the winter darkness. You push open the door, fearing you've come too late, and for a moment you think you see reproach on the exhausted faces that turn to greet you, as if they'd all been devastated by the same illness. I hear names, give kisses, shake hands, exchange words in a low voice; I am the outsider whom they accept because I've come with you. Being part of your life, I, too, belong to this place, to the fatigue and sorrow of people who have spent many nights watching over a sick woman and anticipate the mourning for her. There is an eleven- or twelve-year-old child, and a youngish man who must be his father clasps my hand with a warm and vigorous show of welcome. "This is my cousin, the doctor." Having come here with you binds me to you in a new way, not merely to the adult woman I met not so many years ago but to all your life, to all the faces and places of your childhood, and also to your dead, and to those for whom this house we've just come to is a kind of sanctuary. I see a large photograph of your mother and another of your maternal grandparents, remote and solemn as an Etruscan funeral relief, and atop the ancient television, which is probably the same you sat before as a child to watch the cartoons, is the smiling face of your deceased cousin in a color photo.

I like being nothing more than your shadow here, the person who's come with you: my husband, you say, introducing me, and I become aware of the value of that word, which is my safe-conduct in this house, among these people who knew you and gave you their affection long before I found you, and when I see how they treat you, the familiarity that is immediate among you despite all the time that's passed since you last were here, my love for you expands to encompass that fullness, those bonds of tenderness and memory, bonds that also connect with and nourish me, linking me with a past that until now didn't belong to me, to the photographs of dead relatives unknown to me that were waiting for you with the same loyalty as the worn furniture and whitewashed walls. "How old all this is," you must be thinking sadly, again with a stab of guilt for having waited so long, for living in a house much more comfortable than this one in which your aunt spent the last years of her life, with the same old television that was here when you liked to flop on the sofa and watch the children's programs and an electric heater under the table and a supplementary radiator that did little to dissipate the cold rising from the paving stones, as if seeping up through them, the same floor that has been here always, except more worn, where here and there a stone has worked loose and makes a hollow sound when someone steps on it. Everything is simply old, stripped of the beauty with which memory endows things from the past, the plastic-upholstered chairs that were the latest thing when you were a girl, the brown imitation-leather sofa, the plaster Immaculate Conception with the fine, pale face and cloak of celestial blue. What will happen to them after tomorrow, after the burial, when the house is closed, too uncomfortable to be lived in and too costly to renovate? "Probably it will have to be torn down," someone beside me says, one of your relatives, in that tone people use when speaking of trivial matters in order to break the tedium of a death watch. "It'll be closed up and fall down piece by piece, like so many other abandoned houses here in town."

There is an air of weary insomnia in the house, of waiting for the ponderous arrival of death, which is drawing near on the other side of a half-opened door, the one that separates the living room from the bedroom of the dying woman. "She's sleeping now," we are told by the man with the white hair and the pleasant but melancholy expression, your mother and your aunt's brother, the father of the physician and also of your deceased cousin whose photograph sits staring into the monotony of the waiting, a young and very attractive young girl with green eyes and shining chestnut curls and something of you in her features—maybe the strong chin and broad smile, or the cinnamon tone of her skin. In this room that breathes the presence of death, I observe what you do and see and say and maybe feel as you sit here beside me on the sofa, holding my hand but at the same time far away, lost in the invocations of this place, of all these relics of your childhood I am seeing for the first time, talking in a low voice with people who have known you since you were born.

We never see people who were young adults when we were children exactly as they are today; we superimpose on today's gray hair and wrinkles the splendor they once radiated in our innocent eyes, the face of the old man, for example, who hugged me when he said hello as if he had known me forever; you still see, beneath the insults of age, the energetic features of your uncle, who looked so much like his sisters, your mother and your dying aunt, the younger brother who now will be the only survivor of the three, the man whose daughter's death may have turned his hair gray and given him a burden of mourning that is renewed as he awaits death's arrival again, guarding his sister's bedroom door, wanting to hear her should she wake from her morphine-induced sleep long enough to know that you've come and that she will see you before she dies. "She's been asking about you all day, whether you called, whether you're really on the way."

Now the doctor, who has been with your aunt, appears in the doorway, and with a gesture signals you to come in. He bends down a little to tell you in a low voice that she's awake and has just asked for you. I hang back a little, unsure, feeling cowardly about what I will witness if I go through that door, but you pull me with you, holding my hand hard, and your uncle's large, friendly hand on my shoulder encourages me to follow you. With the same shiver—not of sorrow but in response to a strangeness you cannot absorb—with which twenty years ago you pulled back the plastic curtain around the bed where your mother had just died, you walk into the darkened bedroom, which has the thick fug of old age, illness, and medications, but also the cold of ancient winters, along with some acrid, unhealthy scent that must be the exudation of death, the last secretions and breaths from that body lying on the bed in a stiff fetal position, its volume so reduced that it is barely visible beneath the blankets. Your uncle bends over his sister, brushes back the hair from her face, and pats her cheeks with a tenderness that is much younger than him: perhaps he patted his daughter this way in her cradle. "Look and see who's come from Madrid," he whispers.

The eyelids, bare of lashes, scarcely part, but there is a gleam of pupils in the dark and a rictus that is almost a smile on the swollen lips that dentures have been pushing out as the face shrinks. One hand lifts very slowly toward you, bones and blue veins and ashen skin; it finds your hand, reaches farther, touches your tear-wet face, recognizes it, feeling it as a blind person would. She murmurs your name, using a diminutive I've never heard, undoubtedly the name your mother and she gave you when you were little, and sitting on the edge of the bed you put your arms around her, sinking into the odor of sickness you kiss the unrecognizable face, the hard bones of death beneath transparent skin, you call to her quietly, as if wanting to wake her from all this. You will remember all the times you snuggled near her in this same bed as a child, looking for warmth on cruel winter nights, and how again, when you were sixteen, you sought that same solace on the night they buried your mother.

For the moment I have disappeared, become invisible, blending into the shadow of the corner where I stand, neither guest nor spy, a mute presence from another world and another time. But she, the person I have seen only as she is dying, who seemed to have her eyes closed, has noticed me and motions me forward with a faint gesture of a cadaverous hand, the hand that for you was as warm and reassuring as your mother's. You smile and look toward me as your aunt tells you something in a hoarse, whispery voice I can scarcely distinguish from the rasp of her breathing. "She says come over here, she wants to see if you are as good-looking as I've told her."

I walk toward her with respect, at first uncertain and clumsy, like someone moving in the sanctuary of a religion not his own. The slits of her eyelids open a little wider. As I bend down, I peer into a life and eyes that are fading, and my lips brush skin that will be like ice in a few hours or minutes. The face so near my own is that of a stranger already lost in the shadowy land of death, and the hoarse voice is a death rattle, an anguished effort to breathe, in which words, barely formed, fall from pale, dry lips. Your aunt's hand holds mine for a long moment, and I feel as if I am receiving the affectionate pressure of your mother's hand from across time and from the other side of death, as if she too were seeing me through your aunt's last gaze, and as if seeing you with me so many years later will dissipate a part of her sadness and uncertainty about your future in this life in which she is not at your side.

In the Greek funeral stelae we saw together at the Metropolitan Museum in New York, the dead serenely clasp the hands of the living. The hand holding mine is slightly sweaty, and the pressure ceases at the same time the eyelids close. I panic, I've never seen anyone die, but when I move back a little, the eyes open weakly, a movement as faint as the voice was, as the smile on lips the same yellowish hue as the face. Her hand drops from mine; the scratch of her voice becomes a moan, and the doctor, who has a hypodermic syringe in his hand, gently moves me aside. "I must give her morphine before the pain gets worse." But she shakes her head, her thin gray hair stuck to her temples in swirls from having been pressed so long against the pillows. She says no and murmurs something; the doctor leans down to hear. "Cousin, she's calling you, she says bend over." She's using the name no one has called you since you were a baby, and when you are near, she opens her eyes wide, as if to assure herself that it's really you. She strokes your wet face, and with her other hand she tries to hold both yours, patting and pulling, as if to tell you something or to kiss you. The hand never lets yours go, but after a slight shudder it is no longer squeezing yours, and the open eyes do not see you. She's left you without your realizing, just as your mother did, slipped away so stealthily that you are stunned death can happen so quietly, like the faintest ripple on the surface of a lake.

WHO CAN SLEEP THIS NIGHT, in which so much is under way, the prelude to a burial overseen by women trained in the rituals of mourning, in dressing the dead woman before she stiffens, in ordering the coffin and the catafalque on which it will rest, and the candles and large crucifix that for a few hours will lend the somber air of a sanctuary to the house, a place where the cult of the past and death is honored. I hear your soft breathing in the darkness and know you're not asleep, even though you haven't spoken for a long time and are lying as still as possible in order not to disturb me. The bed with its cold sheets and the room that smells of mildew and gloom feel strange to me, but must feel stranger to you, who haven't slept here since the end of your teenage years, the first bed and the first room you slept in alone after you outgrew the crib in your parents' bedroom, the room where you knew terror and sleeplessness on stormy nights, when rumbling thunder shook the windowpanes and a lightning flash blinded you with its white blaze, where you were afraid to fall asleep and dream of the horror movie your cousin and you saw at the theater that opened in the summer, the two of you huddled beneath the sheets and talking all night long, trading secrets of shameful intimacies, your first period and first boyfriends, slow dancing at the town fiestas with boys who were also summer residents, or in the sinful reddish darkness of the first discotheques you visited, you always tagging along behind your cousin, who introduced you to the giddiness of beer and cigarettes and didn't seem to recognize any of the limits that held you back—not modesty, not danger. Who could have said then that your destinies would be so different, that she, so like you, born at almost the same time, would slowly disappear into the dark maze of misfortune? She never made her way out, and it would have been so easy for you to wander into it, not consciously but just drifting, as she did. One year your cousin didn't come back to spend the summer with her parents and the brother who became a doctor, so serious and docile from the time he was a little boy, always the exact opposite of his sister.

Green eyes—her father stares at the photograph in silence, as if asking a question whose answer he must await forever. Curly hair, suntanned skin—hair made blond by the summer sun and swimming pool—the still plump cheeks of a teenager, the smile like a declaration of complacency or defiance, and the chin so like yours. She was very thin the last time I saw her, but still pretty, tall, with curls falling into her face and that gleam in her green eyes and the same crazy laugh I remember from the times we set out on some risky adventure. But by then she'd become so pale, and she spoke with a slur I'd never noticed before, and although she was married and had a child, she kept telling me the same kinds of crazy things she had told me when we started going out with boys in the summer. For instance, that she met a man on a train, and within a few minutes they'd locked themselves in the bathroom for a quick fuck. We were in a cafeteria, and she was smoking too much and glancing around, nervous, making a great effort to contain herself. I could see that she enjoyed being with me, but also that she wanted to leave, to get something she needed, something that made her bite her fingernails and chain-smoke, and we both also saw that despite our mutual affection and memories we weren't alike anymore, we didn't have things to talk about and just sat there sometimes in silence, then she would turn and look outside or put out a just-lit cigarette in the ashtray, crushing it violently. We agreed that the following summer we'd go back home together, but I couldn't because I had too much work, and she didn't go anyway, and I never saw her again. Not until after her parents had lost track of her completely. By the time my doctor cousin learned what hospital she was in, it was too late. An ambulance had picked her up in the street. He told me she was so wasted he could recognize only her green eyes.

YOUR ARMS ARE AROUND ME, hugging me tight, as you do when you're asleep and have a bad dream, you snuggle your icy feet between mine, shivering from the same cold you felt as a little girl, an ancient cold of long winters and houses without heat, cold retained in the rooms of this house as faithfully as the photos of the dead, as the most vivid memories older than reason but already brushed by melancholy and the inkling of inevitable loss: a child's sudden fear of growing up, the cruel knowledge, which comes from nowhere, that your parents will grow old and die. Also the fear that clutched you in its pincers those nights after your mother's death, when you didn't dare go from your bedroom to the bathroom lest you see her in the shadowy hallway in her nightgown, her hair all wild, the way she looked when you came home and were there only a few days before she had to go back to the hospital. You closed your eyes and feared that when you opened them she would be standing at the foot of your bed, asking you something wordlessly, and if you felt you were falling asleep you feared that she would appear in a dream, and you would jerk awake with anguish, thinking you heard the sound of doors opening, or footsteps, and again you felt the raw pain of her death and of being so alone, and shamefully afraid she would come back as a ghost.

FROM BELOW COME THE sounds of conversations and footsteps, a car starting, a telephone ringing, male voices issuing instructions, large objects being shoved around or set down. They're moving furniture to make room for the coffin. But you don't want to give in to that thought, you resist imagining the face of your dead aunt, ravaged not only by cancer but also by the old age your mother never knew, a delicate woman young forever because the images you have of the time she was ill are nearly erased and because you happen to have no photographs from her last years. That's how I see her too, assiduous spy that I am, researcher of your memory, which I want to be as much mine as your present life is. I can't imagine the woman your mother would be now had she not died: seventy-some years, heavyset, probably with dyed hair. I see her as you do, as you sometimes dream of her, a young woman who still has the smile of a girl, the shadow of which I sometimes intuit on your lips, just as I can see her gaze in your eyes, and that from her—like a ring spreading on the surface of time—comes your inclination to melancholy, your way of building illusions about anything new, the care with which you arrange the objects around you, your devotion to this house in which you and she both were girls, to this oasis with the desertlike hills in the background, this place where she wanted to rest forever and be with her own, with those who gradually have been joining her in the small cemetery with the earthen walls: first her niece, who died even younger than your mother, forever safe from time in the photograph on the television, and tonight her sister, another name added to the tablet in the family pantheon, which you will see tomorrow morning during the burial, and think—maybe for the first time, and without my knowing, without your wanting to say it to me—"When I die, I want you to bury me with them."

oh you, who knew so well

THEY DISAPPEAR ONE DAY, they are lost, erased forever, as if they had died, as if they had died so many years ago that they are no longer in anyone's memory and there is no sign they were ever in this world. Someone comes along, suddenly enters your life, is part of it for a few hours, a day, the duration of a journey, becomes a presence so insistent that it's difficult to recall a time he wasn't there. Whatever exists, even for an hour or two, seems permanent. In Tangiers, in the dark office of a cloth merchant, in a Madrid restaurant, in the dining car of a train, one man tells another fragments from the novel of his life, and the hours of the telling and of the conversation seem to contain more time than will fit within ordinary hours: someone speaks, someone listens, and for each the other's voice and face take on the familiarity of a person he has always known. Yet an hour or day later, he isn't there, will never be there, not because he died, although he might have, and his presence for those to whom he was so close dissolves into nothing. For fourteen years, beginning July 30, 1908, Franz Kafka punctually went to his office in the Society for Prevention of Workplace Accidents in Prague, and then one day in the summer of 1922 he left at the customary hour and never returned, because of illness. His disappearance was as inconspicuous as the way he had sat for so many years at his neat desk, where in one of his locked drawers he kept the letters Milena Jesenska wrote him. For some time afterward an old overcoat that he kept there for rainy days hung in the closet, then it too disappeared, and with it the peculiar odor that had identified his presence in the office for fourteen years.

The most stable things vanish, the worst and the best, the most trivial along with those that were necessary and decisive: the years one spends in a dismal office or endures remorsefully indifferent and distant in a marriage, or the memory of a journey to a city where one had either lived or promised oneself to return to after a unique and memorable visit. Love, suffering, even some of the greatest hells on Earth are erased after one or two generations, and a day comes when there is not one living witness who can remember.

In Tangiers, Señor Salama told of going to Poland to visit the camp where the gas chambers swallowed up his mother and two sisters, and of having found nothing but a large clearing in a forest and a sign bearing the name of an abandoned railway station, and of how the horror of the fact that there were now no visible traces of the camp was somehow contained in that name, in the rusty iron sign swinging above a platform beyond which there was nothing but the sweep of the clearing and gigantic pines against a low gray sky from which a silent rain was falling, rain scarcely visible in the fog but dripping from the roof of a shed at the station. It was a camp so unimportant that almost no one knew its name, said Señor Salama, and he pronounced a difficult word that must have been Polish—but then the name Auschwitz hadn't meant anything to Primo Levi either the first time he saw it written on the sign of a railway station. In a place like that, far from the principal camps, it was easier for deportees to be lost, for their names to disappear from those detailed records the Germans always kept. With that same fanatic administrative zeal they organized the transporting of hundreds of thousands of captives by rail in the midst of the Allied bombings and military disasters of the last months of the war.

Railroad tracks were just visible in the wet grass, rusted rails and rotted ties, and one of Señor Salama's crutches snagged or got tangled in them, and he nearly fell, fat and clumsy and humiliated, onto the same soil where his mother and two sisters perished, over which they'd walked when they reached the camp and got down from the train that had carried them like animals to the slaughterhouse: three familiar faces and names in an abstract mass of unknown victims. The guide steadied him, the survivor who had driven him here in an old car, and pointed out the now barely visible outlines of walls, the rectangles of cement on which the barracks had stood, a low line of bricks that someone who didn't know the place well wouldn't have noticed, it was all that remained of the courtyard where the crematory ovens had been, because the Germans had blown up the buildings at the last moment, after the sky had been red every night for weeks on the eastern horizon and the earth trembled with reverberations from the ever closer Russian artillery. Tens of thousands of human beings killed there over four or five years, unloaded onto this platform from cattle cars and lined up on the cement platforms, with orders barked in German or Polish and cries of pain and desperation, echoes of screams and commands lost in the enormous thicket of conifers, military marches and waltzes played by a spectral orchestra of prisoners . . . and of all that, nothing was left but a clearing in a forest drenched by a wet mist, and the fog wiping out the view, the places the prisoners would have seen every day through the barbed wire, knowing they would never walk in the outside world again, excluded from the number of the living as if they were already dead.

That skinny, evasive, servile man who accompanied Señor Salama to the site of the camp, what could he have experienced to make him choose this strange duty of acting as guardian and guide of the hell he had survived yet still did not want to leave? Guardian of a large deserted area in the middle of the woods and of a platform that now had no connection with any railroad; an archaeologist of blackened brick and slowly rusting hinges and oven doors; a seeker of remains, testimonies, relics, the metal bowls and spoons the prisoners used to eat their soup; a guide through traces of ruins increasingly overgrown and erased by the simple passage of time or sometimes enhanced by the white winter snows. When he died or was too old or tired to accompany the rare traveler who came to visit that unimportant camp, when he was no longer there to point out the sooty brick wall or line of cement platforms or peculiar undulation beneath the unbroken snow, no one would notice those minor irregularities in the forest clearing, or realize that the metallic crunch beneath their boots came from a spoon that once was the most valuable treasure in a man's life, and no one would guess the atrocious significance of a few piles of burned brick or, lying in the grass, a post to which a curl of barbed wire was still attached.

THEY DISAPPEAR, left behind by time, and distance falsifies memory as gradually as the rain. The years, abandon, and deteriorating materials all obliterate the ruins of a German death camp lost in the woods on the boundary between Poland and Lithuania, meticulously burned and destroyed by its guards on the eve of the arrival of the Red Army, which found only cinders, debris, and hastily filled-in ditches where countless layers of human bodies were piled, preserved by the cold, clustered and tangled, naked, skeletal, frozen limb to limb, tens of thousands of nameless bodies among whom were Señor Isaac Salama's four grandparents and most of his aunts and uncles and cousins, along with his mother and two sisters, who weren't saved as he and his father were, because the passports came too late for them in the summer of 1944, issued by the Spanish legation in Hungary, acknowledging the Spanish nationality of the Sephardic families living in Budapest.

"Our neighbors, my friends from school, my father's colleagues—they took all of them," said Señor Salama. "We wouldn't go out of the house for fear they would pick us up in the street before the papers the Spanish diplomat had promised us arrived. We heard on the radio that the Allies had taken Paris and that to the east the Russians had crossed the border with Hungary, but it seemed as if the only thing that mattered to the Germans was exterminating all of us. Imagine the enterprise required to transport all those people by train across half of Europe in the middle of a war they were about to lose. They chose to use the trains to send us to the camps over sending their troops to the front. They went into Hungary in March—March 14, I will never forget, although for many years I didn't remember that date, I didn't remember anything. They came in March and had deported half a million people by summer, but since they were afraid that the Russians would come too soon and not leave enough time for them to send all the Hungarian Jews to Auschwitz in an orderly fashion, they shot many of them in the head right in the street and threw their bodies into the Danube, the work of the Germans and their Hungarian friends. The men of the Cross Arrow, they were called; they wore black uniforms that copied the SS and were even more bloody than the Germans, if much less systematic."

You live all the days of your life in the house you were born in, a haven where you always had the warm protection of your parents and your two older sisters, and you expect to have that forever, just as you expect to have the photographs and paintings on the walls, and the toys and books in your bedroom. Then one day, in a few hours' time, all that disappears forever, without a trace, because you went out to do one of your usual chores, and when you came back, you were prevented from going in by an uncrossable chasm of time. "My father and I had gone to look for something to eat," said Señor Salama. "And when we returned, the concierge's husband, who had a good heart, came out and warned us to go away because the soldiers who had taken our family might come back. My father had a package in his hand, maybe one of those little packets of candy he brought home every Sunday, and it fell to the ground at his feet. That I remember. I picked up the package and took my father's hand, which was ice cold. 'Go away, far away,' the concierge's husband told us, and quickly walked off, looking from side to side, fearing that someone might have seen him talking to two Jews as if he were their friend. We walked for a long time without exchanging a word, I clinging to my father's hand, which no longer warmed mine or had the strength to lead me. I led him, keeping an eye out for patrols of Germans or Hungarian Nazis. We went into a café near the Spanish legation, and my father made a telephone call. He fumbled through his pockets for a coin, but he kept getting tangled up in his handkerchief and his billfold and his pocket watch. I remember that too. I had to give him the coin to buy the token. The man came whom my father had visited before, and he told my father that everything was arranged, but my father didn't say anything, didn't answer, it was as if he didn't hear, and the man asked him if he was ill. My father's chin had sunk to his chest, and his eyes were empty, the expression he would wear till he died. I told the man that they had taken our whole family, I wanted to cry but the tears didn't come, and a suffocating heaviness gripped my chest. Finally the tears burst out, and I think that the people at the nearby tables stared at me, but I didn't care; I threw myself at the man, clutching the lapels of his overcoat and begging him to help my family, but maybe he didn't understand because I spoke in Hungarian and with my father he'd been speaking French. We were driven in a large black car bearing the flag of the diplomatic legation to a house where there were a lot of other people. I remember small rooms and suitcases, men wearing overcoats and hats, women in kerchiefs, people speaking in low voices and sleeping in the corridors, on the floor, using bundles of clothing as pillows. My father was always wide-awake, smoking, trying to make a telephone call, from time to time badgering the employees of the Spanish legation to bring us something to eat. We searched for the names of my mother and sisters on the list of deportees, but they didn't appear. Later we learned—that is, my father learned years later—that they hadn't been taken to the same camps nearly everyone else was sent to, to Auschwitz or Bergen-Belsen. The Spanish diplomat who saved the lives of so many of us was able to rescue some Jews even from those camps, endangering his own life, acting behind the backs of his superiors in the ministry, driving from one end of Budapest to the other at all hours of the day or night in the same black embassy car he'd taken us in, picking up people in hiding or those who'd just been arrested. If they didn't have authentic Sephardic blood, he invented identities and papers for them, even relatives and businesses in Spain. Sanz-Briz, his name was. He located many people and managed to have some sent back from the camps, he snatched them from hell, but of my mother and sisters there was no trace, because they'd been taken to that camp no one had ever heard of, and of which nothing remains except the roof and the sign I saw five years ago. I would never have chosen to go. I can't bear to set foot in that part of Europe, I can't bear the idea of standing and looking at a person of a certain age in a café or on a street in Germany or Poland or Hungary; I wonder what they were doing during those years, what they saw, whom they'd sided with. But shortly before my father died he asked me to visit the camp, and I promised I would. And do you know what's there? Nothing. A clearing in a forest. The roof of a railway station and a rusted sign."

I wonder what happened to Señor Salama, who in the middle 1980s was the director of the Ateneo Español, the Spanish cultural center in Tangiers, working in a small office decorated with once brightly colored tourist posters now crumpled and faded by time and with old furniture in fake Spanish style; he also managed, grudgingly, the Galerías Duna on Louis Pasteur Boulevard, a fabric shop established by his father that took its name from a river in that other country that they, unlike most he knew, had managed to escape from, unlike the sisters and mother they didn't even have a photograph of, nothing to use as a crutch for memory, as material proof that would have helped against the erosion of memory.

Duna is the Hungarian name for the Danube River. Señor Salama, with his rich vocabulary and strange accent punctuated with dim tonalities, musical embers of the Jewish Spanish he'd heard spoken in his childhood and the few lullabies he still remembered, with his laborious way of pulling himself along on two crutches and with his eyes that watered so easily, his sparse gray hair, his forehead always gleaming with sweat he constantly dabbed at with a white handkerchief embroidered with his initials, with his breath ragged from the effort of moving a large clumsy body whose legs no longer served it, bone-thin legs beneath the cloth of his trousers, two appendages swinging beneath the weight of a large belly and thick torso. But he insisted on doing everything for himself, without help from anyone; lurching skillfully along, breathing rapidly, he would open doors and turn on lights and explain the small treasures and souvenirs of the Ateneo Español, framed photographs of a famous visitor many years ago, or of performances of plays by Benavente and Casona, even Lorca, a diploma issued by the Ministry of Information and Tourism, a book dedicated to the center's library by a writer whose fame had been fading with the years, until even his name was no longer familiar—though you had to hide that from Señor Salama, you had to tell him that you'd read the book and that his inscribed first edition must be very valuable by now. Awkward, expert, chaotic, tireless despite his difficulty breathing and his crutches, he would point out old posters announcing conferences and plays in the Ateneo's small theater, and even in the large Teatro Cervantes, which now, he says, is a shameful ruin infested with rats, invaded by delinquents, a jewel of Spanish architecture the government pays no attention to at all. They don't want to know anything of what little is left of Spain in Tangiers, they don't answer the letters that Señor Salama writes to the ministries of Culture and Education and External Affairs. He sets the posters to one side, looks through the papers on his desk, and pulls out a folder stuffed with carbon copies bearing the stamp of the main post office, clear proof that they've been sent, though never answered. He points out dates, quickly thumbs through papers—from a petition to a document dated several years before—all written on a typewriter, in the old-fashioned way before the age of word processors and photocopiers, always with several carbon copies. The stage of the Ateneo Español was the setting for the first theater company of Tangiers, although, he explains, "it is composed of amateurs who don't get a peseta for it, including me—who can't act, as you may imagine, but I often direct." Along the walls of a corridor, he points out poorly framed black-and-white photographs in which the actors hold exaggerated, theatrical poses, enthusiastic amateurs declaiming in front of modest sets of the inn in *Don Juan Tenorio,* the stairway of a tenement in Madrid, the walls of an Andalusian village. "We've done Benavente and Casona, and every year on the first of November we perform the Don Juan play, but don't judge us too quickly, because we also presented *The House of Bernarda Alba* long before it made its debut in Spain, when the only person to have performed it was Margarita Xirgu in Montevideo."

THE MELANCHOLY AND PENURY of Spanish colonies far from Spain. Fake-tile roofs, mock-whitewashed walls, imitations of Andalusian railings, regional bullfight posters, Valencian and Asturian schlock, greasy paellas and large Mexican sombreros, grimy decor inspired by the romantic prints and films of Andalusia that played in Berlin during the Spanish Civil War. The red tiles, the wrought-iron light fixtures, and fancy iron railings of that place in Copenhagen called Pepe's Bar, the imitation caves of Sacromonte at a crossroad near Frankfurt, where they served sangria in December and hung copper sauté pans and Cordovan and Mexican sombreros on the walls. The red tiles and inevitable white stucco wall in the Casa de España in New York in the early nineties; the Café Madrid, which appeared unexpectedly on a neighborhood corner in the Adams Morgan district of Washington, DC, amid Salvadoran restaurants and shops selling cheap clothing and suitcases and bellowing merengue music in places that were emerging from absolute desolation overnight, ruined neighborhoods with whole rows of burned or razed houses and parking lots encircled with barbed wire. Beside the empty lot of a burned house would be a shop for Ethiopian brides, and beyond that a Catholic funeral parlor. Suddenly you would see an eye-catching sign: Café Madrid, right next to a Santo Domingo Bakery and a little Cuban restaurant called La Chinita Linda. It was an icy morning in Washington, and the winter sunlight shimmered on the marble of the monuments and public buildings. You would go up a narrow stairway and on the second floor come to the swinging door of Café Madrid and breathe in warm air carrying odors that were familiar but as rarely experienced as the hiss of the sizzling oil used to deep-fry the white dough of the

churros, or as the sight of the round, oily face of the woman waiting on tables, who had the brassy air of a churro seller in a
working-class neighborhood in Madrid but who by now spoke
very little Spanish, because, she said, in an accent flavored with
the cadences of Mexico, her parents had brought her to America
when she was a kid. Old bullfight posters on the walls, a montera, a toreador's hat, on two crossed banderillas in an arrangement that suggested a display of military trophies, the paper of
the banderillas stained an ocher color that could pass for blood
and the montera covered with dust, as if coated with years of
heavy smoke from boiling oil. Color posters of Spanish landscapes, ads from Iberia Airlines or the old Ministry of Information and Tourism. In his office, Señor Salama had a poster of La
Mancha, an arid hill crowned with windmills, all with the flat,
overlit tones of color photographs and films of the sixties. There
was a poster of the Del Tránsito Synagogue in Toledo, and beside
that, equal in the favor and almost the devotion, of Señor Salama,
another picturing the monument to Cervantes in Madrid's Plaza
de España: it had that same clean winter light of a cold, sunny
morning, and Señor Salama remembered childhood walks through
that plaza he was so fond of, although it seemed strange now, almost impossible, to believe that he had been a slim young man
who didn't need crutches but walked on two efficient and agile
legs without a thought for the miracle of their ability to sustain
him and take him from place to place as if his body were weightless, believing that everything he had and enjoyed would last
forever: agility, health, being twenty, the happiness of living in
Madrid with no ties to anyone, being nothing more or less than
himself, as free from the force of the gravity of the past as from
the earth's, free, temporarily, from his former life and maybe from
the future life others had planned for him, free from his father,
his melancholy, his cloth business, his loyalty to the dead, to
those who couldn't be saved, those whose places they, father and

son, had occupied or usurped, merely by chance not ending up in that obscure camp where so many of their family, their city, and their lineage had perished without a trace. Franz Kafka's three sisters disappeared in the death camps. In Madrid, in the mid-1950s, Señor Salama took courses in economics and law and planned not to return to Tangiers when the period of freedom granted him came to an end, and for the first time in his life he was completely alone and felt that his identity began and ended in him, free now of shadows and heritage, free of the presence and obsessive enshrining of the dead. It wasn't his fault he had survived, nor should he have to be in mourning any longer, mourning not just for his mother and sisters but for all his relatives, for his neighbors and his father's colleagues and the children he'd played with in the public parks of Budapest—for all the Jews annihilated by Hitler. If you looked around, in a tavern in Madrid, in a classroom at the university, if you walked along the Gran Vía and went into a movie theater on a Sunday afternoon, you wouldn't find a hint that any of it had happened, you could let yourself be borne off to a life more or less like that other people lived, his compatriots, classmates, and the friends who never asked about his past, who knew scarcely anything about the European war or the German camps.

In Madrid his memory of Tangiers sank out of sight like ballast he had shed at his departure, and by now he felt very little remorse for having abandoned his father or for the fact that he was living off a business he had no intention of devoting himself to. Of his earlier life, Budapest and panic, the yellow star on the lapel of his overcoat, the nights huddled beside the radio, the disappearance of his mother and sisters, the travels with his father through Europe carrying a Spanish passport, amazingly few images remained, only an occasional physical sensation, as unreal as early childhood memories. "I saw an interview on television," he said, "with a man who went blind in his twenties; he was nearly fifty now, and he said that gradually he had been losing images, they were being erased from his memory, so that he couldn't remember the color blue, for example, or what a certain face looked like, and his dreams were no longer visual. He retained only bits and pieces, and even those were going, he said, the white blur of an almond tree in bloom in his parents' garden, the red of a balloon that he'd had as a child and that was like a globe of the world. But he realized that in a few more years he would lose everything, even the meaning of the word *see*. In Madrid, during my years at the university, I forgot about the city of my childhood, the faces of my mother and sisters, and the irony that I didn't have so much as a snapshot to help remember them when there'd been so many in our house in Budapest, albums filled with photographs my father took with his little Leica, because like music, photography was one of his hobbies, one of the many things that disappeared from his life after we came to Tangiers and he didn't have either time or energy for anything except work— work, mourning, religion, reading the sacred books he'd never opened in his youth, and visits to synagogues, which he'd never attended until we came here. At first I wasn't interested in going with him. But I would take him by the hand and lead him as I had that morning in Budapest when we learned that they arrested my mother and sisters."

After he died, Señor Salama's father regained the place in his son's life that he'd occupied many years before, and was the object of the same devotion he'd received when he led his son through the streets of Budapest or Tangiers, a placid boy, obedient, plump, seen smiling in a lost photograph, hazily remembered, in which he was wearing a goalkeeper's cap and the wide-legged pants of the period between the wars, a proud boy looking up at his father, both wearing a yellow star on their lapel. One June day his father bought a newspaper and after first glancing right and left pointed to the front page, where there was news of the Allied landing in Normandy. Then he folded the paper and put it in his pocket and pressed his son's hand tightly, transmitting in that way his joy, alerting him not to show any sign of celebrating the invasion in the middle of a street filled with enemies. "When I die, you will say the Kaddish for me for eleven months and one day, like a good firstborn son, and you will travel to the northeast corner of Poland to visit the camp where your mother and two sisters died."

Now Señor Isaac Salama, who had no son to say the Kaddish for him after his death, regretted that he had been a prodigal son and that the tenderness he was feeling now could not make amends to his dead father, whom he missed as much as he would have missed a wife and children. They had always been so close. As long as he could remember, every afternoon his life lit up because he knew his father would soon be home. He had been sheltered by him, had admired him as he would the hero of a novel or movie, had seen him crumble in the middle of a street and felt the terrifying weight of responsibility and also the secret pride that his father's hand, resting on his shoulder, was not protecting him but was finding support in him, his son, the heir to his name.

But when he was sixteen or seventeen, he didn't want to live with his father any longer, all the things they'd shared since it had been just the two of them were beginning to stifle him—more than anything the endless mourning, the endless guilt. As the years went by, instead of consoling his father, the mourning had pushed him deeper into the shadows of silent injury in a world where the dead didn't count, where no one, including many Jews, wanted to hear about or remember them. He tended his business with the same energy and conviction he had dedicated to it when they lived in Budapest. Within a few years, out of nothing, he had succeeded in establishing a shop that was one of the most modern in Tangiers, and whose glowing sign, "Galerías

Duna," illuminated the bourgeois, commercial section of Pasteur Boulevard by night. But Señor Salama realized that his father's untiring, astute activity was only a facade, an imitation of the man his father had been before the catastrophe, in the same way the shop was an imitation of the one he'd owned and managed in Hungary. He became more and more religious, more obsessed with fulfilling rituals, prayers, and holy days, which in his youth he'd thought of as relics of an obscure and ancient world he was glad to be delivered from. Perhaps he gained a feeling of expiation with this growing religion; in any case, he prayed now, docilely, to the very God that in sleepless days and nights of despair he had denied for having allowed the extermination of so many innocents. His son, who at thirteen or fourteen accompanied him to the synagogue with the same solicitude as he prepared his evening meal or made sure he had ink and paper on his desk every morning, now found this religious fervor irritating, and any time he was with his father he felt a lack of air, the musty, sour odor of the clothing of Orthodox Jews and of the candles and darkness of the synagogue, as well as the dusty smell of cloth in the storeroom where he no longer wanted to work and from which he didn't know how to excuse himself.

But when finally he dared express his wish to leave home, to his surprise and, even more, remorse, his father not only didn't object, he encouraged him to go study in Spain, believing, or pretending to believe, that his son's aspiration was to take over the business when he graduated and that the knowledge he acquired in Spain would be very useful to both of them in renovating and developing the company.

"I would hear the siren of the boat leaving for Algeciras and count the days until I made that trip myself. At night, from the terrace of my home, I could see the lights of the Spanish coast. My life consisted solely of the desire to get away, to escape all that weighed on me, crushing me like the layers of undershirts,

shirts, sweaters, overcoats, and mufflers my mother used to pile on me when I was a boy getting ready for school. I wanted to put the confinement of Tangiers behind me, and the claustrophobia of my father's shop, along with my father and his sadness and memories and remorse for not having saved his wife and daughters, for being saved in their place. The day I finally left dawned with heavy fog and warnings of high seas, and I feared the boat from the Peninsula wouldn't arrive, or that it wouldn't leave the port after I'd boarded with my suitcases and reservation for the Algeciras-to-Madrid train. My nerves made me irritable with my father, quick to be annoyed by his concern, his mania for checking everything over and over: the ticket for the ship, for the train, my Spanish passport, the address and telephone number of the pension in Madrid, the papers for enrolling in the university, the heavy clothing I'd need when winter came. I don't think we'd been apart since we left Budapest, and he must have felt like my father and mother both. I would have done anything to keep him from going to the port with me, but didn't even hint at it for fear he would be offended, and when he came with me and I saw him among the people who'd come to see the other passengers off, I was mortified, wild for the boat to get under way so I wouldn't have to keep looking at my father, who was the caricature of an old Jew. In recent years, as he grew more religious, he'd also grown old and stooped, and in his gestures and way of dressing he was beginning to look like the poor Orthodox Jews of Budapest, the eastern Jews whom our Sephardic relatives looked down on and whom my father, when he was young, had regarded with pity and some contempt as backward, incapable of adapting to modern life, impaired by religion and bad hygiene. I felt guilty for being embarrassed and guilty because I was abandoning him, and I truly felt sorry for him, but none of that could put a dent in my joy at leaving, and I cut my ties to my father and to Tangiers and to my shame the minute the boat set sail, the instant I could see that we were gradually separating from the dock. We were only a few meters away, and my father kept waving good-bye from below, so different from all the others in the crowd that I hated being linked with him. I waved back and smiled, but I was already gone, far away, free of everything for the first time in my life—you can't imagine the weight that was lifted from my shoulders—free of father and his shop and his mourning and all the Jews killed by Hitler, all the lists of names in the synagogue and in the Jewish publications my father subscribed to, and the ads in the Israeli newspapers where you asked for information about missing people. I was alone now. I began and ended in me alone. Someone nearby on the deck was listening on a transistor radio to one of the American songs that were popular then. It seemed to me that the song was filled with the same kind of promise the trip held for me. I have never had a more intensely physical sense of happiness than I felt when the boat began to move, when I saw Tangiers in the distance, from the sea, as I saw it the day my father and I arrived, escaping Europe."

WHAT WAS IT REALLY LIKE, Tangiers? Distorted in memory by the passing years, for memory is never as precise as literature would have us believe. Who can truly remember a city or a face without the help of a photograph? But they are lost, all those albums of a former life, a life that seemed unchanging, suffocating, and yet evaporated almost without leaving a single image, like the ruins of a camp or like colors gradually forgotten by a man who has gone blind, like the city where Señor Isaac Salama lived until he was twelve, like the faces of his sisters and mother, like the city where a young man feels as if he is a prisoner and will never escape, and yet he does, and then one day he doesn't come back to the office, never again sits at the desk where, in one of the drawers, among official and now useless papers, there is a packet of forgotten letters that someone will throw out during the next cleaning: the letters from Milena Jesenska that Kafka didn't keep.

Ships' horns and the muezzin's call at dusk, heard from the terrace of a hotel. A Spanish pastry shop like those in the provincial cities of the sixties, a Spanish theater called the Cervantes, now in near ruins. Large cafés filled with men only, thick with smoke and humming with conversations in Arabic and French. Gilt teapots and narrow crystal glasses filled with steaming, very sweet, green tea. The labyrinth of a market redolent of the spices and foods of his childhood. A blind beggar wearing a ragged brown hooded cloak that seems made of the same cloth as Velázquez's *Water Seller of Seville*; the beggar wields a cane and murmurs a little chant in Arabic, and beneath the hood all you can see of him is a chin covered with a scraggly white beard, and a shadow hiding his eyes like a mask of melancholy. Idle young men loiter on street corners near the hotels, and as soon as they spy a foreigner they besiege him, offering their friendship and help as guides, trying to sell him hashish or provide him with a young girl or boy, and if he says no it doesn't discourage them, and if he's embarrassed and ignores them, pretending not to see them, they still don't give up but trail behind this person who doesn't know how to elude them but at the same time, plagued with the bad conscience of the privileged European, doesn't want to seem arrogant or offensive. Pasteur Boulevard, the only street name that sticks in his memory: bourgeois buildings that might be found in any city in Europe, although the Europe of a different time, before the war, a city with streetcars and baroque facades, maybe the Budapest in which Señor Salama was born and where he lived until he was ten but never returned to and of which he has only a few sentimental impressions, like postcards colored by hand. The most beautiful city in the world, I swear, the most solemn river—pure majesty, none can compare with it, not the Thames or the Tiber or the Seine—the Duna, and all these years later I still can't get used to calling it the Danube. And the most civilized city, we believed, until those beasts awakened, not just the Germans, the Hungarians were worse than the Germans, they didn't need orders to act with brutality, the Arrow Cross bands, Himmler's and Eichmann's pit bulls, the Hungarians who had been our neighbors and who spoke our language, which by now I have forgotten, or nearly, because my father insisted on never speaking it again, not even between the two of us, the only ones left of our entire family, two alone and lost here in Tangiers, with our Spanish passports and the new Spanish identity that had saved our lives and allowed us to escape from Europe, which my father never wanted to return to, the Europe he had loved above all else and of which he had been so proud, the home of Brahms and Schubert and Rilke and all that great cultural dreck that made his head spin, rejected later in order to turn himself into a zealous Orthodox Jew, isolated and reticent among Gentiles, he who never took us to the synagogue when we were children or celebrated any holiday, who spoke French, English, Italian, and German, but knew scarcely a word of Hebrew and only one or two lullabies in Ladino—although when we lived in Budapest he took pride in his Spanish roots. Sepharad was the name of our true homeland, although we'd been expelled from it more than four centuries ago. My father told me that for generations our family kept the key of the house that had been ours in Toledo, and he detailed every journey they'd made since they left Spain, as if he were telling me about a single life that had lasted nearly five hundred years. He always spoke in the first person plural: *we* emigrated to North Africa, and then some of *us* made our homes in Salonika, and others in Istanbul, to which *we* brought the first printing presses, and in the nineteenth century *we* arrived in Bulgaria, and at the beginning of the twentieth one of my grandparents, my father's father, who was involved in the grain trade along the ports of the Danube, settled in Budapest and married the daughter of a family of his own rank, because in that time the Sephardim considered themselves to be above the eastern Jews, the impoverished Ashkenazim from the Jewish villages of Poland and Ukraine, the ones who had escaped the Russian pogroms. *We* were Spanish, my father would say, using his prideful plural. Did you know that a 1924 decree restored Spanish nationality to the Sephardim?

THE ATENEO ESPAÑOL, the Galerías Duna, the lights of the Spanish coast shimmering at night, so close it seemed they weren't on the other side of the Mediterranean but on the far shore of a very wide river, the Danube, the Duna that Señor Salama saw in his childhood, the river into which in the summer of 1944 the Germans and their lackeys threw the Jews they'd murdered in the street, in broad daylight, hurriedly because the Red Army was approaching and it was possible that the rail lines would be cut and there would be no way to keep sending convoys of the doomed to Auschwitz or Bergen-Belsen, or to those lesser-known camps whose names no one remembers. Spain is a stone's throw away, an hour and a half by ship, witness those lights visible from the terrace of the hotel, but in a conversation with Señor Salama, in the Galerías Duna or in the Ateneo Español, Spain seems thousands of kilometers away, across oceans, as if one were remembering it from the Hogar Español in Moscow one waning winter day or in the Café Madrid in Washington, DC. Spain is so remote that it is nearly nonexistent, an inaccessible, unknown, thankless country they called Sepharad, longing for it with a melancholy without basis or excuse, with a loyalty as constant as that passed from father to son by the ancestors of Señor Salama, the only one of all his line to fulfill the hereditary dream of return, only to be expelled once again, and this time definitively, because of a misfortune that he no longer considered just another injustice of chance as the years went by, but a consequence and punishment for his own pride, for the self-indulgence that had pushed him to be ashamed of his father and to reject him in his deepest heart.

If he hadn't been driving that car so fearlessly, he thinks day after day, with the same obsessive mourning his father had devoted to the wife and daughters he didn't save, if he hadn't been going so fast, wanting to get to the Peninsula as quickly as he could, to go up to Madrid not on one of the slow night trains that scored the country from south to north like dark, powerful rivers but in the car his father gave him as a reward for completing the two degrees he'd studied for concurrently and completed with such brilliance. By now neither father nor son maintained the fiction that these university diplomas were going to help the business on Pasteur Boulevard prosper. Tangiers, Señor Salama told his father when he went home after his last courses, would not much longer be the lively and open international city it had been when they arrived in 1944. Now it belonged to the kingdom of Morocco, and little by little foreigners would have to leave—"we first," said the father with a flash of the wit and sarcasm of old. "I only hope they throw us out with better manners than the Hungarians, or the Spanish in 1492."

That's what he said, *the Spanish,* as if he didn't consider himself one of them anymore, even though he held that citizenship and during a period in his life had felt such pride in belonging to a Sephardic line. Señor Salama realized that his father was calculating the possibility of selling the business and emigrating to Israel. But the last thing in the world he wanted to do was to change countries again. "I should have paid attention to my father," he says now, in another of his episodes of repentance, "because Spain doesn't want to know about anything Spanish in Tangiers—or about those of us Spaniards who are still here. In Morocco there is less and less room for us, but they don't want us in Spain either. With the pension I'll get when I close this shop, from which I get next to nothing now, when I retire I won't have enough to live on the Peninsula, so I'll stay here to die in Tangiers, where we are less and less Spanish and more and more old foreigners. I could go to Israel, of course, but what would I do at my age, in a country I know nothing about, a place where I have no one?"

If he had paid attention to his father then, if he'd had a little patience, if he hadn't been driving so fast along one of those Spanish highways of the 1950s, so full of himself, he says, his fleshy lips twisted in a sardonic smile, believing he could do anything, in control of his life.

A little before dawn, as he came out of a tight curve, his car drifted to the left of the road, and he saw the yellow headlights of a truck coming toward him. "I should have died right there," Señor Salama says, and realizes he is reprising the words he heard his father speak so many times, the same desire to go back and correct a few minutes, a few seconds—if we hadn't left them at home alone, if we'd returned just a little earlier—an entire life shattered forever in one fraction of a moment, an eternity of remorse and shame, the horrible shame Señor Salama felt when he found himself paralyzed at the age of twenty-two, walking with crutches and dragging two useless legs, knowing he could never stand on his own again, that he lacked not just the physical strength but the moral courage to pursue the life he had wanted so much and thought he had right at his fingertips.

"I didn't want anyone to see me, I wanted to hide in the dark, in a cellar, like those monsters in the movies. It was years before I went outside with any feeling of normality, or walked through the shop on my crutches." He noticed that gradually he was becoming deformed, the way his legs grew weaker and his torso more massive, his shoulders unnaturally broad and his neck sunken between them. He would fall in the shop in front of some customer—in those days when there were still a lot of them—and when the clerks came running to pick him up, he despised them even more than he despised himself, and he would close his eyes as he had in the hospital and want to die of embarrassment.

"How can you understand—forgive me for saying so—when you have two good legs and both arms? When you don't, it is like having a grave illness, or a yellow star sewn to your lapel. I didn't want to be a Jew when the other children threw rocks at me in the park in Budapest where I went to play with my sisters, who were older and braver and defended me. At that time in my life, being a Jew gave me the same sense of shame and the same rage I felt after I was paralyzed, crippled—none of this 'impaired' or 'disabled' drivel, which is what those imbeciles say now, as if changing the word could erase the stigma and give me back the use of my legs. When I was nine or ten, in Budapest, what I wanted was not for us Jews to be saved from the Nazis. I say it now, to my shame: what I wanted was not to be a Jew."

A WARM BREEZE WAFTS through the open window of Señor Salama's small office, the breeze of a May afternoon, though the visit came in December and he can hear the clear call of a muezzin, amplified by one of those rudimentary loudspeakers dangling precariously from a few wires, as well as the hoarse blast of a ship's horn entering or leaving the port. With an expression of annoyance, he has called the shop to ask if there's anything he should know, and in French told someone who took a long time to answer the telephone that he can't come before closing time because the concert begins at eight in the recital hall of the Ateneo. Spanish Culture Week was inaugurated yesterday with a lecture on literature, and there was a respectable audience, but today Señor Salama is worried because the pianist scheduled to perform is not very well known and may not be very good either. If he were, why would he come to Tangiers to give a concert for so little money? It's frightening, and depressing, to picture the hall with only a few seats occupied, the Andalusian white stucco wall arching above the stage, and the pianist in a travel-rumpled dinner jacket making an overly emphatic bow before an unenthusiastic public, the locks of a romantic mane covering half his face when he stands back up. There weren't funds to print enough posters or send invitations in time. Besides, it's Wednesday, and there may be an international match on TV. In the large, dark cafés of Tangiers, which assault the nostrils with the stale odor of male sweat and black tobacco reminiscent of Spanish bars thirty years before, you sometimes see a mass of dark faces raised toward a television screen, unshaved cheeks and unblinking eyes: a soccer match on Spanish television or one of those competitions of miniskirted airline stewardesses leaning against late-model cars. "That's the cultural contribution Spain is leaving here," rages Señor Salama, "television and soccer, while the language is being lost and our Ateneo goes without any help, eaten up by debts while on the Peninsula thousands of millions are wasted on that Babylon of the Seville Expo. Look at the French, in contrast, compare our Ateneo with the Alliance Française, their opulent palace, the film series they organize, the exhibitions they bring from the Continent, the money they spend on advertising—which they paste over all our posters, the few we can afford. You've noticed that French flag on high, haven't you? I go there because they're always inviting me, and I die with envy. The French invite me, yes, but the Spanish forget, I don't matter, I'm no one. But the Ateneo itself... The people at the embassy and the consulate shove us aside every chance they get, as if we didn't exist." Señor Salama breathes heavily, his elbows propped on the desktop, his broad torso spread over the papers, his hands searching among the disorder: concert programs, letters, unpaid bills, invitations. It's getting late, and he can't find what he's looking for; he checks his watch and verifies that it's only a few minutes before the concert begins: the piano recital performed by the acclaimed virtuoso D. Gregor Andrescu, works by F. Schubert and F. Liszt, open to the public, please be punctual. Panic that almost no one has shown up, torture at the thought of being seated in the first row and seeing at such close range the disappointment and obligatory smile of the pianist, who according to Señor Salama was a figure of the first magnitude in Romania before escaping to the West and finding political asylum in Spain.

Señor Salama has found what he was looking for, an invitation written in French and printed on stiff, shining stock bearing the gold seal of the republic and, at the bottom, on a dotted line, his name written in exquisite calligraphy with China ink: *M. Isaac Salama, directeur de L'Athénée Espagnol,* the invitation unmistakable proof that foreigners have more consideration for him than his compatriots. "This exhibition was unforgettable," he says, taking back the card, which he looks at again as if to check that his handwritten name and title are still there. "We will never be able to do anything like that: Baudelaire manuscripts, first editions of *Flowers of Evil* and *Spleen,* proofs with corrections and deletions made by Baudelaire himself. How strange it is, I thought, that these very personal things have survived so long, that they're here and I can see them." And his eyes nearly mist over when he remembers the emotion of seeing, copied cleanly by the hand of the poet, the sonnet to the unknown beauty, "A une passante," which of all Baudelaire's poems is the one Señor Salama likes best, the one he knows by heart and recites in the admirable French he learned from his mother in childhood, pausing with delight and a certain melodrama on the last line:

O toi que j'eusse aimé! O toi qui le savais!

He sits as if swamped in tragic silence, in an inscrutable pose of penitence. Eyes fixed and moist, he seems about to say something; he opens his mouth, taking a breath to speak, but just as he begins there is a knock at the office door. A thin older woman enters, eyeglasses hanging from a chain around her neck: the librarian and secretary of the Ateneo. "When you gentlemen want to come down, Maestro Andrescu says he's ready."

ONE DAY THEY DISAPPEAR, dead or not, they are lost and fade from memory as if they never existed, or have become something different, a figure or phantom of imagination greatly changed from the real person they were, from the real life they may still be living. But sometimes they rise up again, leap from the past, you hear a voice you haven't heard for years or someone casually speaks the name of someone dead or a character in a novel. Far from Tangiers, many years later in another life, at such a great remove in time that memories have lost all precision and nearly all substance, on a train where a group of writers and professors are traveling through green hills and mist, someone mentions Señor Salama's name, followed by an expression of mockery and a deep laugh.

"Don't tell me you knew him, too, old Salama? It's been years since I thought of him. What a mess the guy got me into. If someone had just warned me, I wouldn't have gone anywhere near Tangiers, especially for the shit they paid, the place was falling apart, you know. Very accommodating that Jew was, almost to the point of fawning, didn't you think? And an awful bore; he just kept at you. He'd pick you up at the hotel first thing in the morning and take you everywhere, practically to the bathroom too, and all the while the same thing, that song and dance about how no one in Spain paid any attention, and those long-winded stories about how he arrived in Tangiers, wasn't it in the forties? It seems he came from a moneyed family, from Czechoslovakia or somewhere like that, and they had to pay an enormous sum to the Nazis to get out. I can't remember the details, it was a thousand years ago. That was in the days when you had to travel, give performances wherever people asked you. Tedious as he was, he was very pleasant on the phone, lots of flowery talk, right? What an honor it would be, although unfortunately the *emolument* couldn't be very generous, but on and on about how important it was to support Spanish culture in Africa.... What a drag, that Jew, all day long, back and forth with the crutches—from an automobile accident, I think. I am not disabled or impaired, he would say, I am crippled. And speaking of crippled, did he tell you about his train trip to Casablanca, when he met this dame? That's strange, he told everybody after he'd had a couple of drinks, and he always began the same way: some Baudelaire poem, didn't he recite *that* to you?"

Without your knowledge, other people usurp stories or fragments from your life, episodes you think you've kept in a sealed chamber of your memory and yet are told by people you may not even know, people who have heard them and repeat them, modify them, adapt them according to their whim or how carefully they listened, or for a certain comic or slanderous effect. Somewhere, right this minute, someone is telling something very personal about me, something he witnessed years ago but that I probably don't even remember, and since I don't remember I assume it doesn't exist for anyone, erased from the world as completely as from my mind. Bits and pieces of you are left behind in other lives, rooms you lived in that others now occupy, photographs or keepsakes or books that belonged to you and now someone you don't know is touching and looking at, letters still in existence when the person who wrote them and the person who received them and kept them for a long, long time are dead. Far from you, scenes from your life are relived, and in them you're a fiction, a secondary character in a book, a passerby in the film or novel of another person's life.

If the details are lost, the easy thing is to invent them, falsify them, profane what was a painful part of another human being's experience by claiming it as your own. On a train in Asturias, on the way to a writers' conference, to while away the time of the journey, or for the simple vanity of telling with appropriate irony something that doesn't matter to you at all, or to anyone listening, the writer who has spoken Señor Salama's name aloud, although he can't remember whether it was Isaac or Jacob or Jeremiah or Isaiah, begins a story that will last only a few minutes, but he doesn't know that he is compounding an affront, aggravating an insult.

Isaac Salama boards a train bound for Casablanca, where he's going for reasons of business. He's in his forties and for several years, since his father's retirement, has been managing the Galerías Duna, which is going downhill, like those large department stores in Spanish provincial capitals that were fashionable at the end of the 1950s and early 1960s, but after that seemed to be frozen in time like archaeological relics. When he travels by train, Señor Salama likes to be at the station early, that way he can take his seat before the other travelers and avoid having them watch him—so clumsy, so exhausted-looking—struggling along on his two crutches. He tucks them beneath his seat or stows them unobtrusively in the overhead net for the luggage, if possible behind his suitcase, although not without first calculating what moves he must make to recover them without difficulty, and leaving the things he will need during the trip well within reach. He also tries to wear a lightweight raincoat and throw that across his legs. This is during the time when trains still had small compartments with facing seats. If someone takes a seat next to his, Señor Salama will sit the entire trip without getting up, hoping the other person will get off before he does, and only in an extreme case will he rise and collect his crutches to go to the lavatory, braving the risk that people will see him in the corridor, step aside and watch him with pity or derision, or offer to help him, hold a door for him or hold out a hand.

It is almost time for the train to leave, and, to Señor Salama's pleasure, no one has come into his compartment. Which is frequently the case when he travels in first class. Just as the train has begun to move, a woman bursts in, perhaps agitated because she had to run to catch it at the last minute. She takes the seat facing Señor Salama, who pulls up his inert legs beneath the raincoat. He has never married, in fact he has scarcely dared look at a woman since he was injured, as embarrassed by his stigmatizing plight as he was as a boy obliged to wear a yellow star on the lapel of his jacket.

The woman is young, very pretty, cultivated, clearly Spanish. Despite his reticence, in only a short while after beginning the trip they are chatting as if they had known each other forever, because the woman has the gift of expressing herself clearly and easily, but also of listening with flattering attention to what is said to her, and then, without prying, asking further details. Without realizing it, they lean toward each other, and it may be that their hands brush as they gesture, or their knees—hers naked, bare of stockings, his pulled back and hidden beneath his raincoat. As they speak, their heads, profiled against the window, never turn to observe the rapidly passing countryside. Señor Salama is strongly attracted to her but also shivering with tenderness, the physical promise of happiness that he believes he sees reflected and returned in the woman's eyes.

Both wish that the journey would last forever: the pleasure of being on the train, of having met, of having so many hours of conversation before them, and of discovering mutual affinities never shared with anyone until then. Señor Salama, whom the accident has left arrested in the tormented timidity of adolescence, finds an ease of conversing he never knew he had, a hint of seductiveness and audacity that after all these years restores the fun-loving impulses of his first days in Madrid.

She tells him she is traveling to Casablanca, where she lives with her family. He is about to tell her that he's going there too and they can get off together and make plans to see each other during the next few days. Then he remembers what he has put out of his mind for the last few hours, his obsession and his embarrassment, and he says nothing, or he lies, he says what a pity, he must go on to Rabat. If he gets off at Casablanca, he will have to use his crutches, which she hasn't seen, just as she hasn't seen his legs, although she's brushed against them, because they are covered by the raincoat.

They keep talking, but now there are occasional periods of silence and both realize it, and although she tries hard to fill them there is already a pool of shadow, of curiosity or suspicion, behind her words. Maybe she thinks she's done something wrong, said something she shouldn't have. In the meantime Señor Salama looks out the window every time the train comes to a station and calculates how many stops are left before Casablanca, before the inevitable farewell. He berates himself with secret rage, sets himself periods of time in which to express his feelings, postpones them, and all the while she is talking and smiling, her eloquent hands brushing his, her knees so close that they bump his when the train brakes, and then he surreptitiously adjusts the raincoat over his thighs so it won't slip to the floor. He will tell her that he too is going to Casablanca, he will pull himself up in the seat as soon as the train has stopped and take down his crutches, he won't let her try to help carry his luggage, because after so many years he's acquired an agility and strength in his arms and torso that he never imagined having, and when he doesn't have enough hands, he holds something with his teeth, or catches his balance by leaning against a wall.

But deep down he knows and has never doubted for an instant that he won't do that. As the train gets closer to Casablanca, the woman writes her address and telephone number for him and asks for his, which Señor Salama scrawls illegibly on a scrap of paper. The train has stopped, and the woman, standing before him, pauses for a minute, confused, surprised that he doesn't get to his feet to say good-bye, that he doesn't help her get down her suitcase. She probably hasn't seen the crutches hidden behind his bag, although it is also tempting to imagine that she did see them, with a woman's keen perceptiveness, and also noticed something strange about the legs placed so close together and covered by the raincoat. She decides not to bend down and kiss Señor Salama goodbye, instead she holds out her hand and smiles, and the shrug of her shoulders expresses fatalism, or capitulation, and she asks him to call her if he decides to stop in Casablanca on the return trip, and says that she will call him the next time she goes to Tangiers. At the last instant, he is tempted to stand up, or not to release her hand but allow her to help him up with her strong grip. The impulse is so strong that it almost seems he has enough strength in his legs to stand up without help from anyone. But he sits quietly, and, after a moment's hesitation, the woman releases his hand, picks up her suitcase, turns toward him for the last time, and goes out into the corridor. Once she's on the platform, he can't see her anymore. He leans back in the seat when the train starts off toward a city where he has nothing to do, where he will have to look for a hotel to spend the night, a hotel near the station because he will have to take the first train back to Casablanca. *Oh you, whom I would have loved,* he recited that evening in his office in the Ateneo Español, moved as deeply as if he were chanting the Kaddish in his father's memory, the sound of a ship's horn and the music of a muezzin's call came through the open window. *Oh you, who knew so well.*

münzenberg

I SIT UP UNTIL VERY LATE, fighting back sleep in order to read a little more, to learn more about the life of this man I had never heard of before yesterday, Willi Münzenberg, who at the beginning of the summer of 1940 is fleeing west along the roads of France in the great flood of people occasioned by the advance of German armored cars. Now that he is seeing things quietly and with clarity for the first time in the fifty years of his life, and has acquired enough experience and courage to do openly the things he should, nothing matters and there isn't enough time. This isn't the first time he's fled, but it is the first time he's fled on foot, with no resources and without a place to go, knowing that on whichever side of the front lines he tries to find refuge there will be people ready to betray him and turn him in, if he isn't machine-gunned—unknown and unidentified—among a line of hostages chosen at random, or blown up by a bomb or mine. He will be executed if the Germans capture him, but he will also die if his former comrades and Communist subordinates come across his trail. If he tries to reach England, a nearly impossible proposition, he knows that there too he will be arrested as a spy, and that surely the English will use him as a pawn in an exchange with the Soviets or the Germans. He had everything, and now he has and is nothing, although someone says, no, he had two thousand francs in his pocket, which he planned to use to buy a car and escape to Switzerland.

He knows that even the little that's left of him, this fleeting shadow on the roads of France, is unacceptable to many, an irrelevant or harmful witness whom it would be very good to eliminate. What he thought to be his strength, his life insurance, is actually the reason for his sentence. He knows something more: in the English secret services there are Soviet moles who will send news of his presence in England to Moscow, so that he won't be safe there even if the British government offers him asylum.

MY EYES CLOSE, the book nearly slips from my hands, as Münzenberg walks on among the throngs that flood the highways and scatter into nearby fields like a swarm of insects every time the low-flying German fighter planes swoop down over them. First comes the sound of engines in the distance, then the metallic silhouettes glinting in the June sunlight, and finally their shadows, huge raptors with fixed, widespread wings, machine-gunning a convoy of retreating military vehicles, dropping bombs on a bridge where escaping soldiers are clustered around a broken-down truck. Scurrying insects are what the pilots see from the air: tiny figures, oblique black scrawls. But each of those little creatures is a human being, having a name, a life, a face unlike that of any other person. Münzenberg is trying to blend in, to be a nobody and escape the claws and gullet of the cyclops. But the eye of the cyclops he knows best and fears most, Joseph Stalin, sees everything, scrutinizes everything, will not allow anyone to save himself. Not even by shrinking to the size of the most insignificant insect can a marked man escape his hunters, not even in a fortress in Mexico protected by high walls, barbed wire, armed guards, lookout towers, and iron gates, could Trotsky escape a pursuit that lasted more than ten years and encompassed the entire world.

Who among the masses fleeing around him could imagine Willi Münzenberg's story? A corpulent foreigner, badly dressed and unshaven, who has spent the last few months in a concentration camp, one of those camps in which the French government is incarcerating the refugees and stateless persons who according to the criminal logic of the times have most to fear from the Nazis: if war breaks out against Germany, the German refugees living in France become the enemy, so they must be locked up even though it is the Nazi regime they want to escape. Once imprisoned, they are perfect prey for the German army and the Gestapo they believed they eluded when they fled to France. In 1933 this man, Willi Münzenberg, came to Paris with the first wave of fugitives from Nazi persecution after the fire in the Reichstag, where he had held a seat as a Communist deputy. That time he escaped in a large black Lincoln Continental driven by his chauffeur, not on foot, like now, when he has nothing and is nobody, when he doesn't know where his wife is or if she's alive or if he will see her again. Both of them are caught in the chaos of the war, she too a tiny figure among the fleeing multitudes, in the uncountable census of the displaced and deported, the millions of people forced onto the highways of a Europe suddenly thrown back into barbarity. Crowds wait on train platforms, on the docks of seaside cities, line up on sidewalks outside the closed doors of foreign legations to get the passports, papers, visas, and administrative seals that can stamp on their destinies the difference between life and death.

I HAVE PUT THE BOOK on the night table and turned off the light, and as I lie here with my eyes open in the darkness, the sleep that only moments before was sweeping over me now evaporates. I've missed falling asleep the way you miss a train, by a minute, by seconds, and I know that I will have to wait for it to return and that it may be hours before it comes. The last time Münzenberg was seen alive was at a table in the town café, sitting with two men much younger than he and speaking with them in German. It's possible that they too were fugitives from the camp, and that one of them killed him; maybe they'd been sent to the camp as prisoners to win the confidence of the man they'd been ordered to shoot.

I lie quietly in the dark, listening to your breathing. Münzenberg flees in advance of the German army, accompanied by two men, and he doesn't know they are Soviet agents who have been watching him ever since they arrived in the camp as prisoners, with others whose executions have been assigned to them. Or maybe he knows but doesn't have the strength to escape, to keep pushing on in an exhausting and futile flight, the dragging out of a hunt that has lasted several years. Past the balcony, across the rooftops, I see the great face of the clock in the Telephone Building, which from this distance suggests a Moscow skyscraper, maybe because it isn't difficult to imagine that the red light at the pinnacle is a huge Communist star. Years ago, before I ever went to New York, I saw in my dreams an enormous building of black brick with a large red star at its pyramid-shaped peak, and someone beside me, someone I couldn't see, pointed and said, "That's the Bronx star."

When I can't sleep, the ghosts of the dead return, the ghosts of the living as well, people I haven't seen or thought of in a long time, events, actions, names from earlier lives, laced not with nostalgia, but rather with regret or shame. Fear returns too, a childish fear of the dark, of shadows or shapes that take on the form of an animal or a human presence or of a door about to open. In the winter of 1936, in a hotel room in Moscow, Willi Münzenberg lay awake and perhaps was smoking in the dark as his wife slept by his side, and every time he heard footsteps in the corridor outside their room, he thought with a shudder of clear-sighted panic, "They've come, they're here." Out the window he saw a red star, or a clock with numbers in red, glowing at the pinnacle of a building above the vast darkness of Moscow, above the streets where nothing was moving at that hour but the black vans of the KGB.

My grandmother Leonor—may she rest in peace—whom I can scarcely remember now, told me when I was a boy that her mother appeared to her every night after she died. She didn't do anything, didn't say anything, didn't evoke fear, only melancholy and tenderness and a sense of guilt, although my grandmother never used that word, *guilt* wasn't part of her country vocabulary. Her mother would look at her in silence, smile so she wouldn't be afraid, make a movement of her head as if to point to something, ask for something, and then she disappeared, or my grandmother would fall asleep, and the next night she would wake and see her again, motionless and faithful, at the foot of the bed, which is the same bed you and I are sleeping in now.

"Mama, what do you want? Do you need something?" my grandmother would ask her, as solicitous as when her mother was alive and very ill and would stare at her without speaking, her face pale against the pillow and her eyes following her daughter around the room.

The ghost repeated this nightly gesture, like someone who wants to say something but has lost the use of her voice. One Sunday morning in church, my grandmother realized what it was her mother wanted to say. She was so poor, and had so many children, she hadn't been able to pay for masses for her mother, and although she wasn't a dedicated believer her remorse wouldn't leave her in peace; a mute uneasiness developed that she shared with no one. Without the masses maybe her mother hadn't been able to get out of purgatory. My grandmother managed to scrape a little money together by borrowing from a sister-in-law, and with the coins and worn five-peseta bills wrapped in a handkerchief she went to the Church of Santa María to schedule the masses. That night, when her mother visited, standing by the bars of the brass footboard, my grandmother told her not to worry, soon she would have what she needed. Her mother never came again, there was never another "visitation," as my grandmother said in her language from another century. She felt relieved, but also sad, because now she would never see her mother again, not even in dreams.

The bed you and I are sleeping in now is the one my mother was born in. My parents were surprised that we wanted to bring this cumbersome old bed back to Madrid with us after all the years it sat in the attic. It was against those same bars I can see outlined in the dark, now that my eyes have adjusted, that my grandmother's mother rested her pale hand, my great-grandmother, from whom some part of me comes and whose name I don't even know, although I must have inherited from her some of my face, or character, or erratic health. How strange to live in places where the dead have lived, to use things that belonged to them, to look in mirrors where their faces were reflected, to look at oneself with eyes that may have the shape or color of theirs. The dead return during the sleepless hours, people I have forgotten and people I never knew, all prodding the memory of one who survived a war sixty years ago, telling him not to forget them, to speak their names aloud and tell how they lived, why they were carried off so early by a death that could have claimed him. Whose place in life have I taken? Whose destiny was canceled so that mine could be fulfilled? Why was I chosen and not another?

During nights when I lay in the darkness, waiting in vain to fall asleep, I have imagined the sleepless hours of Willi Münzenberg, the insomniac who couldn't sleep when he began to understand that the time of his power and pride had come to an end, and that all he had before him was running without hope of respite or possibility of safe harbor and finally dying like a dog, a hunted and sacrificed animal, just as so many friends of his friends had died, former comrades, Bolshevik heroes transformed overnight into criminals and traitors, into insects that must be crushed, according to the harangues of the drunken and demented prosecutors of the Moscow trials. Executed like a dog, like Zinoviev or Bukharin, like his friend and brother-in-law Heinz Neumann, director of the German Communist Party, who was living as a refugee or trapped in Moscow and who died in 1937, perhaps shot in the head, as unarmed and surprised before his executioners as another accused man, Josef K., whom Franz Kafka invented during the feverish insomnia of tuberculosis, unaware how prophetic he was. But it has never been ascertained exactly how Neumann died, how many weeks or months he was tortured, or where his body was buried.

In the death camp of Ravensbrück, Neumann's widow listened to stories her friend Milena Jesenska told her about Kafka. During many sleepless nights, Babette Gross lived minute by minute the torture of not knowing whether her husband was dead or in one of Stalin's prisons or in a German concentration camp. Years later, when she finally was told the truth, she imagined his hanged body in a forest, swinging from a tree branch, swaying back and forth until the branch or the rope broke and his body fell to the ground to rot without anyone's finding it, and all that long time she couldn't sleep, wondering whether she should or shouldn't think of him as a dead man. With autumn, falling leaves began to cover him.

You were sleeping beside me, and I was imagining Willi Münzenberg smoking in the dark as he listened to the quiet breathing of his wife, Babette, a stylish bourgeois blond, daughter of a Prussian beer magnate, an undoubting Communist in the early twenties, who lived much longer—nearly half a century—than he, an ancient woman who on the eve of the fall of the Berlin Wall received an American historian and whispered into a tape recorder stories of a vanished time and world, images of the night the Reichstag burned, of the first parades of the Brownshirts through German cities, and of Moscow in November 1936, when she and her husband waited for days in a hotel room for someone to come for them, waited to be called and given a day and an hour for an appointment with Stalin, a call that never came, until they heard pounding at the door: the men who had come to arrest them.

There are people who have seen these things: none of it has sunk into the absolute oblivion that claims events and human beings when the last person to witness them, the last person to hear a certain voice or meet a certain pair of eyes, dies.

I know a woman who wandered lost through Moscow the morning Stalin's death was announced. Eight months pregnant, she went back home because she was afraid that in the throng of people in the streets the creature kicking in her womb would be crushed. As I speak with her, I feel the vertigo I would feel crossing a soaring bridge of time, almost as if I were experiencing the reality she has seen, a reality that would be no more than a description in a book for me if I hadn't met her. I know a man who won an Iron Cross in the battle of Leningrad, and when I was very young I shook the hand of another whose pale, skinny forearm bore the tattooed identification number of a prisoner in Dachau. I have spoken with someone who at the age of six clung to his mother in a cellar in Madrid, terrified of the air-raid sirens, and of the airplanes and exploding bombs, and at ten he was interned in a barracks in Mauthausen. That man was small, polite, and detached; his name was half Spanish, half French, though he didn't really belong to either country. The black hair, combed straight back, the strong features and coppery face were Spanish, but his behavior and language were as French as those of any of the writers talking and drinking at that literary cocktail party in Paris where we met briefly, the beginning of my friendship with Michel del Castillo.

By chance, the way you meet a stranger at a party, I met Willi Münzenberg in a book I'd been sent. Begun half-heartedly, it turned into my insomnia. At some moment in the reading, without my knowing, there came a shift in attitude, and the person who had been nothing more than a name, an obscure and minor character, struck me as a powerful presence, someone intimately related to me, to the things that matter most to me, to my deepest being. You are in large part what others know, or think they know, about you, what they see when they look at you; but who are you when you're alone in the dark and can't sleep and your inert body is anchored to the bed and your untrammeled imagination confronts the intolerably slow pace of time? You don't know the hour but don't want to turn on the light and wake the person sleeping beside you; it might be the middle of the night or near the first light of dawn.

FROM AMONG THE GHOSTS of the living and the dead rises the specter of Münzenberg. He was with me that sleepless night, and he has returned often since; unexpectedly, over the years, I find him in the pages of other books, or he comes to me in my thoughts. All his life was a game between show and invisibility, between veiled power and the weightless splendor of appearances, and in the end he *was* invisible, erased from history by the same powerful people he served so well, the ones who in early June of 1940 hanged him from a tree in a forest in France.

Just yesterday I discovered that I had an excellent photograph of him. I found it in the second volume of Arthur Koestler's autobiography, *Invisible Writing,* published in London in 1954. Coincidences suddenly fall into place: I had bought that volume with the red binding and coarse yellow paper in a secondhand bookstore in Charlottesville, Virginia, one winter day in 1993. The store was in a red wooden building that reminded me a little of a cabin or a barn, at the edge of a snowy woods. One day as I flipped through the book, looking for the publication date, I saw something I'd never noticed: on the inside cover was an illegible signature, and beside that a place and date: Oslo, January 1959.

I hadn't remembered the photograph either, which has that chiaroscuro of portraits from the thirties. Münzenberg looks directly into the viewer's eyes, with arrogance and firmness, perhaps with a hint of loss and anticipated desperation, and with the sadness witnesses to some terrible truth exhibit in photographs. He is a strong man, rough, but not vulgar, with a thick, strong neck and broad shoulders, slightly lifted chin, shrewd eyes ringed with fatigue, broad brow, carelessly combed hair, a sign either of constant activity or the beginnings of neglect. He is dressed in a formal but very modern mode: suit jacket with a fountain pen in the upper pocket, vest, tie, and a shirt with an attached collar. Koestler says his face had the solid simplicity of a wood sculpture, but was lightened by an open and friendly expression. Koestler worked on behalf of Münzenberg in Paris during the period the photograph was taken: a short man, squarely built, robust, with the look of a small-town cobbler, but one who nevertheless projected such an hypnotic air of authority that Koestler saw bankers, diplomats, and Austrian dukes bow before him with the obedience of schoolboys.

Münzenberg was born in 1889 to a poor family in a proletarian suburb of Berlin. His father was a brutal, drunken tavern keeper who blew his head off while cleaning his shotgun. At sixteen Münzenberg was working in a shoe factory and taking advantage of the educational activities of the unions. He had always shown intelligence and had a talent for organization as well as an energy that instead of being depleted by controversy and hard work seemed to thrive on them. To avoid serving in an army involved in a war whose internationalist principles he repudiated, he escaped to Switzerland, where in the refugee circles of Bern he met Trotsky, who was immediately taken with his intelligence, his revolutionary passion, and his organizational skills. Trotsky introduced him to Lenin, and soon Münzenberg was part of Lenin's most loyal inner circle. One author reports that he was one of the Bolsheviks who traveled to Russia with Lenin in a sealed railroad car on the eve of the October Revolution. *Dear friend,* it's said he told Lenin, *you will die of your convictions.*

But he was always a little different from his Communist comrades. There was something excessive about him, even when he was most orthodox. He liked the good life, and having been born into and lived in poverty, he had an appetite for grand hotels, expensive suits, and luxury automobiles. He was made of the same stuff as the great American plutocrats who rose out of nothing, energetic impresarios of railroads or coal mines or steel who had grown rich because of their clear vision and villainy, but especially because of the compelling force of a practical intelligence joined with a resolute and merciless will. Those who knew Münzenberg say that had he chosen to serve capitalism instead of communism, he would have been a Hearst, a Morgan, or a Frick, one of those colossal entrepreneurs never satisfied by any possession, no matter how excessive, and who never lose their rough edges; age or power or wealth do not slow their ardor for acquiring, and despite boundless wealth, they remain jovial boors.

During the first years of the Soviet Revolution, when Lenin, hallucinating on the country estates of the Kremlin, intoxicated by his own fanaticism, surrounded with telephones and lackeys, still imagined that at any minute all Europe would explode in the flames of proletarian uprisings, Münzenberg understood that world revolution would not happen immediately, if ever, and that communism would spread in the West only in an oblique and gradual way—not with the loud, crude, and monotonous propaganda that pleased the Soviets but, rather, through seemingly neutral and apolitical causes and with the complicity, in great part unwitting, of intellectuals of great prestige, unaffiliated celebrities who would sign manifestos promoting peace, culture, and goodwill among nations.

Münzenberg invented the political technique of enlisting wealthy intellectuals with flattery, of using their self-idolatry and their minimal interest in reality to manipulate them. Not without scorn, he referred to them as the Club of Innocents. He sought out moderates with humanitarian inclinations and bourgeois solidity, if possible with the added virtue of a patina of money and cosmopolitanism: André Gide, H. G. Wells, Romain Rolland, Ernest Hemingway, Albert Einstein. Lenin would have shot such intellectuals immediately, or consigned them to a dark cell in Lubyanka Prison or to Siberia. Münzenberg discovered how enormously useful they could be in making attractive a system that to him, in the incorruptible inner core of his intelligence, must have seemed frightening in its incompetence and cruelty, even in the years he considered it legitimate.

Little by little he was becoming the impresario of the Comintern, its secret ambassador in the bourgeois Europe he was so fond of, the same bourgeoisie to whose destruction he had dedicated his life. He founded companies and newspapers that served as covers for handling the propaganda funds sent from Russia, but he had such an innate talent for business that each of those ventures prospered, multiplying clandestine investments into rivers of money with which he then financed new projects of revolutionary conspiracy. His audacious business ventures ceased to be covers and became true capitalist successes.

He was a director of the Third International, but he drove through Berlin, and later Paris, in a large Lincoln, always accompanied by his blond wife swathed in furs. He invented grand and noble causes that no one of goodwill could fail to support. The measure of his triumph is equaled only by that of his anonymity: no one knew that the international movements of solidarity and the international congresses of writers and artists promoting peace and culture were the brainchildren of Willi Münzenberg. From his own experience, he knew that hard-nosed Bolsheviks like Stalin, or Lenin himself, would rouse very little public affection in the West, so to attract a Nobel laureate in literature or a Hollywood actress to the cause was a formidable coup in public relations. He discovered that radicalism and distant revolutions were irresistibly attractive to intellectuals of a certain social position.

His first success in large-scale organization and propaganda was the world campaign to ship foodstuffs to the regions of Russia devastated by the great famines of 1921. The international fund for aid to workers, which he directed, was responsible for delivering dozens of shiploads of food to Russia and also for creating a powerful current of humanitarian sympathy around the world for the suffering and heroism of the Soviet people. The indifferent charity of other times was transmuted into vigorous political solidarity in which a benefactor could always feel he was a comfortable step away from active militancy. Münzenberg contrived seals, insignias, and propaganda fliers illustrated with photographs of life in the USSR, color prints, paperweights with busts of Marx and Lenin, postcards of workers and soldiers, anything that could be sold at a low price and would allow the buyer to feel that his few coins were a gesture of solidarity, not charity, a practical and comfortable form of revolutionary action.

In 1925, with countless committees, publications, marches, and images in movie newsreels, he plotted and created the great wave of support for Sacco and Vanzetti. In the terrible years of inflation in Germany, the Japan earthquake of 1923, the general strike in England in 1926, he filled the coffers of resistance and organized soup kitchens, schools, and shelters for orphan children. It was the need to print and distribute massive numbers of political pamphlets that awakened his interest in publishing. In 1926 he owned two mass-circulation dailies in Germany, an illustrated weekly magazine that had a circulation of a million— and was, says Koestler, the Communist counterpart to *Life*—as well as a series of publications that included technical journals for photographers and magazines for radio and movie fans. In Japan, directly or indirectly, his organization controlled nineteen newspapers and magazines. In the Soviet Union he produced films on Eisenstein and Pudovkin, and in Germany he organized the distribution of Soviet films and financed the vanguardist spectacles of Erwin Piscator and Bertolt Brecht. All around the world, film clubs, sports clubs, reading clubs, touring societies, and groups of activists in favor of peace became unimpeachable branches of the Club of Innocents.

With Hitler's arrival in the chancellery, Münzenberg lost everything he possessed or controlled in Germany. But he was like those American magnates who suffer horrific bankruptcies only to claw their way up out of nothing and create new fortunes with the same invincible energy. As soon as he arrived in Paris, he bought a newspaper and organized financial support for the underground in Germany. The German Communist Party had believed up to the last hour that the Nazis were minor adversaries and that the true enemies of the working class were the Social Democrats. The disaster of January 1933 convinced Münzenberg that the suicidal sectarianism of his fellow party members had to be abandoned in favor of a great alliance among all democratic forces prepared to resist the sinister tidal wave of fascism. Within a few months, he had published one of the best-selling books of the twentieth century, *The Brown Book of Nazi Terror*, and achieved his greatest success, the masterpiece of his instinct for mass propaganda, the international campaign on behalf of Dimitrov and others arrested and put on trial for the fire at the Reichstag.

Just as the blackest period of Stalin's terror and extermination was drawing near, Münzenberg's flair for publicity ensured that in the eyes of the world's progressives the Soviet Union was the great adversary of totalitarianism, more valiant and resolute than any corrupt bourgeois democracy.

He never paused, the flow of schemes and proposals never slowed, ideas for books and articles, for new forms of political activism, clubs and committees and campaigns, lists of prestigious names needed for each new cause, aid to workers in the Asturias uprising of 1934 and the protest against the Italian invasion of Abyssinia. He stormed into his offices in Paris like a cyclone, yelled over the telephone at the top of his lungs, smoked his excellent cigars while absentmindedly sprinkling the ash over the broad lapels of his expensive suits, dictated memorandums until three or four in the morning, sent telegrams to Moscow or New York or Tokyo, checked the sales figures for books and print runs of newspapers, improvised the rules for the World Committee for the Relief of the Victims of German Fascism, drew up the list of foods and medicines to go on a ship leased by his organization in Marseilles and destined for striking workers in the port of Shanghai.

He is everywhere, directing a prodigious variety of tasks, feared and obeyed by people working in several countries, and yet he's invisible, hidden in shadow. Both conspirator and a deputy in the Reichstag, both entrepreneur fond of expensive cigars and chauffeured cars and a militant Communist, a man of the world who enters salons on the arm of a woman taller and more distinguished than he and a critic of the idiocies and depravities of the rich, whom at the same time he admires with the fascination of the poor boy who watches the dazzling lives of the powerful from a distance, who smells the perfumes of women swathed in fur stoles and desires them with a passion fed by social outrage.

IN OCTOBER OF 1936, an emissary presented himself in Münzenberg's Paris offices, a man whom he had never seen and whom he disliked because of his surliness and obvious air of an informer or jailer. When the man entered, he examined the office out of the corner of his eye, disapproving of the luxury of the carpet, the curtains and paintings, the solid, bold shapes of the furniture, the tubular chairs, the art deco table at which Münzenberg was seated, leaning on his elbows, surrounded with documents and telephones. Without preamble or ceremony, the man told Münzenberg that his presence was required in Moscow.

There is also a traitor in the story, a shadow at Münzenberg's side, the rancorous and docile, cultivated and polyglot subordinate—Münzenberg spoke only German, and that with a strong lower-class accent—Otto Katz, also called André Simon. Slim, elusive, an old friend of Franz Kafka, Katz was the organizer of the congress of antifascist intellectuals of Valencia, Münzenberg's and the Comintern's representative among the intellectuals of New York and the actors and screenwriters of Hollywood, a perpetual spy, the fawning adulator of Hemingway, Dashiell Hammett, Lillian Hellman, all fervent and cynical Stalinists. The éminence grise behind Münzenberg's grand machinations, he also reported on his superior's every action and word to the new hierarchs of Moscow.

Münzenberg quickly pledges his loyalty, of course, but in spite of how perceptive he is about character and weakness he fails to detect the edge of resentment beneath Katz's suaveness, or the meticulous patience with which Katz secretly collects small IOUs for the insults he suffers or imagines, the humiliation that Münzenberg's uncontrolled and baroque energy has inflicted through the years. Koestler writes that Katz was dark and distinguished, attractive in a slightly sordid way. He spoke and wrote fluently in French, English, German, Russian, and Czech. He had discussed literature with Milena Jensenska in the cafés of Prague and Vienna. He always squinted one eye when he lit his cigarettes or was absorbed in something. During the Spanish Civil War, he directed the official news agency of the Republican government, which entrusted him with secret funds allocated to influence certain French publications and politicians. Münzenberg rescued him from poverty and despair in Berlin, where at the beginning of the 1920s Katz was frequenting the haunts of beggars and drunks and loitering near bridges favored by suicides. In 1938, when Münzenberg was expelled from the German Communist Party, accused of secretly working for the Gestapo, Katz was one of the first to repudiate him publicly and call him a traitor.

That rat Otto Katz gave him the Judas kiss, plotted his death, even if he didn't personally tighten the noose around his neck.

Many years later, an ancient woman of ninety speaks into a microphone in the dusk of an apartment in Munich. Age has erased the haughtiness from her face but not her imperious bearing or the glitter in her eyes, just as time has not calmed her scorn for that long-ago traitor, who also was eventually expelled and condemned, executed in 1952 in a cell in Prague with a rope around *his* neck. There was no mercy for executioners either, it seems. "Otto Katz!" says the old woman, pronouncing that name as if spitting it through her tightly pressed lips painted with a ragged streak of crimson.

I also track this woman through literature, seek her face in photographs, browse the labyrinths of the Internet, hoping to find the book she wrote in the 1940s to vindicate her husband's memory and denounce and shame those who plotted his death. I see scenes, images not invoked by will or based on any recollection but endowed with a somnambulist precision in which imagination does not intervene: curtains drawn in the Munich apartment, in October 1989, the tape whirring with a slight hiss in the small recorder before her, an archive where her voice will be preserved, a voice I never heard, it came to me through the soundless words of a book discovered by chance and read voraciously during a sleepless night.

For two or three years I have flirted with the idea of writing a novel, imagined situations and places, like snapshots, or like those posters displayed on large billboards at the entrance to a movie theater. That these stills were never in narrative sequence made them all the more powerful, freed them of the weight and vulgar conventions of a scenario; they were revelations in the present, with no before or after. When I didn't have the money to go inside, I would spend hours looking at the photographs outside the theater, not needing to invent a story to fit them together like pieces of a jigsaw puzzle. Each became a mystery, illuminating the others, creating multiple links that I could break or modify at my whim, patterns in which no image nullified the others or gained precedence or lost its uniqueness within the whole.

The creaking of the parquet floor in our new house, or a bad dream about illness or misfortune, woke me suddenly, and I was Willi Münzenberg waking in the middle of the night in his house in Paris or in the icy room of a Moscow hotel, fearing that his executioners were approaching, wondering how long it would be before a shot or knife brought an end to the great illusion and delirium of his public existence, and the long tenderness of his married life with Babette, who lay sleeping at his side, hugging him in her sleep the way you hug me, with the determination of a sleepwalker.

The local train stops at the small station of La Sierra de Madrid: drizzle, hillsides covered with trees and fog, the strong scent of wet vegetation—rockrose, pines, cedars—and steep slate rooftops give the impression that you have traveled much farther, to a hidden mountain retreat where there might be sanatoriums or homes for patients in need of rest and cold, clean air. The train is rapid and modern, but the station building is bare stone and the windows are set in red brick, and the sign with the name of the town is written on yellow tiles. There's no one on the platform, and no one else has stepped off the train. A scent of forests, of drenched trees and earth, floods my lungs, and the touch of the still, misty air on my face gives me an immediate sense of calm. The train pulls away, and I begin walking along a dirt road, suitcase in hand, toward some farms where lights are just going on. In 1937, fearing for his life, so agitated and exhausted that at times he felt a sharp pain in his chest, the warning of a heart attack, Münzenberg hid for a few months in a clinic in a place called La Vallée des Loups, the valley of the wolves. The name of the director also seemed an indication or promise of something: Dr. Le Savoureux. But Münzenberg is as ill suited for physical repose as he is for intellectual calm, and the minute he arrives at the clinic he starts spending his nights writing a book. As I step onto the platform of the small train station of La Sierra, alone, I am Willi Münzenberg looking in the dark for the road to the sanatorium.

We have come on a winter afternoon to a hotel in the north, in Vitoria. They have given us a room on the top floor, and when I open the window I see a snow-covered park with little squares and statues and a bandstand and, in the background, above the white rooftops, a gray sky stretching like a receding plain. Münzenberg and Babette succeeded in getting out of Russia, and after a long night on the train they found lodging in a hotel near the station of a Baltic city, still worn out from lack of sleep and the tension of approaching the border, fearful that at the last moment the Soviet guards who inspected their passports would order them off the train.

I walk through Madrid or Paris, and a passing metro train makes the pavement tremble beneath my feet: Münzenberg feels that the world is trembling beneath his feet, that no one but he sees the disaster coming, no one on the terraces of the cafés or walking under the bright lights of the boulevards, as the ground begins to shake beneath marching boots and the weight of armored cars, beneath the bombs falling in Madrid and Barcelona and Guernica that no one in Europe wants to hear, and all the while Hitler is preparing his armies and consulting his maps and Stalin is concocting the great public theater of the Moscow trials and the secret hells of interrogation and execution.

I attend a performance of *The Magic Flute*, and for no reason, in the middle of the verve and joy of the music, the man sitting beside a blond woman is Münzenberg, and the flight of the hero lost in a forest and chased by dragons and faceless conspirators is also his flight. Maybe he slipped into Germany, and although he doesn't like opera came to this performance of *The Magic Flute* in a Berlin theater filled with black and gray uniforms to make contact with someone. But that scenario isn't realistic; Münzenberg could have come into Germany incognito, but in the Berlin opera Babette would have been recognized immediately, the Red *bourgeoise*, the scandalous and arrogant deserter of her social class, of the great Aryan nation.

REAL EVENTS WEAVE dramas that fiction would never dare: Babette Gross had a sister named Margarete, as romantically enchanted as she with radical politics in the early hallucinatory and convulsive days of the Weimar Republic. Margarete, like her sister, married a professional revolutionary, Heinz Neumann, the leader of the German Communist Party. In early February 1933, when Hitler was recently named chancellor of the Reich, Münzenberg and Babette flee from Germany in the large black Lincoln to take refuge in Paris; Neumann and Margarete escape to Russia. There he falls from favor and is arrested and executed, shot in the nape of the neck; his wife is sent to a camp in the frozen north of Siberia.

In the spring of 1939, when the German-Soviet pact is signed, one of the clauses guarantees that German citizens who fled from Nazism and took political asylum in the Soviet Union will be sent back to Germany. No frontier is a refuge; all close like traps on the feet of the hunted. Margarete is transferred by train from Siberia to the border of a recently divided Poland, and the Soviet guards hand her over to the guards of the SS. After three years in a Soviet camp, she spends another five in a German death camp.

In Ravensbrück, where Communist prisoners treat her like a traitor, she meets a Czech woman, Milena Jesenska, who twenty years earlier was the love of Franz Kafka's life and who moved in the same radical and bohemian circles frequented by Otto Katz before he emigrated to Berlin and there crossed paths with Münzenberg. In that Ravensbrück camp, Margarete, who never heard of Kafka, listens as Milena tells the story of the traveling salesman who wakes one morning turned into an enormous insect, and the story about the man who without knowing what crime he has committed is subjected to a spectral trial, found guilty before he is tried, then executed like a dog in an open field in the middle of the night. Milena, starving and ill, dies in May 1944, only shortly before news reaches the camp that the Russians are advancing from the east and the Allies have landed in Normandy. But the proximity of the Red Army offers no hope of freedom to Margarete, only the threat of a new captivity, of the repetition of a nightmare. She escapes from the German camp in the confusion of the last days, flees through two European armies—Germans in retreat and Soviets advancing—two hells and eight years that she survived with unbelievable fortitude.

IN 1989, AT NINETY, her sister Babette relates it all to an American journalist named Stephen Koch, who is writing the book about Willi Münzenberg that I will discover by chance seven years later. Babette lives in Munich, alone and lucid, still ramrod straight, the youthful gleam in her eyes undimmed. There is a fanatic intensity in the way she sometimes focuses on the young man, the diabolical determination to live and endure that sustains some extremist elders. Shortly afterward she moves to Berlin, and her apartment is not very far from the Wall; some nights she must have heard the sound of the crowds demonstrating on the other side, and the roar of skyrockets and songs of celebration would have reached her bedroom on the night of November 9 when the Wall finally came down, the world that she, her husband, her sister, and her brother-in-law believed in sixty years before, the world they helped create.

The woman speaks in a low, clear voice, in the accented but perfect English of the upper-class British of the 1920s, and that voice, like her eyes, is much younger than her years. Everything happened so long ago, it's as if it never happened. Everything she knows and remembers will cease to exist in a few months, when she dies. The face of Willi Münzenberg will be lost with her, the smell of his body and the cigars he smoked, his enthusiasm, and the way he was sapped first by losing faith, then by the suspicion that he was being followed and the conviction that there would be no forgiveness for him. His intelligence, too, was eroded by the discovery that he, the inventor of lies, had himself been deceived, that he hadn't wanted to see what was right before his eyes—all this he tried to tell in a hastily written, tumultuous book when it was already too late, when the intellectuals he had bewitched, used, and scorned for so long turned their backs on him, and his name was carefully being eliminated from the annals of his time.

Messengers came to transmit the order that he was wanted in Moscow. He invented delays, pretexts for postponing the trip, because it was unthinkable that he would openly refuse to obey. Others he knew had gone to Moscow and never returned; all trace of their activities was erased, even their names, or they were publicly denounced in Party newspapers as monstrously disloyal. Münzenberg knew all too well how a campaign of international indignation was organized, how easily reality could be reshaped with the clever use of publicity techniques such as tedious and relentless repetition.

He couldn't go to Moscow now, he said, during that first summer of the war in Spain, just when he was called on once again to summon all his talents as organizer and propagandist in defense of the last of the great causes, the one closest to his heart after the fall of Germany: international solidarity with the Spanish Republic, with the government of the Popular Front.

But the messages and secret orders kept coming, briefer and more urgent, more threatening, even as news was filtering through of arrests and interrogations. In November 1936, Münzenberg and Babette Gross traveled to Moscow. He was still a high official of the Comintern and the German Communist Party, but there was no one to greet them at the station. A couple of foreigners dressed in opulent winter clothing stood in the grit and poverty of a Soviet train station, the man in his felt hat and long custom-made overcoat, the woman in high heels and silk stockings, her face powdered and her blond hair peeking from the collar of her fur coat. Beside them were piles of luggage appropriate for deluxe trains and the best cabins on transatlantic steamers, leather suitcases with brass fittings and stickers from international hotels, trunks, makeup cases, hatboxes: they are a portrait for an ad printed on the glossy pages of a 1930s magazine, one of those publications Münzenberg dreamed up and directed.

No one waits at the hotel they were assigned to, and there is no message for them in their room. From the window, from one of the top floors of an enormous hotel only recently constructed but already dark and depressing, where uniformed, armed women stand guard at the end of the corridors in a silence uninterrupted by voices or ringing telephones, Münzenberg and Babette can see in the distance, high above the dark rooftops, a red star shining at the very top of a skyscraper. This is the world they have dedicated their lives to, the only country to which it was legitimate for an internationalist to swear loyalty. It is so cold in the room they don't take off their coats. There is a black telephone on the night table, but it's disconnected or out of order. Even so, they look at it with the hope, or the fear, that it will begin to ring. As is routine, their passports were taken from them as they entered the USSR, and they have no tickets or return date.

The only word Münzenberg has received is that he is to wait. He will be received and heard in good time. His inability to do nothing at all makes the waiting worse than the fear. The man and the woman, accustomed to the good life, to the brilliant social activity of Berlin and Paris, are left alone and confined to a Moscow hotel, reluctant to step outside into the wintry streets that seem so gloomy compared with the lights of the capitals of Europe where they have always lived. If they go out for a walk, there will be someone following them. If they go down to the lobby or the dining room, someone will make note of their every move, and if they speak above a whisper, the waiter who serves them tea will remember every word they say. They will be overheard if they make a telephone call, and if they send a letter to Paris, someone will scrutinize it under a strong lamp, inspect it for secret messages, and keep it as material proof of something, whether espionage or treachery.

At the end of several identical days, someone knocks at the door. After an instant of uncertainty, Münzenberg and Babette, tense and pale, find themselves confronting the familiar and yet by now nearly unrecognizable faces of Heinz and Margarete Neumann, the only ones who have decided to, or dared to, visit them. Perhaps they dared because they know they are already condemned, because they too are living the isolation of a contagious illness. Once infected, you can approach only someone who suffers the same illness. The two blond sisters and the two men of working-class origins: four lives trapped together. They speak in low voices, huddled close, all wearing their overcoats in the icy hotel room in Moscow, whispering for fear of microphones, so many things to tell after so many years of separation, so little time to say it all, to exchange warnings, for at any moment men in black leather coats very much like the uniforms of the Gestapo can knock at the door, or kick it down.

They say good-bye, knowing that the four of them will never be together again. Within a few months Neumann is arrested and disappears into the offices and dungeons of Lubyanka Prison, where just outside the front door stands a gigantic statue of Feliks Dzerzhinski, the Polish aristocrat who founded Lenin's secret police, a man Münzenberg knew very well in the early years of the Revolution.

But the past counts for nothing, it can even become a basis for guilt. Koestler writes that ministers and dukes once bowed before the decisive and rough authority of Willi Münzenberg, but in Moscow no one welcomes him, no one returns his calls. He was everything, and now he is no one: the past is as remote as the bright lights of Paris and Berlin remembered in the gloomy monotony of a Moscow where the only illumination in the streets comes from the black cars of the secret police.

He organized the international campaign that made Dimitrov a hero, not of communism but of popular and democratic resistance to the Nazis. Thanks to him, German judges had to let Dimitrov go free, and now, in Moscow, he is the head of the Comintern. But Dimitrov doesn't return Münzenberg's messages; he is never in his office when Münzenberg tries to call on him, and no one knows how long it will be before he returns to Moscow.

The Club of Innocents, the credulous, the idiots of goodwill, the deceived and sacrificed who receive no reward—I have been one of them, Münzenberg thinks during sleepless nights in his hotel room. I helped Hitler and Stalin destroy Europe with equal brutality. I helped invent the legend of their struggle to the death. I was a pawn when in the intoxication of my pride I thought I was directing the game from the shadows.

Maybe his life isn't that important to him, less important even than all the money, power, and luxury he has had and lost. What matters is that Babette may suffer, that she may be dragged down and have to suffer for the mistakes he made, all the lies he helped spread. To save her, he does not yield, he besieges the directors of the Comintern who once were his friends or subordinates and now pretend not to know him, he brandishes old credentials that now have no currency: his world campaign for aid to Soviet workers during the years of hunger, his early loyalty to the Bolsheviks during the mythological times of the Revolution, the confidence Lenin placed in him. *You will die of your convictions.* In the sinister and icy mausoleum on Red Square, in a faint illumination reminiscent of a chapel, he has gazed upon the mummy of his former protector, an unrecognizable face with the dull consistency of wax, lids closed over Asiatic eyes. We have come to the kingdom of the dead, and they will not let us return.

At last he wrangles an appointment with a powerful bureaucrat, one of Stalin's protégés. In Togliatti's office, Münzenberg shouts, vindicates himself, pounds the table, puts on an impressive spectacle of power and rage, as if he still possessed newspapers that printed millions of copies, and luxurious automobiles. He must return posthaste to Paris, he says, he must organize the greatest propaganda campaign of all time, recruit volunteers, collect funds, medicines, food, he must supply weapons, cement the solidarity of world intellectuals with the Spanish Republic.

Togliatti, who is blunt, quiet, twisted, and cowardly, a hero of the communist and democratic resistance against Mussolini that was almost entirely invented by Münzenberg's political publicity, agrees, or pretends to agree, to his request; he picks a day for the return trip and assures Münzenberg that passports will be waiting for him and Babette at the office of the station police. Perhaps Münzenberg asks whether he knows anything about Neumann, whether he is able to do anything for Heinz and Greta. Togliatti smiles, servile but also reserved, demonstrating with restrained villainy his present superiority over the former powerful director of the International. He says that he can't do anything, or that nothing will happen, everything will work out; he implies that this is not a particularly good time for Münzenberg to ask, just as he is about to leave.

Again the man and woman wearing hats and voluminous overcoats stand on the train platform, shoes shined, their great stack of luggage beside them; they look out of place, and insolent, in their broad lapels and fox furs. They cast sideways glances, nervous, uncertain as to whether they will in fact be allowed to leave.

The hour of departure is near, but their passports are not in the police office as Togliatti promised. All around them they sense the net, perhaps with the next step they will fall into it, perhaps each moment of delay is a planned stage in the culmination of their sentence. But they are not going back to that hotel now that the train is ready to depart, they are not going to give up, lock themselves in a room, keep waiting. Münzenberg grips the arm of his wife, so tall and graceful at his side, and guides her toward the steps of the train as he gives instructions for their luggage to be taken to their compartment. If they are going to be arrested, let it happen now. But no one comes near, no one stops them in the corridor of the train, which slowly begins to pull away at the announced time.

At each station stop, they look toward the platform, searching for the soldiers or plainclothes officers who will come on board to arrest them, ask for their passports, shove them around, and make them get off the train, or maybe surround them without a word, lead them away quietly in order not to create unnecessary alarm among the passengers.

"It was the longest train trip of our lives," Babette Gross tells the American journalist fifty-three years later. In the dim light of the second morning, they come to the border station. "We thought they would be waiting for us there, prolonging the hunt to the last instant." With a firm step, as the other travelers fell into line on the snowy platform to have their passports checked, Münzenberg strode toward the police office, the belt of his overcoat drawn tight, the lapels of his coat turned up against the cold, the brim of his hat snapped down over his rustic, fleshy, German face.

Both passports were waiting in a sealed envelope.

I feel their anguish, I lose sleep imagining it was you and I on that train. I am terrified by documents, passports, certificates that can be lost, doors I can't open, borders, the inscrutable or threatening expression of a policeman or anyone wearing a uniform, displaying authority. I am frightened by the fragility of things; the order and quiet of our lives always hangs from a thread that can snap so easily; our everyday, secure, familiar reality can suddenly shatter in a cataclysm.

The remaining years of Münzenberg's life are spent on the defensive; he doesn't give up, but lives with the awareness of approaching horror; his light-colored eyes dilate with fear, though his intellect is still sustained by a relentless will. In 1938 he is expelled from the German Communist Party, accused of being a spy and of working for the Gestapo, and no one comes forward in his defense. He has enough energy left to found another newspaper, to denounce in its pages the dual threat of communism and fascism and urge popular resistance against them. Let all the democracies that have abandoned the Spanish Republic and tolerated the aggressive rearmament and brutality of Hitler, to whom they have handed over Czechoslovakia, hoping to sate his hunger, to appease him at least temporarily, awake from their idiotic and cowardly lethargy. In his newspaper he predicts that Hitler and Stalin will sign a pact to share domination of Europe, and also that after a brief period Hitler will turn against his ally and invade the Soviet Union, but no one reads that newspaper, no one gives any credence to the ravings of a man who seems mad.

AS STRANGE AS THE FACT that this man once existed is the fact that there is almost no evidence of his sojourn in the world. Perhaps no one now lives who knew him and remembers him. Babette Gross, who lived so many years after his death, is a shadow herself. On the tape recorded by Stephen Koch you can still hear the sound of her voice, speaking English exquisitely. Her memory of that man fires a gleam in eyes recessed in sockets that already betray the shape of her skull.

There is a final part of the story that this woman didn't know and that no one can ever tell, unless the man still lives who in the spring of 1940 tied the rope around the sturdy neck of Willi Münzenberg and hanged him from a tree branch in the middle of a French forest. There are no witnesses; no one ever learned who the two men were who were with him the last time anyone saw him, when one mild June afternoon he was sitting at the door of a café in a French town, drinking and talking, giving every appearance of naturalness, as if the war didn't exist, as if German armored cars weren't racing along the highways toward Paris.

The three men left the café, and no one remembers having seen them, three nameless strangers in the great floodtide of the war. Months later, in November, at the first light of dawn, a hunter walks deep into the woods with his dog, which is sniffing excitedly, muzzle to the ground, following a scent to a place where he roots out a corpse half hidden under the autumn leaves, a body pulled into a peculiar position, knees to chest, skull half split by the rope that bit into it during the process of decomposition.

Staring into the darkness of insomnia, I imagine a faint light, bluish gray, hazy in the fog, the sound of the hunter's boots swishing through the leaves, the panting and grunts, the impatience, the choked breath of the dog as it noses the soft, loamy dirt. I wonder how Willi Münzenberg's identity was attributed to that disfigured and anonymous cadaver, and whether the fountain pen I've seen in the photograph of Koestler's book was still in the upper pocket of his jacket.

olympia

DAYS BEFORE LEAVING, my life had already been turned by the magnet of the journey, pulled toward the hour of departure, which approached with agonizing slowness. I was still here yet distant, though no one noticed my absence, not from the places where I lived and worked, not from the things that were extensions of myself and indicated my existence, my immobilized life, confined to a single city, to a few streets, which I traveled at fixed times between house and office, or between the office and the café where I went every morning to have breakfast with my friend Juan, in the half hour of freedom granted me by labor laws and administered by the clocks where we had to insert a punch card as if it were an open sesame.

Never was I so obsessed with impossible journeys as then, so distanced from myself and from the tangible and real around me. It wasn't that an important part of me was hidden from others' eyes; my whole self was hidden. The shell that others saw didn't matter at all, it had nothing to do with me. A municipal employee, low-grade, an administrative assistant, although having everything in place, married, with a small child. With literary vanity, I sought refuge in being unknown, hidden, but there was also a conformity in me at least as strong as my rebellion, with the difference that the conformity was practical while the rebellion showed only occasionally as a blurry discontent—with the exception of those daily morning conversations with Juan, who was then living a very similar life, working a few offices away from mine.

Against my principles I had married in the Church, and in precisely nine months my son was born. Sometimes I was struck with remorse for not having dared to live a different life, with a sharp longing for other cities and other women, cities where I had never been, women I remembered or invented, whom I had loved in vain or whom I imagined I had lost for lack of courage. I remembered one woman especially, even though it had been five years since I saw her. She lived in Madrid now and was married, with one or two children; I wasn't sure of the number because I had only indirect news of her from time to time. I still shivered when someone spoke her name.

There were two worlds, one visible and the other invisible, and I adapted tamely to the norms of the first so I could retreat without too much inconvenience into the second. Many years later, I occasionally dream about those days in the office, and what I experience is not depression but a quiet melancholy. I dream that I go back to work after a long absence, and I do it without distress or any hint of the old bitterness.

Now, at the end of my years, I realize that my docility wasn't a mask, the false identity of a spy, but rather a substantial and true part of my being: the intimidated and obedient part that has always been one aspect of my nature, the satisfaction that I looked respectable to others as son and student, and later as employee, husband, and father. When I dream of going back to the municipal office I abandoned so long ago, my fellow workers welcome me with affection; they are not surprised to see me and don't ask about the long absence. For years I liked remembering—embellishing the memory of—my turbulent adolescence, but now I believe the love of conformity dominated my youth, not rebellion, and that love undoubtedly returned to influence me in my adult life, when I accepted marriage and went along with the obligations and little humiliations that made me boil inside: the church wedding, the ritual communion, the family banquet, everything that had been prescribed for an eternity and that I obeyed, unresisting, to the letter of the law. I knew I was deceiving myself, just as I was deceiving the woman I had married without true conviction, as well as the relatives in both families who congratulated one another that finally such a dubious, erratic, and long courtship was over. I never thought about the irresponsibility of my silence, about the bitterness and lies it sowed outside the boundaries of my secret fantasies, seeds that flowered in the real life of the person at my side.

As a boy I obeyed my parents and teachers happily, and the fact that I got excellent grades and was considered an exemplary student filled me with pride. I was the envy of my friends' mothers, and if a teacher favored me, I felt literally paralyzed with satisfaction. I wasn't pretending, as I later invented, wasn't striving to get good grades so I could escape the hidebound life of work in the country that my origins foreordained. I studied because I was supposed to and because fulfilling obligations gave me as much pleasure as living by religious precepts. Until I was fifteen, I went to mass faithfully, and confessed and took communion without once feeling I was performing a ritual alien to me, and for a time I entertained the possibility of becoming a priest.

I have actually had very few outbursts of true rebellion in my life, and most of them were clumsy, senseless, leaving nothing but a memory of humiliation and failure. Once, when I was twenty-two, I gave up everything, my sweetheart and my respectability along with any consideration for my parents or her parents, who had already accepted me as a model son. I had fallen in love with another woman, and when she went off to Madrid I couldn't get along without her. One night at the end of term, I caught the express train and showed up the next morning at the supermarket that belonged to my lover's family. From the way they looked at me I realized that what had happened between us was over for her, and had never really been very important, never reached full bloom. I returned that same night, feeling ridiculous and that I had learned a lesson. I made up with my fiancée, and when she put her arms around me, weeping and saying she had always been sure I would come back to her, I thought, with a flash of miserable lucidity, that I was fooling myself, but I did nothing, and for many years I did nothing but drift, and do everything expected or demanded of me.

For a long time, while I worked in that office in the provincial city I had moved to, I remembered a phrase of William Blake that I'd read somewhere, something like "He who desires, but acts not, breeds pestilence." I was a mass of aspirations unacted on, of fantasies as unreal as those that kept me company in the quiet solitudes of my childhood. I was always wanting to go somewhere, a misfit never pleased with anything, and suddenly I found myself settled down, paralyzed, in a rut at the age of twenty-seven, making payments on an apartment, receiving good bonuses at work, going from house to office, office to house, imagining trips, daydreaming, escaping through books, hazily surrounded by family and fellow workers, and every morning from nine thirty to ten, during that half hour for breakfast, sharing thoughts with my friend Juan.

Wild sexual interludes with the women we passed in the street, with clerks in the shops, models in magazines, and the satiny, totally untouchable stars of black-and-white movies, that is what my friend and I dreamed about, hopelessly, that and travel, places it was unlikely we would ever be and women who would never go to bed with us and in fact never gave us a second look when we passed them in the streets near our office, the alleyways of the *centro*, the downtown business district, the cafés where we went for breakfast every morning, always at nine thirty, nine thirty-five, newspaper tucked under one arm, bought every morning at the same kiosk, the mineral water and *café con leche* and toast the waiter brought without our asking. We had become habitual presences in the morning routine of other people, figures circling round and round like the mechanical dolls that march out to mark the hour on clocks in German squares.

Every morning we walked past the large window of a travel agency featuring a huge poster of New York. We liked that agency because of their posters of faraway places and because a very pretty woman worked there, whom we never saw outside her office or even away from her desk. She was blond and slender, with an extraordinary profile; every morning she was talking on the phone or working at her typewriter, almost always wearing a turtleneck sweater, her back straight yet inclined slightly forward like the wooden bust of Nefertite I saw years later, when I did do some traveling, in the Egyptian museum of Berlin. This girl had a narrow face, large mouth, large, slanted eyes, and a nose with that pronounced tip some admirable Italian noses have. As she talked on the phone, head tilted to clamp the earpiece to her shoulder, she would gesture with a slender hand holding a pencil as she turned the pages of a schedule or catalog with the other, and we would watch with furtive passion, pausing only a moment every morning at the window, afraid of attracting her attention. We saw both her and her reflection, because facing her in the agency office was a large wall of mirrors. Each time we liked to observe some new feature of her beauty: her hair might be loose, or she had pulled it back into a ponytail to emphasize the purity of her profile, or maybe into a bun that revealed the splendid line of her throat and the back of her neck. Behind that glass window, facing the mirror that multiplied the plants adorning her desk and the posters of foreign cities and views of beaches or deserts, she belonged both to the everyday life of the city and to the exotic places of her profession, and part of her appeal to us were the names of foreign countries and cities, and the large color photograph of New York in the window added luster to her image. She may have been no less deskbound than we were, but as she spoke on the telephone and read schedules and made hotel reservations, jotting down things in her agenda, she seemed endowed with a dynamism that was the opposite of our dull work as minor officials; without moving from her desk, she took on the golden tones of East Indian beaches and the bold freedom of the most beautiful women on the Via Veneto, or Portobello Road, or Calle Corrientes, or Fifth Avenue. We fantasized about walking into the agency one morning and asking in a normal way for a brochure, some information about hotels or flights. But of course we never did, and we never saw her going in or out of her office, never met her in the streets we walked. She existed only inside the travel agency, behind the glass window and in the mirrored wall, just as Ingrid Bergman or Marilyn Monroe or Rita Hayworth lived in the black-and-white world of movies; she was as unchangeable and distant as they, and so we watched her a few seconds every morning and continued our brief half-hour routine, the newspaper kiosk, the *café con leche* and toast in the Café Suizo or the Regina, maybe a stop at the post office, for Juan to mail a letter, and then back to the office before the time clock we had to punch reached five after ten.

There was a sweetness in that routine, in the predictable familiarity of street corners and plazas, the sunlit clarity of Bibrrambla and the shadows of the narrow little streets leading to it, the repeated faces, the synchronized appearances, the same girl in dark glasses who arrived every morning at the same hour to raise the iron shutters of a shop with mannequins and mirrors, the officials and the clerks, the woman in the Olympia Travel Agency, whom we'd named Olympia after the Greek goddess and Manet's nude, the lottery-ticket vendors, even the beggars and bums were there every day, following a routine similar to mine, each with his own life, with his secret novel, background figures in the novel I was living or inventing for myself, not the novel of what I did but of things that didn't happen, the trips I never took and the plans my friend Juan and I postponed for a future neither of us much believed in but that served as an excuse for our present inertia.

Our friendship itself was routine and habit: meeting every morning at the same place, walking to a café, hands in our pockets and newspaper tucked under one arm, talking with no obligation to say anything new or too confidential. We were both crushed by the same docility and indolence, shyness or cowardice or lack of drive. Our friendship was surely based on that dismal reality, and it cost us nothing to share the irony with which we viewed the mediocrity of our lives and the deterioration of our ambitions. Each saw in the other the mirror of his insufficiency. We were united by the person neither of us dared to be. With identical correctness, we carried out our duties as employees, husbands, and fathers, rarely dropping the neutral sarcasm of our conversations for a true complaint. Many mornings during our walk to breakfast, Juan dropped a letter in the box at the post office located in the arcade of Calle Ganivet. Like everyone absorbed in his own melancholy, I was not too observant then. I had some vague idea that those letters were office business, until I noticed one that had a stamp for foreign mail. Juan gave no indication that he was trying to hide them from me, but there was something in his attitude that kept me from asking about them. Once, when we were having breakfast at the Suizo, he excused himself to go to the bathroom, leaving his newspaper behind on the bar. I picked it up, and two letters slipped out. One of them was from New York, addressed to him, but at his home address, not his office. The other letter he had written, and it bore the name of the woman who had written him from New York. In a couple of seconds I put the letters back inside the folded newspaper, and when Juan returned I said nothing but thought, with a certain desolation, that in my friend's life, which I'd thought was an open book, there was a part he chose not to reveal.

COMING OUT OF THE small lane where the Club Taurino used to be, we sometimes ran into our friend and office mate Gregorio Puga, who also worked as acting associate director of the city band, after having lost a much more prestigious job in the band of another city, and who even at that early hour was always a little drunk, smelling of stale alcohol and nicotine despite the coffee beans he sucked. Gregorio was the first friend I made when I started working, maybe because everyone had given up on him and he had to latch onto new employees when he wanted company at breakfast or for having a few beers or glasses of wine in the little hideaway taverns in the *centro*. It was said that were it not for his fondness for drink he would have been a major composer and conductor. He had a different version of his failure, which he would deliver with the whining monotony of a drunk: people had pushed him over the edge, they'd made him give up his promising career, begun under the best auspices in Vienna, and all in exchange for what, a pittance, the petty security of a steady job. He would sit with his elbows propped on the bar, drink in one hand, cigarette in the other, held between the yellow tips of his second and third fingers, the languid, soft fingers of an old office worker, although I don't think that he was more than forty-five at the time.

"They bait you with the promise of security, and you get used to the money coming in every month, and then you don't have the will to keep studying, even less when your wife burdens you right off with kids and is always going on about how you're useless and why don't you stop all this foolishness and dreaming and do something to get ahead in the office or go out and look for a job in the evening. At first you don't, of course, your evenings are sacred, you have to keep writing, rehearsing with other musicians until you get out of them what not even they know they have inside, and you want to direct an orchestra, not a city band, that was my life's dream, but you get depressed, and besides it's true, you need money, so you agree to give private classes, or you get a place in a school, and before you get paid at the end of the month you've already spent or budgeted the money, it's clothes for the kids, and books and uniforms for school, because of course we had to take them to a Catholic school. Midafternoon you leave the office, and because you dread going home you stop for a couple of glasses of wine, you get a bite of something and go to your evening job, and when that's over, well, it's the same: Gregorio, let's go have a drink. At first you say no, then all right, just one rum and that's all, the old lady will be pissed if she hasn't seen the whites of my eyes by dinnertime, so you have two rums and one for the road or to help you face the uproar you know is waiting at home, and you forget to look at the clock and when you go outside to the Plaza del Carmen, it's striking eleven and there's hell to pay. I'll buy some cigarettes and pull myself together, but you don't have coins to put in the machine, and you're too tired to ask for change for a bill, so you ask for a glass of wine, and maybe if you're lucky you run into a friend who's alone at the bar, and he treats you to the next one, or it's the waiter who invites you, because all his life he's been seeing you come in and out, he's served you the coffee, or coffee and cognac, at dawn, the rums for an aperitif, and coffee and drinks after dinner—though in all honesty you haven't eaten, just nibbled to fill your stomach."

I remember Gregorio with affection and pain, Maestro Puga, whom I haven't seen for several years now, and I wonder if he's still making the rounds of the bars in the *centro* where the office workers go, whether he's still alive and clinging to the dream of a symphony premiere, elbows on the bar, wearing his suit that is getting more and more frayed and dirty, a cigarette in his nicotine-stained fingers, a glass of wine held loosely in the other hand, and maybe a coffee bean sucked in a mouth now missing a few teeth. Some mornings Juan and I met him as we turned a corner and didn't have time to avoid him, so we had to stand and listen to his whining and persistent invitations to come have a drink, just a quick cognac or anisette in the few minutes left of the half hour allotted for breakfast. When I was less cautious, I agreed to have a rum with him after work, and didn't get away until eleven, ending up so drunk that the next morning I didn't remember anything we talked about all those hours. I remember only one thing, and I've never forgotten it, because since then Gregorio has repeated it many times, grabbing my arm, pulling me toward him, enveloping me in a cloud of stale wine and black tobacco as he pierces me with those reddened eyes and says:

"Don't get stuck in this rut, don't let what happened to me happen to you, get out while you can, don't cave in, don't let yourself be bought."

I avoided Gregorio, as everyone did, because he was a bore and a drunk, and even if you were fond of him you couldn't take his bad breath or the tedium of his increasingly disjointed stories, his detailed account of the intrigues and tricks he was victim of in the office, or about the city band, where another man with fewer qualifications but more connections had been named director. But I also avoided him because I was ashamed to have him see the fulfillment of his prophecy about me: the years went by, and I went to work every morning punctually at eight o'clock, I had obligations now, was married with a child and making payments every month on a car and an apartment, and although my wife earned more than I did, the money didn't always stretch to the end of the month, so I was considering looking for a second job. In this way I'd gradually given up all the plans that seemed so courageous when I started working: preparing myself for a better career, say, university professor, or researcher in art history, or even geography teacher in some institute. But I didn't have the time or the will, and my free evenings got away from me without my noticing, and besides there were only a few openings every year for a history professor and thousands of university graduates, many of whom I'd gone to school with and who were desperate after years of being unemployed, and looked with envy at even a job as unappealing as mine. I would occasionally meet Gregorio in the corridor, each of us carrying a briefcase loaded with files, or I would see him at a corner of the alleys dotted with bars where office workers escaped at midmorning for a quick coffee, but my repugnance for his bad breath and shabby air was more powerful than any gratitude I felt for his friendship. I would look away, or slip through a side door to escape his red eyes, not wanting to hear again what I knew he would say: "What are you doing? Why haven't you got out of here? How many more years are you going to take it?"

ONCE IN A WHILE I did go somewhere, but only for a few days; they would send me to Madrid to get papers signed in a ministry or to place an order for supplies I was charged with inspecting. The trips were brief, the per diem insufficient, and my low rank limited me to moderately priced hotels and meals in modest restaurants, yet the anticipated departure acted as a stimulant, pulling me toward the future like a giant magnet, giving me back the childish happiness of looking forward to an outing.

Several days before the train pulled out of the station, I had already left in my mind. The night express with its blue sleeping cars that reminded me of the Orient Express would be sitting there when I arrived with my suitcase a little before 11 P.M., filled with the heady relief of being alone, of having temporarily freed myself from the oppressive sameness of office and home, from the schedules and scares and bad nights that go with having a very young son. The preparations for this short trip contained all the excitement of a real journey, of any one of the journeys I'd read about in books or seen at the movies or imagined for myself as I studied maps and glossy guidebooks. In the midst of such a low-key, shallow life, the trip was an almost physical pleasure, a sensation of freedom and lightness, as if leaving the station would free me from all the obligations and habits that weighed me down. With the slam of the door of the taxi that would take me to the station, my old identity would be entirely sloughed off.

Since I was going somewhere, I wasn't myself; I luxuriated in the intoxication of being no one. I dissolved into the moments I was living, into the pleasure of being borne away by the train and looking out the window of my compartment at the lights of highways and cities, cheerful windows where stay-at-homes lived, at that hour watching television or going to bed in miserably hot bedrooms beneath a suffocating conjugal blanket, the "watered-down coffee of married life" referred to by Cernuda, a poet I was reading a lot at the time, his disciple and apprentice in the bitterness of the distance between reality and desire.

Those trips were so rare that the administrative monotony of the tasks I had to perform at my destinations didn't affect my intense and childish sense of adventure. But I traveled seldom not only because so few opportunities presented themselves. Sometimes I sacrificed a trip in order not to upset my wife, who didn't like my being away from home, and who was exhausted from her own job and from caring for our child and didn't always want to understand that my stays in Madrid weren't some capricious escapade but required by my administrative position and that carrying them out well could be to my advantage when eventually it came time for promotion.

Whenever I agreed to go, I had difficulty telling my wife, I would keep putting it off, until in the end I was forced to break the news with insensitive haste, or, worse, she would get wind of it from someone who called from the office or the travel agency that handled the ticketing. I didn't have to be unfaithful, my natural state was guilt, and the innocuous secret of the upcoming business trip would be as much of a strain on me as an actual affair. I helped weave the entangling web of reproaches and resentment with my cowardice. And up to the last minute I was never sure I was going, because our son might get a fever, or my wife might suddenly be under the weather with a lumbago attack or a difficult period, complaints it seemed I was entirely responsible for, and that would become much worse in my absence, my desertion.

Finally I would leave and still couldn't believe it, and as the taxi took me to the station I would get a rush of happiness mixed with panic, the fear that I might not get to the station on time because the road was blocked, or because I'd waited too long disentangling myself from my family and my life, from the stifling conjugal heat of my apartment, from the irritation and accusation radiating from my wife as she stood with her arms around my son, who would cry even harder when he saw I was leaving; the two of them would be there in the doorway as I waited for the elevator, and my wife's face would be pale, her eyes sad.

ONE WINTER MORNING, on one of those trips to Madrid, I finished my errands at the Ministry of Culture early and found myself with nothing to do for the rest of the day. My train didn't leave until eleven that night. Disappointment was quick to come in Madrid, a vulnerable feeling of being alone in such a big city, where I didn't know anyone, where there was uncertainty and danger everywhere. When you crossed one of those broad avenues, the light always turned red before you could get to the other side, and when you went to a movie at night, you ended up in a labyrinth of dark streets where you could easily be attacked by someone with a knife, one of those pasty drug addicts who loitered on the corner of the Gran Vía and Calle Hortaleza. I was dazed with loneliness, not because I didn't know anyone anymore, but because I was a nobody, a lowly provincial official who was pulling back into his shell like a snail only three days after fleeing in search of greener pastures and richer air, wandering in circles around the city, carrying his depression with him as if it were a fever that made him long for the shelter of his home and the familiar narrow streets in which he lived his life.

Walking around in a dense fog with no idea of where I was, I ended up at the Retiro, crossing streets that seemed not to be in Madrid, not even Spain, streets with noble buildings and luxuriant trees, the blacktop wet with drizzle, the sidewalks yellow with the newly fallen, broad leaves of plane trees and horse chestnuts. The Prado Museum, the Botanical Garden, the Cuesta de Moyano. At the peak of a wooded hill was a building that resembles a Greek temple: the Observatory. Things opened before me as I approached them through the fog: motionless statues, threatening or serene, a statue of Pío Baroja or Cajal or Galdos, alone in the groves of the deserted park, lost and melancholy in an ostentatious oblivion of bronzes and marbles.

I remember my amazement at the sight of a glass building on the other side of a pond, with columns and filigree of white-painted iron, a white liquefied in the translucent grayness of the morning mist, in the motionless, dark green of the water. I had read in the newspaper that there was an exhibition dedicated to the exile of Spanish Republicans in Mexico in the Crystal Palace of the Retiro. It all comes back, after so many years, an ordinary day of an uneventful trip to Madrid, a walk that by chance led to the Retiro, where amid fog and trees I came upon the Crystal Palace, like one of those enchanted houses that materialize before lost travelers in storybook forests.

I remember glass display cases with newspaper clippings and ration cards, TV monitors showing old films of soldiers wrapped in rags fleeing along the highways toward France, clustered at the border crossings at Port-Bou and Cerbère after the fall of Catalonia. I remember a blackboard and a desk that had been in the first school for Spanish children in Mexico, and a navy-blue student smock with a white celluloid collar, which shook me with unexpected anguish, as did the pages of penmanship exercises written in pencil by children forty years before, and the boxes of paints identical to ones I'd had in school. The smock, too, was very similar to those we wore, and there were the same creased, colored oilcloth maps of Spain that I saw the first time I walked into a schoolroom, except that on these the flag was tricolor: red, yellow, and purple. There was a large photograph of people crowding onto a steamship in a French port. A woman of about fifty was standing next to me, staring at it, murmuring something in a Mexican accent, although there was no one with her. She was breathing hard; I looked at her and saw that she was crying.

"I was on that boat, señor," she said, hiccuping. She had large eyeglasses and dyed hair and was the only person besides me that morning in the glass building enveloped in fog, as if padded with silence. "I am one of the persons in this picture. I was eight and trembling, afraid my papa would let go of my hand."

NOW I AM IN A different past, a different morning, not the one in which I walked through the Retiro and fog to the weightless shape of the Crystal Palace, the beautiful and melancholy purple of Republican flags on the shelves of an exhibition, insignia of a country I had lost before I was born. I leave the Ministry of Culture on Plaza del Rey and start walking aimlessly, disheartened before I begin by the hours ahead, in which I have nothing to do and no one to talk to, hours in which I will slowly become infected with the unreality of being alone in a large, unfamiliar city, of turning into a ghost that from time to time stares back at a stranger reflected in a shopwindow. I look at my watch and calculate that at this hour my friend Juan will be finishing breakfast, reading his newspaper in the Suizo, or maybe he will already have used the pedestrian crosswalk to the post office to mail one of those letters he doesn't want me to know about. Instead of walking back toward the office beside him, both of us dragging our feet, I am wandering around Madrid, leaving to chance the route and choice of streets, and after half an hour I am totally lost, or maybe I've let myself be guided by an old memory independent of my consciousness, rising from the blind and persistent impulse of my feet. *On a certain street there is a certain heavy door,* says one of Borges's poems. I walk along streets with narrow sidewalks and recessed doors, with fish markets and fruit stands and old-fashioned stationery shops and stores selling groceries and notions more antiquated than the ones in the city where I live, with a pullulating mass of cars and people and the strong, working-class voices of Madrid. Remembering, drifting, I head toward a place I shouldn't go, a place I visited only once: Fernando VI, Argensola, Campoamor, Santa Teresa. At some moment, unknowingly, chance has become purpose, and the sequence the street names trace upon the city in which I am a stranger is a coded map, a wound that hasn't hurt for a long time but can still be felt as a slight scar.

Calle Campoamor, at the corner of Santa Teresa; it was here, five years ago, in that time when the years seemed to last much longer, not slip away as they do now. Half a lifetime fit within those five years. I recognize the white shutters on the second-floor balcony. If she comes out on the balcony, she will recognize me, and if I climb the two flights of wooden steps and press the button, the bell will ring not in a dream but in reality, intruding upon the lives of other people, an unwanted surprise. I've heard almost nothing about her all this time, we barely know each other, we were together only briefly, long ago.

My thoughts and actions are not in sync, just as there is no correspondence between this place and my being here. I walk back and forth, looking up at the balconies, thinking at one point that I see a figure behind the windowpanes. I walk into the foyer, which is open and has that strange smell of damp and old wood that doorways have in Madrid. On one of the mailboxes I see her name, handwritten, beside that of her husband. The name that once made me shiver as I spoke it, and in which are codified every degree of tenderness, uncertainty, pain, and desire, is a common name written by hand on a card on a mailbox, among the names of neighbors who meet her every day in the foyer or on the stairs, and for whom her face is part of the same trivial reality as these streets and this city, where I, the traveler, float among mirages of loneliness.

The bravery of cowards, the strength of the weak, the daring of the faint-hearted: I have come to the landing and without hesitation ring the doorbell. An old door, large, painted dark green, with a brass peephole. Every detail falls back into place, and my agitation and the weakness in my legs are the same as then, even though I am a different person. "Maybe she isn't home," I think with both hope and disappointment. A few seconds pass, and I don't hear anything, not footsteps, not voices, only the resonance of the bell in silent rooms.

The door opens, and she is looking at me. At first she doesn't recognize me; she wears the suspicious and questioning expression of someone expecting a door-to-door salesman. I realize that I am much heavier now, and I don't have my beard, and my hair is shorter than it was five years ago, thinner too. In her arms she holds a large child with dark skin and curly hair who has a pacifier in his mouth and a dirty bib over his pajama top. A little girl wearing glasses peers cautiously from behind her, peering at me with her mother's eyes. The boy has stopped crying and is staring at me intently, sniffling and making a slurping, sucking noise with his pacifier.

I recognize the slender face and light gray eyes, the two locks of almost blond hair framing her face, but I can't associate the girl I knew with this carelessly dressed woman who holds in her arms a child so big that he must exhaust her, and who has a little girl who looks so astonishingly like her.

"What a surprise," she says to me. "I wouldn't have recognized you," and she smiles a smile that lights up her eyes with the gleam of old times. I apologize. "I was just passing by, and I thought I might as well see if you were in." I hear my own voice, hoarser than it should be, a voice that hasn't spoken with anyone for hours. "It's a miracle you caught me at home, I was going to take the boy to the doctor, but since I don't have anyone to leave my little girl with I was going to take her too. He's not sick," she explains, "at least not really sick. As soon as his tonsils get a little inflamed, his temperature shoots up, and I shouldn't get frightened, but I always do." I am a little deflated by the natural way she's talking, with no trace of surprise, as if I were an ordinary acquaintance. She feels the boy's forehead. "I gave him an aspirin, I think his fever is coming down." We give aspirin to my son too, and the same thing happens. I'm about to tell her that but don't, held back by a strange shyness, as if to hide from her that I'm married too and a father, that my son is more or less the same age as hers and also sick, according to what my wife told me last night on the phone.

I make some show of getting ready to leave, having been so flustered that I didn't kiss her when I first saw her. "But come in, don't stand there in the doorway; since you've come to see me, I'm not letting you go without at least giving you a cup of coffee." Her apartment has long hallways, high ceilings with elaborate plasterwork, and wood floors. It must have been very luxurious once, but now it's half empty and looks almost abandoned; maybe it belonged to her parents, or her husband's, and now they don't have the money to keep it up. She didn't give me the impression of money, or at least she wasn't taking care of herself as she did when I knew her, she wore old jeans and canvas shoes with no laces. Her skin had lost its transparency, and her hair was messy, like that of a woman who doesn't get out of the house all day and, worn down by her children, doesn't have the time or the energy to put on makeup.

She clears toys, scribbled papers, and colored pencils from a large, old chair and asks me to have a seat while she makes coffee. I find myself alone in a living room dominated somehow by both emptiness and disorder. On the table is a blender just like the one my wife and I use to blend fruit for our son, a dirty bib, a jar of liquid soap for babies, and a disposable diaper that smells strongly of urine. Street noise comes through the two balconies where sheer curtains filter the wan light of a cloudy day. In an adjoining room I can hear the little boy crying, accompanied by the loud strains of a morning cartoon show. What am I doing sitting here? Absurd and correct as a visitor, rigid in this armchair, not daring to so much as cross my legs, waiting for her to appear in the doorway, as I once waited, eager yet frightened of her presence, covetous of her every feature and gesture, the way she dressed—a little extreme for a provincial city—and her Madrid accent.

She comes back carrying coffee on a tray, and as she sets it down on the table, she sees the dirty diaper and looks away with an expression of annoyance and weariness. "I forgot the sugar, I don't know where my head is." She takes away the diaper, the pacifier, and the blender, and I hear her say something to the little boy, who has stopped crying, and she appears again, smiling with a look of "Sorry!" and brushing a lock of hair from her eyes. Then, as if in a painting, I see her as she was five years ago, as precisely as the clear view you get after you clean a cloudy pane of glass, and I think she looks a lot like someone I know, although it takes a while to realize whom: the woman in the travel agency, the Olympia my friend Juan and I are so crazy about. The same foreshortening as she lifts the hair from her face, the same chestnut hair, the large mouth, the line of her chin and jaw, the glint in her light-colored eyes.

Just as when I was so much in love with her, I can't concentrate on what she's telling me, I'm too absorbed in the fantasy of love, of the contemplative, paralyzing, adolescent passion that reaches its tortuous culmination in impossibility, that nourishes the desire for powerlessness, for the suffering and cowardice of literature. "I left medical school when I got pregnant, you remember? I tried to go back when my daughter was a little older, but then I got pregnant again, and now I'm thinking about entering nursing school. It doesn't take as long, I can handle the assignments, and I'm pretty sure it will be easy to find a job. Imagine, with my experience they could make me head of Maternity."

She gets up because the boy has started crying again, very loud, and when she comes back, he is in her arms. His face is red, and his eyes shine with fever. Suddenly I'm jealous, looking at the boy, recognizing his father's features, the man I begged her to leave and come away with me. From the next room the girl calls to her, because something has fallen to the floor with a crash. As she leaves the room again, I observe her from the rear. Her face is the same, but her body has filled out, she has lost that sinuous line I loved so much when she was twenty. When she handed me my coffee I noted, furtively, that her breasts are larger and heavier now, the breasts of a woman who has had two children, and nursed them, and not taken very good care of herself afterward. I remember her tight-fitting jeans and her soft shirts buttoned low, blouses with a liquid, silky touch that felt like her skin the few times I dared caress her. I invited her out for dinner one night in early summer, and she came downstairs wearing sandals and a dress of a fine plaid material with her hair caught back in a pony-tail and two curls at her cheeks, so sexy and desirable that it was a torment not to grab her.

"But don't go, tell me something about yourself, you haven't said a word, you haven't changed a bit in that regard." The boy isn't crying now, and I can hear the television again in the next room. She sits down across from me and asks me to tell her about my life these days, and I notice, with a glowing coal of satisfaction, that she's combed her hair and dashed on some lipstick. "I heard that you got married too, to your old sweetheart." "Like you," I find the courage to say, and for a moment we are truly ourselves and the void between us is a narrow void, we crossed it only once a long time ago but it never entirely closed. We smile, shaking our heads politely, acknowledging the objective vulgarity of real life. "At least you did something, finished your degree. I remember how much you liked art history, how excited you were about it, the Assyrians, the Egyptians, Picasso, Bosch, Velázquez, Giotto. I still have the postcard you sent me from Florence."

And a lot of good that did. I remember that card, the exact moment I wrote you sitting on the steps of Santa Maria del Fiore; how I loved you. I explain to her that I found a temporary job as an administrative assistant, and that the next year I took the competitive exams, "although I don't plan to stay in that office forever. As soon as I can I'll go back and work on my thesis in earnest, or I'll start taking my exams to teach at an institute." "That's what Victor is doing, he's studying for exams for the post office. We'll see if he has as much luck as you." Victor. She says that name so casually. If she'd stayed with me, she'd be saying my name as easily as my wife does; maybe she'd have some loving nickname for me.

The telephone rings at the far end of the room. She speaks in a low voice, not looking at me, telling someone that she will take the child to the doctor, although she thinks his temperature has stopped going up. "Ciao," she says, "come soon." What am I doing here? A ghost, a visitor, not even an intruder. Ciao, come soon. People say words without stopping to think what they mean; entire lives fit in the simplest phrase, and a personal insult can hide in a polite formula of courtesy: "What a shame you didn't run into Victor, he would have enjoyed seeing you."

This time when I get up, she doesn't ask me to stay. I notice the smell of domestic life in the hallway, which she doesn't: the funk of a sick child, kitchen odors, a whiff of sheets and bodies, of a not very well ventilated apartment, these are made up of the everyday events of her life, her real life, which for me is as foreign as this large, disorderly, somber house. There must be a particular smell to the small apartment I bought through a government program, and it must be similar: stale milk and talcum powder. She walks me to the door, holding her son in her arms again. He is red-faced and bawling, his chin wet with slobber. She gives me two kisses, one on each cheek, not touching the skin, barely stirring the air between us. "Will you be in Madrid long? Why don't you come see us if you're going to be here awhile?" Perhaps she says that to eliminate any hint of our old relationship. This isn't the woman who loved me and was ready to live with me; now she speaks in a plural that includes her husband, offering me the kind of matrimonial friendship that is the worst offense to an ex-lover. "I don't think I'll have time, I'm going back tonight and I still have things to do."

THE REST OF THE DAY I walked around Madrid, weary and bored. I chose a restaurant to eat in, after much looking and hesitation. The minute I went in, I realized I'd made a bad choice, but a waiter in a dirty red jacket was already coming toward me and I didn't have the courage to leave, so I ate a fillet that smelled slightly spoiled. In a large bookstore on the Gran Vía I got dizzy looking at titles and ended up buying a novel I wasn't interested in and have never read. I went to a movie, and it was dark when I came out, but I still had several hours to kill before the train left. I called home with a touch of guilt, although I'd been gone less than three days. The minute my wife picked up the phone, I knew there was a problem. Our son had woken up that night with a new cough, and choking, and she'd taken him straight to the emergency room, where they said he had laryngitis.

A few minutes before the express pulled out, I saw a young woman running along the platform. It had occurred to me, as I waited, that she might come to say good-bye, that that was why she'd asked me what time the train left. Five years before, that other time, I'd waited till the last moment on this same platform, watching the clock and the faces of the people pushing through the glass doors. I'd looked for her when I arrived at dawn and again that night—on the same train I'd come on—and she hadn't been there either time. Subconsciously, I'd repeated the wait, not because I thought it was likely she would come, not even that I wanted her to, but out of a sentimental inertia.

Now, shivering, incredulous, almost frightened, I watched her come running toward me, five years too late, and the person who was excited was the person I was then, revived, not as yet humiliated by surrender, by the excessive price of work and family life, but unfortunately not improved with time either, as bewildered and foolish as ever.

Then I saw it wasn't she, although the woman kept looking toward me as she came nearer and smiled at me and held her arms open for a hug. She was tall, slender, with curly hair. But she went past me and threw her arms around a man standing behind me. I boarded the train and watched them through the window. The man was carrying a large suitcase, but neither of them looked up when the whistle blew. I watched them grow small in the distance as the train pulled away, arms around each other and alone in the darkness of the platform.

berghof

A DARKENED WORKROOM, abstract as a cell, with white walls, wood floor, and a table of sturdy, rough wood, like the tables you used to see in kitchens, in our kitchen when I was a boy. Places become echoes, transparencies of other places, they rhyme with austere assonance. Walking into the room at this indeterminate hour of the winter afternoon, I am reminded of García Lorca's room in Huerta de San Vicente, and of the one he had in Madrid, in a student dormitory, and from Madrid and García Lorca and the set of transparencies and assonances of places my thoughts go to Rome, to the room in the Spanish Academy where I slept a few nights in March or April of 1992, where I imagined long industrious days of solitude and reading, monkish days of work and tranquillity of mind, the retreat it seems one carries imprinted in one's soul, is always dreaming of and looking for, the room with only a few necessities: bed, bare wood table, window, perhaps a bookcase for a few books, not too many, and also one of those portable CD players. I would spend the whole day walking around Rome in a state of intoxication, a trance accentuated by solitude, and at night I fell exhausted onto the narrow bed in my room at the academy, and in my agitated dreams, powerful and dark as the waters of the Tiber, I continued my wanderings through the city, seeing columns and ruins and temples magnified and blurred as if in a delirium. I would wake up exhausted, and in the cold, olive-green light of dawn my newly opened eyes would focus on the cupola of the small temple of Bramante.

Another place rises before me as shadow begins to turn to darkness lighted only by the phosphorescence of the computer and the lamp that illuminates my hands on the keypad. The hand resting beside the mouse isn't mine any longer. The other hand, the left, distractedly rubs the worn white shell Arturo picked up two summers ago on the Zahara beach, the afternoon before we left, one of those luxuriously long afternoons at the beginning of July when the sun goes down after nine and the sea takes on the blue of cobalt, slowly retreating from the still-golden sand where the footprints of homebound bathers become delicate hollows of shadow.

From the darkness around by the computer screen and the low lamp, from the two hands, from the smooth feel of the mouse and the roughness of the shell and without any premeditation on my part, a figure emerges, a presence that is not entirely invention, or memory either: the doctor alone in the shadows, waiting for a patient, moving the mouse with his right hand, searching for a file in the computer, a medical history opened not many days ago, to which he added several test results just yesterday.

I OFTEN SEE THAT FIGURE, the hands especially, typing in the light of the screen: they are long, bony, sure, with a lot of hair on the back, not as gray as the hair and beard of the doctor, whom I don't envision standing, although I know he is very tall and so slender that his bathrobe hangs loose from his shoulders. I see him seated, white bathrobe and gray hair and beard, in a room with the curtains drawn, although there is still some time before nightfall.

The computer is on one side of the table, and on the other there is nothing but a white, rounded seashell, smaller and more concave than a scallop, stronger, too, as worn and eroded on the outside as the volute of a marble capital eaten by sea air and weather, and on the inside it is soft as mother-of-pearl, a pleasure to brush with fingertips that run over it as if of their own volition as the doctor speaks to the patient who has just arrived, trying to choose his words carefully—or earlier, when he is still alone, reviewing once again the test results lying open on the table. His mind wanders to a different time, luminous days invoked by the feel of the shell, which is a modest shell, not at all flashy, grayish white patterned with ridges opening from its base like the ribs of a fan, each following an exquisite curve, the beginning of a spiral interrupted by the outer edge, which is worn and nicked, presenting the fingertips with the irregularity of a piece of broken pottery.

One image evokes another, as if joined by the slim thread of coincidence: shells on the seashore in Zahara de los Atunes, curved bits of a broken amphora. He must let the thread roll off the spool, or pull lightly lest it break. He is on the verge of a discovery, a sensory memory like a bubble of air from millions of years ago captured inside a blob of amber. The wood floor of the large, dim room where the doctor works is as old as the building, and when someone walks across it, it creaks. He will hear the buzz of the intercom and tell the nurse that the patient can come in now, and footsteps will resonate as they would on the wood deck of a ship.

In the house of one of my grandmother's sisters there was a room with a wood floor. I liked going there with my grandmother just to enter that room, to feel the floor give a little beneath my feet, and to hear the sound of it. It was like being in another place, another life. I have a similar sensation when I hear a cello. Again time leaps from one thing to another, an almost instantaneous impulse between neurons: Pablo Casals playing Bach's suites for cello in Barcelona, in the fall of 1938 when the Battle of the Ebro has been lost and Manuel Azaña and Juan Negrín are listening from a box in the Liceo Theater. Behind the table, on a shelf holding a small number of books, most on medicine and history, the doctor has a CD player, which sometimes plays softly as he interviews or examines a patient lying on the cot in a dark corner of the room, in front of a screen. On the cot, the patient becomes more vulnerable, surrenders to the illness, to the doctor's examination, to what he already sees on the other side of the invisible but definitive line that separates the healthy from the ill, deep in the prison of his fear, pain, and, perhaps worst of all, shame. *The healthy flee from the ill,* Franz Kafka once wrote Milena Jesenska, *but the ill also flee from the healthy.*

Before he tells the patient what the tests reveal—there is no way to say it without awakening terror, without feeling a knot in the throat, though it has been said so many times—the doctor will ask him to lie on the cot with his clothes on, all he has to do is lower his trousers a little and pull up his shirt, so the doctor can auscultate the abdomen, palpate the viscera with his long fingers, quickly, smoothly, precisely. The patient suffers the ignominy of lying on his back on a cot, flat and passive, his trousers pulled down to his scrotum, while the intrusive hand seeks what should not be there.

In the background, behind the sounds of breathing, the patient's and the doctor's, so close to each other and yet separated by a line, a Bach suite for cello is playing, performed in 1938 by Casals, on a night when the sky over Barcelona may have been pierced by the reports of antiaircraft fire and the flames of exploding bombs may have illuminated the dark city already defeated by hunger and a harsh winter.

Although the sound is low, the patient recognizes both music and the recording. For a few awkward minutes they speak of

Bach, of the sound of the cello, of the technical marvel of digital recordings that allow buried musical treasures to be rescued, performances that took place on only one night. They talk, and the sheet with the test results lies on the table in the space bracketed by the doctor's quiet hands, which in turn rest beside a shell that fingers instinctively reach out to touch. Until Casals exhumed these scores, the Bach suites had never been performed. He found them by chance one day as he was looking through old papers in a stall on a narrow street near Barcelona's port, just the way Cervantes says he found the Arabic manuscript of *Quixote* in a secondhand clothes shop in Toledo. Pure coincidence hands you a treasure, triggers a memory hidden for years. That long-ago afternoon on a train: a tall woman in high heels, the beginnings of uncertainty and vertigo, of intoxication, in the green eyes glittering in a dark frame of curls, an unprovoked smile on thin lips set above a firm chin that looked Scandinavian or Anglo-Saxon.

BUT I DON'T WANT HIM to come yet, though he must already be on his way, uneasy but still not terrified, still living a normal life, which he will remember as a land to which he can never return when he leaves here. The doctor knows that the patient won't want anyone to know what the tests reveal, won't meet the doctor's eyes, although a few minutes before, or during his previous visit, they were talking comfortably enough, perhaps about the Bach suites for cello. Now the patient is excluded, expelled, from the community of the normal, like a Jew in a Vienna café reading the newspaper in which the new German race laws have just been published. The café is the same, and the newspaper is the one he's read every day for years, but suddenly everything has changed, and the waiter who used to speak his name so obsequiously and who knows what to bring without being asked, the same waiter he has every morning, might refuse to bring him a cup of coffee if he learned the truth, though there is nothing in the customer's face—blondish brown hair, light-colored eyes—that says Jew.

I hold the shell in the palm of my hand. The still-childish hand of my son fits into it so easily, my son who takes my hand so naturally when we go for a walk, even though he's thirteen. He would say to me when he was young, "Let's measure hands." We would hold them up, palms together, and his wouldn't be even half as long as my bony, angular hand, the back covered with dark hair, not the hand of a doctor but an ogre's paw making him giggle with happiness and terror. "Swallow up my hand with yours, the way the big bad wolf swallowed the little lambs. Tell me another story, don't leave yet, don't turn out the light." He marveled that when I opened my hand, his was whole, not devoured, not even bitten, like the white lambs rescued by their mother from the belly of the wolf.

We would go outside the hotel and take a sidewalk lined with palm trees and hedges, and soon we would be at the Atlantic, dazed by the light, by the breadth and depth of the horizon, which didn't end at the sea but farther out, at a line of blue mountains that were North Africa. At night we would watch the flickering lights of Tangiers through the ocean fog. I was in Tangiers once, many years ago, in another lifetime. As the doctor squeezes the curve of the shell, he is squeezing the hand of his son two summers before. His wife is pressed to his other side, to protect herself from the west wind off the sea, blowing from the direction of the dark mass of Africa and the lights of Tangiers, a wind smelling of seaweed. Every night, somewhere along that enormous beach, furtive emigrants disembark, or boxes of contraband tobacco and bricks of hashish are unloaded stealthily. Sometimes the powerful tides of the Atlantic carry cadavers of Moroccans or blacks swollen by the water and nibbled by fish, or bits of old rusted metal or rotted wood from the ships they went down on.

ONLY WHEN THEY REACHED the beach that first afternoon were they aware of the weariness they had brought with them, of how light they felt after shedding it, like leaving their luggage back in the room, along with the sweaty clothing they'd worn that morning as they left Madrid. So many months closed up in that dark room, waiting for visitors, for test results, seeing the faces of men and women marked by illness, chosen by the cruel hand of fate. The boy ran ahead, impatient to get to the shore, kicking across the sand the seemingly weightless blue-and-white ball the wind kept blowing away from him. The sun was still up, but there were few people on the beach, or else it was its length that made it seem bare, almost deserted, offered to them alone. He was a little reluctant to take off his shirt, he was so pale and skinny in that golden light, so resistant to tanning, unlike his wife and son, who had the same cinnamon skin, one of the primary genetic traits the mother transmitted to her son. I wonder what you inherited from me, child of my heart, leaping so intrepidly that afternoon into the first high wave crowned with summer's foam, tumbled by it, jubilantly rising from the sea with the gleam of water and sun on skin not yet abused by time.

As I dropped facedown onto the sand, I felt, like a tangible plenitude, the curvature and solidity of the world. Jorge Guillén wrote: *And walking, my foot knows / the roundness of the planet.* I examined the tiny grains, the infinitesimal bits of rock and shell, glass, broken amphorae, worn and pulverized through geological spans by the monotonous force of the sea, which was working this very moment, resonating like a drum in my ear, in my body weak with fatigue, gnawed by months of work, anxiety, insomnia, emergencies, remorse, months of witnessing the pain and infirmity of others, the panic, the progress of their deaths. I took a handful of sand then opened my fingers to let it trickle away in a thin thread. First it was something solid inside my closed fist, closed like the valves of a mollusk to the small fingers of my son, who tried to pry it open but couldn't; if he managed to pull up one finger, breathing hard, the finger would lock back into place. Then the hand would open, slowly, and the sand that had been so compact would dissolve, leaving nothing but a few tiny grains on my broad, open palm, mineral dots glinting in the sun. Eleven years old but still enjoying that game, still futilely challenging his father, struggling and panting as he tried to pry open a fist where sometimes he found a caramel or a coin. Defeated, he would throw himself on his father and hug him with all his might, with a rough, deep-seated tenderness, and rub his hand against the grain of his beard to feel the prickles. And I had only to touch two fingers to my son's side, just below his ribs, to make him fall to the sand, laughing and kicking his feet in the air.

"What a pain, you two, as big as you both are now." Stretched out beside us, her eyes hidden behind her sunglasses, my wife brushed off the sand the boy's kicking had sprayed over the magazine she was reading. Hours of idleness on the beach and in the hotel pool and siestas in the cool darkness of the room had removed all the fatigue from her face, and she wore the same smile of happiness that had dazzled me the first few times we saw each other. So desirable and young, as if twelve years hadn't gone by, as if it weren't her son who had sat down near her and slowly buried her red-toenailed feet, pouring from his half-opened fist a thread of sand that slipped across her arch and between her toes like a caress.

But I didn't want to deny time, it had been kind as it went by, bringing us so many blessings, which were right there before me in those July days. My wife's body pleased me more than ever, because for twelve years I had been learning it, with a desire that only familiarity can give, and also because it had sheltered and given birth to my son. I remember the rich threads of milk it spilled in drops from her breasts after the baby finished nursing. The same hand that felt the abdomen of the patient lying on the cot, searching for disease, twelve years earlier caressed that taut, round belly crisscrossed with powerful currents and quivering from the heartbeat of the child about to be born; I felt its planetary curve on the tips of my fingers. Who knows whether a physician can leave his profession behind the way he leaves his white coat in the darkened consulting room and walks toward the exit? My footsteps echo on the polished wood that glows with the luster of things well cared for over time, and I am blinded when I reach the street by the still-summertime brightness of the sun, forced to put on dark glasses and remember that my wife had bought them two years ago, two summers ago, in the same hotel shop where as soon as we arrived we made all the necessary purchases for our days at the beach: bathing suits and sandals, sun cream with maximum protection, a cap for the boy bearing the emblem of Zorro, a large inflatable rubber ball, so light that the breeze from the sea was always carrying it away, frogman goggles and fins, because the boy wanted to spear-fish as he had seen it done on a television documentary.

Now, in the half-light of the consulting room, there is something more. I didn't see it until this moment, on the shelf with the CD player: the photograph of a child who is still a boy but growing out of boyhood, mussed hair and delicate features, goggles pushed up on his forehead and laughing so hard his eyes squint, with dabs of sand on his nose and in the black hair falling over his forehead.

TO THE WEST, THE BEACH stretched toward the white blur of houses in the town, mist blending the whitewashed walls and the sand into a single sunlit dazzle. Only with the first light of day, or at sunset, did colors show clearly and the forms of things come into focus. To the east, an abrupt hill covered with wild growth stood out sharply above the sea, framing the bay. In the setting sun the windows of expensive homes glittered half hidden in the dark green of hedges and palm trees, enclaves surrounded by high white walls interrupted by the strong purple of bougainvillea. We were told that multimillionaires, primarily German, spent their summers in those houses. At the foot of the cliff, on a large rock that became an island when the tide was in, was a concrete bunker that stood like a mineral cancer on the landscape, as resistant to the assault of the sea as the rock onto which it had been fused. For the boy it was an adventure to hold his father's strong hand, climb up to the bunker, and through a corridor with a sand floor reach an interior room illuminated by the dusty, slanting ray of sunlight that fell through the narrow embrasure cut into the concrete, where guards could keep watch with their binoculars and rest the muzzles of their machine guns. On a cloudless morning, through the slit, you could see the coastline of Africa in great detail. The father took delight in explaining everything to his son, observing his concentration, pleased by his interest, the courteous and attentive way he listened. In 1943 the Allies defeated the Germans and Italians in North Africa and began preparing for the invasion of southern Europe. Look how close they would have been had they wanted to land on this beach instead of in Sicily; imagine the poor Spanish soldiers cooped up in this bunker, waiting for the American warships to appear.

They started back after the tide began to rise. Small, translucent fish fled between their feet as they splashed through the clean water. They walked along a smooth outcropping of rock that was slippery with seaweed or else covered by a dark, spongy moss that was soft beneath their feet. A wave retreated and left behind a pool in which tiny creatures worked busily, and father and son knelt to watch them more closely. The immediacy of human action shifts to the inconceivable slowness of natural history. Primary organisms dragging themselves from the sea to the land, teeming in pools, in the dense fertile ooze of salt marshes, armoring themselves in order to survive, developing valves and shells over millions of years, feet and pincers that leave a faint trail in the sand, a trail no more fleeting, though, than the marks our footsteps leave, our lives, the father thinks with no drama or melancholy, a fortyish man walking along a beach holding his son's hand in a state of perfect and tranquil happiness, of gratitude, of mysterious harmony with the world, on one of those long early-July afternoons when the heat is not yet overwhelming and summer is still a perfect gift for a child.

The boy let go of his father's hand to dive into the waves, and the father veered away from the shore and walked through warmer sand toward his wife, of whom he also has a photograph in the darkened consulting room: wide smile, fine lips always red with lipstick, even that afternoon at the beach, sunglasses like the ones film stars wore in the forties. I liked to think she watched us from a distance, the boy and me, easy to pick out on the beach that was nearly empty at that hour but still warm and bright, a time when there are already puddles of shadow in the footprints and on the sides of the dunes: the two of us kneeling, heads together, observing something in a brilliant sheet of water left by a retreating wave, then walking hand in hand along the shore, the pale, thin man and the plump, dark boy with the embers of a setting sun glistening on his wet skin and rolls of a little boy's tummy showing above the elastic of his bathing suit. The two so different, separated by more than thirty years, and yet astonishingly alike in some expressions, in the complicity of their gait and their lowered heads, although the boy resembles his mother more, not only in skin tone, but also in the way he laughs, in the strength of his chin, in his hands, in the unruly hair curling in the damp sea air.

There is a salty taste on her lips and a more carnal feel to her kisses when I caress her beneath the slightly damp cloth of her bikini during the siesta, behind the drawn curtains. Her breasts and lower torso are white against her dark tan. I put my hand on the fuzz between her thighs and am reminded of the damp moss along the shore that my toes sank into until they touched the smooth rock. We couple slowly, desire building with the gradual tide, then our two bodies are used and exhausted by love, mutually fondled, gleaming in the shadow.

As a young man he'd believed like a religious fanatic in the prestige of suffering and failure, in the vision of alcohol, and the romanticism of adultery. Now he could conceive of no deeper passion than what he felt for his wife and son, a love that enfolded the three of them like a magnetic field. Shared fluids, chromosomes mixed in one cell, the recently fertilized egg, the saliva exchanged and digested, saliva and vaginal secretions, saliva and semen sometimes glistening on her lips, dissolved into the nutritive current of her blood, mixed odors and sweat impregnating skin and air and the sheets they lay on, sated, asleep, while from beyond the drawn curtains came the splashing and cries of the children in the hotel swimming pool, and, farther still, if one listened carefully, the powerful roar of the sea, the wind lashing the tops of the palm trees.

WILD PALMS WAS THE TITLE of the novel his wife had been reading on the train and had carried to the beach in her large straw beach bag. He often asked her to tell him about the novels she was reading, and those summaries, along with a few movies, also chosen by her, satisfied his appetite for fiction. To him reality seemed so complex, inexhaustible, labyrinthine, that he didn't see the need to waste time and intelligence on invention, unless it was filtered through his wife's narrating or endowed with the ancient simplicity of fairy tales. In art he was moved only by forms in which something of the harmonic unity and functional efficiency of nature shone through. The ruins of Greek temples in the south of Italy or of the spas of Rome awakened in him an emotion identical to what he felt in the huge forests he had visited in New England and Canada. In a classic column, a great fallen capital, he found a correspondence with the sacred majesty of a tree, or with the precise symmetry of a seashell. He showed his son the spiral of a small shell and then, in a book on astronomy, the identical spiral of a galaxy. He led him to the bathroom and showed him the spiral the water made as it flowed down the drain of the sink. He caught a gleam of intelligence in his son's dark eyes, which had the same color and oblique slant as his mother's, and identical to hers in expressing, without pretense, wonder or disappointment, happiness or sadness.

He doesn't remember having asked the patient whether he has children. Probably he does, because the man carries an old-married or fatherly look, there is a certain physical wear and tear, a burden of responsibility on his shoulders, of worry. It was the weariness, the vague overall exhaustion, that brought the patient here. The doctor didn't tell the man that in the blood test he was ordering a specific analysis would be included. He didn't want to alarm him, to offend him. "Who do you take me for?" the patient might have said. "What kind of life do you think I live?"

The man will be there in a few minutes, and the doctor will have to say those words, the name of the illness, spoken cautiously, with clinical objectivity, using the euphemism of the initials. *Of course we will repeat the test, but I must also tell you that the chance of error is small.*

Those words, spoken so many times, always neutral and yet horrible, the panic and the shame, and so much predictable anguish, and the never-mitigated bitterness of the doctor's impotence. That is almost another form of contagion, a fatigue like the one his patients suffer, a vague, persistent, and inexplicable malaise, the awakening in certain specialized cells of the unnoticed guest, hidden for years, but also obedient to genetic codes that even now no one knows how to decipher, just as the ultimate nature of matter is not decipherable, the whirlwind of particles and infinitesimal forces of which all things are made, the light of my computer screen and the lamp above the keypad illuminating my hands, the shell I am feeling this moment, remembering a summer, two summers to be exact, alike and yet so different.

You will not swim twice in the same river, nor will you live the same summer twice, nor will there be a room that is identical to another, nor will you walk into the same room you left five minutes ago, the same darkened doctor's office where you were only once, sitting across from a doctor who spoke slowly and asked shocking questions, and who nodded as he listened to your answers, attentive, fingering a white shell on his desk at the left side of his computer keypad, symmetrical with the mouse he touches almost secretively with long, white, hairy fingers as he looks for a file, the data the patient gave by telephone to the nurse when he called the first time asking for an appointment.

FROM THE BEACH we could see a row of white houses on the cliffs to the east, half hidden in the foliage of their gardens and surrounded by high whitewashed walls, their large windows and terraces facing south, toward the bluish line of the coast of Africa. We were told that high up in the naked rock, where no vegetation grew, was a cave with Neolithic paintings and the remains of Phoenician sarcophagi. I got up very early one morning, just as it was getting light, quietly put on my clothes and running shoes, trying not to wake my wife, and left the hotel, cutting through the deserted garden reflected in the mauve, motionless water of the swimming pool. In the restaurant, beneath unflattering electric light, the waiters on the first shift were setting up trays for the buffet, arranging china and silver on the tables, silent as sleepwalkers. I noticed with pleasure the spring in my step, the comfort of the running shoes in which I'd walked and run hundreds of kilometers. The cool air numbed me in my T-shirt, so I began jogging slowly, breathing easily, but instead of heading toward the beach, as I did every morning, I followed the highway curving up the hill. Because the hill was so steep, I quickly grew tired and slowed to a walk. Seen at close range, the houses we had viewed from the beach were even more imposing, protected by walls topped with broken glass, by security company warnings, and by dogs that barked from gardens as I passed and that sometimes hurled themselves against the gates, rattling bars as they stuck their muzzles through and growled. Except for the barking and the sound of my steps on the gravel, the only thing I could hear was the methodical click of sprinklers watering lawns that I couldn't see but that emitted a strong aroma of sap and well-fertilized soil.

Now and then I glimpsed the silvery body of an enormous German-made car through the bars of an iron fence. I turned a corner, and before me lay the vertiginous expanse of beach and sea. The hotel looked like a scale model, or one of those cutouts my son liked to put together when he was younger: a picture-postcard blue pool, the line of windows. Behind one of them, my wife was still peacefully asleep in a night preserved by drawn curtains.

I found no path that would take me to the top, to the cave containing the Neolithic paintings. I abandoned the asphalt road, striking out through thick clumps of rockrose in which I thought there might be a path. I came to the road again, which narrowed between rocks and weeds before ending abruptly at a wall with a tall metal door painted a military green. Several dogs were barking behind it. I recognized the high terraces and arched windows we had seen from the beach: the house on the highest point of the hill. Beside the door, on a ceramic plaque, was a name in Gothic characters: BERGHOF. I had read that name somewhere, in some book, but I didn't remember which one.

I turned back. I was tired. When I reached the hotel, it was no later than 9:00 A.M., but it was already beginning to get hot, and the first German tourists, red from the sun and stuffed from breakfast, were beginning—with careful deliberation—to claim the best chairs, the reclining loungers arranged on the shady side of the pool. I opened the door of my room cautiously and listened in the darkness to my wife's breathing, and smelled the shared scents of our lives. I sat on the bed beside her; she was wearing nothing but her panties and was sleeping on her side, curled up and hugging her pillow. *To see you naked is to remember the earth.* I brushed the hair from her face and saw that her eyes were open and that she was smiling at me. I remembered that word: Berghof.

I wish I could hold every detail of those July days in my mind as completely as I hold this white shell, because if any of it, essential or trivial, is lost, the equilibrium of things may tip out of balance. In my student encyclopedia I read the story of how for want of a horseshoe nail, an empire was lost. How many small coincidences were needed for Pablo Casals to find Bach's suites for cello in a stall in Barcelona filled with old manuscripts? This shell is dragged by waves for a year or for two hundred, and is thrown so hard against a rock its outer edge is nicked, then it lies buried in the white sand of a beach that fades into the horizon toward the west so that one July afternoon Arturo can find it, and so that I in turn may have it here now within reach of my hand, as part of the familiar kingdom of the sense of touch: the plastic of the computer keyboard, the rough wood of the table, the porcelain of the coffee cup, and paper shining in the light from the lamp where I am writing words that are indecipherable to anyone except a pharmacist.

THE DOCTOR IMAGINES he is speaking with a friend, telling him the story, he who confides in no one but his wife, the story of those two summers, of the second summer, the one of repetition, the return two years later. If there is something I truly yearn for, it isn't youth, it's friendship, the mutual affection that joined me to others when I was fifteen or twenty, the ability to talk for hours, walking around my deserted city on summer nights, recounting every detail of who you are, what you want, what you suffer, to do nothing but talk and listen and be together, because often we didn't have money to go to a bar or a movie or play billiards. Hands in our empty pockets and heads sunk between shoulders, we leaned toward one another to share thoughts and conspirings. I miss that bashful male tenderness, feeling accepted and understood but not daring to express gratitude for it—not the rough male camaraderie, that boasting or poke of the elbow or drooling wink at the sight of a desirable woman.

He imagines he's talking now to a friend from thirty years ago, they've kept in touch and maintained the old loyalty, strengthened and improved by time and by the experiences and disappointments of their two lives. He invented friends when he was twelve or thirteen and found himself alone, no longer a child but not yet an adolescent, not a *youth,* as they used to say—too bad such a beautiful, precise word isn't used anymore.

Now my son is at the point of entering *his* youth, beginning to be independent of me, though he isn't aware of it. He would tell his friend this, if he had one, if he hadn't lost the ones he had because of distance or negligence or a slightly bitter current of skepticism that the years have accentuated and from which only the core of his life is safe, his wife and son, and maybe also his work in this darkened consulting room. It is calming to tell things to a friend, though words are imprecise, and it is worth the effort to transmit an experience in every detail in order to make it intelligible, free of the melancholy and self-pity that slip into a memory that hasn't been shared. When I go home and my wife notices I am self-absorbed and asks me if something is the matter, and I say nothing—the strain of work, the oppressive persistence of illness on those new faces that keep showing up every day, faces of the newly exiled—it is a silent betrayal.

We went back that summer, the doctor recounts, or he would if there were a friend to listen. We had only ten days there, and did almost nothing but swim and sunbathe, read on the beach or by the hotel pool, go out occasionally in a rented car to have dinner or drive around the town. I got up early, ran a few effortless kilometers along the hard sand near the shore where the tide had just gone out and the sand stretched smooth and shining in the first light of day. I liked coming back to the hotel and waking my wife and son, having breakfast with them by a window in the restaurant that overlooked the palm trees in the garden. In everything we did there was perfection, a harmony among the three of us that corresponded to the external beauty of the world, to the full moon and the wind at sunset the first night we walked down to the beach and huddled together to protect ourselves against the cold, corresponded to the purity of the form of a shell, and to the taste and aroma of fish roasted over coals that we ate on the terrace of a restaurant beside the sea. My wife and I, my son and I, my wife and my son, my son watching as we hugged or kissed, my wife watching the boy and me as we walked with our heads close together along the beach, looking down, searching for shells and crabs, I watching the boy as he dribbled sand over his mother's feet.

Two summers later, they return to the same hotel, during the same days of July, with afternoons that stretch with golden laziness toward the dinner hour. Everything is the same, and yet he catches himself spying on himself, looking for some flaw in the repetition of his earlier enjoyment, uneasy, disheartened without reason, irritated by inconveniences that he knows he should attach no importance to, the room that this year doesn't look out over the sea but onto a patio with palm trees and the windows of other rooms, the east wind that keeps them away from the beach the first few days, provoking a bad mood in his son, who turns surly and locks himself in his room to watch television hour after hour. He's thirteen now, and the shadow of a mustache darkens his upper lip. He has lost his child's voice; it changed without our noticing, and we will never hear it again. Two years in our lives as adults are nothing, but in his life they are a leap from larva to butterfly. His big eyes, crinkled in laughter, the expression so like his mother's, don't look the way they used to. You look into them, and he isn't there. His father must convince himself not to feel desolation and resentment. "The boy misses his friends in Madrid," his wife tells him, smiling with a benevolence he envies. "Don't you realize that he's going to be fourteen? I wonder what you were like at that age." He watches himself as carefully as he examines the face of a patient or palpates his abdomen or listens to his breathing through the stethoscope, looking for symptoms.

One night while he is waiting for his wife to get ready for dinner, as she is talking to him from the bathroom, combing her hair before the mirror, trying a new lipstick, he sees a blond woman lying on a bed in a room on the other side of the patio. It's too far away to be able to make out her features, to tell whether she's young or attractive or just a figure his imagination is crystallizing, the blond, barefoot foreigner on the steps of a train one early summer night long ago. She is gesticulating, talking to someone he can't see. A man's silhouette appears in the window. The man bends down to the woman, and something slow and hazy takes place. The doctor presses to the window, to see more clearly, excited, because the movements of the two bodies in the room across the patio are rhythmic; his mouth is dry, like that of a teenager choked with desire.

It lasts only an instant. He turns away from the window when his wife comes out of the bathroom; he fears being discovered by her, or blushing and causing her to ask the reason, which would make him blush even more. The two figures in the other window dissolve like fragments of a dream in the clarity of waking up. His wife wears a form-fitting black dress and black high-heeled sandals; she has put on eye shadow and painted her lips a new, softer shade of red that goes with the deep tan of her skin, and she smiles, offering herself to his male scrutiny, seeking his approval. Now the troubled, secret inspector finds no flaw in the quality of his emotion, he hears no false note, senses nothing feigned or forced; his delight in looking at his wife is the same as it was two summers ago, or twelve years ago, it hasn't waned, hasn't been contaminated by habit. He looks at her dark, bare legs and is as captive to desire as the first time, in another hotel room, and he drinks her in with all the lust women have always kindled in him. Even when he was twelve he would stand bewitched after school, watching the girls in the first miniskirts, and once one of his young and beautiful aunts bent over him to set down his dinner and before his eyes was the white, trembling flesh of her breasts in her low-cut dress, perfumed, shadowy—the delicate female flesh he now smells and strokes and gazes at as he puts his arms around his wife, trying to pull down the zipper of her dress, to run his hands up her thighs with urgent need.

She bursts out laughing and tries to draw away, flattered and annoyed, always amazed at the suddenness of male desire. "My lipstick is all over your face, we're late for dinner, and our son's waiting." "Let him wait," he says, breathing through his nose as he kisses her neck, and when, as if invoked by their words, their son knocks at the door and tries to turn the doorknob, he sighs,

"It's a good thing we locked the door." That will give them time to compose themselves, to calm down, and when they come out, the boy gives them a look that may be slightly censorious, or maybe it's only questioning, even a little mocking. "What took you two so long to open the door?"

THERE ARE RAPIDLY blinking lights in the darkness beyond the broad white band of waves breaking on the sand; with the new moon, the speeding launches of the tobacco and hashish smugglers breast the foam, along with emigrants coming from the other side, from the darkest line of shadow, the coast of Africa. Aesthetic contemplation is a privilege, but sometimes a lie: the beautiful, dark coast we are seeing this night from the restaurant terrace, the scene onto which we project tales and dreams, adventures from books, is not the coast seen by those men crowded into boats rocked by the sea, on the verge of capsizing and dying in waters murkier than any well, dark-skinned fugitives with glittering eyes, pressed against one another to protect themselves from cold and fear, trying to conquer the feeling of being impossibly distant from those lights on the shore they have no guarantee of reaching.

Some are returned by the waves, swollen and livid and half eaten by fish. Others you see from the highway, dashing across open land, hiding behind a tree, or flattening themselves against the bare ground, terrified, tenacious, looking for the road north taken by those who preceded them, beleaguered heroes of a journey no one will speak of. When we drive back from the restaurant toward the hotel, we come upon two Guardia Civil jeeps beaming their spotlights on the dunes near the highway; with his face against the back window, the boy, as excited as if he were at a movie, watches as we pass silently whirling blue warning lights and the silhouettes of two armed *guardias*. What would it be like to hide in this moonless night, wet and panting, lying in a ditch or one of those cane fields, a nobody with no belongings, no papers or money or address or name, not knowing the highways or speaking the language, the doctor thinks later, in bed, lying close to the woman sleeping with her arms around him, both of them exhausted and drained by the greed of love.

He wakes with the first light, clearheaded and rested, but doesn't get up, he barely moves in order not to leave her arms. He watches the gradual dawn like a silent and patient witness, drowses with eyes half closed, then feels the spirit and energy to get up and put on his running clothes: a favorable sign that their happiness will be repeated, that things will be exactly the same, his wife's and his son's love, the fullness of every sensation, as strong as his pleasure in thrusting deep within her. That memory is so vivid that he gets out of bed with an erection.

At that hour of morning, the colors on the seashore have the faded tones of an old postcard, the blues, grays, greens, and roses of a hand-colored photograph. He begins running along the highway curving up the cliff, at a fast pace, with long, energetic strides, pumping his arms rhythmically, noting in his Achilles tendons the effort of the climb, his lungs expanding in the sea air, his whole body weightless, moving with a physical joy he never experienced in his youth. With every curve the precipice is more dizzying and the view more sweeping: Tangiers in the distance to the west, a white line in the fog-free blue, the Rif Mountains, where flat-roofed villages cling to ravines just as they do in Alpujara de Granada.

Large silver German-make cars, dogs barking behind the walls of houses isolated amid rock gardens and palm trees. In the hotel they'd told us that the Germans arrived when there was nothing at all along the coast, except the bunkers erected against a possible invasion that happened much farther away: first in Sicily, in the south of Italy, then in Normandy. The Germans began coming at the end of the war, their war; they chose to build their houses and plant their gardens on those heights battered by the winds, where no one ever climbs and where there is nothing but that cave with the black drawings of animals and archers and buried amphorae in which the skeletons of Phoenician travelers were later discovered.

This time he is determined to reach the peak, to find the grotto. He's been told that after he passes a certain curve where a large pine twists out above a ravine, he should leave the highway and follow a path that winds upward through thickets of rockrose and a kind of acacia with sharp thorns and clusters of yellow flowers whose seed, he's heard, has been carried by wind or birds from across the water, because it's a variety that grows in the desert. If he had a friend, he would tell him that almost as soon as he took what he thought was the path, he realized that he was mistaken, because it quickly became overgrown by brush. He made his way through harsh branches that raked his skin, through the sticky leaves of the rockrose, trying not to become disoriented, although soon he could see only a few steps ahead. He could hear the sea crashing against the cliff but didn't know the direction it was coming from. He stumbled over fallen branches and feared he might loose his footing, get too near the edge of the cliff. But he kept going and fought the feeling he was lost; soon he would come to a clearing, find one of those rocks that rose above the vegetation, and climb up on it to get a sighting of the road.

He was so absorbed in the task of pushing through the thorny brush that he was slow to hear the ferocious barking of dogs. A few meters in front of him, invisible till that moment, was a high whitewashed wall topped with jagged glass. He followed it, without coming to a door or window, until he turned a corner and immediately froze. In terror and vertigo he pressed his body to the wall: only one step away was the edge of the cliff and, far below, the splendor and roar of the foam crashing upon the rock that was the base for the bunker.

He stood motionless against the wall struck now by the sun, his eyes closed, not daring to open them and look into emptiness. Then he stepped back, moved away from the precipice, and again heard the dogs. Clinging to the rough wall, he advanced in the narrow space between it and the brush.

He reached an open area in front of the main gate of the house just as a heavyset blond woman came running toward him, sobbing and saying something in a language he didn't understand. Even before he saw the writing on the ceramic plaque, he remembered that he'd been in this place before. Berghof.

He thought at first that the woman was scolding him for having invaded her property. But she didn't have the look of the owner of the house, more that of a servant, the hands she was waving so frantically as she shouted to him were the large, reddened hands of a domestic, a scrubbing maid or cook from a different epoch. She screamed and pulled him toward the half-opened iron gate, where the barking was louder. With dreamlike naturalness, he accepted that the woman knew he was a doctor and was asking him to help someone who was ill.

But she can't have known I was a doctor, she can't have been waiting for me to come. From the moment he enters the house, dragged in the woman's tight grip, he imagines he is telling his wife this adventure, telling her later this morning when he is back at the hotel, sitting beside her on the bed, bringing her a story as he would breakfast: I wish you could have seen what happened to me, what I saw.

Led by the woman, he crosses a patio of white walls and marble paving and arches where sheer curtains flutter, offering a view of the sea and the coast of Africa, those same arches we've so often seen from the beach, wondering who had the privilege of living there. There is a marble fountain in the middle, but the sound of the water and our footsteps is masked by the barking that becomes even fiercer as I step inside the house. The woman is sobbing and rubbing her hands on her voluminous bosom, looking much older now: the blue eyes, light hair, pug nose, and round, rosy face made her look young, but now I realize she must be over sixty. With tear-filled eyes she gestures for me to hurry. The place is a pastiche of Andalusian and German decor, with huge iron grilles at all the windows and dark, paneled doors. But I see all this very quickly, blurred by confusion. We enter a large room where the woman points to the floor, waving her arms, crying openmouthed, tears streaming down her round, withered cheeks, but my eyes, accustomed to sunlight, are slow to adapt to the shadow, and see nothing.

The moan is the first thing I hear, although not clearly because of the woman's screams and the barking dogs, who must be penned up nearby, since I also hear them clawing. A moan and the whistling breath of a sick person's lungs, then I see the figure on the floor, an old man in a silk bathrobe, his yellowish pallor in sharp contrast with the bright red of his gaping mouth and the tongue waggling in search of air, thrust out like a grotesque marine creature struggling to escape a crevice in which it has become wedged. He is clutching his neck with both hands, and when I bend down to him, he grabs the front of my T-shirt, his eyes as wide as his mouth, the color so light that it's difficult to say whether they're gray or blue. He pulls me to him with fanatical strength, as if grabbing on to me to keep from drowning, as if he needs to tell me something. His face is so close to mine that I can see his long yellow teeth, the red tear ducts and tiny veins in his eyeballs, and his breath is like a sewer. *Bitte,* he says, but it's a death rattle more than a word, and the woman who is sobbing beside me repeats the word, shakes me with her big red hands, urging me to do something, but the man has pulled me closer to him, and I can't free myself to listen to his chest or attempt in some way to revive him. Beside him on the dark, polished wood floor is a puddle I had thought was urine, but it's tea. I also see a broken cup and a spoon.

"This man is choking," I tell the woman, absurdly spacing the words, as if she would then understand me better, and I point to a telephone: You must call an ambulance. What I want most, however, is to leave, get away from there, go back to my hotel room before my wife wakes up. I manage to get to my feet, and when the old man lets go, his breathing is somewhat improved, although his eyes are turned back in his head.

On the telephone table is a small red tray with a swastika in the center, inside a white circle. I haven't looked around the room since I came in, only now, while I'm waiting for the emergency call to go through. On one wall is a large oil painting of Adolf Hitler, bracketed by two red curtains that turn out to be two flags with swastikas. In the illuminated interior of a glass case is a black leather jacket with the insignia of the SS on the lapels and with a large, dark-stained split on one side. In an ostentatiously framed photograph, Hitler is bestowing a decoration upon a young SS officer. In another glass case is an Iron Cross, and beside it a parchment manuscript written in Gothic characters and with a swastika pressed into the sealing wax.

I see all this in one second, but the number of objects around me is overpowering, they make the room seem crowded although the space is enormous: busts, photos, firearms, burnished, sharp-pointed shells, flags, insignia, paperweights, calendars, lamps, there's nothing here that isn't connected with the Nazis, that doesn't commemorate and celebrate the Third Reich. What I first perceived as confusion is actually in a perfect order that suggests museum cataloging. Meanwhile, the man lies gasping on the floor, calling out to me in a voice so hoarse it seems scarcely to escape the cavern of his chest. *Bitte,* he says when I hang up the telephone and again bend down to him; he stares at me, terrified.

"Be calm," I tell him, although I'm not sure whether he's learned any Spanish in all the years he's lived as a refugee on this coast. An ambulance is on the way. Saliva drools from one side of his mouth. He feels my chest, my face, as if he were blind; he asks me something, orders me to do something, in German. Now he is breathing a little more regularly, but his eyes are still turned back and half closed. When I check his wrist for a pulse—skin and bone and a sheaf of twisting blue veins—he digs his fingernails into the back of my hand.

WHEN THE DOCTOR RETURNS to the hotel, he will show his wife the physical marks the fingernails made as proof of what happened, the things he will tell her with such relief, still feeling a trace of revulsion. He wants to leave but can't, even though he doesn't know if it's his duty as a physician that holds him there or some form of malevolence he can't shake, no more than he can free himself from the perhaps dying man's fingernails digging into his hand. Time crawls. His wife will be awake by now and wondering why he isn't back. She'll fear suddenly that something happened to him, and be irritated about his mania for running and walking at dawn. We two are most alike in our fear that everything will fall apart, that our life will go down the drain. He needs to pull away from the old man's hand and call the hotel to calm his wife, but he doesn't know the number, and the task of finding it seems too great an obstacle.

The old man's pupils are again visible in the slit of his eyelids and fixed on him. The doctor looks away and makes a sign as if to get up, but two skeletal hands stop him, tugging at his T-shirt. He hears the old man's breathing, smells it, becomes conscious of the monotonous roar of the sea at the foot of the cliff. Between the murmuring and prayers of the woman planted like a monolith and the barking that hasn't let up for an instant, he thinks he can hear, still far in the distance, the wail of an ambulance.

cerbère

THE LETTER FROM THE German embassy must have arrived when we'd been living in the new house for less than a year. I noticed the postmark, that it was dated several months before, and that the address on the envelope was the old one, the one in the apartment building in the Las Ventas barrio where I was born just as the war broke out, and where I saw my father for the last time, the day before the Nacionales entered Madrid, although I was too young to have any memory of that. The letter had been going from place to place for a long time, and the mailman who handed it to me said it was hard work to find us because at that time everything in the barrio where we were living was new and many of the streets didn't have names yet, and sometimes there weren't even streets, just open lots that became mud pits whenever it rained. Now you go to the neighborhood and that seems impossible, everything's so well arranged, so established, and the trees are tall, as if they were planted a long time ago, but then, when we arrived, they were as rare as street lamps, and the first blocks of buildings were far apart, separated by embankments and empty lots, and the country was only a step away. There were wheat fields, orchards, and flocks of sheep, and you could see

Madrid in the distance, looking prettier than ever, with its tall white buildings, like the capital of some foreign country in a movie. People said, mockingly, "You've gone to live in the country," but that didn't matter to me, I actually preferred it. I liked going out on the balcony of my new apartment and seeing Madrid in the distance, liked roaring into the city on my husband's new Vespa with my arms around his waist. For the first time we had rooms with ventilation and a bathroom, and hot and cold water, and as soon as I became pregnant my husband bought me a washing machine, and before long he got his driver's license, which at that time seemed almost better than if he'd had a profession. One morning I heard a horn and went out on the balcony and there was a new car in front of the house, a light blue Dauphine, and my husband was driving. He made the down payment and they gave it to him, just as they gave us the apartment and washing machine with only a down payment. The very words *down payment* scared me, but they pleased me too, and they still sound good if I stop to think about it, because we had the feeling we were starting a new life, exactly as when we walked into the new apartment and smelled fresh plaster, and when I got into the car the first time, it smelled a little like that, new and clean, because where we'd come from everything smelled old, the houses, streetcars, clothes, corridors, closets, dresser drawers, the toilets on the landings, everything was old, dirty, used, sour. Life had been so hard for so many years, everything in short supply, and suddenly it seemed that all you had to do to get something was want it, because they handed it to you with just that down payment, the way they gave us the keys to the apartment even though it would take us more than twenty years to pay it off. The patio of our old building in Las Ventas, near the bullring, was always crowded and cramped, and there were always people around: the neighbor women who listened even though you weren't talking loud and who seized any excuse to come in and snoop around your place, some with no good in mind, so that when I walked into my new apartment in Moratalaz for the first time, it seemed enormous, especially when I opened the living-room window that looked out on wide-open country, with Madrid way in the background: it was like a movie screen in Technicolor. Everything new: my kitchen, which I didn't have to share with anyone, my washing machine that didn't stink of plumbing or other people's filth, my bathroom, with the white ceramic tile, and a toilet and bidet so white that the fluorescent light was dazzling when it reflected off them, a really good light, not those sickly bulbs we had when I was a girl. My mother complained because she'd lived all her life in Las Ventas and couldn't get used to being away from her neighbors and the shops she knew, and in the new barrio she got lost the minute she stepped out the door, she said it was like being an invalid, always at the whim of whoever would take her and bring her back, because in those days neither the metro nor the bus went as far as our barrio, it wasn't even on the maps of Madrid. I didn't want to show my mother the letter. But since she was so suspicious, she shot out of her room to ask who knocked, and when I told her it was the mailman, she wanted to know who'd written us, but I said it was the wrong address and went into my bedroom to open the letter by myself. My heart was pounding, because by that time we'd got over being hungry, but we still had the fear that we'd fall on hard times again, that they'd take my mother away again, the way they did after the war, when it was days before she came back and my grandmother went around to all the police stations and women's prisons asking about her. My father told her, if you don't come with me something so bad will happen to you that you'd be better off hanging yourself or jumping off the balcony, but she wouldn't budge, she didn't want to leave Spain, although she knew perfectly well what lay in store for her, not because she'd done anything, because politics had never mattered to her and she didn't even know how to read or write, but just because she was married to him. I was three years old when the war ended, the day my father showed up one morning in our building in Las Ventas to take us with him. I don't remember anything about it, but I can imagine the scene perfectly. Knowing how hardheaded my mother was, she would have been sitting in a corner, very serious, head down, and no one could have budged her. I can imagine my father, talking and talking and telling her that we all had to go to Russia, trying to convince her, promising her things, arguing just the way he did at his political meetings, where it seems he always won, which was why he rose so high. He had a golden tongue, my grandmother told me, the only person he couldn't convince was his wife, he'd never been able to get her to come to any protest, she was never interested in his meetings and politics and didn't believe a word of anything he promised her, didn't admire him for the higher and higher positions he held during the war, or for the stars he wore on his cap and cuffs. He would go away, leave in the morning and come back maybe that night or not till after a week or a month, he'd come back from jail or from the front, disguised so the police wouldn't find him, or dressed in his military uniform, and she never asked where he'd been, listening without a word to his explanations, which she probably didn't understand. But she always kept a clean house for him and the kettle on the fire, and sometimes she treated his wounds or fixed him bowls of broth or hot coffee at every hour of the day or night to ease his hunger, and when what little money he'd given her ran out she would go out on her own and try to make a living by scrubbing floors or selling water in the Plaza de Toros with a clay jug and tin cup, and if she had to she would go to the parish church to ask for clothing for us, although she hid that from my father, who would never allow any priest to help him. The last time I saw him must have been that night he came looking for us, already in hiding, because if the war hadn't ended it was close to it, and he told my mother that he had a car with its motor running waiting at the door, that he was going to take us that very night, I don't know whether to Valencia, where there would be a boat, or to an airport, and that we'd go straight to Russia and would never be hungry again and have every comfort. In the meantime the car with the driver was at the door, and Franco's troops were at the edge of the city, and my mother sat there as if she were listening to it rain, I can see her so clearly, shaking her head, staring at the floor, saying no, no, he could do what he pleased, he always had, but he wasn't going to take her and their children anywhere, least of all to Russia, so far away, because going was easy, but whoever saw anyone come back from so far? And he paced the room; I have no memory of him, but I can see him, tall, handsome in his uniform, the way he looks in one of the photographs they gave me at the embassy and that later my mother tore into tiny pieces and burned in a pile with all his papers, letters, drawings, and documents, things I'd like to have now as a reminder of him. "Then I wash my hands of anything that happens to you, and to the children," he would have said, and she would have leaped up like a lioness, "As if you haven't always washed your hands of us, you with your politics and adventures and revolutions, if we'd depended on you, your children would have gone begging in the street." Or they'd be in Russia, well fed and cared for, not having to pay the price they had to pay here because of her contrariness, because one other time, when I was two, my father wanted my older brothers to go on one of those expeditions of Spanish children to Russia, but my mother refused then too. She told me that I was sleeping in the room beside theirs, that the shouting woke me up and I came out crying, that when I saw my father I didn't recognize him at first and ran to bury my head in my mother's skirts when he tried to hug me. But there was another woman in the room; as I tell you this, it's as if I remembered it, I see her so clearly, a tall, dark woman, vigorous, beautiful, dressed in black as if in mourning, she had been a neighbor of ours and had a daughter who sometimes looked after me and played with me, a daughter even more beautiful than she was, and she also had a strapping son who was in Russia two or three years. The woman picked me up and sat me on her knees, my mother told me, and said to her, "Please, if not for yourself, at least do it for this child, who isn't to blame for anything." The woman rocked me so I would go to sleep, and sang a song in a low voice while my father kept pacing and arguing with my mother, and all the while you could hear cannons in the distance, but less and less frequently, because the war was in its last hours and everything was lost by then. "And do you know who that woman was?" my mother would ask me, lowering her voice the way she did when she was telling about the things that happened that night. "She was La Pasionaria, who followed the same politics as your father, and she told me that her children already spoke Russian and were getting along stupendously in the Soviet Union, just as we would if we went that night." My mother didn't answer, just sat with her head down, staring at the floor, and my father lost control: talking to you is like talking to a wall. "Whatever happens is on your head," he yelled at her, and again he said that he was washing his hands of it: you'd be better off throwing yourself into a well, because they're ready to take over the city and won't show any mercy. And it was true, because they shaved my mother's head and gave her terrible beatings, just for being the wife of an important Red, and my uncles, his brothers, were all put in prison, and they shot two of them. Every night you could hear shots from the Del Este Cemetery from our house, and as soon as they stopped my mother and grandmother would throw shawls over their heads and go with the other women to look through all the corpses and see if they found anyone from our family. That I do remember, because I was a little older: the two women with their black shawls over their heads, starting off down the street, and me not sleeping until they came back, when the sun was already up, but the part I didn't see I also seem to remember, those two in the light of early dawn moving slowly among the dead bodies, rolling one over in order to see his face. My mother took us to her village, believing that we would eat better and they would pay less attention to her there, but the minute she arrived they arrested her and made her scrub the church floors every morning for two years, and she got so cold scrubbing those paving stones on her knees that she had trouble with her bones for the rest of her life.

THERE'S NO LIMIT TO the surprising stories you can hear if you listen to the novels in people's lives. The woman came about six in the evening, the old hour for making calls, and brought with her the air of a caller from a different time. There was an affectionate formality visible in the care she put into dressing, and also in the pastries she brought, just like the ones from her youth. She's in her sixties, appears to belong to a comfortable though not opulent middle class, but there is a working-class vitality in the gleam of her eyes and the openness of her manner. She no longer lives in her old neighborhood, the one where she went when she married and where her children grew up. She's farther away, in a development on the outskirts, and you can see that she would have preferred not to move, that in recent years the change of address has involved a number of bitter adjustments: her husband's retirement means a decrease in his earnings, which once allowed them to enjoy good cars, good schools for the children, and trips to other countries. But she is strong, a large, solid woman with an open gaze and energetic hands, and has a positive outlook on the world, on whatever life still has to offer, unlike her husband, she says, who hasn't learned how to adapt and is driving her out of her mind because he would like to pull her into his depression, keep her beside him every minute in their small apartment. Suspicious of the world, he has no taste now for traveling or even going out, only nostalgia for what they've lost, both the money and the years. Things wear down, times change, you have less business, suddenly you're retired and must live on a pension, and your savings have shrunk like your energy, the money's gone and time's run out.

So he's at home, she says, sitting on the sofa with the thermos of coffee I left for his lunch, and when I told him where I was going, he perked up a little, and I think he was just about ready to come with me, but laziness got the upper hand, and cold as it is these days, a person has to be careful about going out, he tells me, particularly at eighty, and he's always complaining about how far out we live and how long we have to wait for the bus, not like it used to be, when you could be in the heart of town in fifteen minutes. I just cut him off, "All right then, you stay here," and he asks me again where I'm going, as if he's afraid I'll be gone a long time. By now he'll be worried, checking his watch, wandering around the house in his bathrobe and slippers. "You dress like a sick person," I tell him, but he doesn't care, he's lost his dignity, like so much else he once had.

She looks at her little gold watch, a trinket from the old days, like the bracelets and ring with the precious stone on a hand that's no longer young but still has strength. I must be going, she says, or call him, because he'll be nervous, what a trial the man is. But I can't complain, in forty years of marriage he's never given me any cause, he's been so good that I almost want to murder him, and when I get impatient with him I immediately feel guilty.

She doesn't want to go, you can see she's enjoying the visit. She clearly doesn't have the habit of drinking tea yet makes a show of savoring each sip and takes pains to hold the cup just so and praises everything around her, her eyes clear and radiant with appreciation, accustomed as they are to judging the price and quality of objects: the porcelain of the tea service, the fabric of the curtains, the red roses in the middle of the table. If she's comparing this house with hers, she does it without resentment, more with admiration. Just as there are people blind to what's around them, like black holes absorbing all light without benefiting from it, there are others who reflect any brightness near them, beaming it back as if it were their own. Aye, child, how your mother would love this house if she could see it, if only she hadn't died when she was so young. This woman who has known better times is renewed in the presence of youth, in the spaciousness of a house much larger than hers, in the porcelain and roses she can't afford now, and if she sees a painting she doesn't like or tastes a Japanese tea that's strange and bitter, the spur of curiosity in her is more powerful than the reflex of dismissal. She went to school only a few years, but she speaks like a sensible and cultivated woman, and if in the 1960s she lived in domestic servitude to her husband and children, she has the elegance and aplomb of one who can manage on her own. She reads books, loves the movies, has attended night school. I remember your mother, how angry she was that we were so enslaved to our husbands, the effort she made to see that you and your sister studied. She was very clever, realized that times would change, and that's why she suffered even more when she knew she wouldn't live to see you or your sister as adults, independent, not bound as we were.

She takes a sip of tea, nibbles a pastry, chats about a film or conveys a mild piece of gossip, looks at her watch and says it's time for her to go, you must have so many things to do and here I am taking your whole afternoon, besides my husband must be very nervous by now, afraid I won't get home in time to make dinner, he has to have dinner at nine o'clock sharp, not a minute before and not a minute after, he says it's because of his stomach, that any deviation makes his ulcer worse. He's always had this mania for punctuality. My mother told me when she met him, "Daughter, you surely didn't choose him on purpose; your father was exactly the same, his life was governed by the clock."

I saw *my* father the last time when I was three. Sometimes I think I remember him, but what I probably remember is a photograph in which he's holding me in his arms. When I mention my father, something happens, a shift in her gaze, inward, and the smile disappears. A casual comment is enough to make the woman very different, fading from the room where nothing else has changed. The new silence is like a blank page on which words are being printed, the novel of an ordinary life, leaping from one epoch to another, from an apartment building near the Del Este Cemetery in the bloody Madrid of the early postwar years to a recently constructed neighborhood of the 1960s, spanning the Civil War and the vicissitudes of a man who disappears one night, never to return, climbing into an automobile that's been left running, waiting for him. It's learned that he was in Russia but later slipped into France and fought in the Resistance against the Germans, and was arrested and interned in a prisoner-of-war camp from which he sent brief letters and drawings to his children, because he had a great talent for drawing. He escaped from the camp, again joined the Resistance, and again was captured and again escaped. His trail seemed lost forever until one day, more than twenty years after the end of the war in Europe, his daughter, who didn't remember him, receives a notification from the German embassy. She is afraid to open the letter, with its official letterhead, because ever since she was a little girl official letters have announced only misfortunes. She is also afraid to show it to her husband, who never wants to know anything about politics and is doing very well working hard to pay off the bills for the apartment and the car and the washing machine, take her and their small children to the beach during summer vacations, and enroll the children in the best private school. He doesn't want to know about the old days, he never asked about the father who disappeared so many years ago, but it's also true that he fell in love with her even though she lived in a poor neighborhood and was the daughter and niece of Reds.

IF YOUR MOTHER HAD been here, of course, I would have told her about the letter, but we hadn't moved to the barrio yet, and although I was already friendly with a few neighbor women I wouldn't have wanted them to learn about my family's past, not because I'm ashamed of it, don't think that, but as a precaution, because we were still afraid in those days. Your mother, so distinguished, so young, I always remember her that way, not how she was at the end, although even when she was ill she never lost her elegance, but long before that, the first time I saw her, when your family came to the barrio and you were so small they still carried you in their arms or in the buggy. I remember the minute you arrived. I heard the sound of a car and I went out on the balcony and saw the big black automobile your father had then, the 1500, and when I saw all of you get out I was happy because there were so many of you, and there weren't many people in the building or the barrio at that time. You children filed out of the car, bundles came out of the trunk, then your mother got out in a light-colored dress and stood on the sidewalk, maybe a little tired from the trip, and I didn't get the impression she much liked what she saw, the open land with ditches and cranes and Madrid so far away, the broad streets and the trees like lamp poles. She took you in her arms and looked up, and I waved, so very pleased that she was pretty and young and moving into the apartment right above mine. She wasn't sick yet, or at least she didn't know it, paying no attention to the first symptoms, but I remember she was pale, more fragile than the other neighbors our age although she worked in her house and was kept busy with all of you, just like anyone else, and she wore that same smile of enjoying life that you have today. Often in the stairwell I would hear her singing as she worked in the kitchen or laughing out loud at something your father was saying in a low voice. I did tell her about my life and what happened to my mother at the end of the war, and even that La Pasionaria had held me in her lap and sung me a lullaby, and how afraid I'd been when the letter came from the German embassy, several months late, after being sent all over Madrid. I was afraid my husband would be angry if I showed it to him, but your mother laughed when I told her about it several years later: "My dear, why would he be angry, as good-natured as he is?" I didn't dare hope that the letter would tell me my father was alive. As soon as my husband came home from work that evening, I closed the bedroom door and showed him the letter, and he calmed me down right away; it couldn't be anything bad coming from a foreign government, because the only government we had to fear was our own. "It's best, though, not to say anything to your mother until we know for sure what it's all about."

The next morning they got in the car, which still smelled brand-new, a delicious odor of plastic and metal and gasoline, and drove into Madrid like two tourists, she clutching in her lap the purse that contained the letter the whole time. Maybe they would tell her that her father was alive, that he lost his memory because of a head injury and that's why he never came looking for his family, because she'd seen stories like that in the movies, but she also feared they would certify her father's death, one more among the millions of nameless corpses thrown into the ditches and common graves of Europe during the time his last letter came from the German camp, a few lines and on the back the pencil drawing of a mountain village with bulbous bell towers and steep roofs. I usually walked holding my husband's arm, but on that occasion he took mine, gave my name at the embassy office, and showed them the letter and my identity card. I was so frightened among those well-mannered people with blond hair and blue eyes who spoke with a strange accent and were so friendly, not like the Spanish officials who barked rather than spoke and were always in a foul humor. Finally we were taken to a gentleman in a room with a large table in the center, a man who spoke as if to calm me, like a doctor, so I worked up the courage to ask if my father was alive or dead, and he answered, "That's what we'd like to know, because we've been looking for him for years to return his belongings to him." Then he picked up a large cardboard box from the floor and set it in the middle of the table, a box tied with red tape and sealed with wax but battered, as if it had been shuffled around a lot. My husband and I looked at each other, not knowing what to do, and the man said, "It's yours, you can take it; the things your father left behind the second time he escaped from a prisoner-of-war camp in Germany are in this box." I looked at it without daring to touch it, and at my husband, who shrugged, nervous too, though later he didn't want to admit it. They had me sign some papers. I picked up the box, at first expecting it to be heavy, then surprised it was so light. We went outside and walked down Castellana, I carrying the box as if it held something fragile, and my husband told me to give it to him. It was one of those cold, sunny days in Madrid. I couldn't wait till we got home to open it, and besides, I didn't want my mother to see it before I knew what was in it. It weighed little, and I could hear things loose inside. We sat down on a bench, and my husband opened it. My knees were shaking, and I was crying as he took things out, everything my father had owned in the camp. There were letters my mother sent him, letters she dictated to a neighbor, the ones my brother wrote him on lined paper from a school notebook, and also the letters I wrote when I was little, just learning to write, and the drawings my brother and I made for him, and snapshots of us, some with our names on the back, written in my clumsy writing. How poor we looked, with our starved and frightened little faces, and how had I forgotten all that in just a few years? There was a photograph of my father in uniform, holding a little girl in his arms, so small that I wasn't sure it was me, and another of him, very thin, with a shaved head and huge ears and a number underneath, and also papers in French and German, all of them yellowed and so worn that they tore when we tried to unfold them, and lots of drawings on a piece of cardboard or the back of something printed in German, drawings of towns with church towers, trains, and mountains in the background, and portraits of people, men in striped uniforms, with shaved heads, and on a sheet of graph paper a large, pretty drawing of Red Square in Moscow, in color, that looked like a photograph. We closed the box, put it in the trunk of the car, and all the way home I cried as I hadn't cried in years, like a fool, making everything blurry, and my husband took one hand from the wheel to pat my hand, and he said, "Look, woman, calm down, what are you going to tell your mother when she sees you've been crying, she'll think it's something I did."

To make sure her mother wouldn't see the box, she hid it in the back of her armoire. She lay awake nights trying to imagine what became of her father after his second escape from the German camp—in November 1944, they told her. Maybe his face was disfigured in an explosion and his body decomposed so no one could identify it, or maybe he drowned in a river as he attempted to cross it, or was crushed beneath the wheels of a train or the tread of a tank. Night after night she imagined different deaths for her father, with ghostly landscapes of the war, machine-gun fire, barking dogs. One morning she came home after shopping and was surprised not to find her mother. She felt a flash of alarm even before she ran to the bedroom and saw the doors of her armoire flung open. She ran through the apartment, then went out on the balcony. In the open field across from the building, where excavation was in progress for the foundation of a new structure, she saw her mother bent over, dressed in mourning. She remembered the times she watched her go out every dawn to the Del Este Cemetery. Now her mother was standing beside a fire, throwing things into it. When she heard her daughter call, she turned around but only for a moment, and kept on watching the fire. It was a cloudy, humid morning; the daughter cut across the field toward that solitary figure, her heels sinking into the mud. And as she came closer, she saw her mother was old. Her mother had started a fire with the cardboard of the box and was throwing papers, photographs, and drawings into it with an absorbed deliberation.

"Don't look at me like that, as if I were robbing you of what's left of your father." Her voice was clear and dry, toneless, maybe the same voice of a quarter of a century before when she quietly stood her ground as the mustached, uniformed man and the tall, black-clad woman tried to persuade her, predicting disaster. "Your father is alive, and he doesn't want to know anything about you or any of us. At the end of the war, the French government gave him a decoration and a large payment, but he never bothered to send us one centime. The last time he wrote me was to tell me that he had begun a new life and was therefore ending all contact with us. I didn't want you to see that letter. You were still a little girl and always fantasizing about him. He lives in France and has another family, he even changed his name. He's a French businessman now, that's why the Germans couldn't find him. If you want to see the man who was your father, take a train and get off at a French border town called Cerbère."

wherever the man goes

THE NEW HOUSE, recently occupied, sparely furnished, still echoing empty, the paint fresh on the walls, wood floors smelling of varnish, all trace erased of those who lived there until a few months before, presences of long years' standing abolished overnight, like the rectangles on the wall where pictures once hung. Only one thing defines the austere utility of each room, now that it is stripped of decoration: in the bedroom a large iron bed, in the office a table and chair.

The new house, the new life, recently begun in a different city, far from the dreary provinces, in a Madrid neighborhood unknown until now, a small enclave in the heart of Madrid, where the streets are poorer, hidden, working-class, with a blur of strange people of uncertain sex, of skin tones and facial features denoting faraway places, languages heard in passing that carry the sound of Asia, of Muslim settlements and African markets and Andean villages.

Going outside every morning was a journey of discovery, and the customary errands often ended in aimless ambling, in the simple inertia of walking and looking, of hearing indecipherable tongues spoken in telephone booths on Augusto Figueroa, words of the circular and sinister vocabulary of heroin, the ringing, time-less voices of neighborhood women yelling back and forth, of eld-erly ladies who come to their doors in their bathrobes and look with resigned amazement at what they see or choose not to see, the way their barrio has changed, the affected voices of men trans-formed into women, although not completely, as sometimes a manly beard shows on cheeks puffed with silicone, or a male bald spot through a blond, tempestuously back-combed mane, or feet much too wide and sinewy in high-heeled patent-leather shoes.

On every street corner stand the living dead, so pale that the veins snaking up their forearms stand out beneath transparent skin. So habitual and quiet in their waiting are these specters that you quickly learn not to see them, to pass them as if they were al-ready in the world beyond. They stare into space or keep their eyes fastened, vigilant and expectant, on the nearest corner, where sooner or later a dealer or a police car will show up. Then they move, slowly, with the lethargy of saurians, trying without con-viction to act natural before the police who ask for IDs, as if their identity weren't known, their dead faces and names not radioed from patrol car to patrol car. Led off in handcuffs, they go with the weariness of actors in a bad play.

A man or woman follows an individual with dark glasses and a scrawny beard. Shoulders back, hands in the back pockets of his jeans, the individual hurries so that the follower must struggle to keep up, though bent over and abject as an old beggar, holding out a dirty and insufficient amount of money, which the dealer slaps to the ground with one hand, not even turning to the per-son who is now on his knees, scrambling to pick up the bills and coins scattered beneath cars or in the filth of the sidewalk.

At first they are disturbing strangers, these figures who appear on a street corner or at the end of a sidewalk, huddled between cars, defecating or shooting up, curled up in the shelter of a stair-way or entryway. But soon they became familiar presences, as common in the barrio as the transvestites and old ladies in bathrobes and knife-thin silhouettes of the dealers. The dealers walk with a swing of the shoulders, looking to the side, disappearing into an entryway or kneeling behind a hedge in Chueca Plaza, in the miserable garden at the mouth of the metro. They return with what they never show, speak words that cannot be heard, and there is a quick and secret contact of hands, a little packet in the palm of one hand and dirty bills in the other, and they move on, bend down to a car stopped with its motor running, throw the driver a glance, rest reluctant elbows in the open window.

So many voices, lives, and worlds juxtaposed in a narrow space, even the rarest and most sinister things soon become ordinary, each inhabitant an unwritten novel: the young man roaming in search of heroin who on the narrow sidewalk crowded by parked cars passes the neighbor woman who's come down in slippers and robe to buy bread and has learned not to look at him. The women-men babbling away with little squeals and hands flipping; the blind men tapping the ground and walls with their white canes; the Chinese packed tightly into dark apartments and unventilated cellars; the small Native Americans who at three or four in the morning congregate by the telephone booths and hold long conferences in Aimara or Guarani or Quechua with who knows what relatives left behind on the Altiplano or in the jungle. The man in pajamas who sits every evening on a balcony, in a wicker chair beside a butane burner, watching without expression and suffering fits of coughing that bend him double and force him to rest his damp brow on the iron railing.

He was gone for a while, and when he reappeared, in the same pajamas, sitting in the same wicker chair beside the butane burner, he had a white mask across his mouth, and a thin plastic tube emerged from one of his nostrils. He didn't cough now but still sat looking down at the street, at the people passing, the neighbor women, unshaven transvestites, countless Chinese, Andeans with their babies bound in shawls on their backs, the new couple with a baby and a dog who just moved into the apartment across the street. Sometimes after midnight, when the barrio was deserted, a carefully dressed and made-up old woman ventured out. She always carried a chair that looked as if it had been found at the dump and a plastic bag tied in a knot. She would choose one of the garbage pails lined up along the sidewalk and set her chair before it; then, very serious and neat, she would undo the knot of her plastic bag and pull out a checked tablecloth, the remnants of a meal, crusts and crumbs, a plastic glass, a knife and fork, and finally a large, dirty napkin that she tucked beneath her chin. She sat down at her table as if sharing a distinguished meal with someone, sipping water as if savoring a fine wine, and dabbing at the corners of her mouth, smearing crimson and grease across her chin. When she was finished dining, she collected everything and put it back into the plastic bag—empty sardine tins, bakery wrappers, glasses, plates, and silverware—removed the napkin, folded the cloth she used to cover the garbage pail that served as her table, and left with her bag and chair, not be seen outside until the next midnight.

Gradually you become familiar to the stranger watching you, though no words are exchanged, only a glance from balcony to balcony, or a moment when you brush against each other on a narrow sidewalk of the barrio: the man, the woman, the boy, the dog, the workmen who completely emptied the house across the street, erasing all traces of those who lived in it for years, the trash bin by the door, then the new walls painted soft, luminous colors, to eliminate efficiently the marks of the previous neighbors, the way the pavilion of a hospital is painted white for reasons of hygiene.

You are neither your consciousness nor your memory but what the stranger sees of you. Who was the neighborhood drunk whose name no one knew, though we saw him constantly and were no longer afraid of him, who was suddenly there when you turned a corner one night, with his filthy lank hair all tousled and his heavy bearlike body wrapped in rags stinking of piss and vomit? At times his small, watery blue eyes would seem to focus, but he never spoke to anyone or asked for charity, wandering through our streets like the hide-clad Robinson Crusoe depicted in old lithographs, and just as alone. He fashioned his shelter from cardboard, newspapers, and plastic bags in the entry of a building or slept stretched out in the middle of the sidewalk like a Calcutta beggar, his territory marked by the stench he emitted. What are the episodes of one's life seen through the eyes of an indifferent but attentive witness? Every afternoon the man in pajamas on the balcony watched the new boy go into his building carrying his schoolbag, then come back outside a few minutes later, eating a snack and leading the dog, pulling him or trying to hold him back, never able to control him, this outlandish puppy that must have been as new to his owners as the recently painted house, as the new barrio and the new life and the school the boy was attending for the first time.

Things repeated every day seem to have been happening forever. The boy with the schoolbag, the yips of the dog in the house where the balcony doors are always open, the boy tugging at the dog's leash, undoubtedly taking him to Vázquez de Mella Plaza, which is the only open space in the barrio, a large, ugly concrete expanse, nothing but a large platform built above a parking lot, where the locals walk their dogs while neighborhood boys play soccer and the girls jump rope and play hopscotch and the junkies shoot up and none of the groups seems to see the other, although how can you not see the bloody syringes carelessly tossed aside, the squeezed-dry lemon slices, the scorched squares of silver wrap? The plaza is ringed by buildings occupied by questionable hostels and very elderly people who haven't been able to leave. At night, high above the rooftops, the most visible landmark is the telephone tower, its enormity reminiscent of a Soviet skyscraper, topped with the yellow sphere and scarlet hands of a clock that on foggy winter nights emits a gold-and-red phosphorescence.

One afternoon the boy comes running home and doesn't have the dog, and even from his balcony on the second floor the man in pajamas sees that the boy's face is covered with tears as he pushes the button on the intercom panel. The door opens, but the boy doesn't go in, the man and the woman come down, and the boy throws his arms around his mother, barely waist high and crying as if he were much younger; he points toward the corner and wipes his nose with the handkerchief his mother has given him.

The man's entire life is watching and waiting. He monitors his breathing, fearing a blackout, where he would lie motionless on the balcony in his flannel slippers and pajamas, the mandatory uniform of the terminally ill, perhaps already excluded from the realm of the living like the pale shadows that slip along the street, always hunched over in pain, always worried and hurrying after a scornful dealer.

The man, woman, and boy disappear from view at the end of the street at the corner of Calle San Marcos, which is the limit of his field of vision. After a few minutes the man returns alone, calling a name that must be the dog's, trying, inexpertly, to whistle. The puppy is so little it's probably lost forever, run over by a car. But they don't give up, they go back and forth all afternoon, passing beneath his balcony, and go inside only when it grows dark, while at the corner of Augusto Figueroa, the pink neon sign of the Santander Bar has been turned on, a pink as soft as the blue sky above the roof tiles, as the dusk reflected in the windowpanes of the highest apartments when it is already night down in the street.

It's too cold to stay out on the balcony, but the man with the mask over his mouth keeps watch through the window, his back to a room of which all that can be seen from across the street is murky lamplight and occasionally the bluish wink of a television through sheer curtains that have the same fatigued look as the man's pajamas or the neck of his T-shirt. What would it be like to go into that house? Half behind the curtains, the man breathes through his mask and watches the lit balconies of the house across the way, which still have no curtains, and the now nearly dark sidewalk filled with passersby both living and prematurely dead, each seeing what the other cannot. Someone stands in the middle of the street, but the watching man can't see who it is, so when he hears the sharp, short barks of the puppy, he pulls the curtains back and presses his face to the glass to get a better view.

It's the drunk, huge, his face turned up toward the balcony of the new neighbors, weaving slightly as he holds the black-and-white dog, who is barking hoarsely and struggling to escape from the suffocating rags and hands. The drunk does not approach the door or the intercom, he stands waiting for something to happen with the dull patience of an animal. The sickly man knows that one of those balcony doors will open and reveal a recently painted pale yellow interior, that the boy will come out, the first to hear and recognize the barking, and that the vestibule light will go on.

Father and son come down, and the young woman runs out to the balcony, so focused on the street that she doesn't glance once at the building across the street. The boy, containing his impulse to run to the dog, holds tight to his father's hand. The drunk does not walk one step toward them. Slow and bulky, he bends to the ground and sets down the puppy with great delicacy, without a word, and already the boy is hugging his dog and the man is saying something to the drunk and offering him something in an extended hand. The drunk's eyes are very light, colorless like certain Slavic eyes, his round face is purple with bruises and sores, and though he is less than a meter away, he looks at them from a much greater distance. He is like a castaway who has forgotten the use of language and ended up mad. It occurs to the father that when his son is a little older he will help him read the novels about shipwrecks and desert islands that inspired him in the best years of his own childhood.

THERE ARE OTHER FIXTURES on the street corners of the neighborhood, their faces as familiar as that of the woman in the bakery or pharmacy, or the woman-man at the newspaper kiosk; the police from time to time force one of them to put his hands against the wall and frisk him, or they'll ask a Moroccan dealer for identification and take him away in a patrol car, and he might be back in the barrio shortly afterward, or disappear and never be seen again in this squatter's city on the outskirts of Madrid.

Some of those who arrive maintain a certain dignity, manners from a life they still haven't completely abandoned; they are recent converts to the sweet stupor of the barrio. Young boys with new clothes and name-brand shoes, who from a distance seem undamaged but who at closer range show signs of deterioration, usually succumb after a few months, aged, part of a process in which each of them is both vampire and victim. Their arms and neck marked by needles, they tell the boy never to touch the syringes that crunch beneath pedestrians' feet in the park, never to bend down and pick up anything off the ground.

Where did the new arrivals come from? What was in those eyes that were both intense and vacant? A young woman looked like a secretary, dressed in a suit and dark stockings and heels and carrying a leather purse and a folder. She could have been an employee in any of the nearby offices, maybe the manager of a small lawyer's office who had agreed to meet someone on this corner; from time to time she glanced at her watch. Well filled out, rosy-cheeked, and discreetly dressed, ignoring the others who were also waiting, the habitual ones who could barely stay on their feet, who leaned against a wall where they dozed or seemed in a faint, slowly slipping down the wall to the ground. But after a few days, you might notice that her heels were scuffed and worn, or there was a run in her stocking or a hole in her shoe, or her hair needed care and you could see the lighter roots in her part, or that the rosiness in her face wasn't from good health but from makeup, and she no longer had a wristwatch to consult as if she were waiting for an appointment.

As time passed, she clutched the folder with black covers, the last vestige of her dignity, or a laughable attempt to disguise herself from the people she knew or the police who patrolled the barrio, or simply not to feel embarrassed when she saw women she had resembled not long ago, secretaries of small businesses, employees in pharmacies or hair salons.

As she grew paler she applied more color to eyes and lips and used a more strident rouge on her cheeks. Now she wobbled on her run-over high heels, and her blouse was unbuttoned to show off a pouter pigeon bosom, against which she pressed the ubiquitous file (now with the plastic torn along the edges, revealing the cardboard beneath) that spilled out sheets of paper like forms or memorandums collected haphazardly off the ground and shoved in hit or miss.

Sometimes a man came with her: tall, thirty-something, more distinguished-looking than she, maybe an inexperienced and benevolent boss, wearing a sport coat, wool trousers, and leather shoes, with a studied, three-day growth of beard and tousled hair, a man you would guess to be a journalist or architect. Both of them disappeared, and after a few weeks or months she alone returned, her hair more badly dyed, her eyelashes blacker, the look in her round, protruding eyes more anxious, her lips more clumsily reddened. She wore the same high-heeled shoes and perhaps the same stockings, and the same black folder was in her arms.

The next time I saw her, the last, wasn't in the barrio, it was maybe a year later, as I was walking down Calle de la Montera. She was leaning against the corner of a building, and I was slow to recognize her, she was so much like the other miniskirted women with heavy thighs and scuffed heels who clomp up and down those sidewalks, smoking on street corners, watched over by pimps nearly as moribund as they, surrounded by the sex shops and gaming parlors at the mouths of narrow streets where the air is foul with bad plumbing.

PEOPLE LONG FORGOTTEN rise to the surface with a shudder of memory. Recently I walked by the entry of our building now inhabited by others, and from below I could glimpse, through the balcony railing, the ceiling and upper portion of a wall we had painted pale yellow. It was one of those long May afternoons with a hint of summer and pollen in the air, and on the balcony across the street sat the sickly old man in his slippers and pajamas, elbows on the railing, mask over his mouth, and plastic tube in his nose. He was looking down at the street, and he may have seen and remembered me, or maybe not, after all these years in which I have rarely walked down our old street.

There was another witness to everything, I remember now, a large old man with a broad smile and chubby red cheeks, one of those gallant fellows whom age seems to make more compact and sturdy. He always took a slow morning stroll through the neighborhood streets between Chueca and Vázquez de Mella Plazas, looking larger than he really was in his old-fashioned and opulent overcoat and with his singularly small head covered by a Tyrolean hat, complete with a green feather. I always noticed that hat and his enormous shoes, and his perfect complacency toward the world, the way he took levelheaded pleasure from everything around him, sometimes pausing to enjoy the first ray of sun that lit one corner of Chueca Plaza on winter mornings or to contemplate, with interest and approval, the maneuvers of a dump truck in the middle of interrupted traffic or the arrival of the police car or ambulance to pick up someone lying stiff in a doorway. He stopped a moment, observed, then continued his walk, as if the richness of things yet to come on his walk prevented him from staying as long as he would have liked. Satisfied and absorbed, he lifted a finger to his hat brim in greeting to Sandra at her newspaper stand, helped a blind man walk between badly parked cars on the sidewalk, admired the bags of oranges hanging from the stand of a fruit merchant, even devoted a vaguely compassionate glance to the ghosts on the corners, giving equal attention to stern policeman and furtive dealer. The admiring and magnanimous curiosity of the man in the Tyrolean hat was part of the small business activity of the barrio. How strange to meet him every day and suddenly not see him and yet be unaware of his absence. You go away and forget the habits and figures of that little enclave in the heart of Madrid, and years later remember, for no reason, a place, a face, a fragment of a story with no beginning or end, a novel we each carry but never tell anyone. What kind of life did the old woman have who spread her dinner tablecloth over the lid of a garbage can every midnight? Or the young man and woman who came to the barrio looking for heroin and pushing a baby buggy, their child sleeping despite the clatter and jolting, pacifier loose at one side of its half-open mouth, eyes placidly closed? Or, if the child was red and rigid from crying, they didn't hear it, both focused on the corner where the tranquil shadow they were waiting for would appear at any moment. They must be somewhere around there this very minute, if they're still alive, and the child, who wasn't yet two, would be eight or nine by now, and maybe poisoned by the same disease the parents carried in their blood, the disease that has killed so many of the specters of the barrio.

The living dead have disappeared from the corners of Augusto Figueroa. A few may survive in hospitals and jails or are dragging themselves like zombies along the footpaths that wind through the open land leading to the tin-and-cardboard shacks on the outskirts of Madrid, where police have been herding them since the order came down to clear the addicts off the city streets. A flower shop in the arcade has replaced the kiosk where Sandra sold her newspapers in slippers and a track suit, or in a flannel bathrobe and knit cap on winter days, and if some mornings she didn't shave, her eyes were always carefully outlined in the manner of Sara Montiel, her idol.

Other figures drift back from oblivion, the forlorn drunk who brought back our puppy and the tall, slender woman who was with him for a few months and then disappeared.

She was like a model, with Asiatic cheekbones, a large, fleshy mouth, long legs, and a spring to her step as she walked. From the back, or from a distance, you saw a tall figure and long curly hair. Only when she came near did you see her pallor, the cloud over her large eyes, the bruises on her beautiful legs, now too thin, and the black gaps of lost teeth. She went from one end of the barrio to another like a great disoriented bird beating against walls, not knowing how to get out. She lurched along with the stride of a model, still straight-backed, taller than anyone in the barrio, her curls and mannerist neck above figures hunched in councils cooking up schemes or hunched in doorways where the flame of a cigarette lighter heated a square of aluminum foil on which a shot of heroin was turning liquid and smoky. Sometimes she stopped and stood motionless, her body silhouetted against a building, watery eyes gleaming through dirty hair, a drunken, demented smile on her ruined mouth, a cigarette held in her long fingers and smoke seeping from her lips in a photographic pose.

She began sleeping in the entryways of shops and closed bars, where the indigent set up their burrows of rags and cardboard. In winter she wore a tattered jacket of fake fur over the usual T-shirt and light miniskirt. On cold mornings her white face had a violet hue. Her hair was thinning, and her eyes had lost their color. She begged for cigarettes; she would take one in her hand, slowly put it between her lips, and wait for someone to give her a light as well.

Once she asked the barrio drunk for a smoke. He shrugged, grunted, walked on, but that night, when she was shivering in her fake-fur jacket in a doorway on Calle San Marcos, a shadow stopped before her, it was the drunk offering her a cigarette, holding it delicately in his thick, grubby fingers as if it were the stem of a flower. The woman brushed the hair from her face and put the cigarette between lips purple with cold, and the drunk, whom no one had ever seen smoke, lit it, his living-dead face visible in the brief flare.

People in the barrio soon knew what had happened: he had bought the cigarettes and lighter at the same small shop where they stocked his cartons of white wine, and where the next day, contrary to his custom, he bought some custard and chocolate-filled doughnuts. The druggies lived on that kind of food; mixed in with their syringes and scorched sheets of foil were always candy wrappings and empty custard containers.

He began to carry things every night to the doorway where she took shelter, sometimes not waking her in her shivering delirium. He would cover her with his jacket, older than the one she wore, and one night he was seen dragging a filthy, torn comforter down Calle Pelayo, which he must have found in a trash barrel. He began to move with diligence, concentration, like Crusoe on his island preparing a hut or cave in which to spend the winter. During the day he was never far from her, although he didn't approach her or make himself too visible, watching from a corner where he could duck behind a building. Indifferent to the people passing him, who gave him a wide berth because of his smell, he was focused on the tall, young, skinny woman who walked with a long stride past people and cars or huddled pale in arcades or doorways late at night after no one was left in the dark streets except the most persistent dead, those who at three or four in the morning were still waiting for something.

She probably spoke to him first, asking him imperiously to bring her cigarettes again, or yogurt or doughnuts from the shop where he went when no one else was there and wordlessly laid money on the counter. He always paid and was never seen to beg. The shop owner's story was that the drunk was the firstborn of a wealthy family in the north, that a tyrannical father threw him out, disinherited him, yet took care to see that his son had what he needed to survive, enough food and clothing to keep him from dying of cold in the streets.

No one will ever know the true story, just as no one knew his name, unless he told the woman with whom little by little he began to share nightly encampments in the most sheltered nooks of the barrio. No one ever saw them walking together, but they must have kept each other warm during the icy nights of that winter. He wrapped her up and protected her, stayed awake to be sure she was covered, constructed her bed of cardboard and newspapers with an expert hand, and then cocooned her in rags and garments scavenged from the trash. You would see a flickering glow in the dark expanse of Vázquez de Mella Plaza: the drunk had started a fire where the tall, skinny woman warmed herself like a sphinx, smoking the cigarettes he brought her and lighted with a quick gesture every time she put one to her lips, and eating the yogurt or custard he bought for her at the same time he bought his cartons of wine.

Now he did turn to begging. He never said anything, just held out his hand, looked at you, made the gesture of putting a cigarette to his mouth. He begged for money and tobacco and seemed to become more aware of other people, no longer in the solitude of his desert island. He didn't share the woman's tobacco or heroin, and there probably was nothing sexual between them, but he did pass her his liters of white wine, which she poured into her wide, fleshy mouth, her eyes gleaming.

You would see them in the shadows like two animals deep in their den, two untouchables who had regressed to the savagery or innocence of an irreparable damnation, so remote from those of us passing by in our overcoats and normalcy, on the way to our new house and warm, stable life. They truly did live in a different world, in one of caves and hollows in the rock where primitive man and castaways found shelter.

After weeks or months, the woman disappeared, and we would have forgotten her fleeting existence had the drunk not stayed in the barrio, subdued and sedentary, again withdrawn into a seamless self-absorption, apparently not seeking in the haunts of the living dead the figure of the tall woman who looked like a model from a distance. But we did not pay that much attention to him, so accustomed were we to his presence, just as we did not follow closely what happened every day in the barrio, our neglect including the man, the woman, and the boy who now went to school by himself, who came out every afternoon with his snack, tugging at the leash of the ungovernable dog that no longer was a puppy.

They too moved away, habitual one day and the next gone forever, and the man on the balcony saw that the apartment across from him was empty again, and witnessed the arrival of other tenants, months or years later, it didn't matter, because for him life was a slow endurance with little modification. Months or years later, we met a former neighbor who was still living in the barrio. We talked about the days that suddenly had become distant, fading into the sweetness of the past, and the neighbor asked if we remembered the drunk who was always wandering the streets. He told us that the man turned up dead one morning in the Vázquez de Mella Plaza, purple with cold, his beard and eyelashes white with frost, rigid and wrapped in rags like those polar explorers who get lost and go mad in deserts of ice.

scheherazade

I WAS SO NERVOUS as we walked through those gilded salons that my knees were knocking, and I wished I still held the hand of my mother, who was just in front of me, very serious, quiet, like everyone in the group. She was dressed in black for my father and brother, and all the others wore dark suits, very stiff, very formal, some with uniforms and medals, all just as nervous and upset as I although they hid it. The only thing you could hear were footsteps on the marble floor, as if we were walking down the nave of a cathedral, and I beside my mother, as almost always in my life, moved and afraid, with a lump in my throat, looking at her profile because she never turned toward me, so straight, taller and stronger than I was, and proud of being the widow and mother of heroes. My mother would have given me a severe and mocking look if I tried to take her hand as I did when I was little and she took me to a protest march and I held her hand so hard that my fingers hurt because I feared the crowd would get wild and my mother and my father would be separated from me, feared that the *guardias* would charge, or that the people running away—and the horses we heard whinnying and pawing the ground, ready for their riders to spur them to attack—would crush me. Some soldiers, maybe they were ushers, guided us through the corridors, kept going ahead of us to open the doors, some of which were very tall and gilded, and others as plain as office doors, and every time we went by one my heart squeezed and I thought, now we're going to see him, and when I'm so close that I can shake his hand I hope I don't faint or burst into tears like a silly girl. My mother says I have the reactions of a child, although I wasn't one, far from it, I would be twenty-five in January, and this was December 21, 1949, Stalin's birthday, and we were going to have the chance to offer him congratulations in the name of our Party and all Spanish workers, with more solemnity than usual because it was his seventieth birthday and there would be a huge party for all Communists and workers around the world. The salon where they took us was large and filled with people, although no voices were raised, only a little for the speeches, and not much even then. I believe we were all equally moved, overwhelmed, I don't know whether that's the word, since often I'm going to say something and then after I've begun to speak realize I'm saying it in Russian and can't find the words in Spanish. Chandeliers were switched on, but they didn't give much light, or maybe there was smoke, or the sky was dark outside even though it was daytime, I remember, and everything was a little foggy. I couldn't get close to Stalin and didn't shake his hand, either because my mother motioned to me not to get on line or because someone pushed me back and I ended up in a different group. After all, I was nobody, I'd been allowed to come with our delegation because I begged my mother to take me along; when I had children and grandchildren I wanted to be able to tell them that once in my life I saw Stalin with my own eyes, and really close.

I was so nervous that I didn't notice much of what was going on, or didn't understand it, with that dim light and the low voices. But I could see Stalin well; he was seated at the middle of a long table, chatting with someone, very informal, smoking and laughing, and I almost had to pinch myself to believe that I was actually seeing him, the flesh-and-blood man, unmistakable, like a member of my family—he reminded me of the time I was a little girl and saw my father standing among a group of men— but also very different, I don't know how to explain it; he looked as he did in the pictures we'd seen everywhere forever, and yet he wasn't much like them, he was older and smaller, and I saw his short legs beneath the table and his crossed boots, and when he laughed, his face filled with wrinkles and his small teeth were chipped, or black from tobacco, and his uniform was a little big on him, but precisely for those reasons I was more moved than I'd expected, and in a different way, because I thought I would be seeing a giant at the peak of his strength but it turned out that Stalin was a tired old man, the way my father was at the end of his life. Fragile even though he'd had the enormous strength it took to rebel against the czar, oversee the birth of socialism, and win the war against the Nazis; you could see that all those years of effort and sacrifice had worn him down, like the years in the mines and in prison wore my father down, and I thought he looked as if he hadn't slept well, and every so often he'd seem to be somewhere else while someone was talking to him or as he lis- tened to a speech, until I felt sorry for him, for the sickish color of his skin and all those years with no rest, clear back to when he was a boy in the times of the czars and they deported him to Siberia. Later my mother said to me, "You should have seen your face when you were looking at him, your mouth was hanging open, and you'd have thought you were seeing a movie star." But then something happened as I stared at Stalin, not taking my eyes off him as if no one else were there. I wanted to remember all the details of his face and felt sorry for him, he looked so exhausted, and the uniform jacket on him was so big, then I felt a stab, like an electric shock. Someone was looking at me, coldly, with rage, for my bad manners in staring so openly at Stalin, a small, bald man seated near him, wearing those old-fashioned glasses they call pince-nez, and a bow tie and high celluloid collar that were just as old-fashioned. I turned to ice and still get shivers down my spine when I think it was Beria, but I wasn't afraid of him because he was the chief of the KGB, it was those eyes, which cut through the space separating us. He was studying me as you would an insect, as if saying, "Who do you think you are to be staring at Stalin like that? How did you get in here?" But there was something beyond that, and I was so stupid in those days that I didn't realize what it was, although instinctively I felt re-pelled, the way I did by those men who stared at me when I lived in the girls' residence and didn't understand why they breathed so hard and never took their eyes off me and brushed against me in the trolley.

As I'm sitting here, memories come back, and it seems unreal that so many things happened to me, that I was in such faraway places, at the Black Sea and in Siberia and the Arctic Circle, but I'm far from things here too, Madrid is a long way from Moscow. I don't know Madrid as well, I'm afraid to go outside with all those cars and people, afraid of getting lost and not finding my way back, especially since the time I was mugged just outside the front door, thrown to the ground, my purse snatched, and I lay there on the sidewalk screaming, "Thief, thief," but no one came to help, though now that I think about it, I probably shouted in Russian because of the problem I have with the two languages, speaking in one and thinking in the other. I always dream in Rus-sian, and about things that happened there, or happened many years ago when I was little, before they sent us to the Soviet Union for a few months, they said, and then until the war was over, but the war ended and they didn't send us home, and soon another war broke out and then it was impossible, it seemed the world was coming to an end. They evacuated us and sent us a long way away, I don't know how many days we traveled by train, days and weeks, always in the snow, and I thought, I'm getting farther and farther away from Spain, from my mother and father, although I almost didn't remember them, I even began to feel a little hostile toward them, I'm ashamed to say, because they shouldn't have let me get on that boat, leaving me alone again, as they did when they went to their union or Party meetings. My brother and I were left alone all night, he crying because he was afraid or hungry and I rocking him in my arms, although I wasn't much older, such a scared little boy he was and weakly because of our bad diet, but how strong and brave he became later, when at twelve he went out with me to sell the *Mundo obrero,* the Worker's World, that was when we still lived in Madrid. He told me, "Don't be afraid of those fancy young guys, because if they come after us I'll protect you," and later, when he was just twenty and a pilot in the Red Army, he came to see me and lifted me off my feet and whirled me around as he hugged me, so handsome in his air-force uniform and the red star on his cap. Then he came to say good-bye because his squadron had been ordered to the Leningrad front, and he never stopped laughing and singing Spanish songs with me, and he inspired all the girls in the school to be nurses for the troops. That night I went with him to the station, and when the train was pulling out he hopped down and hugged and kissed me again, then jumped back on the train and grabbed the handrail as if he were swinging onto a horse, and he waved goodbye with his cap in his hand, and I never saw him again. That's the strangest thing about life, something I can't get used to, that you have someone you're close to and who's always been there, and a minute later he disappears and it's as if he never existed. But I know my brother died a hero, that he kept attacking the Germans when his plane had one engine on fire, crashing it into the enemy artillery, a hero of the Soviet Union, and his photo was published in *Pravda* looking as handsome as a movie star. I sit here thinking about him, the memory comes without my doing anything, as if I opened the door and my brother calmly walked in, with that smile and poise of his, I see him before me in his pilot's jacket and imagine we're talking and remembering things. I tell him everything that's happened to me since his death more than fifty years ago, how the world has changed, how everything we fought for has been lost, everything that he and so many like him gave their lives for, but he never loses his good humor, he scratches his head beneath the cap, pats my knee, and says, "Here, now, woman, don't go on so." Sometimes I'm awake and see him standing before me as clearly as in my dreams, but strangest of all is not that he's come back or that he's still a boy of twenty, but that he speaks to me in Russian, so fast and perfect and without an accent, because Russian was really hard for him, worse than for me at the beginning, when people spoke to me and I didn't understand, and not understanding was worse than being cold or hungry. Now it's the other way around, sometimes I don't understand Spanish, and I can't get used to how people speak, so loud and curt, as if they were always in a hurry or angry, like the man the day I was mugged, who helped me get up and stand because I was in pain, thinking, "What if my hip is broken? What if they have to put my leg in a cast and then I can't go out? Who will come help me?" The man said, "Damn it to hell, señora, I'll go with you to the station to file a complaint, because we need to crack down on those bastards, it had to be one of those goddamned *moros* who hang around here." I thanked him but kept my dignity and said, "No, señor, it wasn't a *moro* who attacked me, he was white as snow, and besides, you shouldn't call them *moros,* they're not Moors, they're Moroccans, and as for the complaint, that will have to wait, because the important thing to me right now is to get to the protest: this is May Day." The man looked at me as if I were crazy, "Well that's up to you, señora, whatever you say," and I thanked him and went on to the protest, limping, but I went, and when it was over, some comrades took me to the police station in their car and I filed the complaint, but I'm not one to miss a May Day, even though it's not the same anymore, each time fewer people come and it's all so watered down, there's just a few red flags and raised fists, and not even those marching in the front, right behind the banner, know the Internationale.

IT ISN'T THE WAY NOW it was before the war, when we used to go with my mother and father, and my brother and I would look at them, raising our fists just the way they did, there on Calle Alcalá, which turned into a sea of people and red flags, or in the Soviet Union in Red Square on May 1 the year the war ended, where there wasn't room for any more people or shouting or flags or songs or fervor, with millions cheering for Stalin. Squashed in the crowd, I cheered too, excited to think that the tiny figure I could see on the platform atop Lenin's mausoleum in the distance was him, and I cried with joy and gratitude because he had led us in the victory over Germany, which cost so many Soviet lives, my poor brother among them, although now you would think that the Americans won that war, that they were the only ones who fought, and people know about the landing in Normandy but don't know that the German army met its first defeat at Stalingrad, in the bloodiest and most heroic battle of the war. No one even knows there was a city called Stalingrad, they didn't lose any time changing that name, like they did with Leningrad, what a disgrace that now it's called what it was in the time of the czars, Saint Petersburg, and they even want to canonize Nicholas II, who ordered machine guns to fire on the people in front of the Winter Palace. Oh, I see your expression, though you're trying to hide it, don't think I don't know what you're thinking, all those stories about Stalin's concentration camps and Stalin's crimes, as if he had done nothing but kill people, or as if everyone who was sentenced to the camps were innocent. Of course there were mistakes, the Party itself recognized that at its Twentieth Congress, and denounced the cult of personality, and did everything possible to remedy injustices and rehabilitate those who weren't guilty, but how could there *not* be a personality cult when Stalin had done so much for us, for the Soviet people and for workers around the world? He was responsible for the great leap from backwardness to industrialization, the Five Year Plans that were the envy and admiration of all the world, when in only twenty years the Soviet Union moved from being a rural country to a world power. And all that under the worst circumstances, following a war provoked by the imperialists, in the midst of a siege and an international blockade, in a country with shortages of everything and where the great majority of the population was illiterate, a slave to the czar and the popes. Look what they were, or what *we* were, because I've been a Soviet citizen, and look how the country is now, how in a few years they've destroyed what it cost several generations to build, the largest country in the world broken up into pieces and Russia in the hands of the Mafia and governed by a drunk, so don't tell me things are better now than in Stalin's time, or Brezhnev's, when they say the people suffered such oppression. What they don't say is that there were saboteurs and spies everywhere, that imperialism employed the dirtiest tactics to destroy the Revolution, and that Jews had taken over many of the key posts in the government and were conspiring to benefit the United States and Israel.

JEWS, OH YES, SEÑOR, don't give me that look, as if you'd never heard a word about that; don't you know that some Jewish physicians plotted to murder Stalin? There was always someone to take advantage, to abuse the trust that Stalin and the Party put in him in order to line his own pockets or to gain power, but in the end those people paid for their sins, because Stalin was so upright that he wouldn't allow it. Yezhov paid, that man who committed so many abuses, who jailed so many innocents, and then Yagoda paid, although they said that the worst of all of them was Beria, who managed to deceive Stalin to the end but who also got his, and they say that when they came to kill him he fell to his knees and begged and shrieked, so tell me whether or not justice was served in the Soviet Union. But now they want to hide everything, erase it all, even the names, they want to make everyone believe that the Soviet people were oppressed, or paralyzed with fear, or that the death of Stalin was a liberation, but I was there and know what happened, what the people felt. I was in Moscow the morning they announced on the radio that Stalin died, I was in the kitchen fixing myself a cup of coffee—I'd woken up not feeling well because I was pregnant with my first child—and then music began to play on the radio, then stopped, and there was a silence, and an announcer spoke, he said something but his voice broke, he was sobbing, and I almost didn't understand him when he said that Comrade Stalin had died. I couldn't believe it, it was like when they told me my brother had died at Leningrad, or when my father died, but my brother was in the war and I had accepted that he might die, and my father was very old and he didn't have a lot longer to live, but it never occurred to me that Stalin could die, I don't think it had to anyone, for us he was more than a father or a leader, he was what God should be to believers. I ran outside, not knowing where I was going, without a coat though it was snowing, and in the street I met a lot of people just like me, wandering about like sleepwalkers, they would stop at a corner and weep, old women bawling like babies, soldiers crying like little boys, workers, everyone, a crowd that carried me along, like a river of bodies beneath the snow, toward Red Square as if by instinct, but the streets were already flooded with people and we couldn't go any farther, and someone said that Red Square was roped off and we should head for the Union Palace. I'm sitting here now and it doesn't seem possible that I was in Moscow that morning, that I lived all that, that flood of tears and helplessness, women on their knees in the snow and shouting and calling out to Stalin, funeral music on the loudspeakers that had played such spirited anthems on May Day. I was crying too, and hugging someone, a woman I'd never seen, feeling the kicking in my womb, my son who would be born two months later and who, it seemed to me, would be born an orphan even though he had a father, because none of us could imagine life without Stalin, and we wept from pain but also from fear, finding ourselves defenseless after all those years when he had always watched over us.

IN OUR HOME, WHEN I was little, my parents talked to me about Russia and Stalin, and when the boat bringing us from Spain reached the port of Leningrad the first thing we saw was a huge portrait of him, which seemed to welcome and smile at us, just as we had seen him once in a newsreel, smiling at a child he had swept up in his arms. But it was snowing harder now, and there were more and more people in the street, and we couldn't move in the crowd, and above the music on the loudspeakers we heard the sirens blowing in the factories, all the sirens in Moscow blowing at the same time, as they had for air raids during the war. That was when I began to feel trapped, reminded of running downstairs to a shelter afraid I would trip and people would fall over me. I couldn't breathe, with people pressing from all sides, men and women in overcoats and caps, their breath on my face and neck, the smell of bodies that needed to be washed and of damp clothing. My mouth wide open to breathe, I broke into a sweat but also shivered with cold, trying to cover my belly with both hands because the baby was squirming inside me harder than ever, as if he too felt caged and crushed. I pushed, begged, wept, and pointed to my swollen belly, because I wanted to get out of there as quickly as possible and make it to a street that wasn't crowded, where I could hurry back home, gasping for breath, clutching my belly because the baby was twisting so much I thought I was going to have him right there, in the middle of that crowd that wouldn't budge one centimeter, all wrapped in their overcoats and caps, their breath frosty amid the snowflakes, and I like an idiot without a kerchief or boots. Finally I was free, suddenly alone, my hair soaking wet, lost in Moscow with no one to ask for directions. I tell all this to my son, and he says, "Mother, you've told me this a thousand times." He says it in Russian, of course, because he hardly speaks Spanish although he has Spanish looks, which I'm proud of. His father, may he rest in peace, was from Ukraine. I saw my boy dressed as a soldier when he did his military service and I thought I was seeing his uncle, my brother, just as tall and dark, just as happy, with the visor of his cap tilted to one side, a cigarette in his mouth, and his eyes squinted like the movie stars I'd liked so much as a girl. It's two years now since I've seen my son, I don't even know my youngest grandson, because with what I earn I don't have money for a ticket to Moscow, and he's a chemical engineer and his salary barely stretches to take care of his family. Sometimes I send him a few dollars so he can make it to the end of the month or buy a little car for my grandson, although I get only the minimum pension in Spain, a charity case, he has no idea the years and troubles it cost me to earn it, but my Russian pension isn't worth anything, a few rubles after having worked my entire life.

Lenin said it, freedom for what? Why did we mining people want freedom for the Republic if they sent us off to the Legion and the Guardia Civil and chased down the strikers and shot them as if they were animals? They locked up my mother, who hadn't done anything, just for being the wife of a unionist, and tortured my father and sent him to a penal colony in Africa, to Fernando Poo. When the Popular Front issued the amnesty, he

came home sick with malaria, so aged and jaundiced I didn't recognize him and burst out crying when he hugged me. I didn't
want him ever to go away, from the time I was little I couldn't
sleep until my father came home from the mine, and I did everything possible to stay awake till he came, or I woke up if he had
the night shift and came in before dawn. How happy I was to
hear him push the door open and hear his voice and cough and
smell his cigarette smoke, I can smell it this minute, even though
it's been more than sixty years. I sit here and the memories come,
and with them the smell of things and the sounds from those
days that don't exist any longer. I remember my father's eyes shining in a face black with coal dust, the way he had of knocking at
the door, and I would think, he's come, nothing's happened to
him, there hasn't been an explosion in the mine and he hasn't
been carted off by the Guardia Civil. I've lived through so many
things, been so many places, in Siberia, on a ship trapped in ice
in the Baltic Sea, in those garrisons in the Urals where they sent
my husband, when we couldn't go out at night because of the
wolves howling in the forests. I would have given anything to
have a family like other girls, even those poorer than us in the
mining town where we lived, those girls might have gone to
school barefoot and with lice but at least their fathers weren't
arrested from time to time and didn't have to hide for months,
and they didn't leave their children alone all night to go to their
meetings of committees and unions. The only thing I ever wanted
but never had was to live in peace, to have my house, to get along
with my modest lot and not have unexpected things happen. My
first memories are of hurried moves and nights on benches in
train stations, of being afraid that something terrible would happen, that the *guardias* had killed my father or that he'd died in an
explosion or cave-in at the mine. My heart still pounds when I
think of it, I look at him in that photograph on the piano and it
seems he's still alive, at my side with a gift in his hand he brought

me from a trip, that little mother-of-pearl box, for example, when he came back from Russia and had been gone so long I didn't know him and started crying when I saw him. I never told this to anyone, but the dreams I had as a little girl were petit bourgeois dreams. I always wanted my parents and my brother nearby, and to go to school and occasionally to mass, and to take Communion like the girls I saw coming out of church dressed in white with their rosaries and mother-of-pearl prayer books in their hands, and patent-leather shoes, not like me, who wore old espadrilles even in the winter, my feet like ice and mud clinging to the hemp soles. I was always hearing my parents talk about the Revolution, but what I wanted was for my father not to miss his pay and for us to have a warm meal every day, and good blankets and coats and boots in the winter. I was frightened when he talked about emigrating to America or when he told us that we had to go to Russia because that was the homeland of the workers of the world. Our house near the mine was little more than a hut, although my mother kept it swept and orderly, but I cried when we left it to move to Madrid, it felt like they were ripping out my heart. We got onto the train and my brother, being so little, was wildly happy, but I was dying because we had to leave our clean little house and the school I liked so much and my friends. But after a few months in Madrid I got used to it and wanted all the neighbor women and ladies in the shops to know me, I made friends with the girls in the school and with the teacher who scolded them the first day when they made fun of the way I spoke, which must have been with a strong Asturias accent. We lived in a building in the Tetuán barrio, two rooms in a crowded corridor, but my mother fixed them up right away with the few things we owned, and it seemed that finally we'd moved into a real house, and for the first time the toilet—the *servicio* they called it then—was indoors at the end of the corridor, not in a courtyard or out in the field, like a place for animals. My father didn't have to go to the mine anymore, he had a job I didn't know anything about, at a newspaper or with the union, and at first I thought we were going to live a normal life, that I wouldn't have to be afraid every time he was late or they went out on strike and had meetings in our house, which I hated because the men smoked so much you couldn't breathe and they left behind a smell that took days to disappear and my mother and I had to sweep up the butts and ashes.

What I liked was going to school, and that my teacher liked me a lot, and I wouldn't have minded also going to confession and Communion—so young and already with ideological conflicts. I dreamed of getting a job in a dressmaker's shop when I finished school, of embroidering my own trousseau and becoming close friends with the girls who worked with me. I grew so fond of Madrid that I imagined I would live there forever, and quickly picked up the way the other girls talked, and I liked boarding the trolleys and learning to get around on the metro, and when my brother and I could get a few centimos together we would go and sit in the gallery of some theater to watch Clark Gable movies or Laurel and Hardy. I said "there" when I was talking about Madrid, as if I weren't in Madrid this very minute, but I often forget and wake up thinking I'm in Moscow. But if I say "there" it's as if I were saying "then," because that Madrid was a different city from the one I find when I go outside today, or when I go out on the balcony, which I seldom do because of the noise of the cars on the expressway day and night, something I can't get used to. My friends tell me to get double-pane windows, but how can I spend that kind of money on my income? But with all we've gone through, I'm not going to complain about traffic noise, it's not half as bad as the sound of bombing, or spending the winter in a garrison at forty degrees below, and it's a *lot* worse to be dead. This is the best house I ever lived in, and best of all I won't have to move until the day they carry me to the cemetery, and I have my spot assured there too, in the civil cemetery, beside my mother, the two of us together in the tomb the way we always were in life, except for those horrible first years in Russia when I was alone and didn't know if I would see her again or if she and my father were dead, or had forgotten about me, being so busy with their war and their Revolution.

I sit here and things return, as if I were in a waiting room and the dead come walking in, and the living too, who are so far away, like my son who can't visit and can't talk more than five minutes when he calls me on the telephone, he's so worried about the bill, and my little grandson, who doesn't know me, and I hug and kiss him and sing him lullabies, the ones my mother sang to me and my brother and the ones I learned in Russia and sang to my son. I'm afraid to go outside; I order almost everything I need from the supermarket or have a very nice friend who lives near here bring it to me, and that saves me from being mugged again, or getting lost, which is something else that's happened to me often, especially when there are a lot of people. When the Nazi invasion began and we had to evacuate Moscow, I went through the station holding my mother's hand, but in the confusion she let go my hand, and I found myself among thousands of people, stupefied by the loudspeakers I couldn't understand and the trains whistling their departure, so I began to run like a crazy person, not seeing where I was going because my eyes were filled with tears. I ran into people's legs and had to jerk away from a guard who tried to catch me, who already had me by one arm. I ran alongside a train that had already started, and there were clusters of people hanging from the steps and from the windows, clinging to anything they could, then I saw my mother calling me from the door of a car, and I ran faster toward her, but the train picked up speed and I was left behind. It seemed to me I was lost forever in that station, the biggest I had ever seen, with so many trains and people frantic to leave, spilling over onto the tracks. I saw another train starting off beside me, and without thinking I jumped onto it, but at just that moment someone pulled me back. It was my mother. She grabbed me to her, believing she had lost me forever, and she would have if she'd looked one second later at the train leaving, en route to Vladivostok, she told me later, which is on the Pacific. How would she have found me if I'd got on the train going through Siberia? I deserved the whipping my mother gave me that day, she spanked me and kissed me at the same time. "What were you thinking," she asked, "to let go of my hand, you little scatterbrain?"—that's what she always called me.

I GET LOST IN MADRID more than I did in Moscow, and I don't like to ask people because they look at me in an odd way, probably because of my accent, or because I look like a foreigner, like a Russian. So to avoid problems I don't go out, I spend the day here, puttering, it's such a pleasure having a whole apartment to myself, and my central heating never breaks down. The place is so small I don't know where to put all my things, but I can't make up my mind to throw anything away, I'm so fond of every item and the memories they bring. After all a person goes through life losing so many things, you want to keep what's left. Look at those little doilies my mother used to crochet whenever we could find white thread in Moscow, which wasn't always, though she could make them from anything, she was good with a needle and could make something beautiful from any old scrap. I didn't take after her that way; she used to say, "What pretty hands you have, and so useless, they look like a bourgeois girl's hands," and it was true, they got rough and red with the smallest task, and I also suffered from chilblains, but now I can take care of them, although painting my fingernails makes me feel ashamed, because my hands do in fact look bourgeois.

I break things and don't know how to mend them, I drop them, for example one of the knobs came off the television when I tried to turn it on, and you can't imagine the trouble I had finding the knob on the floor, since there's little space and I get around so poorly after I was thrown to the ground when they mugged me. I spent days looking, because without it I couldn't turn on the TV, and when I put it back on, it fell off again, so finally I used adhesive tape, and if I'm careful it works and doesn't fall off. How can I throw anything away when everything has its own story? I tell stories to myself when I'm alone, as if I was a guide in a museum. That Lenin on top of the television set is bronze, pick it up and you'll see how heavy it is, and just look what a good likeness, though friends tell me, "Woman, put that somewhere not so obvious, it will offend people," but no one comes to see me here, and if someone does come and gets offended, well I'm sorry, so be it, as they say in Madrid, don't they have their crucifixes and virgins and portraits of the Pope? Well I have my Vladimir Ilyich, right there on the doily my mother crocheted for me one birthday, ah, look how yellow it's getting, and think of the kilometers it's traveled, for I had it with me when my husband was assigned to Arkhangelsk, and it got so stiff from the cold that it might as well have been tin. Those dolls in the little Siberian dresses we brought from there, and the coat rack too, let me move the coats and show you, those are real hooves, they come from those big reindeers they have. And those little paintings? I've seen how you can't take your eyes off them, they're drawings Alberto Sánchez did with what he had on hand, sheets of paper and school crayons. I remember watching him drawing at the kitchen table in the apartment where we lived in Moscow, the last winter of the war, if you go over you'll see how perfect the details are, and the little squares on the paper. He talked about the days of the siege in Toledo where he lived, and as he was talking he drew what he was telling us, and it seemed as if we were in Spain and not in Moscow, and we could feel the summer heat and the tickle of wheat chaff in our throats. Look at those white shirts, how the harvesters have their sleeves rolled up, and their straw hats and scythes and the cords they wear to hold up their pants, and the sheaves of wheat. And that town in the distance, Alberto told us, you could see it as you came out of a curve, with the bell tower of the church and its nest of storks, and those blue mountains in the background, what we would have given to see them then, because we thought we would never return to Spain, and for many it was true, they never did, like poor Alberto, who is buried in Moscow. A woman friend who knows what she's talking about said I should sell those drawings, I'd get good money for them, she's always overwhelmed when she sees all the stuff I have. "Before long you won't be able to move around in here," she tells me, "get rid of it all, wipe the slate clean." But I can't part with any of it, not even that painting that drives my friend crazy, "Who in the world would think of framing the top of a cookie box?" she says, but it brings back so many memories, Red Square with its colorful onion domes and that blue the sky has on certain summer mornings, and it's in relief, I can touch the towers on the Kremlin wall, the cathedral of Saint Basil, Lenin's tomb. I had that cookie box for years, and I was so fond of it that before leaving Moscow I cut off the cover and framed it.

IN MOSCOW I REMEMBERED Madrid, and now in Madrid I remember Moscow, what can I do? If I carry Spain in my heart, the Soviet Union is my country too, why wouldn't it be when you consider that I lived there more than fifty years, and it hurts me when people say bad things about it, when I turn on the television and see what is happening there, and read what my son tells me in his letters, which are much cheaper than phone calls. Every day I get up early, even though I have nothing to do, and I spend hours cleaning and setting my house in order. It's small and if you're not careful everything gets cluttered and covered with dust, then I think how lucky I am to be here, with my central heat and hot water, my refrigerator and television, my rug in the bedroom so my feet don't get cold when I get up in the wintertime. My brother and parents never had a chance to enjoy any of these comforts, and it turns out that the silly one among us—why should I deny it, I'm the one who had the least to offer—is the one who gets everything. I sit here in the afternoons and sometimes don't turn on the TV, don't even turn on the light when it gets dark, and there are hours and hours of silence, of not doing anything, unlike my mother, who always had some work in her lap. I sit with my hands folded, listening to the cars on the expressway, and I remember, it isn't as if I do it on purpose, the memories come and link together like a chain, like the beads of the rosary in my fingers when I was little and I went to catechism without telling my parents. I see people's faces, hear their voices as it grows dark, and they walk in that door and sit down here beside me, and I hear music too, the Internationale that a band made up of the Party faithful played in our mining town, Chopin's funeral march on the day of Stalin's funeral, and another march I liked a lot, one they always played in Moscow on May Day. It seems I'm walking down the street and hearing it, the triumphal march from *Aida*, and my eyes fill with tears, it must be that I've turned as sentimental as the Russians. But the music I like best of all is *Scheherazade*, that's what played when I opened the little mother-of-pearl box my father brought me when he came home from his first trip to Russia, when I didn't dare look up at him because I hadn't seen him for five or six months and he was like a stranger to me, he even had a black mustache. I kept the box beneath my pillow and would open it very slowly, and the music would begin, and I would close it fast, because I was afraid it would wear out if I let it play too long, like those perfumes that evaporate if you leave the bottle open. Somehow I lost my music box, who knows in what move. But things last longer than people, and someone must still have the box, like those antiques that sit in the flea market for a long time and then are sold, and when that person opens it, she will hear *Scheherazade* and wonder whom it belonged to.

america

I WOULD WAIT IN MY ROOM with the lights off until the bells in the tower of El Salvador Church struck midnight. Cautious, though I hadn't gone outside yet, cloaked so no one could recognize me on the street, although at that hour and on those raw winter nights there weren't many people venturing out to face the wind or rain that beat down on the large open plaza. I would walk across swathed in my cape, which was very heavy and warmer than an overcoat, with a cap pulled down over my eyes and a muffler covering half my face. You have never known winters like those, or nights so dark. There were weak lightbulbs on some corners, and metal-shaded lights strung from cables over the plaza, which shook with the wind so that the light and shadows moved as they do when you walk through a room carrying a candle. On windy nights, the plaza seemed to toss like a ship in a storm. Night was a different world. There were not many radios then, and it was rare to find electric lights in every room of a house. You took a few steps away from the brazier and the light and were immediately in cold and darkness. We would pass the lightbulb and cord from one room to another through an open hole in a corner of the wall. But the current frequently cut off, the bulb would begin to glow yellow, like a candle guttering, and soon we'd be in the dark. The children had a little song for those occasions:

> *Let there be light*
> *so we can be fed.*
> *We'll have a nice salad,*
> *fried eggs and fresh bread.*

When the current failed you had to light a candle or oil lamp to go to bed, feeling your way upstairs to a bedroom so icy that when you crawled in between the sheets, your feet never got warm all night. How you would yearn to press yourself against the warmth of a naked woman! Day was day and night was night, not like now, when the two get confused, as so many things get confused, at least for us, who are too old to adapt to these times. The long winters and endless nights, black as the inside of a wolf's mouth in the alleyways I slinked down after I left the house, going out of my way to avoid Calle Real, where someone might recognize me, just after the clock in the plaza struck twelve, and then the bronze bells of El Salvador, always a little slow, a deeper tone in their tall belfry with the narrow windows making the tower look more like that of a castle than of a church. The minute I heard the first peal, my heart would lurch in my chest. Alone and in the dark, I waited in my room so no one would suspect me, listening to the ticking of the clock, which was so loud it often made me open my eyes in the middle of the night, thinking I heard footsteps. But the thudding of my heart was louder than the clock, and I was so impatient I would start walking in circles around the room, quietly so no one in the room below would hear my footsteps. I would sit on the bed, wrapped in my cape and wearing my cap yet feeling the cold rising from my feet, waiting for the hour to come, for the bells to ring, just as she had told me, rather, ordered me: not one minute before midnight, and not down the main street but through the alleyways, because no precaution could be too great. One or two hours before I was ready, waiting, dying to see her, already as hard and stiff as the bolt on a gate, and from being hard so long I was almost in pain; it seems impossible today, the vigor you had when you were young. "If you love me," she would say, "don't be early, and don't let anyone see you." The first peal of the bells was like a magnet pulling me, and I couldn't resist, I would leave my room and slip down the stairs without lighting the candle, feeling along the walls, careful not to wake anyone, and draw back the bolt. How strange it is that everything that was normal for us has disappeared, big iron bolts and door knockers, house keys so enormous that when I was a boy I imagined they were Saint Peter's Keys to the Kingdom.

SNEAKING THROUGH THE narrow streets, I would come out on the vast dark plaza of Santa María, a solitary figure trying to pass unnoticed along the walls, stopping on the corner of the Ayuntamiento, the government palace, the only inhabitant of the city awake at that hour—almost the only one, because across the plaza, in one of those colossal and somber buildings that at night was reminiscent of a fantastic engraving or opera set, someone else had been counting the minutes and the sound of the bells: every night, after twelve, she slipped back the bolt on a little side door and three times lit and extinguished an oil lantern in the highest window of the tower. That was the signal her lover waited for to cross the plaza and push open the door—the hinges carefully oiled—and then secure it from inside without making a sound.

He climbs slowly: no light, not even a cigarette lighter or a match, count three landings and forty-five steps, on the third landing there will be a large window to the left and a door on the right, knock softly three times so I will know it's you, push it open and I will be waiting for you.

So many memories have been erased, so many itineraries, obligations, and words forgotten, but from time to time a precise voice comes to him, superimposed on the voices of a present in which he often does not know where he is, as if he suffered not so much from amnesia as from sleepwalking, awaking suddenly not in a plaza in his beloved town but in the heart of Madrid, dressed in clothing he is slow to recognize as his, a visitor in an aged, leaden body that can't be his.

"Ave María Purísima," the voices say to him, and he answers, "Conceiving without sin."

He heard two voices, with the sound of the glass door opening, but he didn't look up immediately or interrupt his work, accustomed to this same apparition nearly every morning, to the differences in the two voices and the two accents, as much a contrast as between the figures they belonged to, though seen from a distance the figures seemed identical: two nuns in the same habit, brown robe and black wimple, one taller and younger than the other, both wearing sandals that must have left their feet freezing, feet as white as their hands and faces. One face was translucent, the other dead and muddy, one voice clear, with an accent of the north, the other hoarse, as if from bronchitis, with a rough country intonation. One of the nuns pushed open the door with the badly fitting glass panes, and he didn't have to look up to know immediately what expression he would see on each face: friendly supplication, ill-humored demand. Both stood before his cobbler's bench, asking almost every day for a donation to the poor, a pair of old shoes he couldn't use anymore, a few centimos for altar candles or to buy medicine for an ailing mother. So different, yet identical as they came toward you from the end of Calle Real any morning that winter, a deserted morning, because the olive harvest had begun and half the city was in the country picking the crop, so the street became busy only as dusk fell.

Ave María Purísima.

He acted as if he were irritated by their persistence, but if he was smoking when they entered, he took the cigarette from his lips and quickly extinguished it against the end of the bench, then stuck it over his ear, because you didn't waste a shred of tobacco in those days. He would nod vaguely, or get to his feet before replying, in a mocking tone of resignation, "Conceiving without sin."

Today he is an old man but still impressive, though lately a little strange in the head, but when he was thirty he was so tall you couldn't miss him, and he always joked with the women patrons who brought him their shoes to be mended, jokes that often went too far, although he was so witty he got away with it. After all, he was the director of one of the Holy Week crews, and he marched carrying a candle in the Corpus Christi procession, and his clientele included priests from nearby churches and even officers from the headquarters of the Guardia Civil, which at that time was on a small plaza down a side street. But he conquered the women without saying a word, and you'd be amazed to know how many ladies of good reputation, who took Communion every day, crossed the line, using the subterfuge that he was bringing them a pair of recently mended shoes—at an hour when the husband was at work and the children in school—and sometimes, I know this because he told me himself, he had them step into the room behind the shop, which was even smaller than the cubby where he worked, and there, in a fit of lechery, he lifted their skirts and gave them the benefit of his attentions. Women then were much more passionate, he says, or used to say, because nowadays he doesn't tell many tales, not the way he used to, when as soon as I brought up the subject he would start and there would be no stopping him, and it was fun to walk down the street with him, because he spoke loudly and looked all the women over with a fierceness he doesn't have now and really isn't appropriate for a man of his years anyway. "Look," he'd say, "don't miss that, what an ass, what a pair of tits that woman has, the way she walks." He went to confession and was given huge penances, so that almost every year he walked barefoot in the procession and sometimes carried a heavy cross, and no one knew the reason except his confessor, Don Diego, I'm sure you remember the red-faced man who was the parish priest at Santa María. Every once in a while Don Diego threatened to deny him absolution. "You can do your penance, Mateo, but if you don't mend your ways the sacrament will not cleanse you of your sins." The thing is that deep in his heart he didn't believe that the Sixth Commandment was as serious as the other nine, especially if it was broken with discretion and with the full enjoyment of both parties involved and without scandal or harm to a third party, and in addition you were spared the degradation and lack of hygiene that went with dealing with whores, a very widespread habit when there were still legal houses, places Mateo boasted about avoiding. "How could I enjoy having a woman who was only with me because I paid her?"

That was the year of the new float for the Last Supper, when that sculptor who owed our friend so much money repaid Mateo by portraying him as Saint Matthew. "Look, Sister," said the older nun, "this cobbler has the same face as the Apostle, but what he doesn't have is his saintliness." "We are made of clay, Mother, sinners all though good Christians, and we can't all devote ourselves as exclusively to divine worship as you good sisters. Didn't Christ say that in the home of Martha and Mary? And didn't Saint Teresa say that our Lord also walked among the prostitutes? Well, maybe he also walks here among my old shoes and half soles." "More works of charity and fewer words, cobbler, for faith without good works is a dead faith, and furthermore, only pagans have such a passion for the bulls. Fewer posters of bullfights and more prints of saints."

The other nun, the young one, didn't say anything, she would stand looking at him as if she were thinking of something else, or cast a sideways glance at the older one. Gradually, on those winter mornings when there was so little work, he began to take more careful note of her, to distinguish between her and the other one, as well as between her and the abstract figure of a nun, surprising expressions so fleeting they seemed not to have been there, quick flashes of, perhaps, disgust or boredom, the way the girl sometimes rubs her hands together or bites her lower lip in a burst of impatience that has nothing nunlike about it, that doesn't go with the habit or the crude sandals or the sweet, devout tone he nearly always heard in her voice, in the few things she said, scarcely more than "Ave María Purísima" or "God will reward you." At first he thought the young nun always behaved like a meek subordinate of the older one, the second part in a churchly duet, but as the days went by he perceived discord, an anger revealed only in the quick flash in her pupils, anger at having to trail after an old woman weighed down with ailments and tedious manias, at having to control the natural rhythm of her step to adapt to the older woman's slow pace as every morning they climbed the hill from the bottom of Calle Real, dark silhouettes in a nearly deserted city, the younger woman sometimes lifting her head with an elegance that was perhaps involuntary, or perhaps secretly aggressive, and the old and bent zealot, her face as wrinkled as her mantle, her hands dry, and her toes as gnarled as grape vines in her penitential sandals.

They stopped at every shop as they made their way up the street, shops that have nearly all disappeared now, the candy store, the ironmonger's, the toy and watch shops, the tailor's, the pharmacy, Pepe Morillo's barber shop—the same irritating routine every morning, the sound of the glass doors opening and the tinkling little bell. Sister Barranco was the older one, Sister María del Gólgota the young one, what names! He doesn't remember much of it now, but when I'm with him at his home and his wife can't hear, I say, "Sister María del Gólgota," and he smiles a half smile, as if remembering very well but after all these years still not wanting the secret to be known. Some mornings, if their visit was a little behind schedule, he would go to the door in his leather apron with a cigarette in his mouth and wait until he saw them at the bottom of the street, after they turned the corner from Plaza de los Caídos, and then he would stub out his cigarette and swing the door back and forth to clear away the smoke and tobacco odor, and he would turn off the radio, on which all he listened to were quiz shows, programs about bullfights, or popular poetry. How strange, he thought, not to have noticed until now, to have seen nothing but a nun's face, white and round like any other. Now he realized that the girl had large slanting eyes and long fingers, and hands that were always raw from washing in cold water, but also were very delicate. Her face, even framed by a toque, did not have the rather crude roundness nuns' faces often have, it was a strong face that reminded him a little of Imperio Argentina—as a youth he spent all his time in the Cinema Ideal just across the street from his shoe-repair shop, and when it came to movies he loved the same thing as in real life: women, the bare-legged dancers in the musicals, the actresses who played Jane in the Tarzan movies and wore those short little leather skirts, but especially, more than any of the others, the bathing girls in the Technicolor films of Esther Williams, Esther Williams herself being the greatest of all.

The younger nun, Sister María del Gólgota, had a chin like Imperio Argentina's, and despite her robes it was possible to get an idea of what her body was like, not her bosom, of course, which was starchily concealed, but a knee, or the hint of a hip or thigh, as she walked up the street into a strong breeze, or the line of a heel and an ankle that promised a naked extent of milk-white legs within the dark cave of her habit.

"Ave María Purísima."

"Conceiving without sin."

He answered without looking up from what he was doing, lest Sister Barranco, who always wore such a suspicious expression, discovered an excess of interest in his eyes, and also to postpone the pleasure of seeing the younger nun's face and trying to coax a little friendliness or complicity from her sidelong glances. He tells me, or used to tell me until recently, that one of his rules is to seek out women who aren't beautiful, because beautiful women don't give themselves completely in bed, they don't make anywhere near the effort as one who is a little homely and must compensate for it in other ways. No beautiful screen stars, no models. "If the woman under you is ugly, no problem, just turn out the light or don't look at her face," the reprobate liked to say. "The results are incomparable, and there's much less competition." The narrator of this tale roars with laughter in the bar, orders new drinks and fried octopus and fish, takes a great swallow of beer, smacks his lips, and continues the story, so flattered by everyone's attention that he doesn't notice how loud his voice is.

The nun really pleased him, her beauty notwithstanding. He liked her so much that he began imagining things, and feared he would make a false step and do something stupid. "She stood there looking at me as if she wanted to tell me something, and gestured at the old woman as if saying, if I could get away from her . . . but after they left I wasn't sure whether I'd seen it or imagined it, and the next day they came again, Ave María Purísima, Conceiving without sin, and though I looked carefully, I couldn't see that Sister María del Gólgota was making any sign. She just stared at a poster for a bullfight while Sister Barranco collected my coins for the day and said, as they left, 'God will reward you,' and it was as if all that time she was a nun like any other nun. Maybe I was delirious from being alone so many hours, not talking with anyone and doing nothing but repairing toes and cutting half soles, surrounded by old shoes, which are the saddest things in the world because they always made me think of dead people, especially that time of year, in winter, when everyone is off to the olive harvest and I could spend the whole day without seeing a soul. During the war, when I was a little boy, I saw a lot of dead people's shoes. They would shoot someone and leave him lying in a ditch or behind the cemetery, and we kids would go look at the corpses, and I noticed how many had lost their shoes, or I'd find a pair of shoes, or a single shoe, and not know which dead man they belonged to. Once in a newsreel I saw mountains of old shoes in those camps they had in Germany."

"MAY I HAVE a little water?"

The young nun was paler than usual that morning, her face dull, the rims of her eyelids red, and there were circles under her eyes, as if from sleepless nights. Under the scowling gaze of Sister Barranco, he led her to the narrow, shadowy corridor behind his shop, where the washroom and water jar were, one of those old brightly colored glazed jugs in the form of a rooster with red comb and yellow chest. It seemed improper for a nun to drink from her cupped hands, so he looked for a clean glass. Her hands trembled a little as they took the glass, and he watched her beautiful pale lips, a thread of water trickling down her strong chin. Her hands were shaking now, and when he tried to catch the glass before she dropped it, his hands touched hers, and he could feel how hot they were. He pressed them and was close enough to smell her fevered breath and feel the carnal mass of a body weakened by discipline and fasting, by the merciless cold of the cells and refectory and corridors of that convent that was so old it was practically in ruins. "Then," he said, "I lost my head completely and not even I believed what I was doing, I took her by the waist and drew her to me, I groped for her thighs and ass beneath the habit, and kissed her on the mouth, though she tried to turn away. I thought, she'll scream, the other nun will run in and make a royal scene; I could almost see the people coming out of the nearby shops, but I didn't care, or else I couldn't help what I was doing, drawn to her lips and feeling how hot her face was, her whole body. I expected her to scream, but she didn't, she didn't even resist, in fact she fell into my arms as I felt her all over, felt the body I had so often imagined. Then I saw she had closed her eyes, the way women do in the movies when a kiss is coming but is cut by the censor. But no, it wasn't an amorous trance, she had fainted, and I tried to hold her but couldn't, her eyes rolled back in her head, and she fell to the floor."

How terrified he was to see her lying there, pale as death, her eyelids half closed, as if he'd killed her with the profanation of his advance. He couldn't remember whether he shouted for the other nun or whether she came into the room behind the shop because she was worried about how long the girl had been gone or because she'd heard the thud of her fall. When they managed to revive her, the young nun was paler than ever, and if he spoke to her, she looked at him with an empty face, as if not remembering anything that had happened. She smiled weakly and thanked him for his help as she started back to the convent, leaning upon the strong, stout Sister Barranco, and once again he was unsure about what had happened in those few instants behind the shoe repair shop. Perhaps she was too.

Days went by, and neither of the two nuns appeared. Possibly Sister Barranco suspected something and wouldn't let Sister María del Gólgota leave the convent, to say nothing of going anywhere near the cobbler's door. Or possibly the young nun was very ill and Sister Barranco didn't leave her side, or she had even died of her fever. But if she were dead, it would be known in the city, the slow, widely spaced tolling of the bells for the dead would be heard. Then one day, at midmorning, he locked his glass door and left to wander around the plaza of Santa María, though not too near the convent doors, which opened from time to time to let a nun pass through who always, for a few seconds, was the figure of Sister María del Gólgota, or maybe Sister Barranco glowering at him for his irreverent behavior.

HE DIDN'T ABANDON his other activities, of course, you know how he was. He attended the meetings of the board of the Last Supper crew and of the Corpus Christi Society, which was dedicated to providing medical assistance and modest subsidies to farmers and artisans in those days before social security. Neither did he desert the wife of a second lieutenant who always sent him word as soon as her husband went off on maneuvers. But in the meetings he was more distracted than usual, and his Madame Lieutenant, as he called her, found him cool and asked if he had another woman, threatening in a fit of spite to tell everything to the lieutenant or steal his pistol and do something horrible. "You remember what I told you about beautiful women? They ruin you, make you critical of other women, the way we get used to wheat bread and white potatoes and are no longer satisfied with black bread and yams, and the carobs we ate so greedily during the lean years turn our stomach. After I became infatuated with the nun, so beautiful and young, my Madame Lieutenant began to look old and fat to me, no matter how hot and grateful she was in bed, or how much *café con leche* and buttered toast she brought me afterward. Since the lieutenant was in the quartermaster corps, there was plenty of food in that house. Sometimes when I was leaving, my Madame Lieutenant would give me a dozen eggs or a whole tin of condensed milk. 'Take this,' she'd say, 'to build up your strength.'"

Rounds of foaming beer, waiters' voices, the smell of frying oil, the snorting of the coffee machine, the tinny tunes from the jukebox and cigarette machine. Our storyteller has a somewhat childish face, jovial and very round, but he is bald and wears a suit, like a lawyer or notary, with a small insignia in the button-hole of the jacket and a silver tiepin on which you can make out a tiny figure of the Virgin. He interrupts himself to accept with mock reverence the large plate of steaming sausage the waiter has just set on the bar, and with food crammed in his mouth recites:

Morcilla, blessed lady,
worthy of our veneration.

He drinks some beer and then wipes his mouth where a black sliver of sausage has lodged between his teeth. He lowers his voice: "Imagine you're in that vast Plaza de Santa María," he says, stretching his arms wide, satisfied at having chosen the adjective *vast,* which corresponds to the gesture, evoking the blackness of a broad space surrounded by spectral churches and palaces, in an-other world and another time. One night, when he was in bed after returning from the home of his Madame Lieutenant, after, as he put it, having performed his chores, he lay in the dark lis-tening to the ticking of an alarm clock that was louder than a pendulum clock. He never lost sleep over anything, but he real-ized that night he wasn't going to sleep. He got dressed, put on his cape, muffler, and cap, went outside, and slunk through nar-row streets as if hiding from someone. About midnight, in thick fog, he ended up at the plaza where the only light came from one or two lamps on the street corners, so faint they were nothing but splotches of light glowing like the phosphorus on the hands and numbers of his clock. He could see the dark outlines of buildings, towers, statue-lined eaves, bell towers, the Santa María and El Salvador Churches, the lion sculptures in front of the city hall, and the forbidding, massive facade of the Convent of Santa Clara, which he didn't dare approach, not even at that hour.

A light went on in the highest window of the tower. Now that the fog was lifting, things were more visible but still veiled. He no-ticed, with a stab of fear, a motionless figure that appeared to be looking at him. "At that distance, and in the state I was in, I couldn't recognize a face, yet I was sure it was the young nun, Sister María del Gólgota, who had come to the tower to see me, and she was turning the light on and off to let me know she knew it was me." The light went out and did not come on again, but he stood there looking up, alone in the deserted plaza, with no notion of time or cold, unsure of what he had seen, wondering if he was dreaming. He stood waiting a long while, so still that the sound of the slow, echoing bells striking two sent a shiver down his spine.

THE NEXT MORNING he puzzled over his nocturnal outing, a confused mixture of fantasy and certainty. He had definitely seen a light go on and off, and a figure in a nun's toque, but it might not have been Sister María del Gólgota, though he seemed to remember her features in every detail, down to the yellow glow of the lamplight on her skin. And her lips were painted a bright red, the rough, fever-hot lips he had kissed, but that must have been a hallucination.

"Ave María Purísima."

He was so lost in his work and his thoughts that he hadn't heard the glass door open, and when he looked up he saw before him the very person that had occupied his imagination for so many days. Sister María del Gólgota was taller, slimmer, whiter, not quite as young—perhaps because she did not have the contrast of Sister Barranco beside her—but she was also, above all else, a real woman, not a nun, with a woman's eyes, and in her throaty voice there was no trace of the religious sweetness of her former visits. She was a woman trapped in robes and mantles from another century, and her gaze, for a moment, held a frankness he wasn't used to in his dealings with women, not even those who yielded to him most brazenly. He did nothing, he didn't even make the respectful move to stand up, didn't take the cigarette from his lips or put down the awl and old shoe he had in his hands. He simply heard himself replying, as he did every day, "Conceiving without sin."

She made a gesture of impatience, looked toward the street, stepped forward and said a few words to him, then stepped back, and as he started to ask her to repeat what she'd said, the door opened and the bent and dedicated Sister Barranco appeared, muttering complaints and prayers, brusquely demanding the overdue alms, scolding him for smoking and for cherishing bulls more than novenas and also chastising Sister María del Gólgota because she hadn't waited for her, why only yesterday she'd been in the infirmary with a high fever and today you should see her, so valiant though the doctor never learned what ailed her, cured by special dispensation of our Most Blessed Virgin she was. As he listened to Sister Barranco, Mateo thought back and was able to review the words the young nun had spoken to him so quickly and quietly, hardly daring to believe that he'd heard what he heard, that it was not the fabrication of an inflamed imagination. "Just after twelve, wait until you see me turn a light on and off three times in the highest window, then push the small door around the corner, come up three flights, and on the third landing you will find a large window to the left and a door to the right. Carefully push that door open, and I will be waiting for you."

AN INFLAMED IMAGINATION: as the story progresses, the narrator measures his pauses, emphasizes the expressions he likes best, savors them as he would a swallow of wine or piece of sausage. The group gathers more closely around him, foam grown warm slides down a mug of beer forgotten on the bar, like the remains of the meals that no one will finish and the waiter will not remove.

I picture it, that night, finally, a night of drama, the first of many, because there were many...I imagine him in his cape, muffler, and cap, like the bandit Luis Candelas in that song we listened to on the radio as children, do you remember?

> *Beneath the black cape*
> *of Luis Candelas*
> *my heart doesn't beat faster,*
> *it flies, it flies.*

The plaza is inky black, like the mouth of a wolf, there isn't any of the lighting that they put in later so the tourists could see, something, in my view, that robbed it of its flavor, because when the electricity came, the mystery was lost. He turns the first corner, the one by the city hall, fearful that someone might see him from a window. He sticks to the wall, and doesn't believe that what the nun promised him that morning is true, or that he will have the courage to sneak into the convent at midnight like a thief, or like Don Juan, because even if the girl is hot as a fox, he is a coward, and suddenly he is overcome with panic, he'll be discovered and accused of blasphemy, people will point at him, expel him from the Last Supper crew and the Corpus Christi Society, he may even be forced to close the business that provides him with a living, a modest one but comfortable enough in these difficult times. He'll be denied his place in the presidential box at the bullring, to which he was often invited during the corridas to act as an adviser, where, smoking an extraordinary cigar and wearing a carnation in the buttonhole of his striped suit, the one for grand occasions, he rubbed elbows with the highest authorities of the city: the mayor, the police commissioner, the commander of the Guardia Civil, the parish priest of San Isidoro— that Don Estanislao, who, you remember, was in spite of his cassock and his reputation for austerity a rabid fan of the bulls and in 1947 administered the last rites to the incomparable Manolete, right there in that damned Linares Plaza.

Overwhelmed by the danger he was walking into, he nevertheless didn't stop, didn't turn around and go back home to the safety and security of his bed. There was still time, he hadn't yet walked across the plaza, hadn't yet seen a light in the window, but prudence had no effect on his feet, and to help him on his way toward the small side door of the convent, he told himself it was all a joke of the nun's, or she was still out of her head with fever, so what did it matter if he kept walking? The door would be as tightly locked as any door in the city at that hour, especially as it was the door of a convent, with the wooden bolt shot, the way we would lock up at night during the bad times of the war, when any night they might come looking for you and take you for a little walk and leave you in a ditch with your socks and shoes thrown far from your sprawled corpse.

But the light did go on and off three times, and he did walk to the corner of the convent with trembling legs, telling himself that in spite of everything the door wouldn't open, and in fact it resisted at first, which was both a relief to his cowardice and a painful disappointment to the desire that had flowed through him when he saw the light in the window. The door, compact, low, and narrow, studded with rows of large rusted nails, slipped open silently at a second, more determined push, and when he closed it and found himself in darkness even deeper than that of the plaza that moonless night, he thought, with both terrified fatalism and raging lust, that there was no turning back now, and he climbed the three flights of steps, feeling along the walls, hearing the whispers and faint echoes wakened by his footsteps, feeling cobwebs against his face and the cold sweat from the stones against the palms of his hands. Finally, he saw a narrow window like an embrasure on his left, a strip of faint phosphorescence in the blackness. On the landing, to the right, he felt the wood of a door, and as he reached out to push it, he feared that he might have miscounted the flights he'd climbed. As he stood there like a stone, not daring to do anything, paralyzed in the shadow, his eyes began to adjust, and he could make out the jamb and panels of the door. There was a soft sound, a friction or breathing not his, the door opened, and a hand grabbed him by his cape and pulled him inside. He shuddered as a voice in his ear warned him to stoop because the ceiling was low, then as the door closed he was dragged forward and pushed onto a hard, narrow cot where he was felt, explored, clumsily relieved of his clothes, with a mixture of inexpert roughness and determination, licked, bitten, instructed, crushed by a naked body that became so entangled with his that he couldn't tell, in the daze of his excitement and the darkness, what he was touching or what was touching him. He was shaken like a rag doll, shoved against a wall that chilled and scraped his shoulder, muzzled by a sweaty hand when his breathing became too loud, tossed as if by a powerful wave, then held as he fell to the floor, and when finally he was left in peace and lay exhausted on the hard cot, he touched and smelled the liquid that wet his groin and concluded that it was blood on his fingertips, that for the first time in his life he had deflowered a woman. "Ave María Purísima," she murmured, and he, a little uneasy about the irreverence of it, replied in her ear, "Conceiving without sin."

"Tell me," she asked, "is it true that a cigarette tastes good afterward?"

"Like heaven."

"I will smoke one."

When at last he saw her face in the flare of the cigarette lighter, he didn't recognize her, because he had never seen her hair, which was chestnut, although very short and wiry, almost like her pubic hair. It was also her first cigarette, which she liked immensely despite the coughing and dizziness; it made her think of riding the merry-go-round horses when she was a little girl. "The thing about women," he said, "is that when it's over and the man wants to sleep or go home, they want to talk—to communicate, as we say today." They tried to make themselves comfortable on the cot, piled all their clothing on top of them, but it was so cold they shivered. Afraid they might be discovered, he asked to leave, but she held him captive between her legs and told him there was time for another cigarette, the bells still hadn't struck two.

She spoke in a quiet voice, so near his ear he could feel the moisture of her breath and lips, which she'd painted red for him, she said, with lipstick stolen from the perfume shop on Calle Real at a moment when neither the clerk nor Sister Barranco was watching, and she laughed at the memory. "The witch doesn't trust me, never takes her eyes off me, but I'm quicker than she is, and besides she's getting blind. She deserves it for the venom she spits every time she speaks, even when she's saying her rosary." Her talk seemed to him as improper as the delight she took in smoking, she even learned to blow smoke rings, expelling them slowly from her painted lips. "María del Gólgota, what a cross that name is, my real name is Francisca, or Fanny, which is what my father called me, may he rest in peace, he was a man who liked all things English. He wanted his little girl to learn English, play tennis, use a typewriter, drive a car, and go to the university and study something serious, not such foolishness for idle señoritas as teaching or fine arts but medicine or science. He made my brother study too, and play sports, but I was his favorite; he said that because I was a girl I needed more skills to take care of myself in the world. My mother, although she let him do it because she had a weak character, complained, 'He's trying to make a man out of her. Who will want to be the sweetheart of an engineer?' My father would say, 'I can't believe I have a wife so backward that she's against the progress of women.'"

She imitated their voices, creating a complete play in the secret darkness of her cell and murmuring into his ear: the grave, measured voice of her father, the whining voice of her mother, the voice of her brother, who had been her accomplice and hero from an early age, the croaking frog voice of Sister Barranco, and the various tones of ridicule and treachery used by the other nuns of the convent. "I know they hate me, want to poison me, those dizzy spells I suffer, Sister Barranco brought me warm broth but I don't trust her, 'Here, Sister, this nice broth will make you feel better, it will raise the dead.' Well feed it to your mother, you witch. I began to get better as soon as I stopped drinking her broths and potions, and she with that 'Come, Sister, let's lift that spirit of yours, look how well that tonic did I brought last night, although, of course, our prayers to the Holy Virgin were what helped most.'"

The whispering in his ear made him sleepy but also bothered him, because he might have been a little bit on the libertine side but he was still a good Catholic. That Sister María del Gólgota, or Fanny, was prettier than a fresh-baked loaf of white bread— his words—but she seemed to him too disrespectful of holy things, and his conscience hurt him more for listening and not protesting than for going to bed with her. "All that talking she did, that chatter, right up against me on the cot, which any moment could have collapsed under our weight. She told me stories about her parents and her brother, who she said was in Africa and then in Tierra del Fuego, and about how one of her aunts had her locked up in a convent and forced her to become a novice, 'For your own good, child, not for your happiness in the other world, because I know you don't believe in Him, just like your father, but so you'll have some security in this world and not end up with a shaved head and insulted in public like your poor mother, who wasn't to blame for anything, and look how she fell apart and how we had to put her away for so long.'"

She spoke feverishly, as wound up as when she'd pulled off his clothes or urged him into the painful tightness of her virginity.

She was ecstatic, sucking up a cigarette almost in one breath, pressing him between her thighs until his bones cracked, thrusting her tongue into his mouth, which he didn't like because it didn't seem a thing for a decent woman to do. She consumed kisses, his cigarettes, precious minutes, and maybe took the greatest pleasure in saying aloud all the things that for years had dizzied her in her secret thoughts and kept her in a perpetual ferment of daydream and impossible rebellion. But when the bells struck two, she made him dress with an impatience similar to that with which she had undressed him two hours earlier, put into his pocket an envelope containing all the cigarette butts and ashes to hide the evidence, took his hand and led him down the stairs, with no hesitation, and more than once it seemed she had the gift of seeing in the dark. She peered out the little side door, then gestured for him to go, and a second later he was alone in the plaza, dazed, bruised, unable to believe that he had actually sneaked into a convent at midnight and deflowered a nun.

IN HIS SHOE-REPAIR SHOP, and in Pepe Morillo's barbershop next door, men liked to boast of their conquests and their feats with whores. Mateo kept silent, and smiled inside: If you only knew. He couldn't tell his confessor about his adventure, so he suffered the uneasiness of living in mortal sin. I'm the only one he told, and that was more than forty years after the fact, when he'd been retired for some years and was living in Madrid. You should have seen the grin on his face, the two of us in the dining room of his home, surrounded by souvenirs of our hometown and prints and images of saints, and those bullfight posters. "Ah, my friend, how I've loved the bulls and the women, and what good times I've had, may God forgive me."

Before the television he's addled and forgetful, blinking, dozing, content. He'll watch a cartoon, a contest of long words, or a physician's daily advice, wrapped in a continuous flow of images and talk from films and news and South American melodramas. He'll perk up a little when he sees a beautiful woman on the screen, to whom he may say something, first checking to see that his wife isn't anywhere near, one of those compliments that as a young man he tossed to women strolling arm in arm down Calle Real on a Sunday afternoon. When I was little, the man who owned the only TV in the neighborhood would say obscene things to the female announcers and miniskirted women in the commercials. If people ask Mateo a question, he doesn't hear, or says something confused, or answers a question they haven't asked. He may burst out laughing at some program that earlier made his tears flow. You set his meal before him and he eats every bite, that's one thing that hasn't changed, he hasn't lost his appetite, but after a while he doesn't remember and asks me when we're going to eat, so he's getting fat. I tell him to go outside, to breathe a little fresh air, not to spend the whole day watching TV, but as soon as he goes out the door I'm nervous, afraid he'll get lost, as foolish as he is and as big as Madrid is nowadays, and I have to be careful that his shoes are tied and he's wearing his socks, he who was once so stylish and fussy about what he wore, even if it was only to go to the market around the corner.

He sits for hours wearing the same complacent smile, approving benevolently of everything he sees and hears, the conversations of the neighbor women and the transvestites at Sandra's kiosk, the news programs and bulletins, the shouts of the women selling fish in the market, the medical advice on the morning shows, the faces of the living dead he meets in Chueca Plaza and on the dark corners of the barrio when he goes out wearing his great overcoat and Tyrolean hat. Sometimes when I visit him, he doesn't recognize me at first. I sit down by him in the dining room, and he looks at me puzzled, trying to follow the conversation, and while he's telling me something or I'm trying to get one of his old stories out of him, his eyes wander to the TV and he forgets that there's anyone else in the room. But I have a trick that never fails: I get close to him, when his wife isn't around, and say in a low voice, "Ave María Purísima." His eyes light up, and he smiles the roguish smile he used to have when he talked to me about women, and he replies, "Conceiving without sin."

HE FELT ASHAMED every time he repeated those words, when every morning at the same hour he saw the two dark silhouettes outside the glass door, and he would put out his cigarette, stow it in the drawer, and lower his head, pretending to be absorbed in his work, tearing a worn, twisted heel off an old shoe or putting on those metal reinforcements we called heel plates in our town, routine repairs during the hard times when almost no one could afford a new pair of shoes. He would feel the double scrutiny— alarming and magnetic—of Sister Barranco and Sister María del Gólgota, Fanny in the secrecy of their blasphemous rendezvous, the dark nights and blind lust in the icy cell, and when both nuns said in unison, "Ave María Purísima," he heard in the younger woman's voice invitation, recollection, and challenge, and as he said, "Conceiving without sin," the formula he had repeated since he was a boy without ever having thought about its meaning, he would feel a strange mixture of thrill and contrition.

It was difficult for him to look up at them, and he tried not to meet the two pairs of eyes, lest a sign from Sister María del Gólgota be intercepted by the older nun, yet he also feared to miss the heartening nod that the little door would be open for him that night. He'd slept with many women, but this adventure caused him uncertainty and confusion, contained something that deeply wounded his masculine self-esteem, and disturbed the perfect simplicity of mind he'd enjoyed until now. "I wonder if you can explain this to me, you who have studied and know so many things. Why am I afraid of her? If I decide not to see her anymore, why do I leave my house before twelve and die of impatience for the light to come on in the tower? She's wonderful, that's the truth, better than a hundred loaves of bread and a hundred cheeses, and I go crazy when I think about running my hands over her body in the darkness, about the smell of her, about seeing that white flesh in the flare of the lighter or glowing ash of the cigarette."

But the one flaw she had, which he noticed the first night and only got worse, was how much she talked after the *faena,* the third pass, as he would say, using the language of the bullfight. Before it, no: from the moment he entered her cell until they were both limp, the woman only breathed, panted, and moaned. But as soon as she was satisfied, she stuck to him like a leech, like a clamp locking him between her thighs, and jabbered into his ear, shaking him angrily if she saw he was beginning to doze, and he felt the touch of her lips and the endless hiss of her voice long after he was with her, when he was on his way home after two in the morning, wrapped in his cape, or when he woke from a dream about disgrace or scandal, or when he was alone in his shoe-repair shop and stopped hearing the songs on the radio, because her voice buzzed like an insect in his ear, or like pounding blood or his heart beating, and it turned into other voices that gradually he was becoming familiar with, voices from her long-ago life and ghostly family: the father wanting his daughter to get her doctorate in science or civil engineering, the mother saying her rosary, the venomous aunt clad in mourning, who came to get Fanny and her brother at the police station on the border when they ran away to France hidden in a freight car, planning to join the Resistance against the Germans or to place themselves at the service of the Republican government in exile. They were like Santa Teresa and her brother, when they escaped from their home to the land of the Moors to convert the infidels or die as martyrs, "with the difference that we didn't have a home any longer because the Nacionales shot my father as soon as they came into our town at the end of the war, and they shaved my mother's head and tattooed a hammer and sickle on her skull and paraded her with other women who were Reds or the wives of Reds through the center of the town, and forced her and the other women to scrub the floor of the church, on their knees on the icy stones. All because they hated my father so much, who was the best and most peaceful and meticulous man in the world, even in summer he wore his suit coat, celluloid collar, and bow tie. Just because at the beginning of the war he was walking down the street dressed that way, he was almost shot by some militiamen, and in that same suit, collar, and bow tie the agitators led him to the firing squad three years later, and he told my brother, 'At least it isn't my own who're killing me.'"

Her father shot, her mother crazy, the furtive journey of days and nights toward the border in a trainload of merchandise, her brother and she sleeping on straw that reeked of manure and making wild plans to join the Resistance against Hitler and Franco, the hillsides covered with flowering almond and apple trees and the narrow streets of the town where they had spent the war years in perfect happiness while their mother prayed and their father administered a school for displaced children and kept wearing the suit and tie and hat and ankle-high boots of a meticulous Republican despite the fright the libertarian militia had given him. Then the others came, clubbed him with their rifle butts, and kicked him out of the house with its patio and grape arbor and fresh-water well where they'd lived four years almost like the Swiss Family Robinsons of that book that she and her brother loved so much. "Don't lose heart, nothing will happen to me, this is just a mistake," she spoke into Mateo's ear in her father's voice. When her brother went to take a bit of food and tobacco to the barracks where they had him locked up, what most impressed him was not going inside the pen filled with men sentenced to death but seeing his father unshaven and without the celluloid collar, filthy and in a wrinkled suit.

Yet it wasn't her father but her brother who was the hero of her tales: her comrade in childhood games and adventures among the white blossoms of the apple and almond trees, her reading partner and the instigator of their plans to run away and enlist in social revolutions, partisan armies, clandestine cells of anti-Fascist resistance, to go explore Tierra del Fuego or Patagonia or the Gobi Desert. They caught her, locked her up in a convent, and forced her to become a nun under dark and terrible threats she never explained, though she was so full of other details, but at least her brother managed to escape, and at some point in the course of all those years a letter came to her through circuitous channels. "He's living in America, I don't know whether north or south, and moves a lot and has so many business affairs he can't stay too long in any one place, he might be in Chicago or New York or Buenos Aires. He always wants to know about me, but because of the witches who kidnapped me his letters don't reach me, and I can't send anything to him, can't ask him to help me, to come save me."

"*You* help me," she whispered, and Mateo felt her lips and fevered breath on his ear, "help me escape and we'll go to America together to look for my brother. What's keeping you here, a man is free to go anywhere he wants, not like a woman, who's a prisoner even when she's not locked up in a convent. You don't have anything here, all you do is repair old shoes in that cubbyhole, smelling the old sweat people leave in their shoes, and you so young and strong, with those huge hands and that energy you have, nothing could stand in your way if you got out of here and went to America, where men go who have the courage to make the world their apple, as my brother did, and where women don't live behind closed doors or drape themselves in eternal mourning or kill themselves having babies and working in the fields and scrubbing floors on their hands and knees and washing clothes in winter in troughs of cold water with scraps of soap that tear the skin off their hands.

"Where can a woman who's fled a convent go here if she doesn't have papers or a man to defend her and stand up for her? No father, no husband, no brother, not like America where a woman is worth as much as a man, if not more. There women smoke in public, wear trousers, drive a car to their office, and divorce when it suits them. They race along the highways, which are wide and built in a straight line, not like here, and the automobiles aren't black and old but large and painted bright colors, and kitchens are shiny and white and filled with automatic appliances, so all you do is press a button and the floor is scrubbed, and there's a machine that picks up dust and one that washes your clothes and leaves them ironed and folded, and the iceboxes don't need blocks of ice, and every house has a garage and a garden, and lots of them have swimming pools. At those pools the women wear two-piece bathing suits and drink cool drinks and lounge in hammocks while their automatic machines do the housework. They drink and smoke and no one thinks they're whores, and they not only paint their fingernails, they paint their toenails too, and if they complain about their husband and divorce him, he has to pay them a salary every month until they find another husband. And if they get bored with life in one place, they climb into their big bright cars and move to another city, California or Patagonia or Las Vegas or Tierra del Fuego, what wonderful names, you just have to say them and you feel your lungs fill with air, or they go to Chicago or New York and live in skyscrapers fifty stories high, in apartments that don't need windows because the whole wall is glass, and where it's never cold or hot because they have machines they call climate control."

"But how do we go there, woman? What do we use to buy our passage on the ship?" he said, to be saying something, but she was furious at his lack of spine and scolded him in that murmur that made him want to sleep: "I have it all planned, you sell or lease your business, that will bring in something, since it's in such a good location, and I'll steal some valuable things here in the convent, a silver candelabra, a beaten gold reliquary, I can even cut a painting of the Virgin Mary out of its frame, they say it's by Murillo, so we should get several thousand pesetas for it." He turned to ice just thinking about it, a sacrilege in addition to profanation and blasphemy, not just public dishonor and excommunication but jail besides. Now he began to understand that this demented nun wanted something more from him than just sating her unholy lust, she wanted him to be an accomplice in her criminal plans, but what did he expect from the daughter of a Red who'd been taught free love and atheism?

HE COULDN'T SLEEP, was no good at work or his charitable activities and brotherhoods, he even reached the point of forgetting to listen to his poetry programs and bullfights on the radio. Now he feared not that someone would catch him as he sneaked into the convent or left it on those stormy winter nights that were so dark and deserted, but that she would drag him into her delirium, that he would lose the common sense that had guided him all his life and end up losing everything he had, the person he was, what he'd made of himself. He dreaded seeing her every morning with Sister Barranco and was nervous until she walked out the door, because the old nun was suspicious, watching both him and her companion for signs, for proof that would push them both toward catastrophe. But he was also worried if they didn't come, imagining that María del Gólgota was ill again and in the delirium of her fever divulging the secret of their meetings in her cell, or she might have escaped and was hiding and as soon as it was dark she would come looking for him, as she had threatened so many times. "All this because I broke my rule and got involved with a beautiful woman, a woman, moreover, who doesn't have a husband or anything to tie her down except those old nuns who don't know anything. A man should choose a mistress who's on the homely side, married, and knows how to maintain some decency even in adultery. And if possible she should have a solid financial base, so she won't be swept away by the romantic whim to leave everything behind and run off with you."

"What a philosopher you are, you should write down this advice so your disciples can follow it," I told him, and he laughed and motioned for me to keep my voice down and not let his wife hear. "We need your memoirs, maestro, or else tell me everything and let me be your official biographer."

It's too late now, he doesn't seem to remember, or if he does, he isn't talking. The doctors have checked his head and say he's all right, thank God, he doesn't have that illness old people get, Alzheimer's, when they can't take care of themselves and don't recognize anything. The doctor who examined his head says that he may be depressed from not doing anything and not knowing anyone in Madrid. But what kind of depression is it if he laughs at the least thing, all by himself? When he's watching TV and I'm doing something in the kitchen, I hear him laughing and come out, and he's roaring with laughter although there's nothing funny about the program, which could be one of those news reports about war and hunger.

SHE GREW ROUGHER AND more demanding in her erotic needs; in a few weeks she had acquired all the depravity other women fall into only after long years of vice. Every night she became more talkative, more monotonous in her stories about the past and her mad schemes for the future. She began to discuss the best dates for her escape, to exact promises from him with terrible threats, full of visions of the freedom and wealth waiting for them in America, where in no time she would meet her adventurer, multimillionaire brother and own a long red or yellow or blue automobile with silvery tail fins, and a house with a garden and swimming pool, and the latest mechanical devices.

One night, she did not drag him in silence to her wobbly cot the moment he arrived but pressed against him in the darkness, took his face in her hands, and in a hoarse, altered voice whispered into his ear that before he possessed her—she loved that melodramatic word—he must swear to her that within two weeks, before the end of the olive harvest, they would run away together. Hadn't he told her two or three nights before, blustering, lying his way out, that he had already half worked out a deal for his business with another cobbler? The nun's right hand, which in so short a time had become amazingly expert in sexual manipulation, was like a grappling hook or claw that clutched his crotch and slowly began to squeeze, and she murmured something that years later still made his hair stand on end and produced an erection when he thought of it: "You betray me, I'll rip this thing off."

But that night was the last time. When he awoke the next morning, he was dizzy and shivering and didn't have the strength even to crawl out of bed. He was relieved, however, that he couldn't go to work and didn't have to confront the daily visit and scrutiny of Sister Barranco and Sister María del Gólgota. By the third day his fever was worse, and he called the doctor, who diagnosed pneumonia and ordered him immediately to a hospital in Santiago. Mateo attributed his illness to divine punishment, and in his tormented half sleep he relived all the cold he had suffered during his vigils in the icy plaza and glacial cell of Sister María del Gólgota. The sins of the flesh, aggravated by blasphemy and not dressing warmly enough, had conspired to confine him to a hospital bed, and perhaps would send him to the tomb and the tortures of hell. He prayed, made fervent promises of penitence, swore he would live a holy life, walk barefoot in his procession for the next twenty years carrying a heavy wood cross on his back, subject himself to flagellation and hair shirts, maybe even become a monk and spend the rest of his days in a convent.

AFTER A MONTH HE returned to his narrow workshop and cobbler's bench, but he had the feeling that more than a month had gone by, and he remembered the days before his illness as one coolly appraises the events of a remote past. The first two or three mornings he was back, he scarcely had the strength or will to work, and he awaited the two nuns with only a flicker of desire and fear. They didn't come, however, and his next-door neighbor, the barber Pepe Morillo, told him he'd heard that Sister Barranco was very ill—the years were taking their toll—and that for some reason the other nun had been forbidden to leave the convent.

That night, wearing heavy clothes, he worked up the courage to go down to the Plaza de Santa María. The bells struck twelve, but no light came on in the window of the convent tower, and he decided, with equal measures of disappointment and relief, to go home and get in bed, and to carry out the promises he'd made during the dark days of his illness, from which he was sure he'd been delivered by the double miracle of prayer and penicillin. As he was leaving, he turned his head and saw that the light was on in the tower, and from where he stood he could see the tempting if somewhat ghostly silhouette of Sister María del Gólgota. It wasn't his will or decision to reform that triumphed over the powerful persuasion of sin: it was a shudder that shook his entire body, a hint of renewed pain in his chest, his distaste at having to take off his clothes and later dress in an icy cell. And then there was the woman's voice like an endless reel spinning wild tales in his ear as he drifted off to sleep, and the hard slats of the cot digging into his back, and he imagined the soft, warm bed waiting for him in the security of his home.

He overcame temptation that night, but as he recovered from the weakness following his return from the hospital his old instincts were awakened, and one night found him roaming around the Plaza de Santa María, so excited it was difficult to walk naturally, with a monumentally stiff dick, as he thought crudely, using our rich vernacular. He was wild that night, a Mihura bull, randy as a goat, ready for anything, to give her the ride of her life and then never come back. The light went on in the tower, and with his blood boiling and his heart leaping from his chest he hurried to the little door and pushed it less cautiously than he had other times—but it was locked, and it was all he could do not to beat on it with his fists. He walked away from the building, back to where he could see the window in the tower. The light went on again, but now that he was closer he could see, or thought he could see, that Sister María del Gólgota was smiling at him and lifting her robe and defiantly and sarcastically showing him her naked breasts, motioning to him, indicating that maybe he should try the door again.

He pushed again, but it was locked, and never opened for him again, and he never saw the light in the tower any of the nights he prowled around the plaza.

"AND HE NEVER HEARD from her again, or saw her?"

People always want to know how stories end; whether well or badly, they want the resolution to be as neat as the beginning, they want sense and symmetry. But few adventures in life tie up all the loose strings, unless fate steps in, or death, and some stories never develop, they come to nothing or are interrupted just as they are beginning. The years go by, and our friend has more bullfight and Holy Week posters on his tiny door, and when he runs out of space he pastes new ones over the old. He works his way up to the presidency of his brotherhood, is named official adviser for the bullfights, is interviewed in our provincial newspaper as one of the pillars of our modest local scene, and he pastes the clipping on a glass pane of his door so it can be seen by people passing in the street. The clipping gets yellow with age, some of the shops in the neighborhood began to close, including the barbershop next door, and the business of repairing shoes seems to have little future, because people throw away their used shoes now and buy new ones in the modern shoe stores that have opened in the more heavily populated areas of the city. But he has his savings, he has prepared for old age as prudently as he provided for the regular satisfaction of his sexual needs. Furthermore, he's decided it's time to marry, while he still has the looks to attract a mature and obliging wife who will take care of him when he really begins to lose his faculties. If he waits too long, it will be solitary decrepitude or a nursing home. He is also clear about the kind of woman that interests him, the exact profile: a widow with an acceptable income, some property—a debt-free apartment, for example—and no children. For a while he considered Madame Lieutenant, now widowed and with a solid pension and her own real estate, but she was too old for his purposes, it makes no sense to take on someone who will double the problems of age rather than offset them. Then one morning, unexpectedly, standing in line at the savings bank where he'd gone to bring his precious savings book up to date, he met the perfect woman, one who far surpassed his expectations: a teacher, spinster, nice-looking, with dyed hair and opulent bosom, and a reassuring manner as well. She had a splendid income, a substantial accumulation of bonuses, an apartment in the heart of Madrid—a family bequest—and was currently employed in a school in Móstoles. They were married within six months, and without waiting for the sale of the property where he'd had his shoe-repair shop, they set off for the capital in early September, in time for his new wife to start the school year. On September 27, the eve of our town fair, he was back, because he had to help with the San Miguel and San Francisco bullfights in his role as technical adviser to the president. A possible buyer expressed interest in his shop. He made an appointment to show it to him, on one of those cool, fresh mornings at the beginning of autumn, and it tugged a bit at his heartstrings to walk down Calle Real, as deserted at that hour as it once had been crowded with people, and to open his familiar glass door—after rolling up the metal shade that had been closed for several months. There were old papers on the floor, and a handful of mail he hadn't bothered to look through before he left, probably nothing but ads. Now, however, he went through the letters, blowing off the dust, to pass the time as he waited for the potential buyer. Among them was a brightly colored postcard of the Statue of Liberty, the American flag, and the New York skyline. On the back there was no signature or name, and except for his address he found only these words, written in the careful, rather affected hand the nuns used to teach in the Catholic schools.

Greetings from America.

you are . . .

YOU ARE NOT AN isolated person and do not have an isolated story, and neither your face nor your profession nor the other circumstances of your past or present life are cast in stone. The past shifts and reforms, and mirrors are unpredictable. Every morning you wake up thinking you are the same person you were the night before, recognizing an identical face in the mirror, but sometimes in your sleep you've been disoriented by cruel shards of sadness or ancient passions that cast a muddy, somber light on the dawn, and the face is different, changed by time, like a seashell ground by the sand and the pounding and salt of the sea. Even as you lie perfectly motionless, you are shifting, and the chemistry that constitutes your imagination and consciousness is altered infinitesimally every moment. Whole scenes and perspectives from the distant past fan out, open and close like the straight lines of olive groves or plowed furrows seen from the window of a racing train. For a few seconds, a taste or a smell or some music on the radio or the sound of a name turn you into the person you were thirty or forty years ago. You are a frightened child on his first day of school, or a round-faced young man with shy eyes and the shadow of a mustache on his upper lip, and when you look in the mirror you are a man over forty whose black hair is beginning to be shot with gray, whose face holds no traces of your boyhood, though a sort of unfading youth accompanies you as an adult, through work and marriage, your obligations and secret dreams and responsibility for your children. You are every one of the different people you have been, the ones you imagined you would be, the ones you never were, and the ones you hoped to become and now are thankful you didn't.

And your room is different, the city or the countryside you see from the window, the house you live in, the street where you walk, all of it growing more distant, disappearing as quickly as it's seen through the glass, there one moment, gone forever. Cities where it seemed you would live forever but left, never to return, cities where you spent a few days only to preserve them in memory like a clutter of old postcards in bitter colors. Or cities that are little more than their beautiful names, divested of substance by the passing of time: Tangiers, Copenhagen, Hamburg, Washington, DC, Baltimore, Göttingen, Montevideo. You are who you were when you walked through them, sinking into the anonymity they offered you.

PERHAPS WHAT CHANGES LEAST, through so many places and times, is the room you take refuge in, the room that according to Pascal one should never leave if one is to avoid disaster. "Being alone in a room is perhaps a necessary condition of life," Franz Kafka wrote Milena. There is a computer in it instead of a typewriter, but my room today is much like any of the many rooms I've lived in throughout my life, my lives, like the first one I had when I was sixteen, with a wood table and a balcony that overlooked the valley of the Guadalquivir and the blue horizon of the Mágina Sierra. I would lock myself in to be alone with my typewriter, my records, my notebooks, my books, feeling both isolated and protected. The balcony allowed me to look out upon the vastness of the world, the world I wanted to run to as soon as I could, because my refuge, like almost all refuges, was also a prison, and the only window I wanted to look through was the one on the night train that would carry me far away.

Laura García Lorca, who was born in New York and spoke a careful and proper Spanish that sometimes had a trace of English, showed me her Uncle Federico's room in Granada, in Huerta de San Vicente, the last he had, the room he would leave one July day in 1936, looking for a refuge he wouldn't find. All human miseries derive from not being able to sit quietly in a room alone. I saw Lorca's room, and I wanted to live sometime in a room like that. The white walls, the floor of large flat stones like the ones in my boyhood home, the wood table, the austere but comfortable bed of white-painted iron, the large balcony open to the Vega, to the sweep of groves dotted with white houses, to the bluish or mauve silhouette of the sierra with its snowy peaks tinted rose in the sunset. I remember van Gogh's room in Arles, just as sheltering and austere, but with its beautiful geometry already twisted by anguish, the room that opened onto a landscape as meridional as the Vega of Granada and that contained only the bare necessities of life, yet it, too, failed to save the man who took refuge there from horror.

I wonder what the room in Amsterdam was like where Baruch Spinoza, a descendant of Jews expelled from Spain and later Portugal, he himself expelled from the Jewish community, edited his lucid philosophical treatises and polished the lenses from which he earned a livelihood. I imagine it with a window that lets in a clear gray light like that in the paintings of Vermeer, whose rooms warmly protect their self-absorbed inhabitants from inclement weather but always contain reminders of the expanse of the outside world: a map of the Indies or Asia, a letter from a distant spot, pearls found in the Indian Ocean. One Vermeer woman reads a letter, another gazes seriously and absently at the light falling through the window, and perhaps she is waiting for a letter. Closed in his room, perhaps the only place he is not stateless, Spinoza shapes the curve of a lens that will allow him to see things so small they cannot be seen by the naked eye. With no aid other than his intelligence he wants to encompass the order and substance of the universe, the laws of nature and human morality, the rigorous mystery of a God that is not that of his elders, who have disavowed him and excommunicated him from the congregation, but neither is it the God of the Christians, who might well burn him at the stake if he lived in a country less tolerant than Holland. In a letter to Milena, Kafka forgets for a moment whom he's addressing and writes to himself: *You are, after all, completely Jewish, and you know what fear is.*

Then Primo Levi in his bourgeois apartment in Turin comes to mind, the house where he was born and died, throwing himself, or accidentally falling, into the stairwell. He lived there all his life except for the two years between 1943 and 1945. Before September of 1943, when he was arrested by the Fascist militia, Levi had left his safe room in Turin to join the Resistance, carrying with him a small pistol he scarcely knew how to use and in fact never fired. He had been a good student, earning a degree in chemistry with excellent grades, profiting from what he learned in the laboratories and lecture halls, as well as from literature, which for him always had the obligation to be as clear and precise as science. A young man, slim, studious, with glasses, educated in a renowned bourgeois family in a cultured city, hardworking, austere, accustomed from childhood to a serene life, in harmony with the world, without the least shadow of the difference that would separate him from others, since in Italy, and even more in Turin, a Jew, in the eyes of society and his own, was a citizen like any other, especially if he came from a secular family that didn't speak Hebrew or follow religious practices. His ancestors had emigrated from Spain in 1492. He left the room in which he had been born, and as he walked out the door he was probably struck by the thought that he might not come back, and when he did come back two years later, thin as a ghost, having survived hell, he must have felt that in truth he was dead, a ghost returning to an untouched house, the same door, his room in which nothing had changed during his absence, in which there would have been no change had he died, had he not been spared the cadavers' mudpit in the concentration camp.

"WHAT IS THE MINIMAL portion of country, what dose of roots or hearth, that a human being requires?" Jean Améry asked himself, remembering his flight from Austria in 1938, perhaps the night of March 15, on the express train that left Vienna at 11:15 for Prague, his troubled, clandestine journey across European borders toward the provisional refuge of Antwerp, where he knew the endless insecurity of exiled Jews, the native's hostility toward foreigners, humiliation from the police and officials who examine papers and certify or deny permits and make you come back the next day and the next and who look at the refugee as someone suspected of a crime. The worst is to be stripped of the nationality you thought was yours inalienably. You need at least a house in which you can feel safe, Améry says, a room that you can't be dragged from in the middle of the night, that you don't have to run from as fast as you can when you hear police whistles and footsteps on the stairs.

YOU HAVE ALWAYS LIVED in the same house and the same room and walked the same streets to your office, where you work from eight to three Monday through Friday, yet you are also constantly running and can't find asylum anywhere. You cross borders at night along smugglers' routes, travel with false papers on a train, and stay awake while the other passengers snore at your side. You fear that the footsteps coming down the corridor toward you are those of a policeman. At the border, uniformed men who study your papers may motion you to one side, and then the other travelers, who have their passports in order and are not afraid, look at you with relief, because the misfortune that has befallen you has left them unscathed, and they begin to see in your face signs of guilt, of crime, a mark that cannot be seen and yet cannot be erased, an indelible stain that is not in your appearance but is in your blood, the blood of a Jew or of a sick man who knows he will be driven out if his condition is discovered. Confined in a sanatorium for tuberculosis, Kafka remembers the anti-Semitic remarks another patient made at the dining table, and writes a letter sharpened by insomnia and fever: *The insecure situation of the Jews explains perfectly why they believe that they are permitted to possess only what they can cling to with their hands or teeth, and that only such possession gives them the right to live.*

In the room of a hotel in Port-Bou, Walter Benjamin took his own life because there was no road left to take as he fled from the Germans. Two identities were offered to Jean Améry when he was stopped by the Gestapo, when he was interrogated and then tortured by the SS: enemy or victim. He could be a German, an army deserter, in which case he would be tried and shot as a traitor, or he could be a Jew, in which case he would be sent to a death camp. He was arrested in May 1943, in Brussels, where under the name of Hans Mayer he and his small group of German-speaking resisters printed leaflets and distributed them at night near the barracks of the Wehrmacht, risking their lives on the futile hope that the conscience of some German soldier would be moved by reading them. Primo Levi armed himself only a few months later with the small pistol he didn't know how to use, no more a threat to the Third Reich than Améry's leaflets. Neither man was a practicing Jew; Levi thought of himself as Italian, Améry as nothing but Austrian. But when arrested, both declared themselves Jews and joined the ranks of victims condemned not by their acts or their words, not for distributing pamphlets or plunging into the forest without warm clothes or boots and with no weapon but a ridiculous little pistol, but for the simple fact of having been born.

You are the person who after the morning of September 19, 1941, must go outside wearing a Star of David on your chest, visibly displayed, printed in black on a yellow rectangle, like the Jews in medieval cities, but now with all kinds of regulations regarding size and placement, explained in detail in the decree, which also lists the punishments awaiting the person who does not wear the star when he goes out or tries to obscure it by covering it, for example, with a briefcase or shopping bag or even with an arm holding an umbrella. In the Warsaw Ghetto, the star was blue, the armband white.

YOU ARE ANYONE AND NO ONE, the person you invent or remember and the person others invent or remember, those who knew you in the past, in another city and another life, and retain a frozen image of what you were then, like a forgotten photograph that surprises and repels when you see it years later. You are the person who imagined futures that now seem puerile, the person so much in love with women you can't remember now, and the person you sometimes were whom no one knew. You are what others, right now, somewhere, are saying about you, and what someone who never met you is telling of what he has been told. You change your room, your city, your life, but shadows and doubles of you continue to inhabit the places you left behind. As a boy you ran along the street imagining you were galloping your pony, and you were both the rider spurring on your mount with film-cowboy yells and the galloping horse, and also the boy who saw that horse and rider in a movie, and the one who the next day excitedly told about the movie to friends who didn't see it, and you are the boy who with shining eyes listens to another tell stories, the boy who asks for just one more story so his mother won't leave and turn out the light, the mother who finishes telling the story to her son and sees in his eyes all the nervous enthusiasm of imagination, the desire to hear more, to prevent the loving voice from falling silent or the room from turning dark, when it will be invaded by dark fears.

You change your life, room, face, city, love, but something persists that has been inside you for as long as you can remember, before you learned to reason, it is the marrow of what you are, of what has never been extinguished, like a live coal hidden beneath the ashes of last night's fire. You are uprootedness and foreignness, not being completely in any one place, not sharing the certainty of belonging that seems so natural and easy in others, taking it for granted like the firm ground beneath their feet. You are the guest who may not have been invited, the tenant who may be ejected, the little fat kid among the bullies in the schoolyard, the one flat-footed soldier in the garrison, the effeminate man among the macho, the model student who is dying inside of loneliness and embarrassment, the husband who looks at women out of the corner of his eye as he strolls arm in arm with his wife on a Sunday afternoon in his provincial city, the temporary employee who never is given a contract, the black Moroccan who leaps from a smuggler's boat onto a beach in Cádiz and moves inland by night, soaked to the bone, freezing, dodging the spotlights of the Guardia Civil. You are the Spanish Republican who crosses the French border in February 1939 and is treated like a dog or someone with the plague and sent to a camp on a rugged seacoast, imprisoned in a sinister geometry of barracks and barbed wire, the natural geometry and geography of Europe during those years—from the infamous beaches of Argelès-sur-Mer, where Spanish Republicans are herded like cattle, to the farthest reaches of Siberia, from which Margarete

Buber-Neumann returned only to be sent not to freedom but to the German camp of Ravensbrück.

YOU DON'T KNOW WHO you would be if you found yourself expelled from your home and country; arrested by a patrol of the Gestapo as you distribute leaflets one dawn in a street in Brussels and are hanged from a hook, held by handcuffs behind your back so that as the chain goes up and your feet lift from the ground, you hear the sound of your shoulder joints as they are dislocated; locked in a cattle car in which you spend five whole days traveling with forty-five other people, and night and day you hear the crying of a nursing baby whose mother cannot feed it, and you lick the ice that forms in the cracks between the planks of the car because in those five days and nights there is no food or water for you, and when finally the door is opened on an icy night, you see the light reflecting the name of a station you never heard of before: Auschwitz. "No one knows whether he will be cowardly or brave when his time comes," my friend José Luis Pinillos told me. In a remote life, when he was a youth of twenty-two, he fought in a German uniform on the Leningrad front; when you see the enemy coming toward you, you don't know if you will jump toward him or freeze, white as death, literally shitting your pants. "I am not the person I was then, and I am very far from the ideas that took me there, but there is one thing I know and am pleased to have found out: I wasn't a coward when the bullets began whistling. But I am also alive, and others died, brave men and cowards both, and many nights when I can't sleep I remember them, they come back to ask me not to forget them, to tell the world that they lived."

You don't know what you could have been, what you might yet be, but you do know what in one way or another you have always been, visibly or secretly, in reality and in daydreams, although perhaps not in the eyes of others. And what if you truly were what others perceive and not what you imagine yourself to be, just as you aren't the person you see in the mirror? Hans Mayer, Austrian nationalist, blond, blue-eyed, son of a Catholic mother, himself an agnostic, a lover of literature and philosophy, and who dressed on festival days in the lederhosen, suspenders, and kneesocks of folkloric garb, realized that he was a Jew not because his father was Jewish, not because of any physical trait or custom or religious belief, but because others so decreed, and the indelible proof of it was the prison number tattooed on his forearm. In his room in Prague, in his parents' home, in the office of his company that insured labor-related accidents, in the rooms of the sanatoriums, in the hotel room in the border city of Gmünd where he awaited Milena's arrival, Kafka invented the perfect guilty party before Hitler and Stalin: Josef K., the man who is sentenced not because he's done anything or stands out for any reason, but because he has been found guilty, and he can't defend himself because he doesn't know what he is accused of, and when his execution comes, instead of rebelling he tamely submits and even feels ashamed.

YOU CAN WAKE UP one morning at the unpleasant hour of the working man and discover with less surprise than mortification that you've been transformed into an enormous insect. You can go to your usual café believing that nothing has changed, and learn from the newspaper that you are not the person you thought you were and no longer safe from shame and persecution. You can go to your doctor's office believing you will live forever, and leave a half hour later knowing that a gulf separates you from others, even though no one sees it yet in your face, that you carry inside you the shadow that waits invisible for all. You are the physician waiting in the dusk of your office for the patient to whom you must tell the truth, and you dread the moment of his arrival and the necessary, neutral words. But most of all you are the patient still unaware, who walks calmly down a familiar street, taking his time because he's early for the appointment, leafing through the newspaper that he just bought and that will be left forgotten on a table in the waiting room, a newspaper with a date like any other in the calendar but a date that marks the borderline, the end of one life and the beginning of another, two lives, two yous that could not be more different.

You climb the stairway with the newspaper under your arm. You almost forgot the appointment, even thought of canceling it, the examination and the simple blood test, it all seemed so silly. You push the door of the doctor's office and give your name to the nurse. You make yourself comfortable on a sofa in the waiting room and look at your watch, not knowing that it is marking the last minutes of vigor and health. You look at your watch, cross your legs, open a newspaper in the doctor's office or in a café in Vienna in November 1935, when a news article will drive you out of your routine and out of your country and make you a stranger forever. A guest in a hotel, you woke up one night with a fit of coughing and spat blood. The newspaper tells of the laws of racial purity newly promulgated in Nuremberg, and you read that you are a Jew and destined to extermination. The smiling nurse appears in the doorway of the waiting room and tells you that the doctor is ready to see you. Gregor Samsa awoke one morning and found himself transformed. Sometimes in the streets of the city I thought was mine, I passed impoverished Jews, émigrés from the East, in their long, greasy overcoats and black hats, with sweaty curls at their temples, and felt repelled, glad that in no way did I resemble those obstinately archaic figures who moved through the spacious streets of Vienna as they had the villages they had left in Poland, Yugoslavia, or Ukraine. No one would stop me from walking into a park or a café, or print crude caricatures of me in the yellow press. But now I am as marked as they. The healthy, blond man reading his newspaper in a café in Vienna one Sunday morning, dressed in lederhosen and kneesocks and Tyrolean suspenders, in the eyes of the waiter who has served him so often will soon be as repulsive as the poor Orthodox Jew whom men in brown shirts and red armbands humiliate for sport, and he will travel with him in a cattle car and end up exactly the same way, a walking cadaver slipping in the mud of the death camps, wearing the same striped uniform and cap, sharing the same darkness and panic in the gas chamber. The doctor runs his fingers over a white seashell, strokes the mouse of the computer, seeking in your file the symptoms that confirm the diagnosis, the sentence, the word neither of you utters. When you go back outside, your eyes are at first dazzled by the sun. The passing men and women are strangers. You walk through the city that no longer is yours, and it is with less surprise than shame that you discover, what a bitter awakening, that you are a giant insect. You move through a sinister nightmare, though the places are everyday places and the light is that of a sunny morning in Madrid. You walk along a familiar sidewalk in Berlin, over glass from shopwindows shattered during the night, and smell the gasoline that fired the stores of your Jewish neighbors. Later you will remember the headlines, the photograph of Hitler, the chancellor, on a stage in Nuremberg, gesticulating before a panoply of flags and eagles, the large letters that announced your fate, that identified you as the carrier of a plague. You are Jean Améry viewing a landscape of meadows and trees through the window of the car in which you are being taken to the barracks of the Gestapo. You are Eugenia Ginzburg listening for the last time to the sound her door makes as it closes, the house she will never return to. You are Margarete Buber-Neumann, who sees the illuminated sphere of a clock in the early dawn of Moscow, a few minutes before the van in which she is being driven enters the darkness of the prison. You are Franz Kafka discovering with amazement that the warm liquid you are vomiting is blood.

narva

BACK HOME, I LOOKED in the encyclopedia for that name I'd never heard but kept repeating to myself during the taxi ride, a name I didn't catch at first because my friend doesn't speak very loud and it was noisy in the restaurant where we had lunch. It's November, the evenings are much shorter now, and the winter dusk is still unexpected in the narrowest, darkest streets. We said good-bye at the door of the building he lives in, a block of modern apartments that don't seem to fit his character or age or the life he's led. Who could guess the life of this man, seeing him as he crosses the street or stands in the entryway of that anonymous building? A vigorous old man with a sparkle in his small eyes, a little bent, and with very fine white hair, like Spencer Tracy toward the end, or like my paternal grandfather, who was also in a war, but not one he marched off to voluntarily, and it may be that my grandfather never completely understood why they took him or realized the magnitude of the cataclysm his life had been dragged into, a life of which mine, if I stop to think about it, is in part a distant echo.

My friend is eighty, almost the age of my grandfather when he died, but he doesn't think about death, he tells me, just as he didn't think about it when he found himself on the Russian front in the winter of 1943, a very young second lieutenant soon to be promoted to lieutenant because of valor and having been awarded an Iron Cross. You don't think about death when you're twenty and in peril every minute, when with pistol in hand you advance across a no-man's-land and suddenly your face and uniform are sprayed with the blood of the man beside you, who in one burst of machine-gun fire becomes a mound of entrails sprawled in the mud. You think only about how cold it is, or about the rations that never showed up, or about sleep, because the worst things in war are the cold and lack of sleep, my friend says, taking a brief, reflective sip of wine. He is seated directly across from me, older than any of the diners in the restaurant, all men, all the same age and wearing midlevel-executive suits, some speaking in an elementary but fluent English in that overly loud tone you tend to use when you're on a cell phone in a public place. Their conversations mix with ours, the bleeps and music of their phones, the clinking of dishes and glassware, so I have to strain to hear what my friend is saying. I lean toward him across the table, especially when there's a foreign name, of some German general or Russian sector or city I never knew existed, one of so many cities of the world that you will never hear of, just as millions of people don't know the name of the small town where I was born, though it's completely real to me, clear in every detail, in its census of living and dead, the living whom I hardly ever see now and the dead who are fainter in memory with each passing day, although sometimes they reappear suddenly, like my paternal grandfather who died fourteen years ago.

I remember Pascal's maxim: Entire worlds know nothing of us. Nevertheless, that foreign city is taking on a presence in my mind, which my friend established when he spoke its name in a restaurant in Madrid. The first time he said it, I paid no attention, because the story he was telling was more important to me, then he said it again but I didn't catch it, with the noise. I interrupted him to ask the name of this city in Estonia. But who can imagine what Estonia is like, what lies behind that name, inside that name? It's like trying to put yourself inside those small glass globes with snowy scenes that people used to have in their homes and you shook to make the snow swirl. Snow also falls in winter in Estonia, in that small city in the provinces, beside a river with the same name, Narva—the Narva River carries huge masses of ice in the winter, my friend tells me, remembering, and that recalled detail means it was early winter when he reached the city.

Afterward, I came home in a taxi, from the sunny autumnal openness of the west part of Madrid to the somber streets of the center, where night is closer, night and the damp cold of winter twilights: mist and the woodsy smell of the road that runs beside a river that is beginning to freeze over and that empties into the Baltic thirteen kilometers beyond the city that bears its name. I was in a taxi in Madrid but also traveling through the places my friend had told me about, and a lifetime of vanished years were squeezed together in the ten or fifteen minutes of my ride, just as the Madrid I barely glanced at out the window was also the dark ruined capital to which my friend returned after his adventures in the European war, less innocent but not completely disillusioned, guarding with modest pride the Iron Cross he still keeps as a talisman.

As I listened, abstracted, to the voices on the taxi radio and the driver's diatribe against the government or the traffic, I thought of that name, mouthed it, decided to look it up in the *Britannica* as soon as I got home: Narva, where my friend was in 1943 and where he returned thirty years later with the nearly impossible task of finding a woman he had seen only once, one night at a dance for German officers he'd been invited to because he was one of the few Spaniards in the Blue Division who spoke German, and also because he liked Brahms and at a certain moment had hummed a melodic passage of the Third Symphony. The war was filled with coincidences like that, with chains of random events that dragged you away or saved you; your life could depend not on your heroism or caution or cleverness but on whether you bent down to tighten a boot one second before a bullet or shard of shrapnel passed through the place where your head would have been, or whether a comrade took your turn in a scouting patrol from which no one came back. My friend was saved that way many times, on the edge of disasters that claimed others, by a coincidence, a fraction of a second. By going to that city in Estonia on a two-day leave he may have avoided certain death. The Brahms melody he loved, Brahms being one of the names on which his worship of Germany was based, changed the course of his life, opening his eyes to a horror for which nothing had prepared him, a horror that marked him for more than the unthinking vertigo of courage and danger.

"There was an inspection of our sector, and the commander of my battalion asked me to act as guide for the German officers. I was with them for several days, and although the Germans didn't have much confidence in us, one of them, a captain almost as young as I was, took a liking to me, because of Brahms. We were standing around, not talking, the three German officers and I, beside a parapet between two machine-gun nests, on one of those calm days when it seemed that nothing would happen at the front, and without thinking I hummed a few bars of a melody. The captain began humming the same thing, but with all the notes, and more slowly, the better to enjoy the memory of the music." My friend hums too, right there in the restaurant, lips closed, eyes shut, and I hear the music more easily than his words, despite the voices, silverware, and cell phones. I recognize it immediately, because it's a favorite of mine, a powerful and sentimental melody a little like a film score: the third movement of Brahms's Third Symphony. "The other two officers had dropped behind, pointing out to each other disapprovingly some defect in our Spanish defenses, but the captain at my side closed his eyes and bobbed his head, and with his right hand he seemed to be drawing the music in the air, his black-gloved index finger a baton directing the sad, undulating theme that combined both great pain and great consolation. He told me that in civilian life he was a professor of philosophy in a gymnasium, and that he played the clarinet in his city orchestra and in a chamber group. That prompted me to mention the Brahms quintet for clarinet, and the German was moved to an almost embarrassing display of affectation," though those aren't exactly the words my friend used. "I noticed then," he says, "that he was a bit limp in the wrist, as they say nowadays, in spite of the uniform and how tall and strong he was. He told me that when he played that piece, there were parts where he had to struggle to hold back the tears. It was always as if he were playing that music for the first time, and each time it was more profound, more moving, containing all the grief of Brahms's life. There was only one other quintet for clarinet that he liked as much as the Brahms: I guessed immediately and said, Mozart's, and in the emotion of remembering the music and because of the empathy between us, he told me, lowering his voice, that he also liked Benny Goodman, although in Germany it was impossible to find his records. By then the other officers joined us, and the captain's demeanor changed, he became as rigid as he was at first, as military as they, and didn't say another word about music, barely speaking to me until we said good-bye. Those Germans were very strange," my friend tells me. "You never knew what was going through their head when they looked at you with those light-colored eyes. Some weeks later, the commander of my battalion called me to say that I had been given a few days' leave because the German officers I accompanied as guide and interpreter were pleased with me and asked that I be allowed to attend a dance in that city behind the lines: Narva.

The captain who was a fan of Brahms and Benny Goodman picked me up at the station. I remember that we drove into the city along a road near a river and bordering a forest, and that though there was still a little sun, it was already starting to get very cold.

The person who hasn't lived the experience demands details that mean nothing to the true narrator: my friend speaks of the cold and of the blocks of ice floating down the river, but my imagination adds the hour and the evening light, which is the same as the light in the street as we left the restaurant, and I also added the German officers' heavy gray overcoats with the broad lapels, as well as the dissimilar build of the two men—the Spaniard a little emaciated, at least in comparison with the captain who loved the clarinet, but both alike in the black gloves, black-visored caps, and collars turned up against the cold, talking about music, remembering sad passages from Brahms and Mozart and snappy George Gershwin tunes played by Benny Goodman's orchestra, which had not been heard for years on German radio.

"THEN I SAW SOMETHING I've never forgotten." My friend puts down his knife and fork, takes a sip of wine with a lively and slightly furtive gesture, so rare in a man of eighty, that suggests many tasks ahead in life, things to learn, books to review for the specialized journals of his profession, in which he is internationally eminent, appointments, travels abroad. As he speaks now, his small eyes peer at me behind heavy white eyebrows and wrinkled eyelids, but he doesn't seem to see me, he's not in the same place and time that I am, a restaurant in Madrid loud with voices and telephones. "I saw a large group of people that spanned the road from side to side coming toward us, men only, some almost children and others so old they stumbled as they walked and leaned on one another. They came in rows, close together, in formation, none speaking, heads bowed, as we used to see in the funerals that wound through the narrow streets of our villages, and the men in the lead held in front of them a horizontal pole like the barrier at a border post, with a tangle of barbed wire hanging from it that must have ripped their legs as they walked. You could hear their footsteps, the wire dragging the ground, and the swish of the guards' rifles brushing against their uniforms. The German and I pulled to one side of the road, where we watched. There were hundreds of men, guarded by a few SS soldiers, and in every fifth or sixth row was another bar with barbed wire, perhaps to entangle anyone who broke formation and tried to escape. I had never seen such thin, pale faces, not even on Russian prisoners, or the way those men had of walking, keeping time but dragging their feet, shoulders hunched, staring at the ground. I remember one old man with a long white beard, but I especially remember a young man in the front row, at the center, very tall, with sallow skin and a dead face, he wore an ankle-length overcoat, the kind in style then, and a navy-blue cap. I can see him as clearly as I'm seeing you now, his pince-nez glasses and his face with its dark beard, not because it was several days since he shaved but because the beard was thick and made even darker by his pallor. He was the only one to lift his head a little, though not much, and he stared at me as he passed, turning his long neck with its promi-nent Adam's apple, just at me, not the German. He turned and kept looking between the bowed heads of the other men, as if trying to say something with his eyes, which seemed abnormally large in such a thin face."

The sound of marching feet blended into the sound of the river as the column of prisoners moved on. The two men stood in silence, the German captain and the Spaniard recently pro-moted to lieutenant, both large in their gray overcoats and like brothers in their silver caps with the black visors. The light of the sun had disappeared, and the cold was damper and more intense. Deep in the woods, beyond the road, night would be advancing, as it did in some of the narrow streets in the center of Madrid, where the sun still shone on the windows of the tallest buildings in the pure icy blue of November.

My friend asked the German who those men were. The German was both surprised and amused at the innocence of the young officer so new to the war, the unpolished Spaniard still not entirely worthy of being admitted into their superior German brotherhood despite the purity of his accent, his bravery at the front, and his devotion to Brahms. *Juden!* the German said, and his face took on a strange expression, as if he were sharing a lewd secret or piece of barracks humor. My friend imitates the tone and the look of sarcasm and scorn on the face of the German, who winked and nudged him with his elbow.

"I didn't know anything then, but worst of all was my refusal to know, to see what was before my eyes. I had enlisted in the Blue Division because I believed everything they told us, I don't want to hide anything or try to excuse myself, I thought that Germany was civilization and Russia barbarism, the steppes of Asia from which all the invading hordes of Europe had come for centuries. Ortega said Germany was the West, and we believed him. Germany was the music that touched me so deeply, the tongue of poetry and philosophy, law and science. You can't know the passion with which I had studied German in Madrid, before our war, how vain I was when the Germans I interpreted for in Russia praised my accent. But that German word, *Juden,* was jarring, a discordant warning of something I had not heard until then, although surely I had heard it many times, I will not say what many said later: that they didn't know, that they never saw or heard anything. We didn't know because we weren't of a mind to know. You can make an effort not to know, close your eyes and not want to open them, but once they're open, what the eyes have seen cannot be erased."

FIRST WAS THAT WORD, *Juden.* Then, maybe two hours later, he met a woman at the dance, a beautiful redhead with green eyes. He walked into a room filled with people, noise, and music and immediately picked her out, as if no one else were there, and in the first look they exchanged he knew she wasn't German in the same way she knew that despite his uniform he was not like the other military men there. The city would have been dark, with no lights except at the street corners, a Baltic city in the winter of the war, occupied by the German army, under curfew, split by a river that would soon freeze and from which a fog rose that wets the paving stones and the streetcar tracks and seemed denser in the headlights of the military trucks.

My friend doesn't describe the place where the dance was held, but I imagine it as I listen to him talk: one of those official buildings I've seen in Nordic countries, white columns and pale-yellow stucco, a cobbled square, its stones shining in the night damp, crisscrossed by streetcar tracks and cables, and at the rear a requisitioned mansion that is the only place where the windows are lit and from which music spills out to the square with the unexpected brilliance of ballroom chandeliers. Sudden light in a dark city, music in the terrified silence of the streets.

After the front, that place must have had the unreal splendor of a cinematographic mirage. But my friend goes on, ignoring that kind of detail as he ignores the bellow of laughter from the banking executives who are honoring someone at a nearby table, toasting in Spanish and English the success of some financial venture. He erases it all, the ballroom in 1943 and the restaurant of today, the sound of the orchestra and the sound of the cell phones, the gleam of leather on the German uniforms, the crunch of black boots on the gleaming parquet floor, the heel clicks of salutes.

How intimidated he must have felt among so many strangers, nearly all of them of higher rank. The only thing that stands out in his story is the figure of the woman he was dancing with and whose name he can't remember, unless he said it and I didn't hear, and now I am tempted to invent a name: Gerda or Grete or Anicka: Anicka was the friend of Milena Jesenska in the death camp.

"I NOTICED HER THE MINUTE I walked into the room. There were officers from the army and the SS, and the blue uniforms of the Luftwaffe. Among all those military men I was the only one not German. Maybe that was why the woman stood looking at me when I walked by her, because she wasn't German either. A tall redhead wearing silk stockings and a low-cut gown of some flimsy fabric, she wore a perfume I would like to smell once more before I die. You are still young, so you don't know that some things are not erased by time. So much has happened since then," my friend calculates mentally, with a smile trapped in a memory whose sweetness can't be conveyed: fifty-six years ago, and it was November, as now, and he still holds intact the sensation of putting his arm around her waist, noting beneath the cloth the smoothness of a body made even more desirable by his being so long without a woman.

She was standing, very serious, beside a heavy man in civilian clothes—an ostentatious pinstripe suit—and there was a weary, conjugal air in the way they spoke without looking at each other. My friend doesn't explain whether it was difficult to overcome his shyness, whether he danced with other women before approaching her, and since he isn't writing a novel he doesn't need intermediate episodes, doesn't need to tell me what happened to the captain he came with. Right now, in his memory, he is alone with the redhead, as if silhouetted against a black background, and the woman doesn't have a name, either because my friend has forgotten it or because I didn't hear it and don't want to give her one.

They danced and she murmured into his ear, leaning a little toward him but at the same time looking in a different direction, with a distracted, formal air, as if they were in one of those dance halls of the time where men paid to dance with women for the two or three minutes of one song. He had come a long way to meet this woman, had traveled across Europe and through the devastation and mud of Russia and fought at Leningrad, all to hold her in his arms and gradually press her to his waist as he breathed the scent of her hair and skin and listened to her voice, the two of them, arms around each other, alone among all the people crowding the dance floor, scarcely moving to the music. He would look for her when a piece was finished during which he had felt obliged to dance with a different partner. But for her, this woman in the full splendor of her thirty-some years, it wasn't just interest or desire, there was also a desperation that he had never seen, just as he had never had his arm around a body like hers, it was in her eyes and voice, and also in the way she gripped his hand as she glided lightly across the dance floor, squeezing his fingers as if she wanted to convey an urgency that he first thought was sexual and perhaps was in part. She kept speaking into his ear, at the same time keeping an eye on the couples near them, and never losing sight of the dark-clad man who hadn't moved from the far end of the room all evening. She smiled at her dancing partner, half closing her eyes as if carried away by the delicious and sensual dizziness of the music, but her words had no relation to the calm and somewhat fatigued expression on her face, only with something at the back of her green eyes, with the way her fingernails dug into the back of his hand.

"You aren't like them, even though you wear the uniform. You must leave here and tell what they're doing to us. They are killing us all, one by one. When they came to Narva there were ten thousand of us Jews, and now there are fewer than two thousand, and the way they're going, we won't last through the winter. No one is spared, not the children, not the old, not the newborn. They take them away in trains, and no one ever comes back."

"But you're alive and well, and they invite you to their dances."

"Because I go to bed with that pig who was with me when you came in. But as soon as he tires of me or thinks it's dangerous to have a Jewish mistress, I'll end up like the others."

"Then get out."

"And go where? All of Europe is theirs."

"Why was he invited, if he isn't military?"

"He supplies clothing and food for the army. He buys up the Jews' properties for nothing."

"Must you sleep with him tonight?"

"Not tonight. His wife is waiting for him. They're giving a dinner for some generals."

"I'll take you home."

"You're reckless."

"Tomorrow afternoon I go back to the front."

He wanted to keep holding her and listening to her, he couldn't bear to have her leave without him at the end of the dance, but when the piece they were dancing ended and a German officer moved him aside politely but firmly to dance the next dance with her, he couldn't refuse, because the man in the pinstripe suit was watching her from a distance and maybe had already observed with displeasure that it was a long time since she changed partners, maybe had even guessed what she was saying to the young lieutenant who looked so little like a German despite the uniform. Strong as his desire was, he wanted to protect her and needed to know more, and he began to fear the looming darkness he had ignored until then, the dreadful suspicion of what was unimaginable yet couldn't be denied. He looked around at the red German faces, the elegance of the uniforms identical to his, which had given him such a thrill the first time he put it on, and felt an instinctive revulsion, though the monstrous thing was invisible, like the desperation of the woman dancing with him, moving her head to the rhythm of the music and smiling, closing her eyes and digging her fingernails into the back of his hand, repeating in a low voice the words that my friend kept hearing long afterward and that still return to him on sleepless nights when the darkness is peopled with the voices and faces of the dead. But the two faces he remembers most clearly are that of the young man in the pince-nez who turned toward him on the road as if wanting to tell him something, and that of the woman he danced with over and over, he doesn't know how many times, falling in love with her and being infected by her fear, her clear vision, her fatalism. What would her voice sound like now? With what accent would she speak German? Now, as I write, reliving what my friend told me, I would invent her, say that she was Sephardic by birth and spoke a few words to him in Ladino, establishing with him, in that remote city in Estonia and in the midst of all those German officers, the melancholy complicity of a secretly shared fatherland.

But it isn't necessary to invent or add a thing for that woman to materialize, to appear to me in the restaurant where my friend and I were talking amid all the noise and people, in the mix of conversations, steam from hot dishes, cigarettes, cell phones. He who has not been able to forget her for more than half a century has bequeathed her to me now, transferring the memory of her to my imagination, but I won't give her an origin or a name, I haven't the authority, she isn't a ghost or fictional character but someone who was as real as I am, who had a destiny as unique as mine although far more cruel, a biography that can neither be supplanted by the beautiful lie of literature nor reduced to arithmetical data, another cipher among the immense number of the dead. "Fifty-six years I've been remembering her, and I always wonder whether she survived or died in one of those camps that we knew nothing about then, not because they were run in absolute secrecy, since that is impossible, it would have been like keeping the operations of the railway system of an entire nation secret, but because we didn't want to believe the unbelievable. I went back to Narva thirty years later, when I traveled for the first time to Leningrad, to a psychology conference organized by UNESCO. It wasn't easy to do, but I obtained permission to visit the city, although they assigned me a Soviet guide who didn't leave me alone for a minute. Now the name was written on the station platform in Cyrillic characters, and the road along the river was gone, and in its place was an entire neighborhood of those horrid cement-colored buildings. It must seem absurd to you, and it was so then to me, but the minute I arrived in Narva I started looking at every woman, with my heart in my mouth, as if I might run into her and recognize her after thirty years. Looking not for a woman a little older than I was, which would have made her over sixty, but the same young redhead I danced with that night, falling more in love with her by the minute, weak with desire, so excited that I was dizzy, and afraid she could see, or someone else could, despite the heavy cloth of my trousers, how aroused I was."

The Soviet guide or watchdog made a show of glancing at his watch and gave my friend a disgusted look, and reminded him that they would have to go back to the station soon, they couldn't miss the return train to Leningrad, but my friend kept walking, ignoring his guide and leaving him a few paces behind, slightly bent over and moving quickly, as he did when we left the restaurant, his wise little eyes darting everywhere. Turning a corner, he recognized the cobbled square and the mansion where the dance had been held and the streetcar tracks, which had the same film of dirt and neglect as the facade of the mansion, which now, according to the guide, was the headquarters of Estonia's unions. He didn't recall all the cables strung from one side of the square to the other, and of course the gigantic statue of Lenin in the center, circled by streetcars clanging and jerking along, came afterward. But he perceived the same icy damp edge to the air and the smell of the river that couldn't be far away, now mixed with the general odor of boiled cabbage and bad gasoline that seemed to be the indelible essence of the Soviet Union. Time did not exist; he heard the footsteps of hundreds of men on the hard-packed dirt of a road and the wire barbs scraping the ground, and saw a thin, pale face turned toward him, eyes again appealing to him through pince-nez glasses, then slowly disappearing down the road and the years to fade into the unbridgeable gulf between those who died and those who were saved, those who were now in the ground and those who walked across it with the light-heartedness of people who don't realize that wherever they step, they are stepping on graves.

"HOW STRANGE TO BE standing at a streetcar stop across from the mansion and see yourself as you were thirty years before, because it isn't that I was remembering," my friend says. "I was literally seeing myself, the way you might see someone in the street and have trouble recognizing him because it's been so long since the last time. I was so young, so different, a twenty-three-year-old lieutenant in a German uniform." I could feel what he was feeling at that moment, the excitement and suspense of the waiting, the fear that his friend the captain might appear and suspect something or simply tell him he had to go back to headquarters. Because before leaving him to dance with a commander of the SS, the redheaded woman had told him to let a half hour go by and then meet her on the other side of the square beneath the shelter for the streetcar stop. He watched her move away through the dancing couples, now in the arms of the man in the black uniform, who was a little taller than she, casually turning to look for him while talking to her partner. He had to give her time to make small talk with some friends of her lover, who had never taken his eyes off her and who now and then sent short, precise signals to her, time to say good-bye. He didn't need to have someone take her home since she lived only two stops away on the streetcar. "I won't leave you alone for a moment," my friend told her, not being foolhardy but with the same assurance and absence of fear he felt sometimes as he leaped over a trench, immune to bullets, exalted and agile, pistol in hand, hoarse from shouting orders to the soldiers advancing behind him, fighting through the clay and tangles of wire and cadavers strewn across the no-man's-land. "I won't leave you by yourself," he told her again, when their dance ended and she tried to step away from him because the SS commander was waiting his turn. "If you want to help me, do as I told you," she pleaded, with an urgency that widened her eyes, and immediately smiled at the German officer who took her in his arms with a polite nod to my friend.

Thirty years later he saw himself from the other side of the square, a solitary figure standing at the streetcar stop in a cone of light, the cobbles wet from the fog. He looked at the windows of the mansion where the dancing was still in full swing, and heard very faintly the music of the orchestra and the sound his feet made as he stamped them to keep warm, the echoes that spread across the wide, open space. He was at the same time the young lieutenant who counted the minutes, jumping out of his skin with hope and disappointment every time the door of the mansion opened. He felt both the wrenching impatience of someone who doesn't know what the next minute will bring and the melancholy compassion of knowing what it brought: the young man waited for more than an hour, more desolate by the minute, and then went back to the ballroom to look for the redheaded woman, but did not find her, neither her nor her protector in the garish pinstripe suit, nor the SS commander who had bowed so ceremoniously when he claimed her. The lieutenant looked for her on the dance floor, then in the large room where drinks and canapés were being served, and walked through corridors where there was no one at all and through salons and libraries lit by large crystal chandeliers.

"And I never saw her again," he says, making a gesture with two upraised hands, as if to indicate a thing that vanishes into thin air. It occurred to him that maybe she had left without his seeing her and was waiting for him at the streetcar stop, and if he didn't hurry she would tire of waiting and leave, and then it would be too late to get her address, but in the vestibule he ran into the captain he'd come with and who had been looking for him. The captain said it was late and they had to get back to the barracks.

THERE IS NO NOISE NOW in the restaurant. Without realizing it, we have lingered until we are the only ones left. A waiter helps my friend into his navy-blue jacket, which accentuates the stoop of his shoulders. Watching him walk ahead of me toward the exit, I remember that he is a man of eighty. Outside we are surprised to find the pale light of early dusk, and the air is damp. My friend offers to take me home in his car.

"I still like to drive, although now and then I get into trouble when people see how old I am. One jerk yelled at me the other day at a traffic light, said it was time for me to pick out my coffin. I asked him, 'You want to bury me alive?' He scowled, rolled up his window, and shot off ahead of me. Generalizations are harmful, I should know, but the real problem is our species. We're aggressive primates, much more dangerous than gorillas or chimpanzees; we carry cruelty and the will to dominate in our brains, and we get the oldest part of the brain from our reptile ancestors. It's all in Darwin, to our misfortune. I know the theory that's going around, that in the evolution of the species the instinct for cooperation has served us better than the law of the survival of the fittest. Except that some primates cooperate to wipe others out. Look how well the Nazis and Communists cooperated, how many millions of dead they left behind. But it's not just them, think of Bosnia, or Rwanda just a while back, only yesterday, a million people murdered in a few months' time, and with machetes and clubs, not the technology the Germans had. Who knows what evil is being perpetrated this very moment while you and I are talking? I don't sleep much anymore, I lie in the darkness waiting for the dawn and remember all the dead I've seen rotting between our lines and the Russian positions, the bodies lying in ditches along the highways as we approached the front, or piled into trucks, stiff from the cold. I could easily have been one of them. And I see them all, one after another, and they look at me like that Jew in the pince-nez, and tell me that because I'm alive I have the obligation to speak for them, say what was done, so that the little that remains of them in people's memories will not be lost for all time."

We passed the park where the Egyptian temple of Debod is now, and I remember that the La Montana barracks stood in that very place. Here too we walk over tombs without names, over common graves. I remember black-and-white photographs and films of the first days of the Civil War, when my friend was a boy of sixteen studying Greek and Latin and German in the Institute and staying up late at night reading Nietzsche, Rilke, Juan Ramón Jiménez, and Ortega, when there was no way he could have known that in a few years he would be a decorated war hero. Not far from where we are now, in those gardens where the ruins of an Egyptian temple are enshrined and mothers walk their children and retirees take the afternoon sun, there was an esplanade filled with dead more than sixty years ago. On the same sidewalk where my friend and I are walking bombs fell during Franco's siege of Madrid.

But I don't say anything, I just listen while he talks about how the legs get weak after a certain age and how names become hard to recollect because of the deterioration of the neurotransmitters. When we say good-bye at the door of the modern building where he lives (maybe the one before it was destroyed in the bombardments), I see him from behind as he walks through the entry hall toward the elevator, bent and diligent, with only a hint of hesitation in his movements. If she were alive, if she is alive, the woman my friend met and lost in the city called Narva, she would be ninety. And if she was saved and is still alive somewhere, I wonder if she remembers, now, tonight, as I write these words, the young lieutenant she danced with one January night in 1943.

tell me your name

I SAT QUIETLY, WAITING, killing time, observing things from my window for hours on end, in an office where it might be mid-morning before someone came in—an emissary from the outside world, usually a second- or third-rate artist, a poet from the provinces trying to set up a reading or get a subvention to pub-lish a book of poems, people who knocked timidly at the door and who might sit for hours in the small reception room, waiting for a contract or a payment, a chance for an interview, to deliver a badly photocopied résumé that somehow, through my hands, might reach the manager I worked for, the man who made the decisions, judgments that were a long time coming, bogged down in the archaic lassitude of the administration, or held up by neg-ligence or carelessness: the manager didn't look at the documents I put on his desk, or I forgot to put them there. Sloth, isolation, estrangement, people always going out of focus, less real than the people in my mind or memories, in the fog between the invented and the remembered. In a letter Kafka wrote, I recognized the symptoms of my illness: ennui. *I was like a dead man, having no desire to communicate, as if I did not belong to this world or any other; as if during all the years that led to this moment I had acted mechanically, done only what was required of me, while waiting for a voice that would call out to me.*

I wrote letters, waited for letters, and when one came, I answered it hastily, then let a few days go by before I resumed my attitude of waiting, because it would be at least two weeks before the next letter arrived, that is, if it wasn't delayed like the decisions awaited by the applicants in the reception room of my office. I waited in both expectation and fear, but also out of mere habit, and if I saw the striped edge of an air-mail envelope among the letters and documents my assistant brought every morning, I would feel a senseless surge of renewed hope.

I worked alone, not in the main administration building but on one of the floors rented for new offices, temporary quarters that always had something furtive about them and often lacked an official seal on the door. There might be just an improvised sign at the end of a narrow corridor or steep stairway, a location close to central headquarters but behind it, on a little street with old taverns, dark hangouts for drunks, and shops that not many years back sold condoms and dirty magazines under the counter. Those streets were so narrow the sun didn't reach them, and there was always the hint of a sewer, and dank shadows gathered at the corners that faced the remnant of what once had been the red-light district, in other days a labyrinth called La Manigua. Now the last survivors occasionally emerged from those alleyways, old women, fat and heavily made up, or a few young pale ones hooked on heroin, with scuffed high heels and a cigarette stuck into the red stain of a mouth, specters loitering in lugubrious arcades.

I sat quietly at my desk waiting, and hours could go by before anyone came. Some mornings there might be only one or two visitors beside the person who brought the mail, perhaps a clerk asking me to consult a file in my archives, in which I had arranged the dossiers that came in the mail or were handed to me by the artists alphabetically, and the records of past performances chronologically. I saved every piece of paper in manila folders: posters, tickets, press clippings, should there be any, the count of the house, a number that often was misleading, depending on the reputation and attractions of the acts I booked; they were not for the important theaters in the city but for community centers in the barrios, little more than halls for school plays, or open-air stages in plazas or parks during the summer months, where it was also my responsibility to organize some festival or other that always featured the adjective *popular* on the posters advertising it, shows with lights and local rock groups, and merry-go-rounds and puppet shows.

My office occupied the narrowest angle of a triangular building that had a pastry shop on the ground floor and a small legal office on the first. Sweet, warm aromas wafted up from the pastry shop, and from the legal service came the sounds of voices and telephones and a lot of tramping back and forth that contrasted with the quiet prevailing in my office most of the time. There were two windows, one that looked out over the Plaza del Carmen and the other onto Calle Reyes Católicos, but the entry was on a narrow street with little traffic, so it was easy, when I came to work every morning, to feel that I was entering a secret observatory, as appropriate for spying as for getting away. I would come and go without being seen by anyone, and from the windows I could note who went by at that central crossroads of the city. The people I knew, who walked with no idea that they were being watched, looked different. Who is the person, really, when he is alone, temporarily free from others, from the identity others give him?

LIKE MANUEL AZAÑA when he was a fat, nearsighted adolescent, I wanted to be Captain Nemo. Closeted from eight to three between those walls were Nemo in his submarine and Robinson Crusoe on his island, and also the Invisible Man and detective

Philip Marlowe and Fernando Pessoa's Bernardo Soares and any of Kafka's office workers in that company in Prague for preventing workplace accidents. I imagined that I, like them, was a secret exile, a stranger in a place where I had always lived, a sedentary fugitive who hid behind an appearance of perfect normality, who, seated at an office desk or riding in a bus on the way to work, could conjure up amazing adventures that would never happen, voyages that would never be made. In his office at the water plant in Alexandria, Constantine Cavafy imagines the music Mark Antony heard the night before his damnation, the retinue of Dionysus abandoning him. In a cheap restaurant in Lisbon, or riding a streetcar, Pessoa pensively scans the lines of a poem about a sumptuous transatlantic voyage to the Orient. A bespectacled, self-absorbed man arrives at a hotel in Turin, peaceful, well dressed, although with a hint of oddness that prevents his being taken for the usual traveler; he registers for that one night, and no one knows that it is Cesare Pavese and that in his minimal luggage he is carrying a dose of poison that within a few hours he will use to take his life. I imagined the suicide in morbid detail. From a literary point of view, was shooting oneself or killing oneself slowly with alcohol a form of heroism? I watched the hopeless drunks in the dark taverns of the side streets with both admiration and disgust, for each hid a terrible truth whose price was self-destruction. I walked past men with scowling faces and unsettled behavior and imagined Baudelaire in the final delirium of his life, wandering lost in Brussels or Paris, and Søren Kierkegaard cast adrift in the streets of Copenhagen, composing biblical diatribes against his countrymen and friends, mentally writing love letters to Regina Olsen, whom he left behind, perhaps frightened to death when he found himself betrothed to her, though he never forgives her when she later marries another man. Closeted in my office, I read his letters, diaries, and notebooks, and learned in Pascal that men never live in the present, only in their memory of the past or in their desire or fear of the future, and that all our miseries outlast us because we are not able to sit quietly in a room alone.

Did Milena's letters reach Kafka at his home, or did he prefer to receive them at the office? He sent hers to general delivery in Vienna so her husband wouldn't see them. Reading many books did not tell me that she was something more than the shadow to whom he wrote letters or who occasionally appeared in the pages of his diary: she was a real woman who obstinately, courageously shaped her destiny in the face of hostile circumstances and a tyrannical father, who wrote books and articles in favor of human emancipation. She passionately loved several men, and continued to write when the Nazis were in Prague. Arrested and sent to a death camp, she died twenty-two years after the man whose letters I read in my office.

I surrounded myself with shadows that were more important to me than people, shades that whispered the names of cities I had never visited—Prague, Lisbon, Tangiers, Copenhagen, New York—and the place in America those letters came from bearing my name and the address of my office and written in a hand that became not the anticipation but the substance of my happiness. I kept *Letters to Milena* in a desk drawer, and sometimes I carried the book in a pocket to read on the bus. It nourished my love for the absent beloved, and for the failed or impossible loves I had learned of through films and books. *Dispensing hand of happiness,* Kafka writes of Milena's hand.

I LIVED IN WRITTEN WORDS, books, letters, and drafts of things that never saw the light of day, and in an office that was more in harmony with me than my own house and was, in a strange and oblique way, my intimate dwelling; the outside world was a blur, as if I didn't live in it, just as I performed my job so casually that it might have been someone else doing it. My life was what didn't happen to me, my love a woman who was far away and might never return, my calling a passion I did not devote myself to in real life, although I had begun to publish an article or two in the local newspaper, using a pseudonym, then felt they were letters not addressed to anyone except a few readers as isolated as I was in our melancholy province, so remote from anything reported in the newspapers of Madrid.

I read in Pascal: *Entire worlds know nothing of us.* I read eagerly, with the same will for oblivion that makes Robert De Niro yearn for the opium pipe in the Sergio Leone film that was playing then, *Once upon a Time in America.* I emerged from books as muddled as from the movies, when you come out of the darkness of the theater into bright sun. Some evenings I took on work I didn't need to, or invented an excuse to go to the office for a few hours, then sat at my desk staring at the door of the small waiting room, imagining I was a private detective, as childishly, though nearly thirty, as when at twelve I imagined I was the Count of Monte Cristo or Jim Hawkins, or when I would look down on the street, with no danger that anyone would see me from below or that any visitor would come to interrupt me. I had read in Flaubert: *Every man guards in his heart a royal chamber: I have sealed mine.* My head was filled with phrases from books, films, songs, and those words were my only consolation in the exile to which I was condemned. I read Pavese's diary, poisoning myself with his nihilism and misogyny, which I took for lucidity, just as I sometimes took the effects of too much alcohol for clear-headedness and enthusiasm. *Death will come, and she will have your eyes.* To write and read was to weave a protective and airless cocoon, to drink a potion that would allow me to flee invisible, to take a tunnel that no one knew, to scratch the wall of my cell with the patience of Edmond Dantes. With a silken line of blue ink I spun a world filled with imaginary men and women who softened the harsh edges of reality. The light scrape of pen on paper, the tapping of the keys of the typewriter, which was manual and noisy like the machines of fabulous screenwriters, the ones Chandler and Hammett used, literary gods, drunk, original, solitary men who could not be bought. The alcohol fumes and tobacco smoke of the 1980s, in retrospect as embarrassing as most of my alienated life then, as distant as the memory of that office and the woman to whom I wrote the letters, not realizing that I loved her not *despite* the fact that she lived on the other side of the ocean and with another man but precisely *because* she did. Had she returned, leaving everything to go with me, I would have been paralyzed with terror, I would have fled as Kafka fled before the determined and earthy passion of Milena Jesenska, preferring the refuge of letters and distance.

Everything at my office proceeded at an administrative crawl, and several months would pass before the Department of Internal Affairs installed the appropriate plaque beside the entrance and above the door, that is, assuming there was not an unexpected move to yet another place, another rented suite in the same area or a vacant office in the main building, and I would have to get settled all over again, the desk and metal filing cabinet with the documents and typewriter and folders with drafts that never reached final form, the books that filled the hours of waiting and daydreaming, the letters kept under lock and key in a desk drawer and judiciously reread.

My life had only past and future. The present was a parenthesis, an empty space, like the spaces that separate written words, the automatic touch of thumb to the long bar of the typewriter, the line that separates two dates on a calendar, the pause between two beats of the heart. I lived from one letter, among the ordinary envelopes on my mail tray, to the next, recognizing it from afar, the moment the clerk came through the door with the large folder of correspondence under his arm, unaware of the treasure he was bringing me.

Real life evolved on a distant plane, the space of separation between the remembered and the desired, a space as empty and neutral as the small reception room where someone occasionally waited, hoping for a part or an interview with one of my superiors, the manager if possible.

He was the one who made the decisions and the one to whom I submitted my reports but who rarely appeared, since he was devoted to tasks of greater importance, such as public relations, over in the main building where he welcomed the eminent personalities visiting the city, the first-class artists whose performances were booked in the best theater, the largest auditorium: managers of Catalan avant-garde companies, celebrated soloists, orchestra conductors. First thing in the morning, I would read the arts section of the newspaper, looking for notice of the arrival of these personalities, their interviews and the photographs in which they often shook the hand of one of my superiors, especially the manager, who always wore a big smile and leaned toward the celebrity to make sure he wasn't left outside the frame. I cut the photographs out and put them in a folder after I pasted the clipping onto a page with a typed notation of occasion and date.

The artists I booked rated no more than a small box in some easily overlooked corner of the paper, pieces that were anonymous or signed with initials, sometimes mine, because more than once the editor on duty just reproduced the note I'd sent in. Thespians, many of them called themselves. The word made me think of limited talent, shabbiness of costumes and sets, the weariness of the itinerant ham actors of other days, except now updated with hippie schlock, improvisation, audience participation. They painted their faces and dressed in rags like clowns and played the drum or walked on stilts in their parades and street theater. The women wore sweaty tights, didn't shave under their arms, and moved sexlessly. They were paid almost nothing, and that little money took a long time to reach them. Every morning they would show up at my office, listen to my explanations, not understanding much, probably not believing much. All the forms they had to fill out, the obscure progress of paperwork from office to office, from Administration to Auditing and then to Disbursements, the delays, the carelessness and neglect, which could mean more weeks of waiting, and the lies at which I had become expert: "They told me at Administration that today they're sending the check request to be signed, and tomorrow without fail I myself will take that form to Auditing."

Like me, they lived in unfilled time, in the small waiting room of my office, as grim as that of a backstreet doctor or one of those private detectives in novels. They brought their portfolios, their sorry assortment of photocopies, their mediocre or invented résumés, and I cared nothing about them, indifferent to their lives and their art, though it was my job to give them hope, invent excuses for delays, confuse them with administrative procedures and administrative language. There was a Gypsy poet with sideburns and a thick head of white, curly hair who claimed he had translated the complete works of García Lorca and part of the New Testament into Caló, Gypsy Spanish, and as proof he brought the entire manuscript of his translation with him in a huge satchel, but he opened it only long enough to show me the first page, afraid he would be plagiarized or the translation would be stolen, and he refused to leave the bundle of pages to which he was dedicating his life in my office, lest they get lost among all the other papers or lest a fire break out in the oven of the pastry shop on the ground floor and his Lorca in Romany go up in flames. I asked him why he didn't make a photocopy, saying it would be a good idea for him to have a spare just in case, but he didn't trust the employees at the copy shop either, they might carelessly scorch the pages of his book or make another copy without his knowledge, and sell it or publish it under another name. No, he wouldn't part with his manuscript, clutching it in his arms as he sat across from me at my desk or waited in the reception room for the manager to arrive, because he couldn't rest until it was published, with his name in large letters on the cover and his photograph on the back so there would be no doubt about the author's identity, his Gypsy face recognized by everyone in the city.

I can still see that dark, rustic face and white hair, and suddenly an unexpected detail surfaces, the large iron rings the Romany translator wore on his fingers, adding to the force with which his two hands fell on my desk or on the bulging satchel he was always protecting from the world, from adversity, theft, indifference, and the administrative lethargy he encountered every day in the waiting room or wandering outside the main building with the hope of catching the manager or some superior with greater influence than mine and in that way, by assault in the middle of the street, achieve what patience never accorded: the interview in which he would be granted money to publish his masterwork or at least a part of it, maybe the *Romancero gitano,* which he recited to me first in Spanish and then in Romany, closing his eyes tight, holding up his right hand with the index finger extended like a flamenco singer in a trance.

I watched him from my window, as I watched so many people, men and women, known and unknown, figures that passed across the unreal diorama of my life in those days. I watched him at the pedestrian crossing, walking with a resolute stride, his satchel held in his arms as if to prevent a blast of wind or a thief from seizing it, and somehow that man was not the same one who a few minutes later entered my office and asked if I thought the manager would be in that morning.

I pretended to pay attention to him, and then I pretended to be very busy sorting papers on my desk or checking figures in a financial report. I wanted to be alone, to go back to the book or letter the visitor had interrupted, and my impatience turned to irritation, although I tried not to show it. No, the manager won't be in this morning, he called and had me cancel all his appointments, he has a very important meeting, and the man closed his satchel again, stood up, pressing it between the huge stone-mason's or smith's hands adorned with rings in crude Asiatic splendor, and a minute later he had left the office and I could see him crossing the street, deep in thought and walking a little more slowly, though no less decisively, not yielding to dejection, perhaps reciting in his restless imagination lines from Lorca and evangelical sermons in Spanish and Romany. But now, as I am writing this, I wonder how I would have appeared if someone observed me from a window without my knowledge as I walked through those same streets, as intoxicated with words and chimera as the Gypsy poet: a strange man who sees nothing around him, his city inhabited with the dark ghosts of desire and books. They didn't see Philip Marlowe, the Invisible Man, Franz Kafka, or Bernardo Soares, only a serious and ordinary thirty-year-old employee who left the office every day at the same time and read a book at the bus stop, and who once a week, always at the same hour, slipped a letter into the "Foreign-Urgent" slot of the mail drop on one side of the Post Office Building.

SOMEONE IS WAITING NOW in the reception room, courteously asking permission to come into my office. I hide in the drawer the letter or book I was reading. Of all the names and faces from that time, one figure stands out, nameless now, and another I remember perfectly. Two images, like illustrations from two different stories, but both set in the same place and atmosphere, a gloomy waiting room where applicants wait hours or days. A man and then a woman, their accents not the same. I listen in a silence broken only by the keyboard. The woman has a child in her arms, no, seated on her knees, because he isn't a baby but a child of two or three. "What luck," she is saying, speaking with a Montevideo or Buenos Aires accent. "I'm so happy that he can't remember."

The man speaks a meticulous, slightly formal Spanish, which

he learned in his own country, I can't remember now whether it was Romania or Bulgaria, when he was a teenager and he thought of Spain not as a real country but a fabulous kingdom of literature and music, especially music, the pieces that he studied at the conservatory in his distant past as a child prodigy, when he astounded his professors by playing from memory difficult piano passages from Albéniz, de Falla, and Debussy, invocations of gardens in the moonlight and Muslim palaces with splendors of stonework and murmuring fountains. He read translations of Washington Irving and listened to and quickly learned Ravel's *Rhapsody Espagnole* and *Night in Grenada* by Debussy, who had never seen the city when he wrote that music, the pianist told me, and who in fact never traveled to Spain, though it was not far away and he had written music indebted to it. The pianist told me that the first time he walked through the Alhambra, after escaping from his country, Debussy's music played in his mind, and he seemed to recognize the things around him not from photographs or drawings but from the faint notes of a piano.

AT FIRST HE WAS an applicant like any other, although somewhat better dressed and with better manners, which were as correct as his use of the Spanish language. In the half light of the reception room, he leafed through a magazine on the low table as if he were in a doctor's waiting room. He, too, had brought a dossier, his briefcase with clippings and photocopies, but his were better organized than usual, the pages protected in plastic sleeves, some with color photographs and programs of recitals in the cities of Central Europe, often with text in Cyrillic characters. On the cover of the album was a professional artist's photograph, somewhat dated, a younger and more vigorous version of the man before me; the pose was that of an impetuous, romantic concert artist, long hair, closely fitted tuxedo, elbow propped on the lid of a grand piano, hand on cheek with the index finger touching his temple, a dreamer of consummate virtuosity. Or maybe I'm re-membering the jacket of a recording of Spanish music published at the height of his career, which he insisted on giving me though earlier he told me that there were few copies left, because all his records and books, everything he owned—except his credentials as a musician—had been abandoned, left behind at the border that then divided Europe. "I didn't desert, didn't flee," he said. "*Me fui,* as you say in Spanish: I went away, because I didn't want to spend the rest of my life toeing a line, afraid my neighbor or colleague was a spy or that there were hidden microphones in the dressing room." It wasn't political, he assured me, sitting there in my office while I was willing him to leave so I could be alone again and he was lingering in the hope that the manager would come that morning. "I couldn't bear to live in my country any longer, because everything was always the same, the face of the head of government on all the posters and in all the newspapers and on television, and his voice on the radio, while things that for you in the West are normal, buying a bottle of shampoo or look-ing up a number in the telephone book, were difficult, often im-possible. In my country there are no telephone books, and it is a major undertaking to get a permit for foreign travel. If you try to bring in a typewriter, they confiscate it at customs and put you on the list of suspicious persons. But what am I saying, my coun-try? Now my country is Spain."

He set his dossier to one side, first making sure the album was tightly closed so no photograph, program, or clipping could fall out, and felt for something inside his skimpy jacket—velvet, I remember now, with very wide lapels, a jacket more for an ob-solete crooner than a piano player—and for a moment his ex-pression turned to alarm as he patted all his pockets, looking at me with a smile of embarrassment and apology, as if I were a policeman who'd asked for identification. But then the anxious fingers touched what they were looking for, the flexible covers of a passport so tenderly handled that it looked new, just like the identification card the pianist now showed me, his color photograph sealed beneath the smooth plastic along with his strange Romanian or Slavic name, which I've forgotten.

His long, pale fingers stroked those documents with reverence, with amazement that they existed, with the anxiety that they could be lost. So many years living in a country he wanted to get out of to visit another that he knew only through books and music, through the sonorous names in the scores he learned so well at the conservatory, all that tension on the eve of the final decision, when he climbed out the washroom window of his dressing room on the tour through Spain to avoid being seen by the agents watching him and his companions, all the waiting, giving statements in police stations and presenting papers, living in Red Cross shelters or filthy boardinghouses, with the fear of being expelled or, worse, repatriated, what a horrible word, he told me, with no money, no identity, in a no-man's-land between the life he'd left and the one he had yet to begin, divested of the security and privileges he had enjoyed as a renowned pianist in his country, uncertain about the chances of beginning a new career here, of being unknown.

The bewildered look of one who has nurtured a dream for years and actually accomplished it contrasted, on his face and in his eyes, with the melancholy of one who has gradually capitulated to reality. He had been a child prodigy in the conservatory at Bucharest or Sofia, and his collection of clippings and programs attested to a distinguished career in the concert halls of Eastern Europe. But now he was spending entire mornings in the reception room of my office, awaiting a decision on a contract that would guarantee him, at most, two or three performances in cultural centers on the outskirts of the city, in theaters with bad acoustics and mediocre, badly tuned pianos.

He wasn't allowing himself to be discouraged, and if he came into my office and I told him that the manager wouldn't be in that day or that we hadn't even begun processing the forms for his contract, he would smile weakly, thank me, and bow as he left with a mixture of old-fashioned Central European courtesy and Communist stiffness: a timid deference toward any official that he would probably never lose. He was a young man, small: in my now-faded memory he looks something like Roman Polanski, a fleeting liveliness in the eyes and gestures that at a certain distance erases the signs of age.

He was giving private lessons, and he sought and accepted concerts anywhere, earning almost nothing, a fee sometimes so low that when he was going over the figures, he told himself, using one of those Spanish sayings he liked so much, "Minimum pay, food for the day." He also told himself, "Better than stone soup," and, "A bird in the hand is worth scores on the wing" in the painstaking Spanish so passionately learned in a capital with broken-down streetcars, long winters, and early nightfalls, practiced privately and with the dream of escape and rebellion, much as he learned to play the most difficult passages of Albéniz's *Iberia* or Ravel's *Rhapsody Espagnole*. Now, although the fruits of his dream were so meager, because in Spain his career as a piano virtuoso meant nothing and he had to perform in lamentable venues, wearing worn clothing and living under the constant strain of poverty, he refused to give in to depression and continued to show his gratitude and enthusiasm for his new country. It was a pathetic happiness, as of a man in love who knows he is scorned by his beloved but still gives her his boundless devotion.

ONE DAY THE PIANIST TOLD ME—I don't know whether it was in my office or one of the bars on the side streets where we lower-echelon employees ate breakfast, possibly he had invited me to have a cup of coffee or a tot of rum to celebrate modestly, that he finally got a contract for a concert.

He told me how he was coming back to Spain from Paris on

a night train scheduled to reach the border at Irún by dawn. He had gone to play in a festival benefiting exiled artists of his country, and this was the first time he had traveled with his new Spanish passport. He couldn't sleep all night because of the discomfort of his second-class seat and the added aggravation of rude passengers, and at nearly every station the French conductors forced him to get up because his ticket, the cheapest available, gave him no right to claim a specific seat. And he was nervous: it was the first time he would enter Spain with the new identity papers, which he had been given only a short time before. In the darkened compartment, among the snoring passengers, he kept touching the pockets of his jacket and overcoat, checking again and again for his ticket, passport, ID, and each time it seemed that he'd lost them or that he had one document but not the others, and he kept putting them in a more secure place, inside a lining or in the zippered pocket of his travel case, and when he dozed off and his eyes jerked open, he would forget where he'd put them, this time sure that he'd lost them or that one of those thieves who roam the night trains had taken them. After hours of anguish at border posts in Communist countries, the laborious review of papers and the flash of alarm each time some bureaucratic flaw in a document held him up, he decided not to go back to sleep. He tried to see what time it was by the pale violet light in the car ceiling, and at the stops he noted the names of the stations, calculating how much farther it was to Irún, eager to get there but also increasingly afraid as the train neared the border. Meanwhile the Spanish and French passengers slept tranquilly in his compartment, sure of the order of things and perfectly allied with their world, unlike him, an intruder who took nothing for granted and always feared the unexpected.

Finally, exhausted, he fell into a deep slumber, only to be awoken by a great screeching of brakes. At first, still trapped in the web of a bad dream, he thought the train had arrived at his native country and that gray-uniformed guards would arrest him because he was not carrying the proper identification, his old passport, which he also showed me, a relic of a dark past.

He got off the train, tightly clutching his travel case in one hand and in the other his Spanish passport. He had been told earlier to have all the documents relating to his naturalization easily available in his pocket, in case he needed to produce them. He took his place in the line, on the Spanish side of the border, in front of the guard post manned by two *guardias* looking bored or sleepy. "My legs were trembling, and when I tried to say good morning, my mouth was so dry I could barely speak." Then, as he walked toward their booth, his palms sweaty and his knees weaker by the minute, something happened that he still remembers with amazement and gratitude. One of the guards came toward him, and he thought the man was returning his gaze with suspicion and distrust. But he summoned his courage, as he had the time he jumped out the window of the washroom, and, as naturally as he was able, held out his passport, carefully opened to his photograph, prepared to explain the discrepancy between his nationality and his name and to produce all the necessary papers. But the guard, without even glancing at the passport, without looking at his face, waved his hand and told him with a Spanish obscenity to move on, and that rude gesture and word seemed to the pianist the most beautiful welcome he had ever received. For my benefit he imitated the guard's wave with his slender, white, musician's hand, still stunned by a gift that none of the other weary passengers appreciated, repeating like a spell the guard's expression, "for shit's sake," *joder* with a strong aspirated "j," which he pronounced precisely and with pride.

THE FACES OF THE PEOPLE in the waiting room, or on the other side of the desk in my office, came and went, and I paid little attention to them, half listening to their petitions or demands for things that weren't in my power to grant and that meant nothing to me, although I had learned to pretend to listen carefully, professionally, sometimes taking notes while I gave information about the necessary forms or explanations about delays of payments or the suggestion that a timely word to the manager might help, busy as he was with larger responsibilities. I was waiting, sheltered in my parenthesis of space and time as in a lair, but what I was waiting for beyond the next letter was unclear to me, and I made no effort to dispel the mist of my indecision. I sat quietly and waited, as one who has heard the alarm clock and knows he must get up but allows himself a few minutes more before he opens his eyes and jumps out of bed. Would the woman writing me come back or not? When she lived on this side of the ocean and in the same city, her interest in me did not last very long. I never felt more distant from her than those few times I held her in my arms. If I sought her out, she fled from me, but if I grew discouraged and gave up the chase, she came to me, always full of promises, erasing the resentment and uncertainty from my soul and making me want her again.

The truth is, she was no more tangible to me than the women in the black-and-white movies who seduced me into a kind of hallucinatory love: Lauren Bacall, Ingrid Bergman, Gene Tierney, Ava Gardner, Rita Hayworth. In *Gilda,* which I saw many times, Rita Hayworth runs away from Glenn Ford and Buenos Aires, and in a cabaret in Montevideo, dressed in white, she sings and dances a song called "*Amado mío.*"

> *Amado mío*
> *Love me forever*
> *And let forever*
> *Begin tonight.*

In the film, Montevideo is just a name, not even a set or one of those false panoramas they use when the actors are pretending to drive a car. But the woman who showed up one morning in the waiting room of my office with a child in her arms and a large bag filled with puppets had fled from Montevideo to Buenos Aires in 1974, and four years later from Buenos Aires to Madrid, pregnant, though she didn't know that yet, carrying the child of a man who had been taken away one night by the military or the police and was not heard from again. As we were talking, the child sat on the floor of my office playing with his mother's wooden dolls. She watched him out of the corner of her eye with an uneasiness that never lessened. A little over thirty, she had very dark hair and eyes; the hair was a silky mane, the eyes large and heavily outlined with kohl. Her nose and mouth suggested Italian blood. Her strong, slightly masculine hands were perfect for manipulating the puppets, a few of which she unexpectedly took and began to maneuver in front of me, after first starting a cassette player she also pulled from her peddler's pack. On the gray metal of the desk and atop the confusion of my papers, Little Red Riding Hood, skipping to the rhythm of the music on the tape, entered the forest where the Wolf lay in wait behind a pile of documents, and in her strong River Plate accent the woman narrated the story and reproduced all the voices, the high voice of the little girl, the big deep voice of the Wolf, the quavering, grumbling voice of the Grandmother. The little boy, as if mesmerized, got up and came over to the desk, which was about at his eye level. Bewitched but terrified, as if the Wolf were also waiting for him, he was completely unaware of his mother's hands or the strings dangling from her fingers.

The demonstration lasted only two or three minutes, and when the music reached its final flourish and the tape stopped, the puppets made a great bow together and collapsed, lifeless, upon my papers, but the boy kept looking at them with dazzled eyes, waiting for them to come back to life. "You saw," said the woman, "that I can set up my little show anywhere." She stowed the puppets and cassette player in her bag, but the boy immediately took them out again, one by one, and examined them slowly, as if to solve the mystery of their extinguished vitality, so absorbed in them and himself that he didn't see me or his mother or the rather shabby office, though it probably was not as dreary as the boardinghouse where the two of them had lived since they came to the city. She had the constant worry, she told me, of not knowing how long they would be able to pay for it, and therefore she wanted me to organize a series of bookings for her in elementary schools and kindergartens.

She, too, had brought her dossier, and she spread out her photocopies and clippings, the credentials from another country that were of so little use here, diplomas from drama schools in Montevideo and Buenos Aires that wouldn't have helped her get a job scrubbing floors in Spain. I reeled off the usual explanation about applications and forms and waiting time. She stared at me with disbelief and possibly sarcasm in those dark, kohl-rimmed eyes, as if to let me know that she didn't believe what I was telling her but that it didn't matter. She asked for an appointment with the provincial commissioner, put her dossier on my desk, and on the first page wrote the telephone number of her boardinghouse, which I knew to be a gloomy place, since I had lived there in my poorer days as a student. She knew as well as I did that there was absolutely no point in her leaving her telephone number, that she would have to come back many times, fruitlessly, but we both also knew that there was no other way, she had to persevere and hope to maintain her dignity. Every day she called to see whether I knew anything, whether there had been any decision; every day she pushed open the door of my office and took a seat again in the dark waiting room, always carrying the child or holding his hand because she couldn't leave him alone in the boardinghouse and had no one she could trust to look after him.

Now he must be about twenty: he will look at the photograph his mother showed me one morning and see the face of a man with a boyish air, with the horn-rimmed glasses, long sideburns, and thick curly hair typical of the 1970s, the ghost of someone his age and yet his father, legally neither alive nor dead, not buried anywhere, not listed in any administrative register of the deceased, simply lost, disappeared, and those who have survived and hold his memory dear cannot rest, not knowing when he died or where he was buried—that is, if he wasn't thrown into the River Plate from a helicopter with his eyes blindfolded and his hands bound, or already dead, his belly split open so the sharks would make quick work of the corpse.

THE WOMAN BEGAN CRYING, and the child, playing on the floor and lost in an imaginary game, suddenly turned to her with a serious look, as if understanding what his mother told me in a low voice. She asked me for a tissue, and when she looked up I saw that a black line of kohl was trickling down her cheek. "I'm all right now," she said, apologizing, pushing back the smooth black hair from her face. I lit her cigarette, and her large dark eyes smiled at me, gleaming with tears—not the usual courtesy or fawning in response to my administrative position, the smile was meant just for me, the person who had listened attentively and asked for details, who had offered her the temporary hospitality of his office, an uninterrupted block of time for her confidences. I thought with a touch of male cynicism that she was a desirable woman, that I might be able to go to bed with her.

She told me her name the first day, when I asked her for information to fill out one of the pointless index cards that gave me the appearance of being organized and that I later typed neatly, arranged alphabetically, and filed in a drawer of the metal cabinet on which there were small tags of different colors corresponding to the cards: "Theater," "Classical," "Rock," "Flamenco Music," or "Miscellaneous Artists," a category that included the translator of García Lorca into Romany.

Maybe I have remembered the name because it didn't go with her Italian looks: Adriana Seligmann. Sometimes when you hear a name, the name of a woman or a city, a story resonates in its syllables like a key to an encoded message, as if an entire life could be contained in one word. Every person carries his novel with him, her story, maybe not the entire story but an episode in which that life is crystallized forever, summarized in a name, even if the name is unknown or may not be said aloud: Rosebud, Milena, Narva, Gmünd.

The desirable woman on the other side of my desk sat down again and told me the story of her name. I have often seen a sudden change in someone who decides to tell something that matters very much, who takes a step and suspends the present to sink into a tale, who even as she speaks, driven by the need to be heard, seems to speak alone. I am never more myself than when I am silent and listening, when I set aside my tedious identity and tedious memory to concentrate totally on the act of listening, on the experiences of another.

MY PATERNAL GRANDFATHER'S name was Seligmann, Saúl Seligmann. As a little girl I knew vaguely that he had come from Germany, but I never heard him talk about his life before Montevideo. I remember holding my father's hand to go visit my grandfather in his tailor shop. He would leave what he had been doing and sit me on his knees and tell me stories in a voice that had a foreign accent. Then he retired and went to live outside Montevideo, on the other side of the river, as we say. He had bought a country place in El Tigre where he could be alone, which was what he liked, my father used to say, I think with a touch of resentment. After that I seldom saw him. When I was twelve, my parents separated, and for a while they sent me to live with my grandfather in the house in El Tigre. It was a wood house on a small island, with a high railing painted white and a dock, surrounded with trees. After the last months I'd spent with my parents, that retreat in my grandfather's house was paradise. I read the books in his library and listened to his opera and tango records. If I asked him anything about Germany, he'd tell me that he left when he was very young, that he had forgotten everything about it, including the language. But I discovered it wasn't true. One of the first nights I slept in his house, I was woken by cries. I was afraid that thieves had broken in. But I was brave enough to get up and go across the corridor to my grandfather's bedroom. It was he who was crying out. He was talking with someone, arguing, begging, but I didn't understand a word because he was talking in German. He screamed as I had never heard anyone scream, calling someone, saying a name so loud that he ended up waking himself. I was going to hide but realized that he didn't see me in the light of the corridor, although his eyes were wide-open. He was panting and sweating. The next day I asked him if he'd had a bad dream, but he told me he didn't remember any. Every night the same cries were repeated, the screams in German in the silent house, the repeated name, Greta or Gerda. When my grandfather died, we found a small suitcase under his bed filled with letters in German and photographs of a young woman. Grete was the signature on all the letters, which stopped in 1940. I didn't like my surname when I was a girl, but now I carry it like a gift my grandfather left me, like the letters I would have liked to read but couldn't. I brought them with me when I came to Buenos Aires, along with the photos of Grete. I told myself that I would give them to someone who knew German and ask him to translate them for me, but I kept putting it off. Life gets busy, and you think there will always be time for everything, then one day it turns out it's all over, you don't have any of the things you thought you had, not your husband, not your house, not your papers, nothing but fear that claws inside you and never stops. I do not know what happened to her letters, what the people who raided my house did with them. I took only one thing with me when I escaped, though not knowingly: I'd just become pregnant.

sepharad

I REMEMBER A JEWISH house in a barrio in my native city called the Alcázar, because it occupies the location, still partially walled, where a medieval castle stood, an *alcázar,* a fortified citadel that belonged first to the Muslims and then after the thirteenth century to the Christians—after 1234 to be exact, when King Ferdinand III of Castile, who in my textbooks was called the Saint, took possession of the recently conquered city. To help us children remember the date, they told us to think of the first four numbers—one, two, three, four—and as if it were one of the multiplication tables we would chant: Ferdinand III, the Saint, conquered our city from the Moors in one thousand, two hundred, thirty, and four.

A mosque first occupied the elevated corner of the Alcázar that was nearly inaccessible from the south and east sides; the Church of Santa María, which still exists although it has been closed many years for a never-ending restoration, was built on the same base. It has, or it had, a Gothic cloister, the only truly old and significant part of the building, which has been restored many times without much thought, especially in the nineteenth century, when around 1880 they added a busy and vulgar facade and a pair of undistinguished bell towers. But I could identify the tolling of their bells from the many heard in the city at dusk, because they were the bells of our parish, and I also knew when they rang for a death or a funeral mass, and on Sundays, at noon and dusk, I recognized the rich peals that announced high mass. Other bells nearby had a much more serious and solemn bronze tone—the bells, for instance, of El Salvador Church, and others had higher and more diaphanous notes, and then there were the bells at the nuns' convent, which rang in a fortresslike tower that was as forbidding as the rest of the church, with its huge main door that was always closed and the high stone walls darkened with lichen and moss because they faced the cool shade of the north side. From time to time that enormous black studded door would swing open and two nuns would come out, always in pairs, and so pale I thought they must have come from the tomb, in their dark brown habits and with their faces tightly framed in white beneath their wimples, their skin whiter than the cloth, and they always frightened me terribly because I thought they would kidnap me, and I held tighter to the hand of my mother, who had put a black veil over her head to come to church.

I remember the large uneven stones in the Santa María cloister, some of which were gravestones bearing names of persons from long ago carved into a slab and nearly erased by the footsteps of centuries, and I remember a garden you reached through ogival arches, where there was a bay tree so tall that from a child's perspective the top could not be seen. In the garden shaded by that tree and filled with ferns and weeds, there was always, even in summer, a strong scent of growing things and moist earth, and the garden rang with the uproar of the birds that nested in the thick branches and the long whistles of swallows and swifts in the slow summer afternoons. You could see the dark green thrust of the bay tree from a great distance, like a geyser of vegetation rising higher than the bell towers of the church and the tile roofs in the barrio, and it swayed on windy afternoons. When my mother took me by the hand into the cloister, it made me dizzy to peek out into the garden and see the tree. I always noticed how cool the dirt and the stone were, and I was always deafened by the clamor of the birds, which flew up in a cloud when the bells were rung.

I was sure the tree reached the sky, like the magic beanstalk in the story that my aunts told me and that many years later I read to my oldest son, who from the age of three always begged for a story at bedtime, quickly restless when he knew the story was about to end, asking me to make it last a little longer or read him another or, better still, make up one he liked, and give the characters his favorite personality traits and magic powers, and the names he had to approve. Reading the story at my son's bedside, I imagined his little hero climbing the branches of that prodigious bay tree at Santa María, up, up toward the sky, and coming out on the other side of the clouds, just as I imagined it when I was a boy. If you looked up, looked hard, the tree swayed slightly even when there was no wind. When a strong wind blew, the sound of the leaves was like that of waves on the shore, which I had never heard except in movies, or when I held a seashell to my ear.

I WENT TO THE CHURCH of Santa María every afternoon during the summer I was twelve to say a few Ave Marias to the Virgin of Guadalupe, the patron saint of my city, whom I asked to intercede for me so I would pass gym in September, because in the June examinations I had failed in a truly humiliating manner. I wasn't good at sports, I couldn't climb a rope or vault over a pommel horse, I couldn't even do a somersault. I had a growing sense of being excluded that was bitterly accentuated by the loss of the comfortable certainties of childhood and the first confusion and fears of my transition to adolescence. Pimples were breaking out on my too round face, fuzz was darkening my upper, still childish lip, hair was growing on the strangest parts of my body, and I was suffering sharp and secret remorse about masturbation, which according to the grim teachings of the priest was not merely a sin but also the beginnings of a series of atrocious illnesses. How strange to have been that solitary, fat, clumsy child who all summer long, at dusk, as the heat was fading, walked to the Alcázar barrio and went inside the cool cloisters of Santa María to pray to the Virgin, stepping on the gravestones of dead buried five or six centuries before, devout but ashamed because that summer I had learned to masturbate and was always surreptitiously looking down women's necklines and up their naked legs: the white breast, the large dark nipple, and the light blue veins of a barefoot Gypsy nursing her child at the door of one of the huts of the poor who lived at the edge of the barrio, beside the ruined wall.

Sometimes from a distance I would see four or five of the toughest boys in our class sitting on a stone bench in the large plaza in front of the church. They already smoked and went to taverns, and if I walked by them, pretending not to see them, they made fun of me, the way they had jeered at my physical cowardice in the gym and schoolyard. They made fun of me even more when they realized where I was going, the fat little sissy who got good grades but flunked gym and now came to pray every afternoon to the Virgin and more than once went to confession and then stayed for mass and took Communion, with the remorse and anguish of not having dared confess everything to the priest, who asked the formulaic questions and in the dark traced the sign of the cross as he murmured the penance and absolution—that there was a further sin he couldn't say the name of but only allude to using a vague euphemism: he had committed *an impure act*. The Catholic doctrine accustomed us to the solitary struggle with ourselves at an early age, to the contortions of guilt; an impure act was a mortal sin, and if you didn't confess it then you couldn't be absolved, and if you came to take Communion in a state of mortal sin, you were committing another, equally grave as the first, which was added to it in the secret ignominy of your conscience.

My first marriage took place in the Church of Santa María, when I was twenty-six. Maybe because of the confusion and tension of the ceremony, and the dizzying number of guests, I didn't take a good look at the great bay tree in the cloister, although now I am struck by the alarming thought that they may have cut it down, which wouldn't have been unusual in a city so addicted to arboricide. The young man with the mustache and razor-cut hair, wearing a navy-blue suit and pearl-gray necktie, seems even more remote to me than the pious and ashamed boy of fourteen years before. Throughout that time, he had perfected the skills that he already glimpsed as his in early adolescence: the art of being what he was expected to be and at the same time rebelling in surly silence, the cleverness of hiding his true identity and nourishing it with books and dreams while presenting an attitude of meek acquiescence on the outside. Thus he lived in exile, at a distance as false as a perspective of open country painted on a wall, or as those cinematic backgrounds against which an actor is driving a convertible at top speed along a cliff without ruffling a hair of his head and the passing trees fail to throw a shadow on the windshield.

THE BARRIO OF THE ALCÁZAR, bounded on the south and west by the road that circles the ruined wall and terraced gardens, has narrow cobbled streets and small plazas on which it is not unusual to see a large house with a great stone arch and a few mulberry or poplar trees. The oldest houses date from the fifteenth century. The exteriors are whitewashed, except for the door frames, which have the yellow tint of the sandstone from which they were hewn, the same stone that was used for the palaces and churches.

The white of the lime and the gold and blond of the stone create a delicate harmony that has the luminous elegance of the Renaissance and the austere beauty of vernacular architecture. High, narrow windows with heavy iron grilles thick as shutters, and gardens enclosed in tall adobe walls, recall the impenetrable look of Muslim dwellings that was adopted for the cloistered convents. There are large mansions with windows narrow as embrasures, in which we children sometimes hid, and great iron rings in the facades, so heavy that we weren't strong enough to lift them; to these rings, we were told, the former lords of the houses tied their horses. The mansions were inhabited by the nobles who ruled the city and who during their feudal uprisings against the power of the kings dug in behind the walls of the Alcázar. In the shelter of those walls was the Jewish quarter; the nobles needed the Jews' money, their administrative abilities, the skills of their artisans, so they had an interest in protecting them against the periodic explosions of fury from devout and brutal mobs stirred up by fanatic priests, by legends about profanations of the host and the bloody rituals Jews celebrated to dishonor the Christian religion: that they stole consecrated hosts and spit them out and ground them beneath their feet, and pierced them with nails and crushed them with pincers to repeat on them the tortures inflicted upon the mortal flesh of Jesus Christ, and kidnapped Christian children and slit their throats in the cellars of the synagogues, and drank their blood or with it sullied the sacred white flour of the hosts.

Someone told me about a specific Jewish house, and I wandered around the barrio until I found it. It sits on a narrow street, as if huddled there, and I remember it as lived in, with sounds of people and television flooding out to the street through the open windows, which were filled with pots of geraniums. It has a low door, and on the two extremes of the large stone lintel are engraved two Stars of David, inscribed in a circle, and not so worn by time that you can't make out the design clearly. It's a small but solid house that must have belonged to a scribe or minor merchant, not a wealthy family, or possibly to the teacher of a rabbinical school, to some family that in the years prior to the expulsion would have lived divided between fear and an attempt at normality, hoping that the excesses of Christian fanaticism would die down, just as it had so many times, and that in this small city, and behind the protection of the walls of the Alcázar, the terrible slaughter of a few years earlier in Córdoba would not be repeated, or the pogrom at the end of the preceding century. The house on this little street has an air of watchfulness and self-effacement, like someone who lowers his head and walks close to the wall in order not to attract attention.

What do you do if you know that from one day to the next you can be driven from your home, that all it takes is a signature and a lacquer seal at the bottom of a decree for the work of your entire life to be demolished, for you to lose everything, house and goods, for you to find yourself out on the street exposed to shame, forced to part with everything you considered yours and to board a ship that will take you to a country where you will also be pointed at and rejected, or not even that far, to a disaster at sea, the frightening sea you have never seen? The two Stars of David testify to the existence of a large community, like the fossilized impression of an exquisite leaf that fell in the immensity of a forest erased by a cataclysm thousands of years ago. They couldn't believe that they would actually be driven out, that within a few months they would have to abandon the land they had been born in and where their ancestors had lived. The house has a door with rusted studs and an iron knocker, and small Gothic moldings in the angles of the lintel. Maybe the people who have gone carried with them the key that fit this large keyhole, maybe they handed it down from father to son through generations of exile, just as the language and sonorous Spanish names were perpetuated, and the poems and children's songs that the Jews of Salonica and Rhodes would carry with them on the long, hellish journey to Auschwitz. It was a house like this that the family of Baruch Spinoza or Primo Levi would leave behind forever.

I walked through the cobbled alleys of the Jewish quarter in Ubeda, imagining the silence that must have fallen during the days following the expulsion, like the silence that would linger in the streets of the Sephardic barrio of Salonica after the Germans evacuated it in 1941, where the voices of children jumping rope and singing the ballads I learned in my childhood would never be heard again, ballads about women who disguised themselves as men in order to do battle in the wars against the Moors, ballads about enchanted queens. The Franciscans and Dominicans preaching to the illiterate from the pulpits of their churches, the bells tolling in triumph as exiles left the Alcázar barrio in the spring and summer of 1492, another of the dates we memorized in school because it marked the moment of the greatest glory in the history of Spain, our teacher told us, when Granada was reconquered and America discovered, and when our newly unified country became an empire. *Of Isabel and Fernando the spirit prevails,* we sang as our martial footsteps marked time with the hymn, *we will die kissing the sacred flag.* A feat by the Catholic king and queen as important as the victory over the Moors in Granada, and a decision as wise as that of sponsoring Columbus, had been the expulsion of the Jews, who in the drawings in our school encyclopedia had hooked noses, goatees, and who stood accused of the same dark perfidy as other sworn enemies of Spain of whom we knew nothing but their terrifying names: Freemasons and communists. When we were fighting with other children in the street and one of them spit on us, we always yelled at him: Jew, you spit on the Lord. On the floats during Holy Week, the soldiers and the Pharisees were depicted with the same gross fea-

tures as the Jews in the school encyclopedia. On the Last Supper
float, Judas was as scary to us as Dracula in the movies, with his
hooked nose and pointed beard and the green face of betrayal
and greed that turned to sneak looks at the bag that held the
thirty pieces of silver.

IN ROME'S HOTEL EXCELSIOR, many years and several lives
later, I met the Sephardic writer Emile Roman, a Romanian who
spoke fluent Italian and French, but also a rare and ceremonious
Spanish he had learned in childhood and which must have been
very similar to the Spanish spoken in 1492 by the people who
lived in that house in the Alcázar barrio. "But we didn't call ourselves Sephardim," he told me. "We were Spanish." In Bucharest
in 1944, a passport expedited by the Spanish embassy saved his
life. With the same passport that liberated him from the Nazis he
escaped the Communist dictatorship years later and never returned to Romania, not even after the death of Ceauşescu. Now
he was writing in French and living in Paris, and as he was retired,
he spent his evenings at a club of elderly Sephardim called the
Vida Larga, the long life. He was a tall, erect man who moved deliberately; he had olive skin and large ritual hands. In the bar of
the hotel, an individual with a red bow tie and silver dinner jacket
was playing international hits on an electric organ. Sitting across
from me, beside the windows that looked out on the traffic of Via
Veneto, Roman took sips of an espresso and spoke passionately of
injustices committed five centuries before, never forgotten, never
corrected, not even softened by the passing of time and succes-
sion of generations: the incontrovertible decree of expulsion, the
goods and homes hastily sold to meet the time period of two
months granted the expelled, two months to depart from a country in which your people lived for more than a thousand years, almost since the beginning of that other diaspora, said Roman.

The deserted synagogues, the scattered libraries, the empty stores and closed workshops, one or two hundred thousand people forced to leave a country of barely eight million inhabitants.

And those who didn't leave, who chose to convert out of fear or for convenience, assuming that once they were baptized they would be accepted? But that didn't work either, because if they couldn't be persecuted because of the religion they had abjured, now it was their blood that condemned them, and not just them but their children and grandchildren after them, so that those who stayed behind ended up as alien in their homeland as those who left, perhaps even more so, for they were scorned not only by those who should have been their brothers in their new religion but also by those who remained loyal to the abandoned faith. The most heinous Christian sinner could repent, and if he fulfilled his penance be freed of guilt; the heretic could recant; original sin could be redressed thanks to Christ's sacrifice; but for the Jew there was no possible redemption, his culpability long predated his being and was independent of his acts, and if his behavior was exemplary, he became even more suspicious. But in this respect Spain was no exception, it was no more cruel or fanatic than other countries in Europe, contrary to common belief. If Spain stood out in any way, it wasn't for expelling the Jews but for being so slow to do so, since Jews had already been expelled from England and France in the fourteenth century and not, to be sure, with any more consideration, and when many of the Jews who left Spain sought refuge in Portugal in 1492, they obtained it in exchange for one gold coin per person, only to be expelled again six months later, and those who converted in order to stay had no better life than the converts in Spain; they, too, were tagged with the vile name Marranos, pigs. Some marranos emigrated to Holland after several generations of subjection to Catholicism and, as soon as they were there, professed their Jewish faith: the family of Spinoza, for example, who was too rational and freethinking to conform to any dogma and was in turn officially expelled from the Jewish community.

"To be Jewish was unpardonable, to stop being Jewish was impossible," Emile Roman said, burning with a slow and melancholy wrath. "My true name is Don Samuel Béjar y Mayor, and I am not Jewish because of the faith of my ancestors, for my parents never practiced, and when I was young I cared about religion as much as you cared about your grandparents' belief in the miracles of the Catholic saints. No, it was anti-Semitism that made me a Jew. For a time my Jewishness was like a secret illness that doesn't exclude a person from contact with others because it isn't revealed in external signs, not like the lesions or pustules that condemned you as a leper in the Middle Ages. But one day in 1941 I had to sew a yellow Star of David on the upper chest of my overcoat, and from then on the illness could not be hidden, and if I forgot for an instant that I was a Jew and couldn't be anything but, the looks of people I met in the street or on a streetcar platform (while we were still allowed to travel by streetcar) reminded me of it, made me feel my illness and my strangeness. Some acquaintances turned their heads so they wouldn't have to say hello, or be seen talking with a Jew. Others walked far out of their way, as you would make a wide berth to avoid a filthy beggar or someone with a horrible deformity. As I was walking down the street, anyone at all might insult me, or push me off the curb, because I had no right to be on the sidewalk.

"Have you read Jean Améry? You must, he's as important as Primo Levi, if much more despairing. Levi's family emigrated to Italy in 1492. Both men were in Auschwitz, although they didn't meet there. Levi didn't share Améry's despair, nor could he accept his suicide, though he, too, ended up killing himself—or at least that's how it was reported by the police. Améry's name wasn't really Améry, or Jean. He had been born in Austria and was legally Hans Mayer. Until he was thirty, he thought that he was Austrian and that his language and culture were German. He even liked to wear the Austrian folk costume of lederhosen and kneesocks. Then one day in November of 1935, sitting in a café in Vienna, just as you and I are sitting here, he opened the newspaper and read the proclamation of the Nuremberg race laws, and discovered that he wasn't who he had always thought he was, who his parents had taught him to believe he was: an Austrian. Suddenly he was what he had never considered himself to be: a Jew. He had walked into the café taking for granted that he had a country and a life, and when he left there he was stateless, and worse, a possible victim. His face was the same, but he had become another person. In 1938 he escaped to the west, to Belgium, while there was still time, but in those days the borders in Europe could change into barbed-wire traps overnight, and the person who had escaped to another country woke up one morning hearing a loudspeaker blasting the voices of the executioners he thought he'd left behind. In 1943 Mayer was arrested by the Gestapo in Brussels, tortured, and sent to Auschwitz. After the Liberation, he repudiated the German name and language and decided to called himself Jean Améry. He never again set foot in Austria or Germany. Read the book he wrote about the hell of the camp. After I finished it, I couldn't read or write anything. He says that at the moment your torture begins, your covenant with other human beings is lost forever, that even if you are saved and live many years more, the torture never ends, and you will never be able to look anyone in the eye or trust anyone. When you meet a stranger, you wonder if he has been a torturer. If an old and well-mannered neighbor says hello when she meets you on the stairway, you think that she could have denounced the Jewish man next door to the Gestapo, or looked the other way when he was dragged downstairs, or shouted *Heil Hitler* until she was hoarse when German soldiers marched by."

I WAS INVITED TO GERMANY once, some years ago, to give a talk in a very beautiful city, a storybook city with cobbled streets, Gothic rooflines, parks, and hundreds of people riding bicycles: Göttingen, the home of the Brothers Grimm. I remember the silken sound of the bicycle tires as they rolled over the wet cobbles at night, and the sound of the bicycle bells. It had been a sunny day, and I'd been up since early morning, taken from one place to another all day, always by very helpful and friendly people whose sole concern was to organize the immediate satisfaction of any desire I could dream up, with an efficiency that became oppressive. If I said I was interested in visiting a museum, they immediately began telephoning, and in a short time I had information pamphlets, hours, and possible means of transportation at my disposal. In the morning they took me to give a talk at the university, then agonized over various places to have lunch. Did I prefer Italian food? Chinese? Vegetarian? When I said that I liked Italian, they discussed which of several possibilities would be the best.

That afternoon, drowsy as I was from the food and the accumulated exhaustion of the trip, they took me to a bookstore to give a talk there. I read a chapter from my book, and then a translator read it in German. I became depressed thinking of all the pages I had to go, and I was disgusted and irritated by my own words. I looked up from the book to swallow, to take a breath, and saw serious, attentive faces, an audience listening with great discipline but without understanding a word. I was embarrassed by what I'd written, and felt guilty for the boredom those people must have been experiencing, so to shorten their agony I read as fast as I could and skipped entire paragraphs. I closed my eyes when my German translator began to read, and tried to sit up straight and be attentive, as if I understood some of it, and in the slightly less inanimate faces of the audience I looked for reactions to what I'd written some time ago in a language that had no similarity at all to what they were hearing. I would detect a smile, an expression of agreement with something I'd written, but had no idea what it was. At the end I felt so relieved that it was of no consequence that the applause was enthusiastic, though I smiled and bowed my head a little, with the usual insincerity of a person being praised. I wanted to get out of there as quickly as possible and not have to sign another book or show interest in another explication, and to be free of the crushing politeness of the organizers, who were already plotting my next steps, looking at the clock and calculating how long it was before the museum I wanted so much to see would close, discussing whether it would be quicker and more comfortable for me if they took me in a taxi or by streetcar.

They were completely undone, and I felt inconsiderate and ungrateful telling them that I would rather go back to the hotel, I would just get a bite to eat there; there was no need to call a restaurant and have the menu read to me so I could make my decision. I wasn't hungry and would be happy with a beer and a bag of potato chips from the minibar in my room. Finally they left, saying good-bye at the steps to the hotel with a friendliness I didn't deserve, they being so amiable and I cursing them inside, longing for the moment when I could lie down on the bed, do nothing, not speak to anyone, take off my shoes and fluff up the pillow and stare at the ceiling, enjoying all the hours ahead when I could be alone, take a walk at my pleasure, wherever I pleased, with no one beside me to subject me to implacable courtesy.

I luxuriated for a while in the German comfort of the room, which was small, with beams in the ceiling and a floor of polished wood, like an illustration in a story. I pulled up one of those warm, light eiderdowns that you don't find in any other part of the world, but I didn't want to fall asleep because it was early, even though it was growing dark, if I slept now I might be wide-awake at two in the morning and spend the rest of the night in one of those miserable bouts of hotel-room insomnia. So I went down to the lobby, first looking to see that none of my hosts was about, and when I went outside, I also looked both ways, like a spy in the John Le Carré novels I read as a youth, ordinary-looking men in glasses and overcoat who walk through small German cities, turning from time to time to look in the side mirror of a parked car to be sure they're not being followed by an agent of the Stasi. There was a cold mist in the air, the dampness and smell of a river and wet vegetation. As I walked I began to recover from my exhaustion and drowsiness, and the euphoria began that tends to animate me when I go outside in a strange city and have no obligations to meet and nobody knows me.

I remember a few things clearly: a cobblestone street, houses with peaked roofs on both sides, slate roofs, wood beams crisscrossing the facades, small windows with carved wooden shutters, and through them scenes of well-lit, paneled rooms lined with books. I would hear the sharp sound of a bicycle bell behind me and be overtaken by a placidly pedaling man or woman, not necessarily young, sometimes a white-haired lady in an out-of-style hat, sometimes an executive wearing a navy-blue suit beneath his raincoat. I saw Gothic towers with gilded clocks and streetcars that floated across a street in a silence almost as ghostly as that of the bicycles. On a street corner my attention was caught by a bright pastry shop and busy sounds—though they, too, were muted, as if wrapped in the general quiet of the city—of jovial conversation and the clink of teaspoons and cups, along with the warm, pungent aroma of baking, and of cocoa and coffee, on the cold air. Because I was hungry and I'd grown cold during my long walk, I overcame the timidity that so often keeps me from going alone into a place filled with locals, that Spanish diffidence that becomes more pronounced when I'm in a foreign country. It must have been a shop from the turn of the twentieth century, preserved intact, with stucco and gilding reminiscent of the Autro-Hungarian baroque, mahogany-framed mirrors and ballroom chandeliers, and marble-top tables and slender columns of white-painted iron that gleamed with touches of gold on the capitals. There were racks holding thick German newspapers, the print heavy and black, as if from early in the century, the First World War. The waitresses wore low-cut white bodices and old-fashioned skirts, their blond hair a wheel of braids or curls secured over the ears and their round faces pink from rushing among tables crowded with people, one hand high above their heads skillfully supporting a tray laden with teapots, porcelain jugs of coffee or chocolate, and tarts—the same copious, exquisite tarts so temptingly displayed in the showcases in greater variety than I had ever seen, or have since.

I took a seat at a small corner table and waited for my tea and the cheese-and-blackberry tart I had succeeded in ordering, using sign language. I entertained myself looking at the faces around me, enjoying the warm room and the tranquillity of not having to pay attention to a language I didn't understand. Most of the clientele were older, prosperous retired couples or groups of ladies in hats and coats, and the general tone was one of solid and civilized pleasure, heads nodding and hands with extended pinkies lifting teacups, prudent laughter, lively conversation. Pairs of light eyes sometimes registered my presence with a slight flicker of curiosity, or perhaps rejection. I was undoubtedly the only stranger in the place, and in the mirror in front of me I suddenly saw myself as if from the outside—as the waitress bringing my tea and tart must have seen me, or the man with very blue eyes and very white hair who had turned slightly and was examining me as he continued talking to the lady with gold earrings, jet-black-dyed hair, and white gloves sitting next to him, whose excessive makeup accentuated the countless creases that ringed her crimson lips. I saw my own black hair, dark eyes, white shirt—no necktie—and the five o'clock shadow that gave me the appearance of a Bulgarian or Turk. My suit jacket, wrinkled after several days of travel and neglect, looked like the jackets immigrants wear, the ones you see in 1960s photographs of Spaniards in Germany.

I was tired; professional trips wear me out, and new acquaintances make my head spin, and I sleep badly in hotels. I was beginning to see the faces and objects around me as through a fog, although no one was smoking in the pastry shop and the only vapor came from the cups and the breath of people walking in from the cold. How strange I hadn't noticed earlier that everyone except the waitresses was old, the men and women as carefully preserved as the decor and the plaster molding of the tearoom, and equally decrepit: false teeth, canes, toupees, blond or white-powdered wigs, bi- and trifocal eyeglasses, orthopedic shoes and stockings, Miss Marple hats, and parchment-skinned, arthritic hands tremulously conveying forkfuls of tart and delicate porcelain teacups. Even the rosy, plump waitresses were somehow ancient despite their ballooning skirts, braids and curls, bodices and lace-filled décolletages. I looked at the man who had been examining me a moment before, and it occurred to me that he must be over seventy, maybe eighty. His face and hands were ruddy, as if he spent a lot of time outdoors, and he had the haughty air of a retired military man. In 1940 he wouldn't have been more than thirty. I saw him in a uniform, those light eyes shaded by the visor of a silver cap. In the Germany of the 1930s and later, during the war, what would he have been doing, where would he have been? I must have been staring at him, because I caught an expression of irritation when his eyes met mine.

I considered the other people in the tearoom in the light of the chandeliers glittering in gilded moldings and multiplied in the mirrors, and I imagined every face, man's or woman's, as it might have been fifty or sixty years back. The transformation was at first disquieting, then threatening: those placid features became young and cruel, the mouths sipping chocolate or tea opened in cries of fanatic enthusiasm, the hands with age spots and knuckles deformed by arthritis so elegantly holding teacups shot up like bayonets in an unanimous salute. How many of those around me had yelled *Heil Hitler*? What was on their conscience, in their memories? How would they have looked at me had I been wearing a yellow star stitched on my overcoat? Had I been in this same pastry shop, would one of those men, in a black leather coat, have approached me and asked for my papers? The stranger with the southern European look draws sidelong glances; cupping his tea in his hands to warm them, he doesn't know that some conscientious citizen has already called the Gestapo. So many people called in those days, without anyone forcing them, they called out of a sense of duty, and maybe one of these elderly people in the tea shop made such a call, a denunciation like the ones in the archives, proof that the crime was nearly universal, that a multitude of individuals supported the bloody edifice of tyranny. More eyes are focused on me, and my face in the mirror that expands space and multiplies people has also been modified: I am odder, darker. My discomfort grows. I wish I had a book or newspaper, something to distract me and occupy my hands. I feel through the pockets in my overcoat, but I haven't brought anything except my passport and wallet. Tired of waiting, I gather my courage and stand up to leave, but immediately sit back down—I even think I blush—because the waitress has arrived with the tray and a paper-doll smile, saying something I don't understand. I pay her before she leaves, drink a little tea, and nibble the overly sweet tart. Dizzy from the excessive warmth, I go outside and am grateful for the solitude and the cold, clean air. I start off through a park, believing it's the one I walked through on my

way from the hotel, but when I come out of it along a high railing and see the lights of a modern street I don't remember having
seen before, I realize, with all the sudden lucidity of waking from
a dream, that I am lost.

ONE SOLITARY WALK blends into another, like a dream that
leads into another, and the German night dissolves into a rainy
afternoon ten years later on the other side of the ocean, but there
is the same penetrating odor of wet vegetation and soaked earth,
and the person doing the walking is not the same man he was
then. At some moment in that interval of time, he has discovered
what everyone knows and yet no one accepts: that he is mortal.
Having been on the verge of dying, he also knows that the time
he is living now is a gift half of chance and half of medicine. That
this midafternoon stroll through the tree-lined, tranquil streets
of New York might never have taken place. That if he were not
this minute, slightly dizzy, crossing Fifth Avenue at Eleventh
Street, going west, wearing his raincoat and carrying his umbrella, it would make absolutely no difference, no one would notice his absence, there would not be the slightest modification in
the world, in the redbrick houses with high stone steps that he
likes so much, in the lines of gingko trees with their fan-shaped
leaves, still young and tender green, as shiny as the green of the
wisteria climbing up the house fronts to the cornices, sometimes
curling around the metal geometry of the fire escapes. He might
never have come back to this city, it could easily have happened,
and since it is only one or two days before he leaves it, he fears
this may be the last time, and his awareness of the fragility of his
life, the so easily cut thread of any person's life, makes this walk
he is taking now that much more valuable. Among the names of
cities and women his life and mind have gifted him with, there is
a new name, scrabbling up like a scorpion in his vital lexicon. Just
as Franz Kafka never wrote the word *tuberculosis* in his letters, he

never speaks the word *leukemia,* he doesn't even think it or say it silently, lest with that mere pronunciation he feels the poison of its sting.

He walks west, letting his footsteps lead where they will, looking for the hidden, cobblestone streets close to the Hudson River, on the edge of the vast desolation of the port and the abandoned wharves where transatlantic steamers used to berth. Now the huge pilings are rotting in the gray water, and thick weeds grow in the cracks of the piers as if among the crumbling columns of a ruined temple. Some of the piers have signs forbidding entrance. Others have been converted into children's parks or playgrounds. Countless people fleeing Europe walked across these broad wooden planks, and from here they looked toward the city with fear and hope. Along the river runs a path for runners and bladers, for people who come to quietly walk their dogs. On the other side he can see the New Jersey coast, low lines of trees interrupted by ugly industrial hangars, an apartment tower, a gigantic brick building that from a distance looks like the merloned door of a walled Babylonian or Assyrian city and that has its exact equivalent on this side of the river. Those constructions seemed the more mysterious to me because they had no windows and I couldn't imagine what purpose they served. They were like the towers of Nineveh or Samarkand, erected not in the middle of the desert but on the banks of the Hudson; later I learned that they contain ventilators for the Lincoln Tunnel, which runs beneath the river and is so long that when you drive through it in a taxi you have the sensation that you will never reach the end and soon will run out of air.

In the distance, to the south, rises the cliff of the newest skyscrapers in the lower part of Manhattan, the ones that have grown up around the Twin Towers, which have a certain beauty only when surrounded by fog or when the sun at dusk gives them the splendor of copper prisms. On this afternoon of cloud and mist the waters of the Hudson are as gray as the sky, and the tops of the skyscrapers are lost in the large, dark, swiftly moving clouds in which the red lights of lightning conductors glow like coals beneath a light layer of ash. Almost lost in the fog are the Statue of Liberty and the slim brick towers of Ellis Island.

I have returned to this city and am already saying good-bye to it. I want to treasure every foot of it, every minute of this last evening, the red brick of those hidden streets, the fragrance of the purple blooms of the wisteria, the scent of the small jungle-like gardens you sometimes glimpse between two buildings, behind a wooden fence, where dank shade and thick vegetation remind me of the garden in the Church of Santa María on afternoons of heavy rain, when the water spilled from the gargoyles between the arches of the cloister and echoed within the vaulted ceilings. Between Fifth Avenue and Sixth, almost at the corner of Sixth Avenue and Eleventh Street, I have found the Sephardic cemetery my friend Bill Sherzer once showed me. I never noticed it before, although I am often in this neighborhood, the lower end of the avenues, which become more open and bohemian at the juncture of Chelsea and Greenwich Village, with its street stands of books and secondhand records and shops of outlandish clothing, its sidewalk café tables and showcases of fabulous Italian specialty groceries. We had often gone to one of them, Balducci's, to shop, but never noticed that shaded, narrow garden with the iron fence that at the beginning of the nineteenth century was the cemetery of the Hispano-Portuguese Jewish community, information confirmed by a plaque. Bill pointed it out to us. Fugitives from Russia, from hunger and the pogroms, his grandparents came to Ellis Island at the turn of the century.

Among the trees, ferns, ivy, and weeds are a few headstones so worn that you can barely read the inscriptions: Hebrew or Latin characters, an occasional Spanish name, a Star of David. The fence is closed, so we can't get inside the tiny cemetery, but if you could touch the stones you might make out something more than slabs whose corners have rounded with time, eroded to the point that almost all trace of human labor has been erased, like the broken columns and fragments of capitals returning to a primitive mineral state in the forums of Rome. Who is there to rescue names that were carved two hundred years ago, names of people who lived as fully as I do, who had memories and desires, who perhaps could trace their lineage back through successive exiles to a city like mine, to a house with two Stars of David on the lintel and to a barrio of narrow streets that lay deserted between the spring and summer of 1492? On this foggy, misty afternoon in New York, standing at the fence of a tiny cemetery locked between the high walls of buildings, I reencounter my ghostly compatriots, and sadly say farewell, because I am leaving tomorrow and may not return. There may be no future afternoon when I stand in this place, before these stones with eroded names, lost like so many others to the immemorial catalogue of Spanish diasporas, to the geography of Spanish graves in so many exiles throughout the world. Gravestones, tombs without a name, infinite lists of dead. On the outskirts of New York there is a cemetery of rolling green hills and enormous trees called the Gates of Heaven, with lakes where in autumn large flocks of Canadian geese gather. Among the thousands of headstones, in the midst of a geometry of graves with Irish names, there is one that is Spanish, so modest, so like the others, that it is difficult to find.

FEDERICO GARCÍA RODRÍGUEZ
1859–1945

How could that man have imagined that his grave would be not in a cemetery in Granada but on the other side of the world, near the Hudson River, or that his son would die before him and not have a grave, no simple stone to mark the exact spot in the ravine where he was executed? Modest burial places and common graves line the highways of the great Spanish diaspora. I would like to visit the French cemetery where Don Manuel Azaña was buried in 1940 in the midst of the great upheaval in Europe, and read the name of Antonio Machado on a tomb in the cemetery of Colliure. Legions of other dead who have no tomb or inscription endure in the alphabetized archive of names. On one Internet page I found, in white letters on a black background, a list of Sephardim the Germans deported from the Island of Rhodes to Auschwitz. You would have to read them one by one, aloud, as if reciting a strict and impossible prayer, to understand that not one of these names can be reduced to a number in an atrocious statistic. Each had a life unlike any other, just as each face, each voice was unique, and the horror of each death was unrepeatable even though it happened amid so many millions of similar deaths. How, when there are so many lives that deserve to be told, can one attempt to invent a novel for each, in a vast network of interlinking novels and lives?

I REMEMBER THE MORNING of that next-to-last day in New York, when you and I were already a little dazed by the imminence of the trip. We were in that strange nontime of the eve of departure, when a person is not completely in the place though he hasn't left it yet, when the things that seemed to accept him for a while now remind him that he is only a stranger passing through. We were shaken by the realization that no trace would remain of our presence in the apartment we occupied for such a brief time but in which, nonetheless, day after day, we had accumulated the signs of domestic life: clothes in the closet, which when I open it smelled of your cologne, just like our closet in Madrid, our books on the night table, your creams and my brush and shaving cream on the bathroom shelf—the part of us we brought on this trip, the part we must take with us again like nomads, erasing all the marks of ourselves before we go, even the scent of our bodies on the sheets, which we drop off at the laundry on the morning of our departure.

The least gesture casts the shadow of farewell. I was hoarding the count of the days we have left, and this morning I am thinking back on them, completely awake in the bed that belongs to others but has been ours for a few weeks. Still lazy and relaxed, my arms around you as you lie there as though still asleep and drawing pleasure from the deep pool of dream, I am also thinking that we still have this day, and I want very much to keep it whole and enjoy it slowly, like those moments we grant ourselves in bed after the alarm clock has gone off. Later I turn on the radio as I fix breakfast, but despite the announcer this is not a day like any other, and my routine of getting the coffee can from its precise place in the cupboard and the carton of milk from the refrigerator is false, like the ease with which I open the drawer with the spoons or turn the knob for the gas or put the filter in the coffeepot. False because tomorrow afternoon we will be two ghosts in this place, unknown and invisible to the new renter, whom we will not see and for whom we will leave an envelope with the concierge that contains the key to the apartment. The new renter is already an invading shadow, usurping the space of our intimacy, not just the bed where we've slept and made love and the table where every morning before you get up I have set out the coffee cups for breakfast, he also is present in the humid early-morning light that sifts through the glass doors to the terrace, and in the view we saw when, elbows propped on a fourteenth-story cornice as if on the railing of a great transatlantic steamer, we looked out over the city, especially at night. Those May nights of wind and lightning, storms with the fury of a monsoon, lightning bolts cutting across the large black clouds that blocked out the skyscrapers or that turned them into ghosts rising radiant through the downpour in the distance and disappearing suddenly in fog tinted the colors of the spotlights illuminating the highest floors of the Empire State Building, violet at times, red and blue, intense yellow. How reluctant we are to return to our country, for we have received almost daily accounts of obscurantism and bloodshed. We long to remain in exile.

There is still one day to pretend to ourselves, to each other, that our presence in this house, in this city, is real, as real as the doorman who gives us a cordial good morning in his Cuban accent or the Bengali at the shop on the corner where every day I buy a newspaper and telephone cards. I have spent so much of my life wanting to leave the place where I am, but now, when time is moving so swiftly, what I want most is to stay put, to cling like a limpet to the cities I like, to enjoy the calm of habit and familiarity, as when I think of the years you and I have been together. Never, except when I was a child, have I been tempted to collect anything, but now I like to slip ordinary mementos between the pages of a notebook or book: matchbooks with the name of a restaurant, theater tickets, bus tickets, any minimal document that records a date and time, our presence at some site, the itinerary of a brief trip. I'm not attached to things, not even to books and records, but I am to those places where I have known the mysterious exaltation of the best of myself, the fullness of my desires and affinities. What I treasure like an avaricious and obsessive collector are the moments I spend listening to music or looking at paintings in the galleries of a museum, the pleasure of walking with you one afternoon along the banks of the Hudson as the sun tints the glass of the skyscrapers with gold and copper. That captured light continues to glow in a photograph. I treasure the restless sense of adventure and uncertainty that invaded us that next-to-last morning in New York as we watched the last opulent houses of the Upper East Side slip past the bus window and gradually be replaced by the first vacant lots and ruined blocks of Harlem.

Going north, there were fewer and fewer passengers on the bus, and almost imperceptibly the white Anglo-Saxon faces disappeared, and instead of pale old ladies with an air of fragility the passengers now were young mothers, black or Hispanic, holding babies in their arms or leading small children by the hand, fat ladies with the bleach-blond hair, long fingernails, and impudent mouth of the Caribbean, black grandmothers sitting in their seats with the majesty of Ethiopian matrons but moving with great difficulty when they got up at their stop, weaving from side to side in their untied sneakers, their bodies misshapen and twisted as if by a painful bone disease. And as the passengers on the bus ceased to be white, the city changed outside the window, it became wider, emptier, deteriorated. There was less traffic, fewer shopwindows along the almost deserted sidewalks, there were unpopulated spaces, perspectives of properties with wire fences and buildings burned or in ruins, lots with razed houses where maybe one wall still stood, its empty windows boarded up, sinister as blinded eyes. Occasionally we drove through a stretch of street where for some reason there remained a vestige of neighborhood life, a sidewalk, a row of houses spared from destruction, with a moderately prosperous store on the corner and solitary men sitting on the steps, with young mothers leading small children by the hand and pots of geraniums in windows. The last tourists had got off the bus many stops ago, the ones going to the uptown museums, the Metropolitan or Guggenheim, and we no longer saw the trees of Central Park on our left, topped in the distance by the towers of apartments on Central Park West with pinnacles like an expressionist film set: crests and gargoyles, ziggurats, temples of remote Asian religions, lighthouses, cupolas.

The nearly empty bus made much better time, and the conductor turned to look at us, or he studied our strangeness in his rearview mirror. We passed a square that featured a garden in the French style, with a bronze statue of Duke Ellington in the center. The pedestal was like the edge of a stage, and Duke Ellington, dressed in a tux, stood against a grand piano, also cast in bronze. It had been more than an hour since we got on the bus at the Union Square stop. But we'd come so far and moved so slowly that it seemed we'd been gone much longer, and there was no sign that we were near our destination: 155th Street.

Our stop was on the corner of a wide avenue lined with not very tall, widely spaced buildings, and its air of solitude and of being at the end of something was accentuated by the gray day and the low walls of the empty lots. There was no one around to ask directions of. Run-down houses, churches, closed shops, an American flag flapping above a brick building that looked both shabby and official. We were discouraged, afraid we were lost, maybe even in a dangerous area: two foreign tourists you could spot a mile away, who don't know where they are and who realize with apprehension that among the few cars in the streets there's no bright yellow of a taxi.

The two of us walk along the wall of a large cemetery, which at first we took for a park. To the west you can imagine the vast stretches of the Hudson, then on a corner, where the cemetery ends, we see on the other side of the avenue, like a mirage, the building we're looking for, imposing and neoclassic, equally as strange as we are in this place, the home of the Hispanic Society of America, where we've been told there are paintings by Velázquez and Goya and a huge library no one visits, because who will come here, so far from everything and in a neighborhood that from midtown Manhattan can easily be seen as devastated and unsafe.

Behind a fence are a patio and statues between two buildings with marble cornices and columns and Spanish names inscribed across the facades. There is an imposing equestrian statue of the Cid, and on one wall a large bas-relief of Don Quixote on Rosinante, horseman and steed equally defeated and skeletal. Beside the entrance a woman with her white hair pulled back and with a rumpled look smokes a cigarette with that half-stubborn, half-furtive attitude of American smokers who have to go outside to fill their lungs with smoke, protecting themselves against the cold wind behind some column or in the shelter of a building, taking quick puffs from the cigarette and then hiding it, fearful of the censure of people going by. The woman looks at us a moment, and later we will both remember those eyes shining like coals in her aged face, the eyes of a much younger woman. She is an employee or secretary nearing retirement, who lives alone and doesn't care how she dresses, who cuts her hair without fuss and wears dark sweaters, men's trousers, and shoes between orthopedic and running gear, and hangs her glasses on a chain about her neck.

In the vestibule we look in vain for a ticket office. A burly old doorman sitting with indifference in a convent chair indicates that we can go on through, and from his face, attitude, and accent in spoken English we know he is Cuban. He wears a gray uniform jacket resembling that of a Spanish guard, but one from many years ago and threadbare after long service, after many terms of sleepy administrative laissez-faire. The minute we step into the lobby we notice, with misgiving, that there is practically no one there, and the whole place is dilapidated. A sign affixed to the glass of the entry door gives the museum hours; it is printed in an old typeface and badly yellowed, obeying the same principle of time as the doorman's jacket or the framed photographs in a glass case that document the founding, in the 1920s, of the Hispanic Society: the large black automobiles of the Spanish and American officials who attended the inauguration, views of a building that doesn't exist now, arrogant and white in the classicism of its architecture, its recently polished marble gleaming with the splendor of the new and up-to-date, and with the promise of a triumphant future. In the sky, above heads covered with top hats and stylish straw chapeaux, is an airplane that at the time would have been as dazzlingly modern as the cars of the ladies and gentlemen attending the inauguration. But the photographs have warped, and on the inside corners of the frames you can see the work of silverfish.

We enter a dark gallery reminiscent of the patio of a Spanish palace, with plateresque carved-wood choir stalls and arches of a deep red stone that is even darker in the faint daylight filtering through the skylights. The space defies identification: it could be the patio of a palace opening on several galleries, or the enormous desanctified sacristy of a cathedral . . . or a museum shop not organized according to any clear principle. At the beginning of the century, the millionaire Archer Milton Huntingon, possessed of a passion for all of Spanish Romanticism and a man of an insatiable and omnivorous erudition, wandered through Spain buying everything, anything, whether the choir of a cathedral or a glazed earthenware water pitcher, paintings by Velázquez and Goya, bishop's cassocks, Paleolithic axes, bronze arrows, the bloody Christs of Holy Week, heavy silver monstrances, Valencian ceramic tiles, illuminated parchments of the Apocalypse, a first edition of *La celestina,* the *Diálogos de amor* by Judá Abravanel, called León Hebreo, a Spanish-Jewish refugee in Italy, the 1519 *Amadís de Gaula,* the Bible translated into Spanish by Yom Tov Arias, the son of Levi Arias, and published in Ferrara in 1513 because it could not be published in Spain, the first *Lazarillo,* the *Palmerín de Inglaterra* in the same edition Don Quixote must have read, a first edition of *La Galatea,* the successive augmentations of the fearsome *Index librorom prohibitorum,* the *Quixote* of 1605, and a multitude of Spanish books and manuscripts that no one valued and that were sold at ridiculous prices to the man who traveled the impossible roads of Spain by automobile and lived in perpetual enchantment and enthusiasm. Consumed by a prodigious acquisitive greed, Mr. Huntington traveled here and there with his wild American energy through the dead, rural villages of Castile, following the route of the Cid, buying things and having them shipped to America, paintings, tapestries, ironwork, entire altarpieces, the detritus of high Spanish glory, relics of ecclesiastical opulence, but also objects of the everyday life of the people, pottery plates on which the poor ate their wheat porridge and the water jugs that allowed them the luxury of cool water in the dry interior. He directed archaeological digs in Italy and in one purchase bought the ten thousand volumes in the collection of the dead-broke Marqués de Jerez de los Caballeros. And to house the outlandish booty of his journeys through Spain, he constructed this palace at one end of Manhattan, which was never to be blessed with the prosperity or speculative fever he anticipated.

Everything is on the walls, in glass cases, in corners, always with a yellowing label giving the date and place of origin: Roman mosaics and oil lamps, Neolithic earthen bowls, medieval swords, Gothic virgins, like a flea market where all the testimony and heritage of the past has ended, washed up here in the convulsions of the great flood of time, refuse from the homes of the rich and the poor, the gold of the churches, the credenzas of the salons, the tongs that stirred the fires, and the tapestries and paintings that hung on the walls of churches now abandoned and sacked and palaces that may no longer exist, gravestones from the tombs of the powerful now worn nearly smooth, and marble fonts that held the holy water in the cool darkness of the chapels. And names, the sonorous names of Spanish communities on the labels in the cases, and among them, suddenly, beside a large green glazed bowl that I recognize immediately, the name of my hometown, where when I was a boy there was a community of potters whose kilns hadn't been modified since the times of the Moors, all grouped on a sunny street called Calle Valencia that ended in open country. I point out the bowl to you behind the glass in one of the freestanding cases in the Hispanic Society of America. From this remote time and place it has taken me straight back to my childhood: in the center of the bowl is a rooster in a circle, and as I look at it I can almost feel the glassy surface of the glaze and the raised lines of the design on my fingertips, a timeless rooster that looks like one of Picasso's and is also replicated on the plates and bowls in my home, as well as on the belly of the water pitchers. I remember the large bowls the women used for mixing ground meat and spices to make fresh sausage, the pottery plates on which they chopped the tomato and green pepper for the salads—austere and savory food of the common people and a standard subject of still lifes. Those objects had always been on the tables and in the cupboards of our houses, and it always seemed as if they had the status of a liturgical constancy, and yet they disappeared in only a few years' time, replaced by the invasion of plastic and commercial pottery. They have vanished like the houses in whose dark shadow the generous curves of that pottery shone, vanished like the people who once inhabited those houses.

"That bowl holds memories for me too," says the woman we saw smoking outside. She apologizes for interrupting, for having listened. "I recognized your accent, I lived in that town a long time ago." Her voice is almost as young as her eyes, unrelated to the age inscribed on her features and to the American carelessness of her clothes. "I work in the library, and if you're interested I'll show it to you. There are so many treasures, and so few people know about them. Professors come from time to time, very learned people doing research, but weeks can go by, even months, when no one comes to ask me about a book. Who's going to come all the way up here? Who would think that we have paintings by Velázquez, El Greco, and Goya, and that being almost in the Bronx, we would have the first *Lazarillo* and the first *Quixote* and the 1499 *La celestina*? Tourists go up to Ninetieth Street to visit the Guggenheim, and they think that everything that lies north of that is darkest Africa. I live near here, in a neighborhood of Cubans and Dominicans where you never hear a word of English. Downstairs from my apartment is a little Cuban restaurant called La Flor de Broadway. They make the best *ropavieja* stew and most delicious daiquiris in New York, and they let you smoke in peace at the tables, which have checked oilcloth covers, like the ones they had in Spain when I was young. What luxury, smoking a cigarette as I drink my coffee after dinner. You know how rare that is here, that they let you smoke at your table in a restaurant? I love my cigarettes. They're good company, and help when I'm talking with a friend or to pass the time when I'm alone. When I was young, I wanted to run away from Spain and come to America because here women could smoke and wear trousers and drive cars, all the things we saw in the movies before the war."

The woman spoke a fluid, clear Spanish, the kind you hear in some parts of Aragon, but there were sounds of the Caribbean and North America in her accent, and the timbre of her voice became totally Anglo-Saxon when she said a word in English. She invited us to have a cup of tea in her office, and we accepted, partly because we felt that physical exhaustion you get in museums, partly because there was something hypnotic in her way of talking and looking at us, even more in that empty, silent place on the gray morning of the last day of our trip. She still hadn't given us her name, yet she seduced us, speaking in that Spanish from so many years ago and examining us with eyes much younger than her face and figure. Her office was small, cluttered, and smelled of old paper, the office furniture was from the 1920s, like something you would see in a painting by Edward Hopper. She took three cups from a filing cabinet, along with three tea bags, set them on the papers on her desk, and with a totally North American gesture of apology went to get hot water. We looked at each other wordlessly, smiled at being in such a strange situation, and the woman returned.

Her glasses hang from a black ribbon. She looks like a university department secretary who is about to retire, but her eyes question me unabashedly, they are not the eyes of a woman pouring hot water into teacups. She regards at me as if she were thirty and evaluated men only by their looks or sexual availability; and she regards you as if to determine whether we're lovers or married and whether there is desire or distance between us. And while those magnetic eyes study our faces and our clothes, her old woman's hands are involved in the ritual of academic hospitality, serving tea and offering envelopes of sugar and saccharin and those little plastic stirrers that so disagreeably substitute for spoons in the United States. Her clear voice, ancient Spanish with influences of Cuban and English, recounts details about the megalomaniac millionaire who built the Hispanic Society on the corner of Broadway and 155th Street, believing that this part of Harlem would soon be in vogue among the rich, and about how strange it was to spend a life so far from Spain and yet be surrounded by so many things Spanish. She gestures toward the window from which you can see a common, ordinary sidewalk that is nonetheless Broadway, a row of redbrick houses crisscrossed by fire escapes and with water tanks on the roofs, and, in the distance, the gray of a horizon and the large blackened towers of public housing complexes in the Bronx.

"I left Spain more than forty years ago and have never been back, and I don't intend to go now, but I remember some places in your city, some of the names, Santa María Plaza, where the wind blew so hard on winter nights, and Calle Real, wasn't that what it was called? Although now I remember it was called José Antonio then. And that street where the potter's studios were, I'd forgotten the name but when I heard you talking to your wife about Calle Valencia, I realized you meant that street. There's a song we used to sing:

> *On Calle Valencia*
> *The potters, each day,*
> *Make cooking pots*
> *From water and clay.*

"When I was still young I took some Spanish-literature classes at Columbia University with Don Francisco García Lorca, and he liked me to sing him that. He would repeat the words for the class so we could see there wasn't one that wasn't ordinary, and yet the result, he told us, was both poetic and as informative as something out of a guidebook, just like the old *romances,* those ageless ballads."

She is talking a lot, mesmerizing us, but we haven't really learned anything about her, not even her name, although we realize that only later, and not without surprise, after we've left. We wonder what the apartment is like where she lives, undoubtedly alone, maybe with a cat for company, hearing voices and Cuban music from La Flor de Broadway below, where she regularly goes to eat, where she orders beans and pork and rice and maybe gets a little tipsy from a daiquiri, alone at a table with a checked cloth, smoking as she finishes her coffee and watches the street, appraising with unwavering eyes the men and women passing by. What does she do during all those hours and days when no one comes to consult a book in her library, the buried treasures that she catalogues and checks with a look of severe efficiency on her withered face, her eyes half closed behind the glasses on the black ribbon? Unique books that now can be found only here, first editions, entire collections of scholarly journals, seventeenth-century folios, autograph letters—all of Spanish literature and all possible knowledge and research concerning Spain gathered in this one great library that almost no one visits. But she doesn't need to open the poetry volumes of the Clásicos Castellanos collection to recite, because while she was studying with Professor García Lorca, she told us, she had acquired, at his urging, the habit of memorizing the poems she liked best, so she knew by heart a large part of the *Romancero,* and the sonnets of Garcilaso and Góngora and Quevedo, and especially of Saint John of the Cross, and almost all of Fray Luís de León and the Romantics Bécquer and Espronceda, who had been passions of hers during the fantasy and literary adolescence she shared with her brother, who was a little older than her and with whom she had read aloud *Don Juan* and *Fuente Ovejuna* and *Life Is a Dream.* Thanks to her professor, she devoted all the years she worked in the library of the Hispanic Society to memorizing Spanish literature, to reciting it silently or in a low voice, moving her lips as if praying, as she walked to work every morning along the Caribbean sidewalks of Broadway or traveled to lower Manhattan on slow buses or crowded subway cars, as she tossed nights in the insomnia of her solitary bed or walked through the rooms of the museum, almost without noticing the paintings and objects that were etched in her mind, as their layout was, and the names and dates typed on their labels.

But there was one painting she always stopped before and sat down to study with a melancholy that never lessened, that actually became stronger as the years passed and nothing seemed to change, sealed in time as if in a magic kingdom. The labels, posters, and catalogues yellowed, the toilets in the rest rooms became ancient relics, the thick curly hair of the Cuban and Puerto Rican custodians turned white, there were holes in the pockets of their Spanish-guard jackets and the cuffs of their sleeves were rubbed threadbare, and she herself was becoming more a stranger every time she saw herself in a mirror, except for the eyes, which sparkled as brightly as they had when she was thirty and found herself in America, alone and mistress of herself for the first time, possessed of a fever for life stronger even than Mr. Huntington's uncontrolled and lunatic fever for collecting. "I like to sit before that Velázquez painting, the portrait of the dark-haired girl that no one knows anything about, what her name was or why he painted her," she told us. "I'm sure you've seen it, but don't leave without going by again, because you may not be back this way again and will never have another chance. Over the years you don't notice things as much, you get used to them and don't look anymore, not out of indifference, but as a matter of mental health. The guards at any museum would go crazy if they looked at the same paintings day after day, at every tiny detail. I walk in here and after so many years I don't see anything, but that little girl by Velázquez is like a magnet, she's always looking at me, and though I know her face by heart I always find something new in it."

Paintings, in any museum, portray the powerful and the holy, people puffed up with self-importance or crazed by saintliness or by the torment of martyrdom, but that child doesn't represent anything, she isn't the young Virgin or a princess or the daughter of a duke, she's just herself, a solitary little girl with a serious, sweet expression, as if lost in a daydream or some moment of childish unhappiness. She's lost, too, in that place, in the pretentious and somewhat shabby halls of the Hispanic Society, like an enchanted child in a storybook palace where time hasn't moved for a hundred years. She has a frank and at the same time timid gaze, and those dark eyes look straight into mine as I write this, although now I am very far from her and that cloudy day in New York, on the eve of our departure. Only a few months have gone by, and my memories are still clear and strong, but if I think hard about those hours in the Hispanic Society, about the face of the little girl in the Velázquez painting, about the voice and fiery eyes of the woman who never told us her name, everything has the shimmer, the fragility, of something you are not sure really happened. I have kept proof, material evidence, the stub from the bus that carried us there, the postcards we bought in that gift shop, where you can still find black-and-white postcards from a century ago, and guides and catalogs of publications that would be at home on the counters of those bargain bookshops where they sell the most dog-eared and maltreated publications. But this modest shop reminded me a little of a humble state shop in Spain—in contrast to the shops in other New York museums, those spectacular supermarkets of luxury. They occupy enormous rooms lined with large, dark wood counters like shelves of an enormous early-twentieth-century fabric showroom, or like the gigantic wardrobes you see in the sacristies of cathedrals for holding liturgical garments. This museum shop occupies one dreary corner of the hall and a section of the counter where an elderly woman sits, looking for all the world as if she will bring out her knitting at any moment, as soon as these two strange visitors who are thumbing through a collection of faded postcards leave.

Every wall, from floor to ceiling, is covered with enormous paintings, or by a single painting as if in a baroque delirium. Here is a jumble of encyclopedia illustrations representing every regional folk costume, the traditional occupations and dances and geographies of Spain, all the gems of folkloric Romanticism diligently painted by Joaquín Sorolla, like a Sistine Chapel consecrated to the glory of Mr. Huntington's Hispanic passion, celebrating in broad, colorful brush strokes every racial type, every dusty costume closet or ancestral headwear or anthropological peculiarity: Andalusian horsemen in their wide-brimmed hats, Basque villagers in their berets, Catalans in their typical caps and espadrilles, Castilians with furrowed, sunburned faces, Aragonese with red kerchiefs tied around their necks dancing *jotas,* along with orange groves and olive trees, and Cantabrian waters where the fishermen of the north ply their trade, Gallegan granaries and the windmills of La Mancha, Andalusian Gypsies in their tiered, ruffled skirts and Valencian women in stiffly starched skirts and necklaces and with hairdos rigid as those of the ancient stone sculptures of the Damas Ibéricas, lush gardens and high, windswept plains, the violet skies of El Greco and the mellow, clear light of the Mediterranean, paintings by the square yard, a profusion of faces like masks and clothing like disguises that have all the vertiginous animation of a Carnival ball and also the grinding meticulousness of a catalog or rule book, each district with its folkloric characteristics and particular dress, along with its eternal customs and regional landscape, each individual categorized by origins and place of birth like birds or insects in their zoological taxonomy.

I HAVE BEFORE ME NOW, in my study, beside the keyboard of my computer and the white, polished shell that Arturo found two summers ago on the beach at Zahara, one of the postcards we bought in the Hispanic Society gift shop, the portrait of that dark-haired, delicate, solitary girl painted against a gray background. She looks at me today as she did that day on the eve of our return trip, when we went to see her for the last time before leaving the museum, when we were not quite present in New York though it was still twenty-four hours before our flight to Madrid. Time was disintegrating in our hands with the flimsiness of burned paper, pages of ash, anxious minutes and hours, like the agitated and fleeting time of clandestine lovers who know that the countdown to their separation has begun almost as soon as they see each other. When you invent, you have the vain belief that you are controlling places, things, the people you write about. In my study, beneath the lamp that lights my hands and the keypad, the mouse, the shell whose grooves I love to stroke, the postcard of the Velázquez girl, I can entertain the illusion that nothing I invent or remember exists outside me, beyond this reduced space. But the places are there even though I am not and even though I will not go back, and the other lives I have lived, and the men I was before I became who I am with you, may endure in the memory of others, and at this very moment, six hours and six thousand kilometers away from this painting, the girl who watches me from the pale reproduction of a postcard is showing the hint of a smile on a real and tangible canvas painted by Velázquez around 1640, taken to New York around 1900 by an American multimillionaire, and hung in semidarkness in a large room of a museum that few people visit. Who knows whether right now, when it is 2:40 P.M. in New York and here near nightfall at the end of a December day, someone is looking at that girl's face, someone who notices or recognizes in her dark eyes the melancholy of a long exile?

AUTHOR'S NOTE

I HAVE INVENTED very little in the stories and voices that weave through this book. Some of them I was told and have carried in my memory for a long time. Others I found in books. I discovered Willi Münzenberg while reading Stephen Koch's *El fin de la inocencia* (*The End of Innocence*), and I followed his trail in *The Passing of an Illusion* by François Furet, a book as admirable as its title, and in the second volume of the memoirs of Arthur Koestler, *Invisible Writing*, and in a surprising number of Internet pages. I saw the beautiful name of Milena Jesenska for the first time in the amazing *Cartas a Milena* (*Letters to Milena*) by Franz Kafka, in an Alianza paperback that has been with me for a long time. It was that single name in the title of a book, *Milena*, that led me to discover its author, Margarete Buber-Neumann, whom I found a few references to in Koch and in Furet, as a kind of minor character in a footnote. The two volumes of her autobiography, the French version of which I tracked down in the Seuil catalogue—*Déportée en Sibérie, Déportée à Ravensbrück*—was quickly sent to me from Paris by my editor Annie Morvan. It is curious that in this dark affair of the hells created by Nazism and Communism there are so many testimonies by women: they have been vital to me; among them are *Hope Against Hope* by Nadezhda Mandelstam and especially *Journey into the Whirlwind* by Eugenia Ginzburg, whose name I read for the first time in an extraordinary book by Tsvetan

Todorov that I discovered in English translation, *Facing the Extreme: Moral Life in the Concentration Camps.* I learned a great deal from Todorov by reading *El hombre desterrado.* I read extensively on the situation of the Jews in Spain in *The Origins of the Inquisition in Fifteenth Century Spain,* the tendentious and colossal study by Benzion Netanyahu, and from the much briefer and also more balanced classic by Henry Kamen, *The Spanish Inquisition,* not forgetting a book that to me seems extraordinary despite its extreme concision, *Historia de una tragedia* by Joseph Perez. My friend Emilio Lledó has read the extensive diaries of Professor Victor Klemperer in the original German: I know only the English two-volume version published under the title *I Will Bear Witness: A Diary of the Nazi Years.* It is sad to think that books of such depth are virtually inaccessible to readers in Spanish.

It is questionable whether this book would have occurred to me or that I would have found the state of mind necessary to write it without two of the most decisive writers in my education during recent years. I am referring to Jean Améry and Primo Levi. I discovered Améry's book about Auschwitz by accident, and without previous knowledge of its existence, in a bookstore in Paris in 1995. It was published under the title *Par delà de la crime et le châtiment,* and I have no indication that any Spanish publisher is interested in it. Thanks to Mario Muchnick, however, the Spanish reader has access to the great trilogy of Primo Levi: *If This Is a Man, The Truce,* and *The Drowned and the Saved.* What one learns in these three volumes about human beings and the history of Europe in the twentieth century is terrible but instructive, and I don't think it is possible for anyone to develop a full political awareness of the Holocaust or Holocaust literature without reading them.

There are other books, but the ones I have named are those that nourished me most fully as I wrote *Sepharad.* I have also tried to listen to many voices: among them I must name, with gratitude and emotion, those of Francisco Ayala and José Luis Pinillos; the resonant and jovial voice of Amaya Ibárruri, who one winter afternoon invited me to have coffee and told me some episodes in the extraordinary novel of her life; that of Adriana Seligmann, who told me about her grandfather's nightmares in German; and that of Tina Palomino, who came to my home one afternoon when I thought I had finished this book and made me realize, listening to the story that she, unknowingly, was giving me, that there is always one more thing that deserves to be told.